The Orphan the Marine and the Mastiff

Josh Amos

Published by Tiger Shark Mktg Madeline Bartorillo, 2023.

Copyright

---

1. https://jmamos.com/about/
2. https://tigersharkmarketing.net/

Table of Contents

Dedication

For Austin and Penny... and Pop and Auntie.
I love you all very much!

Epigraph

"When you find the right people, you never let go. The people who count are the ones who are your friends in lean times. You have all the friends you want when things are going well." James Lee Burke

"Behavior is Truth." Andrew Vachss

"Since it is so likely that (children) will meet cruel enemies, let them at least have heard of brave knights and heroic courage. Otherwise you are making their destiny not brighter but darker."
— C.S. Lewis

Preface

Welcome!

Come on in and have a seat. Coffee is on and Boudicca (Yes she is real!) is very appreciative of being petted.

I wrote this book because I wanted to tell you a great story about an odd couple that you will be able to let your guard down and enjoy. Brother and Mei Mei are not your usual hero and heroine. They are not magical and their lives haven't been easy. They are the kind of people that you would want to have in your life because after all they have been through they are still kind and brave. Brother and Mei Mei are learning to be generally unconcerned with the kind of standard conventions that cause hesitation and doubt in the rest of us. They certainly have their flaws and faults, but they are learning that they love and are loved. Knowing that, gives them the strength to surmount their pasts and reach for their own stars. Will they reach them? Who knows? Sometimes having the courage to try is the victory... and the story.

A final note. I purposely do not tell you what Brother and Mei Mei's given names are, or what their ethnicity is, or even where they live, because I feel their struggles and triumphs are universal to everyone, and I want you as the reader to be free to imagine what you want, and to see what you want to see. Above all, I want you to root for them. They are sure trying hard.

-Josh Amos

PS Since people have asked.... the phonetic pronunciation of "Mei Mei" should sound like "May May"

Prologue

Mei Mei

Mei Mei pressed her lips together and massaged the back of her neck. The term paper for her English 102 class was giving her fits. Up to now, no other assignment had challenged her academic prowess and work ethic. The assignment topic she had been assigned was "Contemporary Heroism," and the title had been assigned at random. It wasn't even the class per se, it was the assignment.

When Mei had gone to Ms. Kendal's office during office hours and asked her to elaborate, she had been met with the basilisk stare of an academic who was not interested in mercy.

Cussing and grumbling under her breath, Mei planted herself in the family library and tried to work. Despite the comfort of curling up on a comfy sofa with the warmth from the fireplace, her frustration continued to nag at her psyche. Her eyes blurred and slowed her progress to a crawl. Suddenly, a clue flashed in her mind, and an idea began to form

She pledged to use the title "Contemporary Heroism" as her compass to guide her in the right direction. She put her head down and pressed on. She Googled, "What is a hero?" and clicked on "Heroism in Psychology." She jotted down her thoughts and notes on a pad of paper, forging ahead, gradually formulating ideas in her mind.

She began to understand her direction with the project and realized she had always known it. Ms. Kendall had misunderstood Mei Mei's intentions. Mei's frustrations and apprehensions were not caused by the assignment, but how well she wanted to work the project. A contemporary hero? She chuckled to herself. She was rescued and raised by one of the most heroic men she knew.

Her Brother.

How should she tell his story? She certainly didn't want her report to be a pretentious, over-the-top comic book story, or worse, a trite, smug, condescension of heroic deeds.

The clinical truth was so spectacular and outrageous, readers might not believe it. Fortunately, key parts of the story, such as the court cases, the medals awarded for valor, and even the fortune, demanded extensive and meticulous documentation even the smuggest academic couldn't deny.

Mei continued reading, taking notes, and typing on her laptop. She was making progress, but the project taxed her emotions. Many of the ideas seemed to distract her by taking the project in another direction. Normally, when she worked on a project for college, she saw a clear path to the end, but this one remained disembodied and scattered.

Why was her Brother an example of a contemporary hero?

Was it fighting in the war and earning medals? Was it assuming the role of a single father, who rescued her from a traumatic foster care experience? Was it his humility to deal with his own mental health, and refusal to surrender to his own physical disabilities? Was it his refusal to surrender to his attention to humanity and kindness, or his earning degrees to live life for life's sake? Was it not surrendering to the whims and dictates of people who cared only about their own agenda? It was all these, Mei thought, but much more, yet she couldn't talk about one or two without mentioning the others.

Which was most important? Could she talk about one or two without acknowledging the rest? No.

Oddly, when the professor had announced the assignment, Mei considered it just another hurdle on her academic journey. But the more she unpacked her memories, the more responsibility she felt to tell the story accurately. She had much to tell, share, and explain, and vowed to get it right. The project was more than just an assignment; it was an epic story. Yet she knew the project must come before the book.

The main issue blocking the flow of consciousness was still the outrageous nature of the real story. Her memories were clear in her mind, but she struggled to transfer them to the page with as much clarity. Who would believe it even if she could articulate it? She paused and squinted at the last line she typed, and grimaced. Nope. She hammered the back key, deleted what she wrote, and sighed.

She leaned back and perused her surroundings, breathing in slowly. She closed her eyes and shook her head.

"Look at this place," she said aloud. "Who would believe all of this unless they were here? I was here for it all and can hardly believe it myself."

For instance, the library where she was working. It was a magnificent place she and her brother had designed and built. It was the kind of comfortable place of learning that any self-respecting bibliophile would have to be dragged out of kicking and screaming. A large stately hall, filled with overflowing dark wood bookshelves, long wooden study tables, overstuffed chairs, and couches.

A cyber study, complete with computers, printers, and whiteboards, occupied the far end of the hall. A variety of hand thrown coffee cups, books, and notepads were always within arm's reach. Ceiling fans circulated the aromatic aromas of coffee, kindling, well-thumbed books, and the faint but pleasant scent of her brother's cigars occasionally wafting from his office down the hall.

To her, it wasn't only a place to study or learn; it was her sanctuary. She felt comfortable and safe here. As she nestled in her overstuffed chair, the room's atmosphere wrapped itself around her like a down comforter.

She rested her head on the deeply upholstered chair and closed her eyes. All of this came from her Brother's vision and reminded her of his sheer will and stubborn refusal to submit to the ordinary.

Despite the grand and worthy attributes of the library, nothing could quell Mei's growing anxiety as she typed, retyped, deleted, and fretted over her prose. Although her research had revealed most writers struggled to get enough information, she had too much.

For another hour, she tried to organize her outline, but failed to get things right; second guessing herself with each false start.

At a particularly difficult point, she glanced up and remembered her Brother's words—"Take a deep breath and remember Who. You. Are."

Out of training and habit, she took a deep breath, then stood up and ambled the length of the room. She paused to look at the classic maps and framed pictures on the wall depicting brave and learned men and women from many ages noted for their commendable deeds. They all seemed to stare back at her.

Mei studied the pictures of herself her brother had hung despite her heated protests. One showed her scaling a rock in the bright sunshine; another an embarrassing picture of her dancing at swing class, displaying brace covered teeth with a wide grin. Another framed image captured her as she struck a fencing pose with her saber, flashing in mid-cut.

The last picture Mei looked at showed her holding her 8th grade report card with all A's in one hand, her arrest report in the other, with a belligerent smile plastered across a bruised face, with a half dozen stitches above her left brow. Despite the avalanche of trouble that event had caused, she still couldn't help but chuckle.

Brother had been genuinely upset at her over that one.

Mei moved down the length of the room, stopping only to pet "Mr. Big," the cat sleeping on the back of one of the sofas.

She stopped and looked at her Brother's pictures that he, in turn, had protested her hanging. In one, he was standing in front of a platoon of fellow Marines as an officer pinned a medal on his chest. Another showed him on a craggy Afghanistan mountainside, helmet removed, face covered in dirt, wearing a filthy uniform, in full gear and weapons, smoking a cigar. In another, he lay on his back and laughed as mastiff puppies slobbered his face with wet doggy kisses.

Next to that picture, a large frame held a collage of images Mei had arranged which depicted Brother as she saw him; sitting on a sofa reading to a younger Mei, building a stone wall, cooking in the kitchen, and brushing Mei's hair. The last picture showed them together—him standing erect and proud with a young Mei, her head thrown back in laughter as she sat astride his giant shoulders.

He had always lifted her up where she could almost see forever.

Feeling braver, Mei delved back into her treasure trove of memories. Thanks to Brother teaching her how to do mind pictures and Kim's game, the images became almost as vivid as the day they were made. They still had the power to remind her of her younger days. The dreadful times were still there too, powerful enough to roil her gut if she focused on them too long. But she was no longer the little refugee girl. She was stronger. She knew more. She had grown, and now knew how to be brave.

She took another deep breath.

"Shut up and write!" Brother's stern but kind words resounded, gruff, but propelled with a smile.

Motivation.

"It's okay to use adult words and thoughts from the present to describe your child feelings from the past."

Permission.

Mei settled back in front of her laptop and typed. The words came slowly at first. As she wrote, she wished she could see the story from her Brother's point of view, then wondered whether she really wanted to hear his thoughts from those times. She suspected he struggled with life more than he would ever admit.

Mei tapped on the keys. "When I first met my Brother, I was very young, I was scared, and I was an orphan. My first thought was that my Brother looked like a giant scary monster. I didn't know it at the time, but that day would turn out to be the best day of my life."

Chapter 1

Mei Mei

The little orphan girl sat in the caseworker's office, head down, her face buried deep into the top of her stuffed bear's head. Her stomach was knotted with fear.

Her despair was worse. She would have no say in anything; a feeling that might never change. The closeness of the velvety fur of the stuffed bear did little to ease her growing anxiety.

When she had gone to live with the Curley's, she'd hoped to stay there, ending the uncertainty that always happened whenever a caseworker came to get her. The Curley's had been the nicest people she'd known since her mommy and daddy died; much nicer than the people at the first place she was sent to live. The Bad Place.

Memories of the Bad Place upset her stomach even more until she forced her thoughts back on the Curley's. Their smiles and laughs rang sincere. They owned a little dog that yapped and loved being petted. Why couldn't she have stayed with them? The knots in her stomach alternated from tight to loose and back again.

The caseworker's cell phone beeped, and the little girl raised her head from her stuffed bear enough to see the older woman answer. She spoke briefly before putting the phone back into her pocket.

"Your brother is coming up to take you home," she said, flashing her fake caseworker smile.

The fake smile didn't fool the little girl. She knew that once she was taken out of the office, the caseworker wouldn't know, perhaps not even care, what would happen to her.

Two weeks ago, the caseworker showed up at the Curley's with the same fake smile. She said the little girl had a brother. An older brother, not a little one. He was all grown up and she was going to live with him because, "he was her brother." The caseworker said the word "brother" as if it was a magic word, but the little girl was confused.

A brother? What did that mean?

Until recently, she didn't know she had a brother (whatever that meant). When her parents were killed, she thought she'd go live with people she didn't know. The first family wasn't nice at all. Just the flashing memory of the Bad Place caused her to remember the bad things that happened there.

She thought instead of the Curley's' house, the best house she'd ever stayed. Clean, big, she was the only child living there. After a while, she felt at home, relieved to be away from The Bad Place, comforted by their little dog, Bella.

Mr. Curley was a big man, and often made grilled cheese sandwiches for lunch. She liked grilled cheese sandwiches.

Mrs. Curley was pretty, and Mei liked it when she let Bella sleep on Mei's bed at nap time. Whenever Mei woke from a nightmare, Mrs. Curley came in and rocked her back to sleep. Mei felt better at the Curley's house than anywhere else, but didn't stay there for long.

So there she sat, in the office, squeezing her bear, waiting to go to another strange home to live with strange people.

The thump of heavy steps sounded outside the office, followed by a solid knock at the front door. When the caseworker entered, Mei peeked from behind her bear.

The biggest man she ever saw stood in the doorway. He reminded Mei of the giant in a book Mrs. Curley once read to her. Mei knew nothing could stop the man from doing what he wanted to whomever he wanted. Scars dotted and slashed his black tattooed arms protruding from his short-sleeved shirt.

Mei ducked her head back down into the soft safety of the bear and didn't move. She listened for a clue for what this big man was doing there. The caseworker was talking to the giant man, so without moving her head, Mei peeked again. His frame was blocking most of the daylight coming through the doorway. Mr. Curley was big, but this man was even bigger. She noticed he had more scars on his neck and side of his face. Was he a Frankenstein monster? She was fascinated, and accidentally looked him in the eye.

He was looking at her! Before she could react, he winked at her! Startled, she quickly buried her face down into her toy. Oddly, she thought the wink looked...friendly?

She heard his footsteps as he approached her. She froze. He bent down in front of her.

If she looked up, would he be looking right into her face?

Then, in a deep and smooth voice, he said, "Hello little one. I'm your brother."

She didn't move and refused to look up.

"I'm here to take you home, he said, then paused. "May I pick you up?"

Her heart thumped in her chest. She wondered whether he sensed her fear. Her mind raced out of control. He was so big; scary big. But the caseworker confirmed he was her brother, so she had no choice.

Mei didn't want to be under his control. If he wanted to hurt her or carry her away, no one could stop him. She breathed in to force her mind to stop racing, then shook her head. No. She didn't want him to pick her up.

"Now, missy...," the caseworker began in a critical tone, but the big man stood up and said, "it's okay."

She thought she heard a slight grinding noise as he moved, making her wonder whether he was a robot disguised as a person. At least he didn't appear mad when she hadn't let him pick her up.

He walked over and spoke to the caseworker. They talked for a few minutes, and then he signed some papers. The caseworker put the papers into a folder and handed it to him.

He turned and walked back over to Mei, and pointed to a cheap purple travel bag Mrs. Curley had packed for Mei. "Are these your things?"

She nodded.

He reached down and picked up the bag, then extended his other hand.

"I won't pick you up if you don't want me to," he said gently, "but I need you to hold my hand so we can get in the truck."

She didn't want to hold his hand, but knew she had no choice. Clutching her stuffed bear with one hand, she hopped off the chair, then reluctantly took the giant's hand. It felt warm and strong, so big that her own hand felt lost inside. Despite his size, he didn't crush her hand or pull her along.

Together, they walked out of the caseworker's office, down the stairs, and out into the sunshine. The giant took smaller steps so Mei didn't need to run to keep up with him. They walked together out into the parking lot to a black pickup truck. This truck was different than regular pickup trucks she'd seen. The back was smaller than a work truck, and had fancy shiny wheels. To her, it looked more like a fancy race car than a regular pickup truck.

The big man opened the door. "I have to lift you up to the seat."

He reached down for her, but she let go of his hand, then scrambled around him and climbed up into the special seat. She looked up into his face and waited for him to yell or say something scary, but he didn't. Sitting higher, she had a better look at his face. Even with the scars, she was surprised to find he looked more calm then mean.

In fact, instead of yelling at her for climbing in by herself, he just nodded, admiring her spirit. He put the purple bag and folder into the truck, then fastened her seat belt.

She felt relieved to see other stuff from the Curley's house already in the truck. She was tired of losing stuff when the caseworkers sent her someplace new.

He walked around and got into the driver's side. "Are you ready to go, sweetie?"

She stared straight ahead, silent, but nodded.

"Well, maybe not," he said.

She was confused. What did he mean? Could she go back to the Curley's house? Her hopes were dashed when, instead of taking her back, he reached up and took down a pair of sunglasses.

"Do you have sunglasses?"

Mei shook her head.

"Well, maybe these will do," he said, then leaned over and gently put the sunglasses on her face.

She tensed when he reached over, but his hands were gentle. She stared straight ahead without moving. The sunglasses were huge, with black frames and shiny lenses. They kept sliding down her nose, but she liked them. They helped to hide a little bit of herself.

The giant flashed an equally giant smile. "There you go! You look like a rock star!"

Mei didn't know what a rock star was, but liked the sunglasses. She took them off for a moment and held them up, looking into the lenses. They weren't as good as mirrors, but she could still see her reflection. She put them back on. Her special seat allowed her a view through the truck's windows. When the big man turned the key in the ignition, she felt a gentle rumbling through her whole body.

"Okay," the Big Man exclaimed. "Here we go!"

They left the parking lot, pulled onto to the highway and sped down the road....

Chapter 2

The Big Man

The big man sat in his souped-up pick-up truck in the parking lot of the Child Protective Services satellite office. The prescribed pain killers were serving double duty. They limited his chronic pain spikes and slightly numbed his nerves. After his high adrenaline military career, he was pleasantly surprised his nerves still reacted. Like finding a long-lost keepsake.

"Stop it," he said aloud. Then, more calmly, he thought, You know what you're here to do, save the girl. Chaplain Griffin and the others spent a lot of time preparing you for this very moment, so make 'em proud.

He took a deep breath and once again scanned the checklist. Even after his traumatic brain injuries had denied him a once nearly photographic memory, his memory still served him well. However, the ritual of a checklist provided comfort and familiarity. A final scan revealed nothing surprising or forgotten. He tucked the leather-bound notebook into his vest pocket, removed his sunglasses, quickly checked his reflection in the truck's mirror, then got out.

He walked to the CPS building and up the stairs to the door at a slow pace. As he moved, he inventoried himself; full stride, a few twinges of pain through the dulling blanket the pain killers laid down, but tolerable. He climbed the stairs with no issues, suddenly thankful for all the hours of painful physical therapy.

He paused at the office door and took a moment to soften his expression and relax his body posture. He couldn't change his size or repair his scars, but he'd practiced adopting the persona of a character from one of the children's books Chaplain Griffin and the daycare team told him to read—The Big Friendly Giant. He didn't want to scare the little girl. He opened the office door and went inside. He threat-scanned the office as he walked in, (an old habit drilled into him), and saw her right away.

His baby sister.

She sat clutching a stuffed bear with her face buried in the top of the toy's head. When he saw her, his heart skipped a beat, then froze. The clinical part of his brain assessed the situation at a furious speed and the results broke his heart. The ugly results also ignited a cold hatred deep within him. His guilt ugly whispered "Someone has done evil to this child and you weren't here to stop it." He didn't know what kind evil or to what extent, but it was evident this little girl, his baby sister, endured too much trauma during her brief years. She was tiny to the point of appearing malnourished. She wore hand-me-down clothing. She looked clean, but when he saw her sneak a peek at him, he recognized the same haunted look of refugee children he'd seen from the war-torn countries where he carried out his missions.

His stomach clenched at the condition of his only known blood relative, but his years as a Marine Senior Non-Commissioned Officer paid off. He kept his bearings and temper in check, even managed a friendly wink at the girl, who ducked her face into the safety of the bear.

The caseworker came over and began talking to him, but his silent fury at the little girl's condition smothered the bureaucrat's professional sounding words. He smiled and nodded silently, grateful for his inspiration to hire an attorney to smooth the path for him and his sister. He showed his ID, signed papers, then accepted the files the well-meaning caseworker offered, in every effort to expedite. Still, he struggled to restrain his emotions. Finally, unable to tolerate any more, he thanked the caseworker, set down the paperwork, then turned and slowly approached his baby sister. The caseworker followed behind.

He squatted down to get closer, and in his most calm and non-threatening voice, said, "hello, little one. I'm your brother."

Small steps sounded from behind.

"Now missy...," the caseworker broke in, causing the little girl to lock up again.

The big man abruptly shot up to his full height. "It's okay."

The caseworker stepped back.

He guided the caseworker over to the desk, where other employees nervously chatted words sounding more like white noise than intelligent conversation. Fuck the whole lot of this, he thought. He needed to get out of here right away. Actually, needed to get both of them out right away. He gathered everything up, signed a final form, then walked back to the little girl.

He pointed to a cheap little suitcase sitting next to her. "Are these your things?" Without waiting for an answer, he reached down and grabbed the suitcase. He extended his other hand.

"I won't pick you up if you don't want me to," he said gently, "but I need you to hold my hand so we can get in the truck."

Reluctantly, the little girl got up and took his hand.

The caseworker mentioned something about her card in the file and to call with any questions. The big man nodded and grunted a "thank you," as he and his baby sister walked out of the office and into the sunshine.

My God, she's little, he thought, as she wrapped her little hand into his. While they walked, he shortened his stride to keep her from feeling like a rowboat tied to a battleship in full throttle.

They walked up to the passenger's side of the truck and the big man opened the door. "I have to lift you up to the seat," he said.

She looked around as if she was going to bolt for freedom, but instead, surprised him by dropping his hand and climbing up into the truck and into the kid's seat. She sat and looked straight ahead, refusing to look at him, almost as if daring him to say something.

Well now, he thought, there is a spark of life there. He nodded his approval and put the rest of her stuff in by her feet, closed the door, then got in on his side of the truck.

"Are you ready to go, sweetie?"

She slowly nodded.

"Well, maybe not," he mused. "Do you have sunglasses?"

She shook her head.

He had planned for this. He reached up into the visor and pulled out a pair of sunglasses, knowing they'd obviously be too big for her. "Well, maybe these will do," he said, then carefully but deliberately reached over and eased them onto her face.

"There you go! You look like a rock star!" He thought he saw the little girl's icy façade warm up just a little, but didn't dare to hope.

He fired up the big truck's engine. "Okay, here we go!"

Chapter 3

Mei Mei

The big man tried talking to her as they drove down the highway. He said they were on an adventure to start a new life, and asked her questions. What did she like to eat? What's her favorite color? What did she like to do? Did she like to read?

He asked questions most of the adults she'd met in her 8 short years never asked, nor cared to ask. However, she couldn't bring herself to answer him at first. She sat very still and avoided speaking while watching the passing buildings of the city turn to houses, then houses turn to trees.

Mei felt sure the big man wanted to know more about her, but she had no clue why, and felt nervous about it. She knew she'd have to talk sooner or later, so eventually she gave short, guarded answers.

Usually, she sensed when adults were only pretending to care what she said, and could tell when they were trying to trap her or use her own words against her. She didn't know whether this was the big man's intention. He seemed to be like Mr. and Mrs. Curley, but she couldn't be sure, so answered only when she thought he wanted to hear. She sat still, staring out the window and listening to the rumble of the truck's engine.

She could smell the big man. He didn't stink, nor emit an odor as though he'd just shaved. Mostly he smelled like soap, but not like the perfumed soap ladies use, or medicine smelling soap they used in the Bad Place.

With that thought, her stomach lurched. She struggled to make her stomach hold still by concentrating on the big man's smell. Another faint smell she didn't know how to describe. Was it richer? Was it smoky? The smell was unique but somehow friendly, and she felt confused by that.

The big man continued to try to engage her with gentle questions and observations while they drove. He seemed so sincere, it was tempting to feel comfortable with him. A big, friendly smelling man with a deep calm voice who winked at her; taking her from bad things to a new place. But what if he was a new kind of monster, one she hadn't seen before? And what did he want? People always wanted something. Where were they going? She wanted to know more about what was going on and what was going to happen, but hated to make herself more vulnerable by asking.

Her stomach twisted into knots again as she struggled with her questions and feelings. She was losing control. She had held on longer than ever before, but it was getting too hard to be still. Finally, she became frustrated, and decided if there was going to be trouble, it would be better to know as soon as possible.

The next time the big man asked her a question, she answered reluctantly. He didn't act surprised she spoke to him, nodding while she spoke, then answered her.

So far so good. She chanced asking a few questions of her own. She had to pretend to care, so spoke slowly at first, because she learned that, through her mostly awful foster journey, if you had to ask questions, better to ask them quietly and small, as if you were afraid. She could sound small and afraid with little effort. She quickly found out this giant was different. He answered her questions casually but directly, as if he didn't mind her asking him at all. She was surprised to find that the more she asked questions and chatted, the more she sensed his sincerity. The more she spoke, the more she believed he was listening, and after a while, she dared to think he actually cared what she had to say. Maybe she was wrong, and didn't dare hope.

Her stomach was starting to settle. The conversation during this ride was different than before, and it threw her off balance. She couldn't trust him, could she? What did he want? Waves of worry welled up inside her and her stomach started to tighten up again. She got quiet again and fought to hold still, but her stomach started cramping, and was really starting to hurt. Then, to her horror, she lost control and farted, long and loud. The relief overrode her panic and humiliation. She looked at the big man in horror.

He looked at her, chuckled briefly, and said "oops," Then to Mei's horror he followed with "Sounds like you sat on a duck." He was trying to be funny but noticed the expression on her face and quickly said "no worries, it happens," then rolled down his window. The cool wind whistled through the opening and raised goosebumps on her skin, yet, she struggled to avoid a meltdown.

The big man tried to save her dignity without directly addressing the fart. When he asked whether she liked to sing, her stomach clenched up again, and she couldn't make it stop!

He asked her if she knew any songs. Maybe she let her guard down due to stress, and the big man's questions stirred up something in her. Years ago, when mommy and daddy were still alive, she liked to sing, but after they died, she got into trouble when she sang at the Bad Place. They made her stop. She started spinning up inside, unable to stop thinking of that place, and the more she thought of it, the more scared she became. Her stomach felt worse, and she struggled to breath. She tried to keep herself together, keep up her shield, and avoid crying. Her stomach cramped to the point she became terrified that she might mess herself.

"Mei, Mei, are you okay?" the big man asked, then glanced at her. "What's wrong, sweetie?"

She couldn't hold it, and farted again. She tried not to cry, especially in front of this new and unknown big man, but felt so scared. It was all so unfair. The more she tried to refrain, the faster she spun inside. So, despite her effort not to cry, the tears fell.

The more she tried to stop, the more she cried. She hated feeling helpless. As she leaned forward, the sunglasses slid from her face and tumbled to the floor.

He reached over and put a warm and strong hand on the back of her neck.

Despite his attempts to comfort her, her stomach cramped and she farted again. Her dignity gone, she knew her meltdown would continue.

Mei felt the truck pull off the road then roll to a stop. The big man shut the engine off, got out and walked around to her side of the truck. Through her tears, she started to shake and cry. She felt sure the big man had changed his mind about taking her home. He might throw her out of the truck and drive away; or worse, take her back and she'd be all alone again.

She cowered in her special seat as the door opened. Instead of grabbing her roughly, the big man unbuckled her seat belt and lifted her out of the truck. He wrapped his giant arms around her and gently rested her head on his big shoulder.

She struggled and started pounding her little hands on his shoulders and chest, but struggling was a waste of time—he was too strong. After a minute, she stopped fighting and fell into deep breathless sobs.

He continued to hold her, patting her back and gently rocking her back and forth.

Her stomach rumbled, and she knew in an instant this event would be worse than the farting, but she couldn't stop. With a loud burp, she vomited.

He felt her distress but must have anticipated what would happen, and aimed her face away from him just in time. He continued to hold her until she finished.

"You poor little thing," he said in a deeper than usual voice. "There, there, wee girl, go ahead and let it out. I'm right here." He lifted her back up to his shoulder.

His comforting words reached inside her and helped calm her meltdown, but she felt sad. She balled up her tiny fist and wailed her despair and embarrassment into his shoulder and chest. She didn't understand what possessed her to hit him, and she continued to cry.

"There, girl," he crooned. "It's okay, let it out."

She soon stopped pounding on him. His muscles were so solid, hitting him was like beating on the sidewalk.

He continued to rock her. "Poor little thing. It will all be okay."

Cars sped past them on the road, but the big man kept rocking her, and comforting her with his words. Finally, after a while, Mei finally calmed into exhausted hiccupping sobs and stopped crying. She was spent.

The big man rocked her for a while longer, then lifted her up and kissed her forehead. He curled a finger under her chin and lifted her face to look into his warm and dark brown eyes. "Feel better?"

She didn't, but nodded anyway.

"It's okay, baby sister. It's better to get it out, no shame."

Mei didn't know what might happen next. He lowered his head and noticed a big wet stain on his shirt. He looked up, and his eyes were twinkling.

"Hey," he chuckled. "Look at this, you snotted all over me." He flashed a big smile and contorted his face. "Ack! Girl cooties! I got girl cooties on me!" He sounded so absurd, she couldn't help but choke out an involuntary laugh. At least he clearly wasn't mad at her, and wasn't going to hurt her.

"Let's get you cleaned up," he said, as he tucked her back into the truck.

He took a slightly soiled bandanna out of a pocket and crouched down. He wiped her face and had her blow her nose. Then he took out a bottle of water, opened it and had her rinse her mouth and spit out the last of the nastiness on the side of the road. He fussed at her for a minute then paused, and a calm look came over his rugged features.

Out of the blue he asked, "Do you know why I call you Mei Mei instead of the name your mom gave you?"

She shook her head, thinking it strange this giant and her had the same mother. She wasn't sure it was true, but maybe it wouldn't be so bad if it was.

"It's a Chinese phrase that pretty much means, 'my dear little sister.' You can always use the name mom gave you, but I thought a special name would be good to start a new life with. Your real name can be special and private—just for you. Yours to share only if and when you want to, like if you think someone has earned it. Do you understand what I mean?"

She nodded slowly.

"You don't have to agree with me, you can do what you want."

Mei thought about it. A special name just for her on a special day. A new name for a new life. And he asked her what she thought; asked her for her permission. She wasn't used to anybody asking her anything. They had always told her what to do, but here he was, asking her. She was tempted to say, "no," just to see what he would say. But even if she wasn't sure about everything else, she decided she liked the idea. It felt odd to be with someone who cared what she thought. She didn't trust him, but so far, he hadn't been mean to her. Despite her uncertainty, she nodded her head.

"Are you ready to keep on going?"

She nodded and he smiled. He still wanted her to come with him; he wasn't going to take her back. That was something.

"Yes," Mei said quietly.

"There's my girl!" he said with his big, friendly smile. He stood up and scooped up the sunglasses then put them back on her. He buckled her up, then stood up and happily shouted, "Kick the tires and light the fires! We ride!"

He closed the door and trotted around to his side, got in, buckled up, and started the engine. In a silly fakey announcer's voice he said, "Copilot, Mei Mei, are you ready to motate?"

"What does that mean?"

"It means, go on down the road!"

She nodded.

"Let's kick it!" he cheered, then revved the big engine as they pulled out onto the road.

Chapter 4

Mei Mei

Mei tried to be happy, but she was just ...done. They drove along for what seemed like hours.

"Are you ready for me to talk with you?" the big man asked. "There are lots of things for us to say and do, but I don't want you to have too much too fast."

Mei nodded. She wasn't ready to talk, but didn't feel as if she had a choice. Maybe she could find out something that would improve her situation.

"Okay, good," he said, then glanced at her. "If you have any questions or concerns, just ask, I won't get mad."

He turned back to watch the road. "You're my sister and my new crime fighting partner. You're important to me, and there's a lot about you I don't know, so you might have to tell me." He paused and glanced at her sideways. "Can you be a brave girl and help me, sister of mine?"

Could he be for real? No one had ever asked her for help, especially not a scary looking giant.

"Yes, big man."

She named him big man on the spot, just like he named her Mei Mei. She wasn't sure he was her brother, or even what his real name was, but he was a big man.

"Okay, that's the spirit! From now on it's you and me. Now, I'm the adult and have the privilege of being your guardian. I also get to teach you things, and you'll teach me things, and we'll get to do things together."

He didn't say what she thought he would, and despite her general despair, she was curious. "Like what?" she asked.

"Lots of things that are necessary to build a great future. But I promise I'll always do what's best for you, even if you don't understand or like it at the time. You understand?"

"Yes," she said, but wondered what he meant.

"But right now, I give you permission to ask me anything," he continued, watching the road as he spoke. Traffic was getting heavy. "I may not know the answer, I may have to find out, and I may choose not to answer, but you may always ask me. Got it?"

"Yes," Mei said.

"Okay. We're going home to get settled in for tonight, but we have lots of running around to do in the next couple of days. Shopping for things you'll need, doctor and dentist visits for checkups; stuff like that." He turned and winked at her. "Some things are going to be interesting, some boring, but all of it's important."

He changed lanes then said, "since summer is coming pretty soon, you won't have to go back to school, but we both have a lot to learn."

"Like what?"

"Everything." he said in a happy tone. "The world is full of things to see, do, and learn, and I'll teach you all I can. Don't get worried if you don't catch on right away, just be willing to try."

Her stomach twisted. This was so much different than anything she'd known before. Even when her mommy and daddy were still alive. The truck rumbled and the big man continued. "You'll have chores and things to do to help me. Hey, you know what? I have a puppy! You'll love her; her name is Boudicca, and she's going to grow into a giant walking huggy bear." He paused for a moment, then asked. "Do you like dogs?"

"Yes. How big is she now?"

"She's regular-sized now, but she'll grow up to be bigger than you."

"Nu huh" Mei said, with more than a little scorn. A dog bigger than a person? The big man had to be lying.

"For real! She's a Mastiff, and they're known as the gentle giants of dogs. She gives big sloppy drooly dog kisses. Just make sure she didn't drink out of the toilet or eat anything gross first."

"Ooooh!" Mei said "Gross!"

The big man chuckled. "Mastiffs are giant love bugs, but they're not the smartest of God's creatures, so we'll have to teach her how to act. But you'll love her."

"Okay," Mei said, but was skeptical. She liked talking about dogs. It seemed like a safe thing to talk about, even if the big man was lying about a puppy that could grow bigger than a person.

"Oh, and more stuff. About me...I've got some old injuries, so sometimes I ache or limp a bit, but don't want you to worry. It's nothing that'll stop me."

"Did you get hurt?" she asked, then felt mad at herself for asking. Of course, he'd been hurt. His face, hands, and arms were covered with scars.

"Yes, a bit," he said, "but I'm getting better. I still have some work to do."

"What happened?" Mei asked, concerned.

"Well, before I met you, I was a Marine and fought in the war overseas. I got a bit banged up."

"You were in a war?"

"Sure was. But I'm here now, and I'm not going anywhere."

"Was it scary?"

"Sure, sometimes," he said, then snickered "But it was scarier for the guys I was fighting."

Mei looked over and saw a huge smile break across his face.

"Really?"

"You bet, but more on that another time." He continued without missing a beat. "Oh, I cuss, and say things you shouldn't say. You can't use the bad words I use. I'll try not to cuss, but probably will. Try and ignore it." He flashed her a half stern, half playful look.

"When we get home, you get to meet Boudicca, then we'll get you settled into your room and make dinner."

My room?! Her eyes widened. She never had her own room, unless she counted the tiny cabinet those nasty people locked her in when she was "bad." They had called that place her room, but Mei wanted no more of that. She shivered at the memory, which suggested to her maybe she shouldn't trust this big man. He might have a closet at his house.

Mei got quiet for a minute.

"Are you okay kiddo?"

Worried he might sense her doubts, Mei raised her eyebrows and opened her mouth wide.

"My own room?"

"Yes. Your own room, And after I finish fixing up the bathroom next to my room, you get your own bathroom, too!"

Mei's tiny jaw dropped. Using a bathroom and shower with privacy was such a special thing. She didn't dare believe he was honest.

"Is that okay with you?" he asked.

"Uh...Yes?" Mei said, still in shock. She looked out the window and was quiet for a while. She realized her stomach didn't hurt anymore. In fact, she felt hungry "What's for dinner?"

"I was thinking of tacos or spaghetti. What would you like?"

"My tummy is a bit sore. Is spaghetti okay?"

"Are you still feeling okay?" he asked, and looked away from the road.

"Oh yes, it's just a big day," she said quickly. She was worried he knew she didn't trust him.

He spoke with caution in his voice. "Of course. You can help me cook."

"Really?" she asked, faking a smile.

"Sure, cooking is fun." He glanced at her. "Mei, are you sure you're okay?"

"Oh yes," she quickly answered.

"Okay," he said, but his voice tone had changed.

Mei was sure he knew she was lying, but he didn't push her.

They both got quiet and drove on. Mei leaned back in her seat and watched the world pass out the side window. She was just a leaf in the wind, blowing along without any say where she was going or where she would end up.

Chapter 5

Mei Mei

"Okay, here we are."

Mei woke up with a start. She didn't realize she'd drifted off. They were pulling into a driveway at a normal looking house, with a plain front yard with nice grass. The big man turned off the ignition, gathered her things, and went up to the front door.

"Here we are," he said, as he opened the door. As Mei started to step in, the big man put a hand on her shoulder and gently held her up. Mei flinched when he touched her, but once again, instead of an attack, he surprised her with kindness. He turned to her and looked down.

"Mei Mei, this is your home now, too. We'll make it better together, me and you." He ushered her in to begin a new chapter in their lives.

Mei walked into the living room, holding her stuffed bear and looking around as the big man went through the house, to the kitchen and out into the backyard.

The house looked and smelled clean, was tidy, with big, comfy looking sofas and chairs, a fireplace and lamps. Tall and wide bookshelves stacked with books of all kinds, colors, and sizes covered the walls.

Mei gasped when she looked at one wall and saw framed pictures of her! The big man obviously put them there, but where did he get them? It felt creepy. She was going to ask the big man about them when a heavy scampering of feet distracted her.

The cutest puppy Mei had ever seen chugged into the room, furiously wagging its little tail. She lost her breath as the puppy (who really was big for a puppy) galumphed up to her and butted its head into her legs, sniffing and licking. She nearly fell over from the puppy's initial affections, then it plopped onto its stomach and rolled over, wiggling its legs into the air.

"That means she wants you to give her tummy rubs. She's actually kind of a brat about it. Go ahead."

The big man said 'she.' The puppy was a girl. She looked down at the ball of happy puppy for a moment, then leaned down and carefully rubbed its round tummy. The puppy's face was black and squishy looking; its reddish-brown coat as soft as rabbit fur. It thumped its tail and growled happily.

"Mei, this is Missy Boudicca," the big man said, pronounced 'Boo-Di-Ka.'

"She's our dog, and that means we have to take care of her, teach her how to act, clean up after her and care for her; but mostly pet and love her."

A puppy! Mei's eyes unexpectedly and suddenly filled with tears. She set her stuffed bear down, then she laid down and hugged the puppy, who then started furiously licking Mei's face.

"Well, it looks like she thinks you're pretty special," the big man said, and noticed Mei's tears. "Hey, sweetie, are you okay?"

Mei nodded but didn't answer. She didn't want to share her feelings at the moment.

"Aw, its okay. You've had a big day, huh?"

Mei nodded and tried unsuccessfully to fend off the puppy's affections. The big man helped her up, and together they walked her through the house.

He led her down a hallway with hardwood floors and more framed pictures on the walls, past an open bathroom, an open door, and stopped in front of another door.

He opened the door and stepped inside. "This is your room. It's a bit bare now, because I don't know what you like, but we can get some things later." He directed her to a big bed covered with a big fluffy quilt.

"Why don't you lay down and rest for a bit?"

Mei's stomach clenched again. What was he going to do now? He untied her shoes and she lied down.

"I'll go get dinner ready then come get you. I'll leave the door open. If you need to go to the bathroom or get up early, go ahead. You won't get in trouble."

He looked toward the doorway as Boudicca scampered in. "Do you want your pal to come up on your bed?"

Mei nodded.

He scooped up the wiggling pup and put it next to her. The pup walked up to her face, licked her, then burrowed her nose next to her. Mei giggled, and the puppy plopped down and snuggled.

The big man chuckled. "I think she likes it there, but don't let her hog the bed." He leaned over and spread another comfy quilt over the two, then stepped back without touching her. She relaxed a bit.

The big man turned to go but stopped, causing Mei's stomach to tighten again.

"See that lamp over there?" he motioned, and Mei rolled over to look. A tall hour-glass shaped table lamp sat on a dresser. It glowed with a light blue fluid, with a bubble of white jelly-like substance slowly ballooning and swirling inside. When the big man turned off the light, the lamp emitted a soft blue glow.

Mei felt drawn to the image, and surprised she didn't notice it when they came into the room.

"It's called a lava lamp. I thought it might make a neat night light for you."

Mei nodded, suddenly too tired to talk.

"One last thing." He pulled the door partway closed, then reached around and pointed to the lock on the doorknob. "That lock is for you. You can lock it or keep it unlocked as you like. I just want you to feel safe."

He left the room.

Mei was startled. Her own lock? A lock she could use to keep him out? Her head spun for a minute before calming down.

She looked around her new room. It felt too big for one person, but smelled as though it was recently painted. A bed, dresser, and closet was on the far wall. She had nice curtains on the windows, and a coat rack with pegs hanging on the wall.

Mei hadn't had her own room for as long as she could remember. The last closet she had in her room was during her stay with the Curley's. Although the Curley's were gracious to let her stay there, the room was a guest room for a visiting adult, so this was a new experience.

Mei could hear the big man in what she supposed was the kitchen. She thought about getting up and locking the door, but felt too comfy to bother. Before long, her eyes grew heavy with sleep and she no longer focused on the new sounds and smells. She lied down and drifted off, curled up beside Boudicca.

Chapter 6

Mei Mei

The big man woke up Mei a few hours later. "Well now, I wondered if she would stay there," he said, as he brushed Boudicca back onto the floor.

Mei sat up slowly and stretched. "She snores," she said without thinking. "And she's a bed hog."

He chuckled. "Yeah, she does, and it'll get worse as she gets bigger. We'll need to set puppy boundaries before she decides she's your boss."

Mei nodded.

"Dinner will be ready soon, so you might want to use the bathroom and wash up."

Mei nodded, then got up and went into the bathroom as the Big Man went back down the hall.

The bathroom was clean, bright, and smelled fresh. A fragrant bar of green soap sat in the soap dish. Carefully, she sniffed it. The fragrance was the same she smelled on the big man. It wasn't bad, but smelled more like a fresh tree, maybe cedar or pine? She wasn't sure, but it smelled good.

After she finished with her toiletry, she went to the sink and found a step stool next to it. She didn't really need one, but it made washing her face easier. She looked at the girl in the mirror and wondered what she would look like after living here for a while.

Leaving the bathroom, Mei followed the good smells wafting down the hall and the sounds of the big man singing to himself as he cooked dinner. She found her way to the kitchen where the big man was setting a table with plates and silverware.

"Hey. Pick a spot."

She perused the seating arrangement and chose to sit next to the place setting at the head table. The plate and glasses on the table were a pretty blue pottery.

"Pretty stuff!" she said.

"Thanks," he said. "I have a friend who's a potter. She made all of this for us."

"Wow!"

Dinner was spaghetti, garlic bread, and a salad. Mei loved it, but didn't tell the big man. They finished eating and cleared the table. He opened the back door and Mei was greeted by a covered porch with a view of a big backyard filled with another big lawn, trees, and a surrounding fence.

They went out into the yard with Boudicca in tow.

The big man said, "there's lots of room for you to play back here. Just be careful not to step where Boudicca does her business. We have to clean that up."

They ambled around the property while Boudicca sniffed about. Too soon, it was time to go back inside. They went into the living room. Mei kicked off her shoes and sat on one of the big sofas.

The big man went to another room then returned with a big blanket and tossed it to her.

Mei felt a moment of anxiety. Was he going to sit next to her now? But he sat on the other sofa. Boudicca came over to Mei and put a paw up on the cushion.

"Can she come up with me?"

"Yeah, go ahead."

Mei patted the cushion, and the chubby puppy struggled her way up next to her. She sure liked to pet the cute little pup, and Boudicca burrowed next to her. She scratched and petted her new little pal.

The Big Man turned on the TV and found a kid's movie. "I don't know what you like. Do you want to watch this one?"

Mei nodded and they watched it together. Mei enjoyed it, but didn't let her guard down any more than she felt necessary. She just kept petting the dog and watched the movie. After the movie, it was time for bed, and the big man showed her where to find her washcloth, towel, and toothbrush. Mei felt her stomach tense up again but didn't fuss. Was he going to do something now?

After she washed up, she entered her room and found a new pair of jammies lying out on the bed. Reluctantly, she put them on and not only did they fit, she felt better wearing them.

The big man knocked on the open bedroom door. His knocked startled Mei at first, but he stood in the doorway patiently waiting, rather than barge into the room.

"Are you ready for bed?" he asked, then nodded at the new jammies. "Oh good! You found them."

She nodded.

"They were hard to miss," he said, then chuckled and said, "Are they okay for now?"

She nodded again.

He gestured to the bed. "Okay, climb in."

She climbed up and got under the covers. Her stomach clenched a bit when the big man approached the bed. "Okay," he said, then opened a dresser drawer and pulled out a bell with a handle.

"Look here, kiddo, I'm going to put this bell right here on your nightstand." He put it down and it softly clanged. "If you get upset or need me during the night, just jingle and I'll come get you. Don't worry, I won't be mad." He smiled. "Sometimes I take medicine to help me sleep, so ringing the bell loud is the best way for you to let me know you need something."

She nodded.

"But anytime you need to use the bathroom, you just go ahead. I want you to feel comfortable enough to take care of your own business." The big man paused while searching for the right words. "We'll leave the lava lamp on as your night light. If you wake up before me in the morning, shut off the lava lamp then make your bed, go to the bathroom and get dressed. Then you can go play with the puppy or find a book to read."

The big man paused for a moment. "I don't know how many of my books you'll like. Maybe we should get you a library card or go to the bookstore." He paused again "Do you even like to read?"

Mei smiled and bobbed her head.

"Good. Reading is important."

He reached down patted her arm and stroked her hair.

She didn't feel comfortable with his touch, but didn't shrink away.

"I'm new to all of this parenting stuff," he said, "but I'm glad you're here. We have big things to do."

He took her hand and his eyes softened.

Mei tensed.

"I was going to see if you wanted me to read to you or something, but I think it's best if you just go to sleep for now."

The big man leaned down, quickly kissed Mei on the forehead, then got up. "Do you want the door open or closed?"

"Closed, please."

"You got it."

"Good night, Mei Mei." He turned the light off and walked out of the bedroom, closing the door behind him.

The blue glow of the lava lamp filled the room, and Mei watched the swirling liquid slowly roll behind the glass. She felt tired, but her mind was busy trying to absorb the events of the day. This morning she was a scared little girl, all alone. Tonight, she was sleeping in her own bed, in her own room, with a big man there to protect her. Maybe. And, she had a new name, a special name to start her new life. That was interesting. Everything was happening so fast, she had to think on that some more. But not until morning, as she slowly drifted off to sleep.

Chapter 7

The Big Man

The big man closed the door to Mei's room and walked down the hall. He looked at the TV for a moment then pushed the off button on the remote. Television's inanities were more annoying than usual and would only exacerbate today's events. He stood quietly in the living room for a moment as he analyzed the day's events. He felt upset and needed to process what had happened today.

He thought for a moment, then walked over to one of his bookcases and opened a shoe box sized wooden humidor. He paused briefly to inhale the rich tobacco smells wafting up to his nose, then picked out a thick cigar. He started to close the lid, then paused and selected a second cigar. It was going to be that kind of night. He needed to think, might as well make it a full ritual. He scooped up his notebook, pen, and laptop, and as he passed through the kitchen, got two cans of seltzer water on his way out to the porch.

His mind was still whirring at high speed as he settled into a comfy chair. He set his writing materials down, then commenced his deliberate ritual. He smelled the cigar, rolled it between his thumb and forefinger, then clipped off the end. He took a match from the cigar box, lit it, then watched it blaze to life. He carefully brought the match to the cigar while simultaneously rolling it near the flame. A couple of draws and puffs and he was in business. The rich blue grey smoke rolled out from the end of the cigar and lazily spiraled into the evening sky.

The big man hit the mental stop button. Time to sort out today's events. His visceral reaction had started when he first saw his little sister in the caseworker's office. The attorney had warned him she'd had a bad time in foster care, but "Damn!" He grit his teeth in anger. He fought to calm down, because throwing a fit would serve no purpose. After all, what had he expected?

Perhaps he'd thought he'd meet a cheerful little kid who would be all shyness and smiles. Instead, he got a kid resembling one of the refugees Taliban left behind after one of their reprisal raids.

The big man wasn't ashamed to acknowledge how much the events of this new endeavor had unsettled him. The poor girl's state had proven more dire than he'd thought, but he swore to himself he'd do whatever necessary to save her. Starting with sacrificing his ego, accepting his guilt for not getting to Mei sooner, and asking the chaplain for help.

He picked up his notebook and pen to jot down notes. He noted that despite his initial angry response to the girl's condition, he'd kept his cheerful/neutral mask on, and kept his composure. His real desire was to grab the caseworker by the throat and force her to tell him where to find the vermin that did this to a child. He knew just what to do when he found them, because he'd done it before; more than once, and it didn't bother him.

"STOP!"

The big man's internal mind brakes slammed on, and he used logic to check his anger. It's about the child, not your ego. She needs your help. You can't help her from a prison cell. You've indulged your mental tantrum, now get back on the clock.

He drew on the cigar and blew more blue grey smoke into the air. Then he settled back into a logical zone of thinking, and picked up his notes for the Chaplain he'd started when the little girl had laid down to nap.

The drive home had started out okay, or so I'd thought I'd chatted her up with a few easy questions, then the poor kid had a meltdown that started with farting, then sobbing, and ended with her puking on me on the side of the road. I don't care about that, I've been covered in puke and much worse many times before.

What concerns me most is the burning ulcer where the girl's soul should be. This child will need much more than I'd been told, but the situation is clear. It's up to me to help her.

He puffed on his cigar and wrote more notes.

I made the decision to acknowledge and move past the meltdown and continue talking to her, trying to be nonchalant but still present. I don't know where the inspiration came from to rename her, but it sure felt right, as though convincing her a new name would give her a new chance in life. Anyway, it seemed to work.

"Mei Mei...baby sister."

At least she started talking a little on the way home, and that interaction gave me relief. It at least bought me time to get her home, where I could play my Ace in the Hole...Boudicca.

Mei and Boudicca got along really well, and I was pleasantly surprised to see her and the puppy nap together on her bed. That's something isn't it? Anyhow, she napped then got up and we ate dinner. She seemed to eat just fine, but my stomach was so upset, I didn't have much of an appetite.

We finished the night watching a kid movie on TV, then she went to bed without a fuss. The puppy slept with her.

That's all I have for now; I look forward to hearing your input.

Thanks, Padre.

Your favorite crash test dummy.

The big man smiled at the ending. In addition to his education, skills, and bravery, the chaplain had a great sense of humor. He and the big man had spent a lot of time teasing one another.

The big man stubbed out his cigar and opened his laptop. Using his voice to writing feature, it didn't take long to transcribe his notes into an email and send to the chaplain.

He lit a second cigar, turned on music and sat back to relax. Writing the report helped calm him down and focus his thoughts.

He sure hoped the chaplain could make sense out of the day's events.

He looked up at the darkening sky.

"Oh mom, how did you ever do it?"

He sent his question skyward on more curls of blue-black cigar smoke.

Chapter 8

Mei Mei

Mei woke up to her first morning in her new home. Yellow morning light shined through the windows, and gently overpowering the light of the bubbling lava lamp. The big man had been right, the lava lamp was a great night light. She stayed deeply burrowed in her blankets and quilts while listening to the sounds in the house. She heard the big man singing. She didn't care about his singing, but it was good to know she wouldn't have to guess where he was and maybe have a bad surprise.

Mei thought she heard another sound, so peeked out from under the blankets and looked around the room. Her eyes stopped on the door. It was unlocked! The sound seemed to come from the other side. She was surprised and then mad at herself when she realized she'd forgotten to lock the door after the big man left. She'd never dreamed she'd have the luxury of a lock on her door and now that she did, she forgets to use it. Now she's wondering about the noise.

Should she get up and lock the door? Unfortunately, needing to use the bathroom added to her anxiety, so she had no choice. She carefully got up and switched off the lava lamp, then dug through her clothes bag and changed into clothes she'd packed. She looked up at the door again. Did she hear the sounds again? She didn't want to face the sounds, the day, or the big man without being dressed. She couldn't find her shoes, so she'd have to go barefoot. Worse, she realized she'd forgotten her stuffed bear when she went to bed.

Mei really didn't want to leave her room, but really needed to use the bathroom. Besides, sooner or later, she'd have to come out. So, gathering her courage, she opened the door, and immediately a black nose followed by a black smooshy face pushed through.

Boudicca wiggled her chubby puppy body through the door with her tail wagging furiously.

Mei's relief almost brought her to tears. How could she forget about Boudicca? Ignoring her need to use the bathroom, she reached down with both hands and happily petted away her worries.

Boudicca happily accepted Mei's pettings while bouncing around and bumping against her in puppy joy.

With the door open, Mei could hear the big man singing down the hall. Apparently, he was in the bathroom. Of course. Her apprehension made her stomach twitch, but only slightly. Nothing left but to go. Giving Boudicca a final back scratch, Mei followed the sound of the bathroom fan running and the big man's singing down the hall. Boudicca followed along.

The bathroom door was open and steamy warmth rolled out, pushed along by the notes of a song from the big man. She peered around the open bathroom door and saw the him standing at the bathroom sink looking into the bathroom mirror. He was wearing a pair of trunks, a tank top, and had a towel wrapped around his shoulders.

Mei gaped. There he stood, bold as anything, without a care, looking into the mirror and singing in a big deep voice.

Mei wasn't sure if she was comfortable with the sight of the big man like this. He wasn't naked or even indecent (a term Mrs. Curley used), but was more revealed. She ducked around the corner and peeked around to look again. The big man had lots of big muscles and she noticed the black twisty tattoos on his arms covered his shoulders, chest, and back. He really did look like a combination of Frankenstein and a pro wrestler.

Lots of scars on his arms, chest, back and legs, mostly white slashes and lines, dotted his skin and covered his tattoos. He'd obviously been hurt. Bad. Often. Mei wasn't sure what to think.

Boudicca interrupted her thoughts by bumping into her legs, begging to be petted. Taking her attention away from his scars, Mei watched the big man shave. Shaving cream lathered his face, and he hummed and sang while going about his business. She noticed mostly that he used a large, straight-edge razor. She'd never seen anything like it. He might cut himself! The razor was silver with a hinged looking handle and looked like a foot long! She watched him use the razor to skillfully scrape away the foam on his face, leaving big clean patches.

He glanced over and saw Mei watching him.

"Well now!" he cheerfully boomed. "Top O' the morning to you Mei Mei! Did you sleep well?"

Mei shrunk back after he noticed her and couldn't nod, let alone reply.

The Big Man acted as though she'd answered him. "Good stuff," he said, through a foam-framed mouth, then continued to shave.

"I need to use the bathroom," Mei said shyly.

"Oops!" he said. "Yeah, sure. I suppose it's has been a while hasn't it? Don't worry, my bathroom is almost all fixed up, and soon this one will be all yours."

He wiped off the razor and put it away. He used a damp washcloth to wipe his face, then walked past Mei, clean and smelling of fancy green soap.

"All yours," he said, then paused and waved without turning around. "There's soap, wash cloth, towel, toothbrush, and toothpaste for you in there. When you're done, come out to the living room. There's lots to do today, so after breakfast, we'll have to get going."

Mei closed the door and did what would become her morning routine; using the toilet, washing up, and brushing her teeth, although didn't shower. Her first disaster of the day came when she realized her hair wasn't going to cooperate no matter what she tried. She fussed at it for a minute, but nothing worked. She didn't have the right kind of brushes. Finally, she ended up wetting it down and whacking at it with a man's hairbrush, then gave up and went down the hall to the kitchen. She wondered whether the big man would yell at her for having messy hair, so prepared herself.

Boudicca had been waiting for Mei in the hallway. As she came out of the bathroom, the puppy's tail thumped against the wall. The sight of Boudicca cheered Mei up, so she patted its head and went to the kitchen with the puppy following.

He had dressed and was setting plates of eggs at the kitchen table. Sure enough, he was singing a ridiculous song with cheerful enthusiasm. She wasn't sure she'd ever heard the real song, but whatever it was, didn't resemble what he was singing.

"Mei-O!" He loudly sang out when she walked into the kitchen.

"Mei-yay-O!" He belted out again, "Mei light come and me w'an a go hoooome!"

"Mei!" He continued with loud enthusiasm "Me said Mei, Me said Mei, Me said Mei-ya-O. Mei light come and me want go hoooome!"

Mei had never heard a worse song. The terrible sincerity freaked her out and the words pounded like hammers in her ears.

"Work all night and drink-a rum! Mei light come and me wan go hoooome." The big man started an embarrassing shimmying dance across the kitchen floor. "Stack banana 'til the morning come!"

Mei had frozen in place when she first came into the kitchen, but now she was ready to run back to her room and lock the door.

Boudicca started barking.

The big man stopped and looked over and grinned. "There you are, a girl and her dog!"

His cheerful sincerity caught Mei off guard. He thought she would like this...this...whatever he was trying to do. She clapped her hands over her ears.

The big man saw the look on Mei's face and her hands on her ears, then stopped. His face flushed a bit. "No?" he asked tentatively.

Mei shook her head "No."

"No?" he repeated.

Mei shook her head again and took her hands down. "No."

The Big Man cocked his head and asked with a sudden grin. "Maybe a little bit?"

"No," Mei said, then pressed her lips together.

"Okay." Then after a few moments, he said, "but I'm still going to sing."

"Just not that song."

"Not even a little bit?"

"No."

"Are you sure?"

"Yes," Mei said firmly.

"Okay," he said with a shrug, then resumed preparing breakfast as though nothing had happened.

Was that it? Mei thought. The big man was going to just...stop? No yelling, no hitting, no punishment? He didn't even seem to mind, and she was confused. She didn't know what to expect on her first day, but a happy puppy and absurdly cheerful scarred giant were not it.

The big man's voice broke her reverie. "Before we eat, we need to take care of Boudicca. I already let her out, so we just need to give her food and water." He showed Mei how to measure Boudicca's food out of a big bag and pour it into one of two big metal bowls. Next, he had Mei put her step stool in front of the kitchen sink and fill a plastic pitcher with water, then pour into the second bowl.

"Good job!" he said. "Boudicca's going to be very big, so it's important she knows how to behave, and we're the ones in charge. Don't let her push you around."

He looked at Boudicca who was still sitting—wiggling more than sitting. "I don't like hitting dogs to make them mind, so we'll use other ways to make her behave, but it'll take longer. Got it?"

"Yes," Mei said.

"It's okay, Mei, I'll show you how."

He turned and faced Boudicca. In a firm voice he said in two separate commands. "Boo! Down!"

Boudicca reluctantly laid down. "Yes!" he said firmly, and Boudicca thumped her tail.

"Boo, up!" Boudicca popped up and began to galumph over.

"Bo! "Stop! Sit." Boudicca slowed, stopped, then reluctantly sat.

"Yes!" he said. Boudicca thumped her tail and looked at the food.

"Look here!" the big man commanded, then held up a finger.

Boudicca looked up at the big man.

"Boudicca...eat." Boudicca got up and trotted over to the bowl and started eating.

With a big smile, the big man turned to Mei and gestured to the table.

"Have a seat."

He set down two glasses of water and a cup of coffee.

"Let's eat! I put cheese on your eggs. Is that okay?"

Mei nodded and started eating. She didn't remember having cheese on her eggs before, but it sounded good. And it was good, really good. Out of the corner of her eye, she watched the big man pour hot sauce on his eggs, then start eating.

They were quiet while they ate, then he said, "after we get the kitchen cleaned up, make your bed if you haven't. "However, we need to fix your hair. You've a righteous case of bed head." He smiled as she nodded.

She was surprised when he said "bed head," but it was funny. More importantly, she couldn't detect any traps or meanness in his words.

They finished breakfast and cleaned up the kitchen. The big man poured more water in the puppy's bowl while Mei left to make her bed and get ready. She got the brush from the bathroom and returned to the big man.

He took the brush from her and looked at her hair as if it was a brand-new project. She tensed all over as he stood behind her, but with surprising gentleness, he started trying to brush the tangles out of her hair.

Unfortunately, it quickly became clear that despite the big man's best effort, taming her hair was unsuccessful and occasionally painful. They eventually wrestled her tangles into a mock ponytail.

He stepped back and looked at her hair and sighed. "Hmmm," he said and shook his head. "We'll, looks like I need to learn how to do this. Sorry about all the pulling," he said, sincerely petting her smarting scalp.

Once again, Mei was surprised at his genuine concern. "It's okay, you didn't mean to," she said, and didn't know why, but patted his arm. "I know when somebody means it when they hurt me."

The big man caught his breath, and a dark look flashed for just a moment across his face, and although he quickly made a face to disguise his dark thoughts, Mei Mei had still noticed.

The big man paused; momentarily lost in thought. "Let me think on this," he said, then his features brightened. "I have an idea!" he said, then grabbed his phone and tapped the keys. "Go take Boudicca outside for a bit. Make her stop and sit a few times. Remember to say, 'yes!' when she does what you want. Got that?"

Mei nodded and led Boudicca out into the backyard.

Chapter 9

Mei Mei

When she got outside, Mei stopped next to an outdoor table at the edge of the back porch and perused the backyard of her new home. But was it really home? She pushed the thought away and took it all in. The backyard was fairly bare; a fence with gates, but no trees or bushes; like a big pond of green mowed grass. Simple, uncluttered, open. She wanted to like it but wasn't sure if she could, you never knew when you were going to get taken away to a different place..

She stepped out into the yard, feeling the grass press down beneath her bare feet. Boudicca trotted along behind her. When they reached the middle of yard, she stopped to take in her surroundings. She couldn't see through the fence, but could see the street they came in on yesterday. Turning in the other direction, outside of the fence across a small field, she saw a neighbor's house, but it looked far away. Mei liked the wide open look. She stood still, closed her eyes and felt the whole back yard; the morning sun on her face, the grass beneath her feet, and the puppy playing at her feet. It felt good. Her stomach didn't hurt nor even twinge.

She opened her eyes and remembered what the big man told her to do, so she made Boudicca sit and get down several times, then they played for a while.

Soon the big man called them in. He wore a big smile and said, "I have a cunning plan! The game is afoot!"

Mei frowned. "What game and who's foot? What are you talking about?"

"It's kind of a surprise," he said then looked at the clock. "We got lucky we got in on short notice. Get your shoes on."

Mei went to her room and put on her shoes, still confused. She couldn't imagine what the big man had in store.

A few minutes later, the big man came down the hall. He was wearing a clean, tight t-shirt on that showed off his muscles, overlaid with a dressy black vest, and clean jeans that looked brand new. He looked much different than this morning, but mostly looked like the big man that came and got her the day before. Mei couldn't decide if he looked, good, clean, shiny, or handsome. Perhaps all of those.

"Ready?" he asked.

Mei shrugged and nodded.

The big man looked at Boudicca. "Watch the house, big girl!"

Boudicca thumped her tail in reply.

They went out and got in the truck. The big man made sure Mei was buckled in before they drove off.

They drove for a while before she asked, "where are we going?"

The big man chuckled. "Well, Mei Mei, I may know many things, but not everything, and when a smart person doesn't know something, they take time to find the answer. And there are many ways to find things out. You can read up on it online, at a library, you can puzzle it out, or you can get someone to teach you, even if you have to hire them."

Mei never heard someone talk this way before.

The big man continued his monologue. "Today I don't know how to do your hair right? So, we're going to hire someone to teach both of us how to do it. And sometimes, if the opportunity is there, finding out can lead to an adventure." He grinned.

Mei said nothing. He hadn't answered her question, but she didn't want to push him. Instead, she just looked out the window at the passing houses and trees and tried to figure out what he meant.

They got into town, turned into a parking lot and pulled into a parking space in front of a fancy looking salon. The salon had big glass windows with fancy lettering on the door. Mei sounded out the words written on a sign posted in front. "'Le Bon Vie?'" Salon."

The big man turned off the ignition and glanced in the rear view mirror. With a smug grin, he reached under the seat and pulled out a notebook with a pen clipped to it. "You ready?"

Mei shook her head.

"What's wrong?"

"I have no idea what's going on or what we're doing," she said, with apprehension. "I tried to read the fancy words on that door, but they don't make sense." Her stomach twinged a bit.

The big man sat back. "Okay, you're right," he said, nodding. Then with visible effort, he slowed down and spoke clearly. "Okay, so here goes. It's important that little girls feel good about themselves, and looking good is a part of that process. Having her hair done right helps them look and feel good." He took a breath. "Unfortunately, I don't know how to do your hair, so can't help you with that, so I want to learn. I called ahead and made an appointment with one of the ladies here to teach us how to do your hair the right way."

He gestured to the door with his chin. "The words on the door are in French, which is why they didn't make sense to you, but they mean, 'the good life.;'" He looked at her and calmly said, "your questions and concerns are fair and valid. Did I answer you?"

Mei wanted to disagree, but couldn't think of a way, so she nodded.

The big man's face split into a giant grin. "All right!" he said, then opened his door and climbed out. He tucked the notebook in the back of his pants and covered it with the back of his vest.

"Come on, Mei Mei!" He laughed. "Let's have an adventure!"

She got out of the truck, and he helped her close the heavy door, then took her little hand in his big hand, and they went into the salon.

Chapter 10

Mei Mei

Inside, a number of ladies were bustling around and setting things up.

Mei felt as if every eye in the place was focused on the odd couple standing in the lobby.

A pretty lady walked up the front counter and smiled. "Hi! How may I help you?"

In a voice a shade deeper than usual, the big man said, "hello, I called earlier and spoke with Miss Traci about getting some help learning how to do a pretty girl's hair."

"Oh yes," she said. "Just a moment, please." She turned and walked to the back.

More than a few minutes later, she returned with another pretty lady whose face meant business. "Hello, I'm Traci," she said, and extended her hand.

"Hello, Miss Traci," the big man said, and shook her hand. "We spoke on the phone earlier today."

"Yes, ...uhm... you wanted your daughter's hair done?" she asked, then quickly glanced at Mei before looking back at the big man.

"No ma'am. This is my sister, Mei. I'm her guardian. She just came to live with me. And ...I don't know how to do her hair." His lips drew thin with embarrassment. "Can I engage you to show me how?" He flashed a cheeky grin. "I can't have her running around with bed head now, can I? It just won't do."

Miss Traci smiled and nodded. "No, it won't, but I'm afraid we don't provide lessons here. The Department of Licensing would fine me a blue streak if they caught me teaching without a license."

"I understand, and I wouldn't want you to get into any kind of trouble with the civil authority types. But how about this? I hire you to do her hair and let me watch."

Miss Traci cocked her head and held a finger to her lips in thought. "Well," she said slowly, "if you're her guardian, I'd expect you'd want to observe for due diligence for her care and well-being."

"Miss Traci," the big man said, "a man who doesn't look after his people, especially the wee ones, isn't much of a man, now is he?"

"That's right," she said then narrowed her eyes. "But, mind this, big fella, you can't be in the way when I'm working."

"I never get in the way of a professional doing her job," he said, and a grin split his face again.

Traci looked down at Mei. "Well then, let's see what we can do. Come on, Mei, is it?"

Mei nodded.

"We'll make magic for you!" Traci said.

The three moved to the back of the shop. Traci provided a chair for the big man, and had Mei hop up into a big salon chair. Making her comfortable, Traci put a big sheet around her.

Once Mei was settled, Traci went straight to work. Her hands were gentle and sure.

Mei felt important, and while her hair was washed, shampooed, treated, trimmed, and dried, Traci provided clear instructions to the big man.

He wrote everything down and it looked to Mei as though he was drawing pictures as well.

Miss Traci suggested three possible hairstyles; one Mei could do by herself, one he could do, and a fancy one for special events. While she worked, she coached Mei on how to do it herself.

Mei felt good that Traci talked to her just like another grown up, at least as much as Mei could understand. The entire time Traci styled Mei's hair, the other ladies in the salon, both employees and customers, made a point to come by the booth and watch the transformation. From the corner of her eye, Mei noticed most of them paid more attention to the big man than Mei or Miss Traci.

Miss Traci provided good instructions and showed Mei and the big man tips and tricks to make Mei's hair look great. After she finished, Traci asked the big man if he had any questions. Mei's hair looked amazing shining in the shop's lights, and she thought it made her look as pretty as the ladies working in the salon. She was beaming.

The big man looked at Traci, took a breath, then steadily repeated the entire process for each hair style, just as Traci instructed.

Traci widened her eyes and nodded. "Yes, that's right, just like I said. Do you have a photographic memory?"

"Alas, no," he said, "but it's pretty good, especially when I take notes. I usually don't have to read them, but listening, watching, and writing helps the topic sink in." He stood up and walked over next to Mei. "May I?" he asked Traci politely.

Traci frowned but stepped away.

The big man looked at Mei's hair from several angles, then turned her chair to face him. Looking her in the eye, he said, "I need you to trust me. I'm going to do your hair over again, and if I don't get it right, Miss Traci is here to help me fix it."

And then to Mei's horror, the big man undid her hair, took a brush and brushed it out! Both Mei and Traci were shocked, and neither said a word. Mei's stomach knotted up hard.

"What are you doing?!" Traci yelled.

"I'm showing you why you're the best salon teacher in the world."

As Mei sat without a word, holding back tears, the ladies in the salon gathered around. Mei felt a lump in her throat, her stomach ached, and her eyes moistened. Her hair had been so wonderful and pretty, and the big man had ruined it. This was the type of evil thing Mei knew would eventually happen. The big monster was no different than anyone else!

The big man tried to make eye contact, but Mei refused. Not to be deterred, he leaned over and kissed her on the forehead, then in a surprisingly soothing voice, said, "It's okay, Mei Mei, hold fast and be brave. Your big brother is on the job."

That shocked Mei more than anything that had happened so far! She was too startled and upset to do anything but just sit there with everyone watching the spectacle.

Then, to everyone's surprise, the big man slowly and methodically put Mei's hair back together, just like Traci had shown him, including using the fancy brushes. The result closely resembled Traci's finished product. His gentle hands fixed Mei's hair without pulling even once, and Mei eventually became relaxed with his touch. He finished in no time.

He looked at Miss Traci. "Like that?"

"Pretty close," Miss Traci said, "but not good enough for our girl here. Do it like this."

The big man resumed working on Mei's hair with renewed diligence. After several minutes, he stepped back. "Are you happy with my work?"

Mei nodded as Miss Traci scrutinized his work. "It's not bad, but I don't think you'll make it as a hairstylist." She flashed him a snarky grin, then looked him up and down. "I suppose it's a good thing you're pretty, well, pretty enough."

The big man put a hand to his chest and opened his mouth. "Why, Miss Traci, you do know how to make a lad blush!"

"Don't you start that with me, Mister Man," she said. "You might be big, and you might be pretty, or at least kind of pretty, but this is my house, and you don't want me breaking your heart in front of this pretty little girl."

"No Ma Jolie fille," he said smoothly. "I don't want you to break my anything."

Miss Traci blushed.

"Let's go Mei Mei," the big man said. "If I need to learn something else, I'm sure Miss Traci can show me how to fix it."

Mei nodded in amazement. The big man's work on her hair was a bit different than Miss Traci's, but he came close. In fact, even with him redoing it, it was way better than ever before.

The big man unsnapped the sheet covering Mei, and with a flourish, folded it, and with a little bow, handed it to Traci.

"Thank you, my dear lady, you're a very good teacher."

He turned and gave a stage bow to the salon ladies, who applauded.

"Do me next! Me next!" some of them shouted.

"Sorry, ladies, I'm a one-woman man."

They hooted and clapped louder, while Miss Traci rolled her eyes and reluctantly applauded for his theatrics.

"Ladies, will you please excuse us?" he said with a laugh.

The salon ladies returned to their stations and customers.

The big man turned and put his hand out. "Miss Traci, I can't thank you enough for your kindness and understanding."

"Well," she said, "this has been quite a ride." She turned to give him a suspicious sideway glance. "You're a bit of a rogue, aren't you?"

"Me?" he asked in mock shock, then smiled. "Perhaps, but my baby sister needed help." In a more serious tone, he said, "And we all know the rules. For those I love, I will do great and terrible things."

Mei felt goosebumps at the big man's sincerity.

The big man snapped back into his cheerful roguish demeanor. "I realized thus far, my experience with girls' hair is," he paused and waved a hand for dramatic effect, "inappropriate to this situation."

Traci rolled her eyes then chuckled. "You sir, are a bad man."

"Perhaps, my dear lady," he said, then retorted, "but not an evil man."

Traci rolled her eyes again.

"How much do I owe you?" he asked. "With the treatment, wash trim, shampoos, and everything in this "to go" baggie here."

Traci named her price, and the big man didn't flinch at the hefty bill. He pulled out a roll of money, peeled off several bills, handed them to Traci, then peeled off two more.

"Gratuity, and thanks." He moved closer to Traci out of Mei's earshot. "My baby sister, she's had it rough."

He glanced at Mei who was admiring herself in the mirror, pretending not to listen.

"I can't erase it, but can try to make things better from here on out."

Mei looked over noticed Miss Traci's eyes moisten.

"Well, damn you, bad man," she said in a hoarse voice. "I can't take this."

"Yes, you can. You earned it fair and square, TANSTAAFL."

"Well," she said, with a bittersweet chuckle, "the only thing worse than having you two come back is if you never came back. So please do. Besides, I need to check your work, and can't have this little beauty going around looking raggedy." She glared at him, hands on her hips. "And I certainly can't have my student's work embarrassing me in public!"

His devilish grin reappeared. "Yes, Miss Traci. I'm happy to be your most apt pupil."

"Oh you!" Traci said, and slapped his shoulder with a towel, then looked down at Mei with a warm smile. "Miss Mei, keep your eye on your brother here. He's a tough guy, but even tough guys need protecting."

Mei nodded. "Yes, Miss Traci, and thank you Miss Traci."

"Let's go, Mei Mei," the big man said.

They left the shop, and the big man helped Mei into the truck. He got in, buckled them up, then started the truck and pulled out into traffic.

Chapter 11

Mei Mei

As they drove along, the big man asked, "I bet that was a lot to take in for you, huh?"

Mei nodded. She felt as though the air blowing on her scalp and neck was different than before.

"It's okay, Mei," he said, patting her shoulder. "Think on it, and if any questions come up, just ask."

Mei nodded again, and thought about her hair, but wasn't sure she wanted to share anything with the big man.

They passed a bank with a big clock. "Wow! It's later than I thought!" he said, then asked Mei, "Are you hungry?"

"Yes," she said, as her stomach grumbled audibly.

He laughed. "Okay," he said with a grin. "Let the adventure continue."

She wondered what the big man had planned next.

He must have read her mind. "The place we're going is called a farmer's market. It's like an outside shopping mall. People buy and sell things they mostly make or grow at home. Buuutt, it also has several food stands, with different things to eat. I thought we could try different foods and see what you like."

Mei frowned. "You mean, I get to pick?"

"Sure, why not? I might suggest things you never thought of, but you don't have to eat anything you don't want to."

Mei remained skeptical but didn't say anything.

They drove for a few more minutes, then pulled into a big parking lot next to a building with a roof but not many walls. Lots of people were browsing at the tables and walking around.

"Hey, Mei," he asked, as he pulled her out of the truck, "are you allergic to anything?"

"What's that mean?"

"Like, when you eat something, does it make you violently sick? I don't mean you don't like it, but you swell up or throw up, even need to run to the bathroom."

Mei shook her head. "No."

"Good! Now, if there's something you don't want to eat, let me know. Nobody likes everything, so it's okay if you don't either."

Mei looked at the big man in wonder. Was he for real? Was she really going to get a say in what to eat? And she could just not like something? This was so different from what she was used to before. When she thought of "before," the black clouds and a wave of sadness crept up on her. She stopped walking. The bad thoughts had returned.

The big man looked down at her. "What's wrong, Mei Mei?"

Mei teared up and tried not to cry. He picked her up in his big arms, which she didn't like because she felt so tiny. She avoided his eyes because she felt ashamed of losing control.

He gently lifted Mei's chin up with a finger, and she looked into his big, warm brown eyes. She saw kindness and understanding.

"Bad thoughts?"

She looked down and nodded.

"You poor, wee thing," he said gently. "You've had a rough time, but bad thoughts will pop up from time to time. Like a surprise case of the farts, and less welcome, right?"

Mei's sudden laugh surprised even her. He was crazy! But he was making fun of bad thoughts, not her. Although she didn't feel comfortable being held so close to him, he didn't act mean.

He winked. "That's my girl. Bad thoughts come and go, but we'll laugh at what we can, and if we have to, we'll get help for the bad thoughts we can't whip together, okay?"

"You mean, make them go away?" Mei asked incredulously. She thought bad things lasted forever.

"Well, we'll make some go away, take the bad out of others so they don't bother you. But if they do come, they won't know who they're messing with!" The big man held up a giant fist, and Mei knew he wasn't lying to her.

"Do you have bad thoughts?" Mei asked cautiously, and the big man chuckled almost sadly.

"Oh yes, yes indeedy I do, my baby sister! Maybe worse than most people, but I work hard so they don't get the best of me." He wiped Mei's moist face with a thumb.

"And they won't get the best of you. These things I know, and I'm a smart man. And adorable too! Drives the ladies crazy!" He wiggled his eyebrow and laughed.

Mei almost giggled but stopped in time.

"You know what?" Big Man asked.

"What?"

"You're a beautiful girl, and your hair looks amazing! And you know what? I think you should ride on my shoulders so you can see everything and show off your amazing hair at the same time!"

Before Mei could tell him she didn't want to (although the idea intrigued her because she'd be taller than him) he shifted his grip and gently scooped her onto his shoulders.

Mei felt awkward and a bit scared at first, but she felt so tall riding on his giant shoulders, she relaxed and enjoyed it. The big man held her firmly but gently around her calves as he strode across the parking lot and into the market.

People smiled and waved at Mei as she passed by their booths and stands, and she tentatively waved back. Stands sold vegetables, bread, cheese, clothes, candles; so many choices, Mei couldn't take it all in.

They arrived at the far end of the building, and the big man smoothly lifted her down and held her hand as they walked toward the food area. Mei smelled an array of enticing aromas, some sweet, some spicy, others weird.

The big man said, "What I like about this place is there's so many new foods to try. If you don't know what you like, you can experiment." He looked down at Mei. "Would you like me to pick first?"

She nodded slowly, unsure whether she'd like what she ate.

"Okay, but if you don't like something, you don't have to eat it, even if you chose it."

This was another new concept to Mei. She always had to eat what she was fed, like it or not.

They walked up to a booth with a big red circle and stick letters on a banner above. "One chicken yakisoba please," the big man said. He handed money to the person in the booth, and they handed him a paper plate piled with steaming noodles, vegetables, and chicken. He juggled the plate, then reached into a bucket next to a napkin dispenser and grabbed wooden chop sticks in a paper wrapper. He clutched Mei's hand the entire time.

They sat next to each other on a bench, and the big man opened the chopsticks. "This is called yakisoba. It's like Japanese spaghetti. Have you ever eaten with chopsticks?"

Mei shook her head as she eyed the chopsticks. "How in the world do you eat with sticks?!"

"Okay," he said, "watch."

He worked the chopsticks in one hand then dug into the food and ate a mouthful. He then scooped up more, and reaching over, fed it to Mei, who ate it without thinking.

She wasn't sure what to think at first. It tasted different than anything she'd ever eaten, but it was okay. Actually, it was pretty good.

The big man fed both of them with the chopsticks, alternating between each other.

Mei stopped after a few bites and let her stomach settle.

Soon the big man cleaned the paper plate and tossed it into a nearby trash can. "How was that?"

"Okay," Mei said, and wiped her mouth with a paper napkin. They went to another booth, and the big man bought a bottle of water. He cracked it open and gave Mei the first drink. "Just don't back wash into it, okay? I hate that."

She nodded, and they walked on.

"Are you still hungry?" he asked.

"I'm not sure," she said.

"No worries, I can get something else, and you can try a bite if you like."

They strolled down the row of food booths, hands together.

So many smells wafted from so many booths, it was hard to tell what food came from what booth. The big man stopped in front of a big booth where several different aromas wafted. No one else was standing in line, so he stepped up to the little counter and said hello to a lady with black hair and caramel colored skin.

She smiled back and greeted him warmly.

He looked at Mei and pointed to the sign. "Can you read the sign for me?"

Mei looked at the sign. The letters were shaped fancy and hard to read.

"It's ok, we're not in a hurry," he said. "Take your time, sound out the letters, then the words, then try to say them all together."

The lady looked at Mei and smiled with encouragement.

Mei shut out all the noises around her and looked at the letters. "Bom – bay. Curr yah?" She looked up at the big man with uncertainty.

Big man nodded. "Keep going."

"Bombay curryah-ee?" she tried again.

"Closer," he said. "Pronounce the 'y' at the end as '"e.'"

"Bombay Curry," Mei said proudly.

"Yes!" he said and beamed, and the dark-haired lady clapped and said, "well done, Miss! You're a smart girl!"

Mei blushed at the praise.

"Mei, in this case, the polite thing is to say, thank you, Ma'am. It's okay to talk with strangers when I'm with you and give you the okay."

Mei blushed and said, "thank you, ma'am."

"Such good manners, and so pretty!" the dark hair lady said in an accent Mei had never heard. The lady clapped her hands and asked, "if it's okay with your father, would you like a sweet?"

Before she could answer, Mei felt the big man squeeze her hand slightly, and she looked up at him.

He winked. "Go ahead."

Mei wondered why he didn't correct the lady, but she looked back and said, "Yes, please."

The lady stepped back into the booth briefly, then reappeared from behind a counter and handed Mei a small slice of warm, flat bread with melted butter and sugar on top.

"This is for the little miss!" the lady said warmly.

"Thank you," Mei said, and took a nibble. It tasted different than anything she'd eaten before, but it was delicious! Warm, buttery, and sweet all at once.

"Oh!" she said. "It's very good!"

"Oh, thank you!" the lady said with a warm smile. "So happy you like it!"

Mei surprised herself by turning and offering a bite to the big man.

He nodded then leaned down and took a small bite of the sugared bread. "Oh man, sooo good! Thank you, Mei Mei!" He rose to his full height and nodded to the dark-haired lady. "And thank you, ma'am."

"You are most welcome! Now, what can I get you, big fella?!"

"Chicken curry with peas and lentils, garlic naan, and an iced tea, please. We're going to share, so please, go easy on the spice."

"Yes, of course," the lady said, then went to get their order while the big man got out his money out.

Mei munched on the rest of her treat, then looked up at him and smiled. A ring of crumbs circled her lips. The big man laughed, grabbed a napkin from the booth counter, and wiped off her face.

Mei didn't know why she let him wipe her face off. She wasn't a baby and still didn't like him. At least she still didn't trust him.

The lady put their order on the counter. The big man paid, and they both said goodbye before walking over to a picnic table. Mei thought the food looked like stew. It had a strong scent, not bad, just not like anything she'd ever smelled.

The big man pointed at the plate. "This is curry, a blend of spices made into a gravy, or can be like soup, depending on who's making it and what style they're making it from. This gravy kind comes from India, a country in Asia." He scooped up a bite sized piece of chicken and offered it to Mei. "I like it a lot, but don't think you'd like it that way."

She took a bite. It tasted warm and spicy, but not hot. Still, she wrinkled her nose. The aroma and taste filled her senses.

"Here," the big man said, and offered her a sip of his tea after seeing her reaction.

"That's spicy!" Mei said.

"Yeah," he agreed, "but it's good, right?"

"I don't know. I have to think about it."

"Good, girl! Never be afraid to think about something, and maybe try more before you fully decide if you like it or not." He tore off a piece of the flat bread they served with the meal. "Try this."

Mei tried a bite. This bread was warm and buttery like the sugared bread she had tried, but instead of sweet, it was garlicy, and she decided right away that she liked it.

"Mmmm!" she said, licking her lips. "I like it!"

The big man smiled back. "Good. It's called naan, another favorite of mine. You know," he said, gesturing at the plate of food, "I like this, but it gives you dragon breath!"

He finished the plate and shared a few more bites with Mei. They cleaned up the table, waved to the dark-haired lady, and moved on down the row.

"Did you get enough to eat? We can try more or wait and come back another time."

"I'm good for now."

"Sure thing. It's later than I normally eat lunch, and I'm sorry about the delay today."

He apologized. "We'll get on a better schedule as soon as we get settled into a routine, okay?"

Mei nodded.

They wandered through the market and looked at the items people were selling. All the while, the big man talked with Mei, and told her many important things to remember. How to be safe, how to be polite, what to do if she met strange people, and what to do if she ever got lost. They found a restroom and Mei went in by herself. When she came out, she noticed the big man didn't let anyone else come in while she was in there. They wandered around and looked at more booths.

Since Mei was so little, she had trouble seeing what the big man was looking at. She liked the big man more than she did earlier, but still wasn't sure she wanted to be close to him. It was a confusing. After walking farther down an aisle and not seeing much more than grownups' behinds, she tugged at his hand.

"What's up?" he asked.

"I can't see what you're trying to show me from down here," she said with pursed lips.

"Oh yeah, sorry about that," he said, then scooped her up and put her back on his shoulders.

"Now, can you see?"

"Better, thank you." She felt proud she remembered to say thank you.

They continued along down the rows of booths and the big man stopped in front of one with stacks of very brightly colored t-shirts and clothes hanging from racks.

"Do you like these?" he asked.

Mei looked at the clothes and nodded.

"You need some clothes, so let's pick something out for you, any one you like, any colors you like."

She got to pick her own clothes? Brand new and not hand me downs? She felt off balance again, and glad the big man couldn't see her face.

Mei waited for the big man to change his mind, but he didn't. Instead, he asked the man working there what he might have in Mei's size. Together, they found a few shirts that might fit, and she picked out one with cheerful splashes of reds, yellows, and orange. They also found a little pair of bright multi-color overalls she liked. The big man paid the man for the items, and they moved down the aisle.

They found another booth where a lady was selling beautiful summer dresses. She smiled and greeted them politely.

"I think my baby sister would look great in one of your dresses," the big man said. "Can you help us find something in her size?"

"Oh, yes! I'd be happy to!" the lady said. "What would she like?"

"I think she would like to see what you have, so she can make an informed decision."

Mei wasn't as surprised as before, but her hope had soared when they had first stopped in front of the booth. She knew she once had dresses but couldn't remember. These dresses we so pretty, she immediately fell in love with them.

With the lady's help, they perused the racks and found a couple of dresses Mei liked. They decided on a beautiful lemon-yellow dress, and sandals to match. The lady showed Mei a few summer hats, and they bought one that just happened to fit her.

Bidding farewell to the lady, the big man carried their purchases in one hand and held Mei's hand with the other as they headed for the truck. Before they reached the end of the market, he stopped and looked at one last booth.

"She's here," he said, mostly to himself.

"Who?" Mei asked.

"It's ok, Mei Mei."

They took few more steps. An elderly woman sat inside a booth with home sewn stuffed animals.

"Mei," the big man asked, "would you like a stuffed pal?"

Mei felt overcome. The stuffed animals in the booth were amazing; much better than anything she'd ever seen, let alone owned.

"Could I?" she asked and looked up at the big man.

"Absolutely!" he said. "I didn't buy you any toys because I didn't know what you'd like, so I just saw these and thought you might like one."

Mei was flustered. So many choices, so many neat stuffed animals. She looked them over. Bears, kitties, puppies, ducks, tigers, horses, and even a platypus. She liked them all. Then she saw him. A stuffed, smiling bunny, beckoning to her as if it had been made just for her.

"That one!" she said, pointing excitedly. "He's the one!"

The big man nodded at her excitement. "Are you sure?"

"Yes!"

"Positive?"

"Yes!" Mei said, her heart thumping. Was he going to be mean now?

"Cross your heart and hope to die?" He laughed cheerfully. He was acting silly, not mean.

She nodded.

"Stick a dagger in your thigh. Eat a manure pie?" he teased and laughed.

"Aaagh!" she thought to herself and tried to hide her frustration.

"I think she'll take that one," the big man said to the lady.

Soon the rabbit was in Mei's arms, and they were heading for home.

Chapter 12

The Big Man

The big man settled into his comfy chair on the back porch like he had the night before. His lower back, leg, and hip were hurting after his first day with Mei Mei, especially after carrying her on his shoulders, but he didn't care. He was used to pain, and it was worth it to try to bond with the kid.

He went through his cigar lighting ritual and then opened his laptop and re-read the email from the Chaplain. The Chaplain had reassured him of some things, (yep, that's normal) and discussed some of the big man's observations. Reassured, the big man set the laptop down and opened his note pad.

The first full day with Mei had been something special. He wasn't sure what he'd expected with adopting a little girl, hell, he'd never been a parent before, so he had nothing to compare it to. He felt frustrated.

Fuck it! He wasn't going to accept the circumstances and leave the little kid and himself in misery. When he was still in the hospital and had discussed his ideas with the Chaplain, the Chaplain had understood the big man's intent and goals, but he'd cautioned him that he could influence, not force, the process or outcome. So, to achieve his goals, the Chaplain and the big man favored parenting principles and ethics over iron bound rules.

The big man chuckled to himself. The Chaplain was one in a million. He wasn't just a highly educated service corpsman. He tempered his faith and education with continued practical experiences, and had the medals and respect of many to prove it.

The big man almost felt embarrassed at the bad time he'd given the Chaplain when they had first met. Now he appreciated the Chaplain's support and friendship.

The first full day with Mei started off okay. Clearly, she didn't like my singing, and some people would say that's a point in her favor. She didn't speak or acknowledge me a great deal, and didn't initiate conversation, but at least responded when I asked her to do something.

I quickly found my first blind spot when I tried to help her tame her bed head but knew nothing about grooming a little girl's hair. I got inspired and called a local salon and got lucky. They had a last-minute cancelation and we got in. Once I explained my dilemma, the owner took pity on us and helped us out. Man oh man, that wasn't cheap! Those salon ladies must have a license to steal! But it was worth it, not just the hairdo, the teaching, and the experience, but it helped Mei feel pretty and important.

I don't know how to address this next issue, so I'm just going to come straight out. I had my own "emotional landmine" incident. Before we went to the salon, when I had been trying to untangle her hair, I accidentally pulled her hair a few times by accident. I apologized each time because I knew it must have hurt her. The thing is, even though I had hurt her, she didn't cry or complain. And when I apologized, she said with all sincerity and calm, "it's okay, you didn't mean to. I know when somebody means it when they hurt me."

Fuck! That statement speaks volumes, and I'm glad she wasn't looking at me when she said it, because I struggled to hold my emotions in check. For a few seconds, I didn't know whether I should cry or commit murder! Even thinking of it now still spikes my rage...if I could have just gotten to her sooner....

The big man's mental brakes came on and warning signal flashed in his mind. Stop! Get back on the clock!" He took a few deep breaths and then a heavy puff on his cigar, then continued writing in his notebook.

After the salon, I took Mei down to the market to try different foods for lunch and bought her clothes. I suppose I should have bought them from the department store. She'll probably outgrow them soon, but I wanted to set her up with special things she could call her own.

She didn't seem to have a problem holding hands when we were in the market, and seemed to like riding on my shoulders. My old injuries started hurting a bit, but it was worth it.

Overall, I kept it casual, engaging her in conversation by going into teacher mode. I'm also having her interact with people and keep playing with the dog. I would like to think day one went pretty well, but I'm really not sure. I felt as though I was holding my breath most of the day, waiting for something to go wrong, but I'll continue on.

Thanks, Padre.

The big man read his notes then opened his laptop and recorded them in another email to the Chaplain. When he finished, he closed his laptop and finished his cigar while he watched the sun set, pondering his new life. This was going to be one hell of an adventure. Fingers crossed.

Chapter 13

Mei Mei

Brother soon introduced Mei to the important people in his life. Due to his genuine, kind, and larger than life nature, Brother was an influential person and people liked him. During the first few days living with him, he taught Mei what a 'family of choice' meant, and started introducing Mei to those people.

For someone who's family was ripped from her, and who for a long time had no guardians, blood or otherwise, the idea of a family that would choose her only because she was little Mei was a gift beyond belief.

Even now, the enormity of these people choosing to love her for just being her, caused a catch in her throat and brought tears to her eyes.

The first couple of days with the big man were busy. First, he took Mei to two doctors for examinations. The nurses and doctors talked with her, took her temperature, checked her eyesight, and gave her a bottle of chalky syrupy liquid to drink for her upset stomach episodes. Fortunately, the results were mostly favorable.

Then the big man took her to a dentist. Mei couldn't remember ever having gone to a dentist, and it wasn't a terrible experience. The dentist and his assistant lady were nice, but Mei didn't like the scraping necessary for cleaning her teeth.

There always seemed more shopping necessary for more things Mei needed. She continued to keep up her guard up with the big man, but he was always attentive and kind. He sometimes cracked jokes to be funny, but Mei tried not to laugh.

The big surprise in her new life was how much she loved Boudicca. She'd always liked dogs, loved puppies, but with Boudicca's squishy face, giant paws, thumping tail, and love bug personality, Mei was gone on her. The first few days at the new house, Mei always kept the big puppy close to her, even letting her in to sleep on her bed at nap times. Before long, Mei assumed responsibility of Boudicca feeding and watering needs; didn't even mind cleaning up after her in the backyard.

Besides Mei's chores with Boudicca, the big man told her to make her bed, pick up her room, clean the bathroom, and help set and clear the table. Mei didn't like these as much, but these weren't too bad, even if they needed done every day.

Another daily routine for the big man was exercise. "Maybe I can't be what I was, but I can still be flexible, fast, and strong," he said.

The big man practiced a strict routine. Usually, he was up before Mei and would be exercising in the garage. He did a stretching routine called "battle yoga," He would followe that with a complicated martial arts dance as a warmup. Brother would also perform a number of complicated lifts and twist with weights called kettlebells. After, he sometimes he went for a walk by himself, or shower, dress, then come out to the kitchen and make breakfast.

The last thing they did everyday was read. Bookshelves were scattered around the house, at least one in every room. One was taller than Mei and full of books. In the early days, Mei usually didn't pay much attention to them.

On the afternoon of the second day, they'd returned home after running errands, and were putting more of Mei's new things away in her room, when the big man handed her a book.

"Here, have you read this one?" he asked.

Mei tentatively took the book and curiously looked at the cover, which showed a smiling red haired girl dancing with a monkey. She shook her head.

"That's okay, here's your chance!" the big man said with his cheerful enthusiasm.

Mei didn't move or react.

"Tell you what" he said. "Why don't we go to the living room, take off our shoes, and sit on the sofa and read?" Without another word, he turned and went down the hall to the living room.

Mei stood and looked at the book, then slowly walked to the living room. The big man was already kicking off his shoes, while Boudicca tried to climb up on the sofa next to him.

Mei walked over, fussed a bit at removing her shoes, then reluctantly climbed up on the sofa, making sure Boudicca sat between her and the big man.

When she was settled, he said, "why don't you read it out loud to me and Boo?"

Mei had never read to anyone before and didn't want to. She was just a little girl. People were supposed to read to her. She didn't move, but looked at the big man out of the corner of her eye.

"Please begin," he said, in a kind but no-nonsense tone.

"Sound out the big words, or you can ask me to help." He paused. "You're going to like this one. That girl Pippi Longstocking is a riot, and her and her pet monkey have all kinds of adventures. So, let's tackle the first chapter," he said with renewed enthusiasm. "Now, please begin."

Mei opened the book, took a deep breath and started reading as best as she could, but she hadn't read much of anything since before mommy and daddy died and she went to the Bad Place (stomach twinge again). But Mei wasn't stupid, she knew letters and how they sounded, so she pressed on.

The big man stopped her every few sentences and asked her to tell him about what she'd just read. The first time he stopped her, she got mad. Couldn't he see that reading was hard? Didn't he listen to what she'd just said? She scowled, but he just patiently waited with an open expression on his scarred face.

"Mei Mei, don't just say the words, think about what they mean. Are they telling you a story? If so, what is the story about? Are the words teaching you something? If so, what are they teaching you?"

Mei felt really angry! She wanted to throw the book at his head! She didn't like reading out loud especially to this big dummy, and she didn't know she was supposed to be able to answer questions about what she was reading. She didn't even pick the stupid book out. He did!

"No need to scowl," the big man said "Now pause and let your angry slip away, and then tell me about what you just read."

He was relentless!

Mei caught herself winding up, but then thought, he wasn't yelling, He wasn't hitting. He wasn't doing anything mean. He was just reading with her. That's all. She took a breath. She could do this.

"Pipi is a girl who has her own house, and she's the strongest girl in the world," Mei started.

The big man smiled and nodded encouragement as Mei thought about what she was reading and gave voice to the story the book told.

Chapter 14

Mei Mei

After three busy days into their first week together, the Big Man took Mei over to meet Auntie. As they drove across town to Auntie's house in the truck, Mei felt apprehensive. Who was this Auntie person?

"Auntie is one of the most important people in the world to me," the Big Man said.

"Auntie's my mom's, my foster mom's, uhm, my first foster mom's daughter. Sorry, this is a bit complicated. Let me explain."

Mei sat still and kept looking ahead at the road.

"Mom, our mom, had me when she was like 14. She was too young to have a baby, so she was brave, really brave, and made the choice to give me up to people who would love me and raise me as their own. I will always love her and respect her for that decision."

He cleared his throat.

"So, when I was adopted the first time, I was raised by a really great couple who became my parents in every way." He took a breath. "Anyway, they were older, and had a daughter who was years older than me. She became my big sister, and now she's your Auntie. Auntie was almost grown up and gone when I was adopted, but we had great years as a family before Auntie grew up and went onto school. Then Mom passed away, and another family adopted me."

He took another breath, "man, this is complicated," he said, mostly to himself. "But even then, Auntie stayed in touch with me. She didn't have to, but Auntie wrote me letters, emailed, and called on the phone. Sometimes she came and visited. She became like a bridge to my time back with my first mom. It felt good to have her rooting for me and calling me out if I got out of line with my

81

goofing off or made things hard for my new family. She's quite a lady," he said with pride.

The whole time the Big Man was talking, Mei kept looking straight ahead, but listened to every word. She was storing the information to think about it later.

The Big Man continued. "She may seem stern sometimes, but that's just her way. People show their love in different ways but remember this: it's not what people say but what they do that matters. Behavior is truth."

This introduction didn't ease Mei's unease about meeting someone new. After all, there was already so much going on with just coming to live with the Big Man. She wasn't sure she wanted to meet another stranger. She had enough trouble trying to understand the new thoughts and feelings in her new surroundings. Now the Big Man wanted to add more people, giving her new feelings to deal with? She didn't like the sound of this, but put on a poker face and went along with it. What choice did she have?

"Auntie has known me the longest of anyone, and has been real family to me," the Big Man said. "She's wise, tough, and funny. She owns a bunch of cats and feeds all kinds of animals that come to her house."

Mei looked at the Big Man with a frown.

"Yeah, sounds weird. Her house is like a wildlife zoo. Just wait."

Before they arrived at Auntie's house, they stopped at a gardening store. Mei held onto Boudicca's leash as the Big Man purchased several big bags of smelly soil and some plants. As the store's staff loaded it into the truck, Mei felt the truck rock under the weight. Soon, the Big Man and Mei were back on the road and heading to meet "Auntie."

They drove through town and pulled up to a medium-sized house with a big garage. Mei was surprised. She wasn't sure what she'd expected, but it wasn't this. The lawn around the house was almost perfect, with an abundance of flowers, plants, and trees. In the front yard were a riot of wind chimes, fancy clay pots, a fountain, greenhouses, and a big American flag flying on a flagpole. It looked as though it belonged on the cover of a magazine. A tall, confident looking lady with a long, braided ponytail, wearing jeans and a purple t-shirt with a butterfly on the front, stood in the yard watering plants.

"That's her," Big Man said.

When Auntie moved, Mei noticed her ponytail was long, tied together with evenly spaced red, white, and blue scrunchy ties. She couldn't say why, but right then and there, Mei decided someday she wanted a long ponytail just like Auntie's.

They got out of the truck, and the Big Man took Mei's hand and Boudicca's leash and led them over to Auntie. Up close, Auntie was tall, not as tall as the Big Man, but tall.

"Hi Auntie!" he said. "This is Mei Mei."

Auntie looked at him, then down at Mei. "Boy, don't you know you can't go around kidnapping little kids and running off with them?" She squatted to Mei's eye level and looked her in the face. Boudicca charged over for some Auntie pettings.

She petted Boudicca. "Missy-girl, did this big gorilla kidnap you?

"No, ma'am, he didn't," Mei said. "They said he's my brother."

"Sounds like you need to see legal papers to prove that."

Mei shrugged but said nothing.

"It's okay," Auntie said. "You can tell me the truth. He doesn't scare me." She winked.

Mei grinned. This Auntie person might not be a smiley person, but Mei sensed right away not only was she confident and tough, she was also kind, a quiet but strong kindness, like Mrs. Curley. That was okay with her. Mei didn't care about the smiley part, as long as she wasn't mean. She'd been with enough people who would smile and still be mean.

Mei could tell Auntie wasn't afraid of the Big Man either, but could also tell she liked the Big Man.

"Well," Auntie said, "If you really want him as your brother, then I guess I'm your aunt." She stood. "Come on, we can go see the critters while he unloads his truck."

Boudicca stayed with the Big Man while Auntie and Mei walked around the house to the backyard. If Mei thought the front yard was something, the backyard was ten times as impressive. More trees, plants, benches, tables, statues, birdbaths, and glass art items sparkled in the sunlight. It looked like a crazy magical place out of a story book, even more impressive than the garden at the nursery where they bought the dirt. Better than a park. Three big, lazy cats laid around the yard, and Mei saw another a fourth fluffy cat snoozing in the plants in a garden bed.

Auntie walked over to the side of the garage, opened a big plastic container, reached in, and scooped out a handful of peanuts. "Let's see if my critters will come out and greet you."

She started tossing peanuts onto the ground, and in a minute, three big squirrels appeared as if they'd been called. They came right up to Auntie and Mei. Auntie tossed more onto the ground in front of her and Mei, and the squirrels crept up and munched on the peanuts. The cats paid no mind to the squirrels or the people. Auntie tossed out more peanuts. A minute or two passed before a big racoon emerged from one of the plant beds. It shoved its way past the squirrels and helped itself to the food.

"Hey!" Auntie said. "Looks like the gang's all here to say hello."

Mei was amazed. Everything was green and alive here. Besides the racoons, squirrels, and cats, birds gathered on the bird feeder, and Mei thought she saw a rabbit dart between the plants. The entire yard smelled of dirt and flowers.

Auntie picked up a coffee cup from a table. "Come on, let's take a look around."

Mei followed her through the backyard. They walked through a gate, then onto a winding path of paving stones with butterfly images imprinted. They walked past glass mirror balls set on iron stands, locked tool sheds, through another gate, past several green houses, several planter boxes, and through trees. They arrived at a plant-covered gate leading to a small courtyard. Big wooden lawn chairs, potted plants, birdbaths, and a stone bench lined the borders of the courtyard.

The grounds comprised a lawn so immaculate and perfect; it looked as though it belonged in a fancy park. In its center sat a big old stone fountain with a paved stone walkway around the perimeter. Instead of water, several kinds of colorful flowering plants splashed up and out of the fountain. Bees zoomed in and around the flowers, birds dipped around and flew by. The place looked so peaceful. Mei wanted to sit on the cut grass and read a book, or eat lunch, or take a nap. Maybe all three.

The Big Man walked through another plant-covered gate from across the courtyard. "There you ladies are," he said, then looked at Mei. "Are you getting the grand tour?"

Mei nodded.

"Good," he said, then looked at Auntie. "I got the dirt off-loaded; do you want me to move anything else?"

"No, and don't go hurting yourself by lifting things," Auntie said.

The Big Man protested. "I'm fine. I'm not made of glass, you know."

Auntie pointed her finger like a spear. "Don't you start with me, mister."

The Big Man raised his hands. "Auntie, look, I'm doing my exercises and stretching, just what the doctor ordered. Ask Mei!" he said, and pointed in her direction.

Mei seized the opportunity. "I'm not a tattletale." When the Big Man sputtered in surprise, she pushed on with an impish grin. "I'm not saying he does or doesn't, I'm just saying maybe he's doing it when I'm asleep or doing chores."

Auntie laughed. "Ha!"

"Do you see this?" the Big Man complained. "I thought I was getting a little sister, instead I got a......he paused and thought for a second..."a she imp!"

"This is cosmic pay back," Auntie said, then laughed and looked at Mei. "Your brother's the reason I decided not to have kids!"

"Hey now!" he protested.

"Aww, pipe down," Auntie said, good-naturedly. "I'm happy being the old crazy cat lady."

"Well, you're definitely on your way," he retorted.

The three of them spent most of the day talking and working in the garden. Auntie wasn't super talkative like the Big Man, but felt wonderful to be around. She showed Mei how to garden as a matter of course and was an easy person with whom to ask questions. No surprise, the Big Man knew a lot about gardening, but often asked Auntie's advice and opinions.

Auntie's gardens had more than Mei thought. Not exactly a labyrinth, but certainly detailed and busy with lots of hidden nooks, crannies, and various artsy things.

In one of the nearly hidden nooks next to the house, Mei found a place with a stone bench with big, thick candles next to a small brick wall. On the wall were two brass plaques framed with small American flags on one side, and big, sealed boxes set into a cut window in the bricks. The boxes had see-through glass frames stored with items. She climbed up on the bench and looked closer.

On one plaque was a symbol she'd seen at the Big Man's house. He told her it was the Marine Corps Eagle Globe and Anchor. This one had the Big Man's real name inscribed. Inside the glass were two medals attached to a square of polished wood; He had gotten medals when he was in the Marines!

Mei didn't know why, but a wave of pride washed over her. Maybe the Big Man was a hero after all, like Mr. Curley had said. She was so focused on looking at the medal and trying to make out the words on the plaque, she didn't hear Auntie approach. Mei looked up in surprise.

Auntie put her hand on Mei's shoulder and squeezed.

"I may be tough on your brother," she said, "but I'm very proud of the big idiot. He's done a lot for our country; much more than he'll ever admit." She chuckled. "But he's also him, so we've got to look after the big oaf."

Mei smiled. "What's in that glass box?"

"Those are some of the medals he earned in the war, and being your brother, he didn't tell me about them, just sent them to me in the mail," Auntie said and chuckled. "God, sometimes he infuriates me. The other box belonged to our dad. He was an Air Force Officer. He was a hero too." Auntie squeezed Mei's shoulder a last time. "Hop down and let's go make lunch." She guided Mei through the gardens to the back door of her house.

Chapter 15

Mei Mei

They ate sandwiches and drank iced tea in the beautiful courtyard next to the fountain of flowers. It was as awesome an experience as Mei had expected when she first saw it.

The Big Man and Auntie chatted while they ate, then Mei removed her shoes and laid down on the manicured lawn to enjoy the sunshine. Boudicca curled up next to her. She wasn't paying attention to everything they were saying, so caught off her guard when the Big Man turned to her.

"This summer is going to be busy; we have lots to do, but I think you might be a big help to Auntie here. Would you like to come by sometime?" he asked, and muttered, God help me.

Mei sat up and looked at Auntie with wide eyes. "Could I?" she asked. The thought of helping in this magical place, not to mention time away from the Big Man, sounded great.

Auntie rubbed under her chin. "I think," she said slowly, "that you would be a big help here."

"Thank you!" Mei said, then jumped up and ran over to hug Auntie, who leaned back in surprise.

"Mei," the Big Man said, "Auntie isn't a touchy person."

Mei broke the hug. "Oh." She looked up at the woman with sad eyes. "I'm sorry," she said, then looked at the ground.

"It's okay, kiddo," Auntie said. "I'm just not used to little people." She glanced nervously at the Big Man, then bent down to look Mei in the eye. She took the little girl's hands and drew her into a light hug.

"But with you, I'll make an exception this one time, okay?"

88

Mei nodded into Auntie's shoulder, and a tiny smile crossed her features.

Auntie drew away and lifted Mei's chin to look into her eyes with a twinkle in her own eye and a tough smile. "If you want to learn stuff, I'll show you. Maybe that's better than a hug from an old lady, anyway."

"I don't know about that," the Big Man said slyly. "Now and then, a friendly hug from an experienced woman is just what you need."

"You shut up!" Auntie snapped and playfully swatted at him.

He snickered and danced out of range of her playful blows.

They worked around the garden for a few more hours. They took breaks, mostly when Boudicca yapped at a cat or raccoon passing by. By the middle of the afternoon, they bid Auntie goodbye and left. Mei enjoyed the day and looked forward to going back.

In the coming days and months, Mei would spend a great deal of time with Auntie. As Mei grew, Auntie would become one of the most important people in her world.

Chapter 16

Mei Mei

A few days after visiting Auntie, the Big Man told Mei they were going on a trip to meet his "God Pop" out at his farm. So, the next morning, Mei dressed up in her overalls and her working shoes. After breakfast, they loaded up in the truck with Boudicca, and hit the road.

"Pop's farm is a bit far from our house," the Big Man said. "It's out in the country and off the beaten track. It's easy to miss unless you know where it is. In fact, Pop's farm is in a valley with other farms, and unless you went there on business, wouldn't know they were there. An out-of-the-way place, hiding in plain sight."

Just like when they drove to Auntie's house, the Big Man opened up about his past. "A few months after I turned eleven, my mom found out she was sick with cancer. She was brave and tough, but we all knew she wasn't going to last long. She knew it too." He took a breath and spoke carefully, as though trying to remain calm.

Mei broke her rule about being quiet. "But you still had your daddy, didn't you?" she said, and sneaked a look at the Big Man from the corner of her eye.

His eyes were locked on the road. "Dad was a good man, a real good man. Honorable, smart, and quietly brave. He'd always wanted a son, and so I was his boy, and nobody could have asked for a better dad. He was a retired Air Force Lieutenant Colonel, a math teacher, and he loved mom with his whole heart. Mom loved him too." He snickered. "Even when they were arguing about something silly."

He cleared his throat. "When we heard how bad mom's cancer was, Dad was heartbroken. He'd known mom his whole life and couldn't be without her, and got super depressed. As usual, Mom took charge. When I say take charge, I mean she took the leadership role for her family and always put our needs before her own. She did everything that needed to be done while she was still healthy enough. She wasn't mean or bossy, just made sure Dad was eating, Auntie would stay in college, and if Dad couldn't manage me alone, I had a family to go to. A good family."

He took another deep breath. "Mom knew Pop and Miss Janice from the VFW and other places, and got them to agree to be my new family if anything happened to her and Dad. And it might have been one of the most heroic deeds I've ever seen. Whenever I'm hurt or feeling sorry for myself, I just think of my mom, who she was, and what she did. It inspires me to try harder."

"Anyway, when Mom passed, Dad died soon after. He'd lost his best friend and lover. So, I came to live with Pop and Miss Janice and my brothers. And even though I was super sad, I quickly realized I'd been blessed with another great family. They were different from Mom and Dad and Auntie, but were and still are some of the best people I've ever known. And I loved them very much."

The Big Man stopped talking to focus on driving.

Questions raced through Mei's mind. The Big Man had two families? She had liked Auntie, but now she had more people to like? What if she didn't? Her mind started racing, so she clamped down and tried to stay focused on just getting through the day with no trouble.

They turned down several long country roads and drove farther away from the city. The Big Man turned onto a road that wound through a thick forest of woods for a long while. They then turned off the main road and drove down a smaller road past pastures, houses, and farmlands. The scenery reminded Mei of the Hobbit movie they'd watched a few days earlier. She even liked most of the smells of the countryside blowing through the open truck windows.

The truck seemed to know the way all by itself, as they turned onto a one lane road, passing more small houses and farms, then onto a gravel road winding around a pasture. Mei looked at the grazing horses and wondered whether she'd get the opportunity to pet one. She liked horses.

They finally pulled up and parked next to a big red and green tractor sitting in a small gravel parking lot next to a barn with a low roof. Mei noticed a couple of houses and a few more low-roofed barns in the distance.

She let the Big Man help her out of the truck. Boudicca flopped out and stood next to them, wagging her tail and sniffing the breeze. They stood still and quiet for a minute.

"Do you hear anything?" the Big Man asked.

"Nope."

"HEELLOOOO THE FARM!!!" He yelled, startling Mei.

He patted her shoulder. "Sorry, sweetie," he said sincerely. "It's just a way of being polite out here on the farm."

Mei didn't care why he yelled, but didn't like the unexpected loud noise.

The Big Man took her hand, and they walked toward the nearest barn.

"Hello there, son!"

"Hey, Pop!"

An older silver-haired man walked out of the barn. His silver streaks wove through his beard and mustache. Though older and smaller than the Big Man, he was tough looking. He wore a flannel shirt, a worn t-shirt beneath, and faded jeans. He walked straight and proud, then grabbed the Big Man in a bear hug, and they thumped each other on the back.

They separated. Pop looked down at Mei curiously. "Well, son," he said with a genuine smile, "are you going to introduce me to the pretty little lady?"

Mei took the initiative and stepped forward and held out her hand. "Hello sir, I'm Mei."

"What a fine young lady you are, Mei," Pop said. "I'm proud to meet you." He looked up at the Big Man and winked. "Would you like to see my farm?"

"Yes, sir" Mei said.

"Please, dear one, call me Pop."

"Okay, Pop."

"Thatta girl!" Pop said. "Do you mind if your brother comes along?"

"I suppose if he doesn't go, then I can't go."

Pop's expression changed slightly, and he glanced at the Big Man, then looked back at Mei. "Sounds fair."

The Big Man nodded.

As they walked, instead of holding her hand like usual, the Big Man scooped Mei up and put her on his shoulders. She didn't feel super comfortable, and wasn't sure she liked being picked up without her consent, but liked the feeling of sitting high up, able to see far and wide; so it was worth it.

Pop guided Mei and the Big Man to the barn, and Mei needed to duck her head as they went through a big door. The barn had brick and wood walls, and rather than filled with animals, it was actually a workshop full of tools and machines. Mei saw old-fashioned saws, hammers, and blades, and couldn't imagine how someone would use them. She saw a big iron blocky thing and a tank full of something, gloves, and an enormous machine that looked like a furnace. There was so much to see and take in, she didn't know where to look first. Electric machines were scattered throughout the shop, and other tools of all kinds spread out along work benches and of the shelves above benches.

The Big Man put Mei down, and Pop escorted her around, showing her the tools, briefly explaining how they worked, and how to be safe around them. All this was new to her, and she found Pop's teaching interesting. As she listened to Pop and the care he was taking to teach her, she decided she wanted to work with Pop like she did with Auntie.

Pop looked at her with a twinkle in his eyes. "I suppose this is boring to you."

Mei shook her head.

"Oh?"

Mei nodded.

"Well, that's interesting. Would you like to see the horses?"

Mei nodded enthusiastically, but without thinking, took Pop's sleeve when he turned to go outside. Why did she do that? She didn't know what came over her, but pressed on.

"I do want to see the horses and animals," she said, then waved her hand. "But this is interesting, too. Can we make something sometime?"

"Really?" Pop asked.

"Yes, please. I don't even know what's possible, but I want to learn how to fix or build something." Flushed with her own audacity, she turned to the Big Man. "Maybe we could make something for Auntie to use in her garden."

The Big Man smiled. "I think Auntie would like that."

"And how is your auntie?" Pop asked.

"Good!" Mei said. "She has an amazing garden, and I want to learn everything about that, too."

"She sure does. Maybe we can make a surprise for her."

"Whatever it is, I think it will need a butterfly on it, and it should be purple."

"I think you're right," the Big Man agreed. "Those are some of her favorite things."

As they walked around the farm, they discussed what Auntie might need for her garden. Pop also pointed out things he thought might interest Mei as they walked past them; such as chicken coops, rabbit hutches, a vegetable garden, goat pens, and greenhouses. Pop's chubby dog, Charley, came out from somewhere and tried to follow them along, but Boudicca wasn't having any of that, and charged at Charley, straining her leash.

"Looks like Missy Boudicca is protecting you," Pop said.

"Or making sure she gets all the pettings and goodies to herself," the Big Man said.

Pop chuckled, and Mei bent down and stroked Boudicca's fur. "My good girl," Mei said with authority.

They crossed the property to another barn and went inside. From the powerful smells, Mei knew there were horses in this barn, but the stalls were empty. Mei looked up at Pop with wonder in her eyes. "Aren't there any horses?"

"They're out in the pasture," Pop said as he opened a gate. "Come on." They went out to the pasture where three horses grazed.

"Would you like to get close and pet one?"

Mei nodded, though she felt apprehensive. The closer she got, the bigger the horse was.

Pop went back into the barn, reached up to a shelf on the wall and pulled down a pail, then walked over to a big can, lifted the lid and dipped the pail down. Mei heard a grating crunching noise, then Pop lifted the pail up and rattled it. The horses turned and looked at Pop, then all slowly turned and walked toward them. Mei felt more uneasy as they came closer. They looked really, really big!

The Big Man noticed Mei's nervousness. "You're okay, Mei Mei," he said, patting her shoulder. "Breathe in and out through your nose just like I showed you and keep calm."

Mei did as she was told, breathing in the smells of the pasture, the horses, and each individual smell of the Big Man and Pop. When one horse got really close, Pop reached out and let the horse eat what was in the pail, then beckoned to Mei.

Breathing calmly as the Big Man instructed, she tentatively walked over to Pop.

With one arm, he lifted Mei up she could reach the big animal. "Give her a pet," he said.

Mei slowly reached out to pet the horse's neck as it munched. She could see its enormous eyes and the muscles in its jaw and neck move as it ate.

Pop talked to the horse, and so did Mei. "Good horse, nice horse," she said, and soon no longer felt nervous.

"Can I ride her?"

"Well, not today. But maybe some other time."

Mei nodded, but felt a little disappointed. She wanted to see what it was like to sit up on the horse's back. Maybe even better than riding the Big Man's shoulders. Certainly more comfortable.

The horse snorted, bobbed its head, and backed away once it had finished eating.

Pop put Mei down, and they walked back to the barn door where the Big Man had been watching.

"Did you like that?" the Big Man asked.

Mei nodded enthusiastically.

"She's ready to saddle up and ride the range," Pop said with a chuckle.

"That's my girl!" the Big Man said.

They wandered back through the barn and outside. As they passed a shed, Pop stopped. "Look here," he said. A couple of big round log ends on stands leaned against the side of the barn. They looked like targets; each with a red bullseye painted in the center. Chips and nicks were peppered throughout.

"Oh, Pop," the Big Man started.

"Come on now, it's been a while," Pop said with a smile, then walked over to the shed and went inside.

"It's okay, Mei," the Big Man said.

Mei's face held a puzzled look.

"This is ridiculous fun," he said.

Mei wondered what was going on when Pop came out holding a bucket in each hand. As Pop set them down with a clunk and a rattle, Mei noticed several wooden handles sticking out from one bucket.

"Choose your weapon, son," he said.

"Okay," the Big Man said, and nodded. "Just remember, you called me out, not the other way around."

Pop snickered as he pulled three rolls of canvas out of one bucket and rolled them out. Each one held a neat row of knives in pouches. Squares of leather were sewn into the canvas of the last row, with a metal dart tucked into each square.

"Okay, Mei," the Big Man said, "I can see you're wondering what these two crazy old guys are about." He chuckled. "Pop and I used to have throwing competitions." He pointed to each row and the bucket. "Throwing knives, throwing stars, throwing axes, and tomahawks."

"Your brother is overdue for a lesson in humility!" Pop teased.

"Oh, that does it!" the Big Man said. "It's on!"

He snatched up two knives from the nearest canvas and, to Mei's amazement, flipped them in his hands first slowly, then faster, until he broke out into a full juggling act. The knives had no edges, but were still pointy and sharp at the business end.

"Your fancy act won't spare you the taste of bitter defeat," Pop said as he armed himself with a few knives.

"Have at thee, villain!" the Big Man said, as Pop wound up and threw a knife. It flipped and stuck the target just outside the bullseye.

"Do you want me to call that a practice throw and give you another try?" the Big Man taunted.

"Just throw your steel, smart ass!" Pop groused.

In one smooth movement, the Big Man reached back and let his knife fly. It flipped and stuck in the target, just touching the bullseye.

Mei's eyes widened. The Big Man was good!

"Is that a hit?" the Big Man mocked. "I can't see from here, you know, war wounds and all." He winked at Mei. "It looks pretty close. Do you have a ruler or something?"

"Pipe down, boy. Sometimes the sun shines on a dog's..." Pop glanced over at Mei, "behind!" He threw another knife. This one stuck firmly inside the bullseye.

"Score one for the silver horde!" The Big Man cried to the sky, then threw again. This time, the knife didn't flip correctly, bouncing off the target with a clang.

"Steeeerike One!" Pop mocked, then threw his next knife.

Their contest continued for a few more throws as Mei watched in fascination. It looked like fun. The men were teasing each other mercilessly and obviously showing off for her, but it was cheerful. Both were really good, but after a few throws, it became clear Pop was better than the Big Man. Sometimes, Mei thought she could hear creaks and pops coming from the Big Man's body when he threw, but she really wanted to try throwing a knife, a tomahawk, something!

The men moved back to the weapons bucket. Pop picked up a tomahawk, and the Big Man chose a throwing ax, and they started throwing again. They kept on throwing and sassing each other. Both missing, both hitting. After they'd thrown everything but the throwing stars, they went down to the target, picked up the weapons that had missed, and pulled those that hit out of the target.

As they walked back to their starting spot, Mei could no longer contain herself. She jumped up and down and clapped her hands. "Now me!" she cried. "I want to do it!"

The Big Man raised his eyebrows. "Really?"

"Yes!" Mei said, then took a knife from him, spun around in a furious turn, and with all her might, threw it at the target. She missed by a mile. Even though the knife went wild, it didn't go far enough, and hit the ground in front of the target, then skidded to a halt.

"Whoa whoa whoa! Hold on there, you maniac!" the Big Man said, as Mei turned to grab another knife. "Don't you think you ought to have someone show you how?"

Mei shrugged. "Perhaps." She turned to Pop. "Pop, since you're mopping the floor with the big guy here, will you teach me?"

"Hey!!" the Big Man protested as Pop roared with laughter.

"You little fink!" the Big Man said.

Pop was laughing so hard, he had to wipe the tears from his eyes. "Okay, little one, let's get you on target."

He scooted Mei closer to the target, then showed her how to hold the knife, how to stand with the right posture, and how the motion of throwing a knife differed from throwing a ball.

Mei missed with her next five throws, but on the sixth, the knife flipped slowly and stuck in the target with a solid thunk! She did it!

The Big Man and Pop roared with approval.

Mei took another knife, and being careful to duplicate the last throw, threw again. Plunk! That knife stuck, too!

The men whooped again.

Mei raised both of her fists in the air and yelled in triumph. She felt great!!!! Although she missed the next few times, she improved with each throw. Next, she tried throwing the axes, but they were too big and clumsy. The tomahawks weren't as difficult, but still hard to throw. However, she moved closer and stuck with it until, finally, a tomahawk flipped end over end just right, and stuck by the corner of its edge in the target.

Pop and the Big Man looked at each other. "I think we've created a monster," Pop said.

"You've no idea, Pop."

"I want to do the stars before we finish," Mei demanded.

"Okay," the Big Man said, "but they're a totally different throw."

"That's okay," Mei said confidently.

As warned, she had a devil of a time throwing the stars just right. The more she missed, the more she became determined. The Big Man and Pop hung in with her until she finally started hitting the target, then stood back and let her keep throwing.

Pop produced a pipe, thumped in the palm of his hand, and lit it with a long match. The Big Man lit a cigar. The pleasant aroma of their smoke wafted around her. Occasionally, one or the other gave Mei advice, and she improved with every throw. Eventually, she threw one of stars with enough skill (or luck), that it stuck into the wooden target with light sounding plunk.

"Okay!" Big Man said. "Brava! You've got it, but I'm tired, so let's pick 'em up."

Mei took a breath and slumped in place. She'd been working hard, and now realized how tired she was. Her arms felt heavy; her shoulders sore. She thought for a minute and decided she didn't care. She joined the men as they gathered up all the weapons and packed them in the canvas rolls. Pop put them back in the shed on their way back to the shop. Mei, thoroughly exhausted, stumbled along behind until the Big Man gathered her up and carried her. She didn't mind this time.

They settled back in Pop's shop. The Big Man relit a cigar, and Pop lit up his pipe. They continued talking and, though Mei fought off the urge to curl up and nap in a chair, she wandered around the shop, examining the tools, machines, materials, and Pop's other treasures.

"Please look all you like, Mei," Pop said through a cloud of good smelling bluish colored smoke. "And ask all the questions you want. Just remember to ask before touching anything."

"Okay, Pop," Mei said. It all fascinated her, but she couldn't figure out what everything was or its function. When she asked, Pop and the Big Man would patiently explain to her what she was looking at, and its use. Even with their explanations, Mei still didn't totally understand. They noticed her puzzled expressions.

"It's okay if you don't understand everything all at once, Mei," the Big Man said gently, acknowledging her confusion. "It takes time, even if you're a grownup."

"I still want to know. I like knowing things."

"Of course you do, and you should want to know things," the Big Man said. "Knowledge is power." He paused. "Well, actually, it's not that simple. Knowledge combined with ability, skill, and will power is power."

Pop chuckled, and the Big Man shot him a look.

"Knowing how to do something isn't the same as knowing how to do it and having the ability and skill to do it, and then being willing to get it done."

"Huh?" Mei said.

"It's a process that takes work and focus," the Big Man explained.

Pop chimed in. "Little Mei, do you want to learn things?"

Mei nodded.

"Good. The best way to get started is to pick a project and start working on it, then you can learn and ask questions along the way." He looked up and around the shop. "Now, would you like to do a project with me and your brother here in my shop?"

"Yes, Pop!" Mei said excitedly. Suddenly, she wasn't tired anymore.

"Okay," Pop said. "I've been wanting to build another bat house, and I think we can plan it out, and build one. We won't finish it in one day, so you might have to come back here again. Would that be okay with you?"

"Yes! Yes!" she said.

"Well then, let's get started," Pop said. "Miss Mei, do you know what a bat house is?"

"No, Pop," Mei admitted, then paused and thought for a moment. "Is it like a bird house for bats?"

"Yes, miss, that's exactly what it is."

"Can we build one for Auntie?"

"I think that's a fine idea," Pop said. "Bat boxes provide a place for bats to live. Bats are handy because they help by eating mosquitos and insects, and pollinate plants just like bees do. So all of those things will be a help to your Auntie's Garden."

Pop looked around the shop again, then got up and reached into a dusty filing cabinet behind her. He pulled open a drawer and plucked out a worn folder stuffed with papers. He pulled out some papers and showed Mei. "These are the designs we'll use to build the bat box. See here?" He pointed at the writing on the papers. "The plans tell us everything we need to know to build them. What kind of wood to use, the measurements, materials to use, how to cut the wood, and in what order to put it all together."

"It's just like a recipe, Mei Mei," the Big Man said. "Instead of making a cake, we're making a bat box." He paused. "That's a thing to remember."

Mei nodded and thought hard for a minute on what Pop and the Big Man told her, while the two men gathered materials for the project. Then they told her how they were planning what to do, which person would perform which task, and how long the project would take to complete.

As they worked, Pop and the Big Man told Mei the names of the tools and wood, how each of the tools worked, how to pick out the one to use, how to lay the wood out, and how to keep track of their progress.

Mei hung on their every word.

Sometimes, the Big Man and Pop asked Mei to repeat instructions to make sure she understood, and encouraged her to ask questions. She found it was easy to ask them questions and noticed the Big Man paid close attention to Pop when he spoke. She also noticed Pop watched with concern when the Big Man got one of his muscle cramps and needed to "stretch it out." The Big Man grinned through his pain and told Pop and Mei not to worry; he was doing fine. "Real good, all things considered."

"Uh huh," was all Pop would say.

The rest of the day passed quickly. Mei was fascinated at how the project progressed, and how Pop and the Big Man made it look easy. She enjoyed being included in the project, even if she didn't understand everything and wasn't big enough to use some of the tools. They were so engrossed in their work; they ate lunch in the shop while the stain on the box dried.

After lunch, they continued to work on the box and finally, after a couple of hours of diligent work, the box was done.

Mei had been so engrossed in doing her part and listening to the casual conversation of the men, she had lost track of time.

Even better, she hadn't thought about anything bad all day. This was special, and she needed to think about everything that had happened, because besides fun, working on the bat box called to her today.

They gathered up Boudicca, hugged Pop goodbye, loaded up into the truck, and drove off with Pop waving.

Mei settled into her seat as she listened to the comforting rumble of the truck's engine and thought more about the day. She really liked Pop, the shop, the horses, and the entire farm. She felt surprised when she realized she even liked the Big Man teaching her things. Even more, she realized she was okay with him being close. She didn't know what that meant, so thought about it.

The Big Man interrupted her thoughts. "Did you have a good day?"

"Yes, I did," Mei said, instead of her usual nod.

"What did you like the best?"

"I liked it all," she said, and the words tumbled out, "and I want to come back, throw more knives, ride that horse, and build more things!" She thought for a few moments. "Most of all, I want to learn more from Pop. He's a good teacher."

The Big Man chuckled. "He's one of the best teachers I've ever known."

"Really?"

"Yep. Pop is very smart, and loves learning new things. Most of all, he loves to teach, share knowledge, and help other people learn."

They drove through the farmlands as they headed home. Mei was happily squished into her seat with Boudicca, nodding off but still awake, when the Big Man took a breath.

"I call Pop, 'Pop,' because he took me in when my foster mom died and left me alone."

"Really?" Mei asked, suddenly wide awake, her mind trying to process several things at once.

"Yeah."

Mei held still. She had to think. Her mind was racing. There was something there...something important. Her mind clicked, then clicked again. She'd heard the Big Man was her brother (or half-brother) because they had the same mother. And their mother had to give up the Big Man for adoption because she was too young to raise him. So, what did that mean?

There was an answer there. She just had to slow her mind down and focus. She clamped her mind down and tried to think step by step. If mommy had to give up the Big Man for adoption because she was too young to be a mommy when he was born, and the lady who adopted the Big Man and became his foster mom also had died, then he had lost two mommies! The reality clicked, and when it did, it hit Mei. Her eyes opened, and she bolted straight up in her special car seat.

"What's wrong, Mei?" the Big Man asked with concern. "Do you need me to pull over?"

Mei stopped her whirling mind. She didn't dare ask the Big Man if he really had lost two mommies, could she? She couldn't afford to feel sorry for him, could she? Was he more like her than she thought? With effort, Mei pushed the thoughts down while keeping her guard up. He was a grownup and maybe losing two mommies didn't hurt him as much if he was a child like Mei. Were these thoughts mean? Was she being mean? How did she know what hurt him and what didn't? The Big Man had been a little baby when he lost his/her/their mom, and not much older when he lost his second mommy, the one who raised and loved him when he was a little boy. Ugh, this was too much.

"Mei." The Big Man's voice broke her concentration. Concern lined his face as he tried to look at her and drive. "Are you okay?"

What to do? What to say? Mei slowed down her brain, and suddenly, the way out occurred to her. "So, Pop, he really is a 'Pop' then?"

"No one has ever done it better," the Big Man replied, relief echoing in his voice.

"I really like him."

"Good, he likes you, too. I think you'll have fun at the farm, and if you put in some work, you can learn some awesome things."

"Yes!" She really liked the thought of that.

"Are you sure you're okay?" the Big Man asked.

"Yes," she said, "I think I was falling asleep and got startled."

"Oh, okay." The Big Man didn't sound convinced, but he focused back on driving.

Mei felt anxious. She had lied, but why? And when did she start caring? Why did she care about the Big Man? She didn't like being here, did she? She didn't want to feel bad for the Big Man, did she? How did this get so confusing? Mei hated being little and not understanding things! So frustrating!

The Big Man's voice rescued Mei from her thoughts.

"You can ask him anything," the Big Man said. "In fact, if you have questions you don't want to ask me, you can ask him, and it will be just between you two."

"Really?"

"Yes, dear one. It's very important for you to talk to other people."

Mei didn't know what else to say, but nodded and settled down to enjoy the long ride home. She had lots of thinking to do.

Chapter 17

The Big Man

The Big Man emailed his report into the Chaplain

Hey, Padre,

It's been a minute since I checked in, but I thought I'd give you a break from my drama and wait until I had more to report. Thanks for the info on the other stuff. It's good to have someone tell me what's normal behavior and what to be wary of. Did you have to go through this with each kid you adopted? If so, you are much, much man!

I'm trying to be positive so I can report things here are getting into a routine. I took Mei to the doctor for a full checkup. She is underweight and borderline malnourished, but the doctor looked over the diet guidelines I brought and said that should be just fine. With careful monitoring, she won't have any lasting effects. That eased my anxiety a bit, but it was still a challenge to hold my temper when he confirmed what I suspected. Her eyesight and hearing are good too, thank God.

The doctor is also writing a report complete with test results, timelines, and his expert opinion for the attorney to attest that Mei's condition is a direct result of her foster care. He hates people who abuse kids too. That helps a little. It's a good thing I have a lot of experience compartmentalizing my own feelings so I can keep getting things accomplished.

Next stop was the dentist. She's lost some baby teeth and the new ones coming in needed a deep cleaning, but the dentist said she would also write a report showing symptoms of malnutrition in Mei's dental health record for the court case.

On to better things. Mei seems not to mind doing chores and helping around the house. I'm trying to teach her to assume ownership of her bedroom, house, yard, and surroundings, and to care for the dog. That's a cheerful topic. Boudicca is in love with Mei, and rarely far away from her. I'm glad to see that bond growing.

I continue to talk with Mei and engage her in conversation. Unfortunately, I don't think I'm making much progress. I think she's listening, but doesn't engage with me very much. It's probably still too early in the game, but it's still frustrating. Can't she see I'm taking care of everything? I'm not sure how to convince her not to worry. I don't let her see me get flustered. Again, my compartmentalization skills are getting a workout.

I did start her on reading books. My sister-in-law recommended some "girl" type books for her to start with. Mei is a smart kid, but I don't think she's been to school much, at least I don't think she's reading at the level she's capable of, so I'm hoping gentle forward pressure and acting with the presumption she can succeed with to help her reach her potential.

It seems teaching and explaining things to her gives me the excuse to keep engaging, and hopefully she'll feel safe enough to come out of her shell. Or at least, won't completely withdraw into herself.

So, here's a question for you, Padre. If teaching Mei is the only way I can keep her engaged, how do I prevent her from burning out? I don't want to nag or monologue all the time. There must be some kind of balance. As always, I welcome your advice.

I'm trying to build my support network as well as bring Mei into my family, so I started by taking Mei over and introducing her to my big sister. She was the nurse you met when she came and visited me when I was in the hospital. I joke with her and call her "Auntie" all the time now. Sometimes she resists slugging me. Small wins.

Here's the next aggravating situation. When I introduced Mei to "Auntie," they hit it off right away. Mei interacted with Auntie just as if they'd known each other forever, talking and engaging just like a regular aunt and niece. What the hell? I get treated like a stack of rakes at a hardware store sale, but Auntie gets the red carpet?

I guess I should be happy Mei is engaging with someone, but I found myself being hurt and jealous. (God! Can't believe I actually feel that way).

Do you think it's because I'm a guy and Auntie is a lady? Or is it just me?

Anyway, they took off to play in the garden and left me to do the heavy lifting type work, but that's cool. It's nice to do some physical activity in the sunshine and break a sweat. I ached afterward, but it was worth it. My fiendish plot worked. Auntie really likes Mei and now sees what I see in the whole situation. I never doubted Auntie would back me up with this whole adoption adventure, but now that she's seen Mei in real life, she's onboard on a visceral level. She's also furious at what happened to Mei but is careful not to let it show when the kid is around. At least I think the relationship will be healthy for the both of them.

My next big introduction is when I took Mei over to meet my God Pop and Miss Janice on their farm. It felt great introducing Mei to them and showing her around where I grew up. I think she liked it there. It's a great place to be a kid. It took about ten minutes for Mei to accept Pop. They're already crime partners. He had her talking, petting horses, throwing knives, and building things in his shop, again, just as though they'd been grandpa and granddaughter forever.

So, I don't think Mei's shutting me down because I'm a guy. Maybe the size? The scars? It's hard not to take this personally, but I'm glad her meeting everyone on the farm was successful. That was another big relief for me. I wasn't sure how she'd react to being out on the farm with people she didn't know. She seems to have a genuine hunger to learn and know things, so I'll need to find a way to encourage that.

Here's a cool thing. I choked up when Pop pulled me aside and told me he felt proud of me for saving that little girl. Wow! You warned me about being ready to deal with emotional landmines, but you forgot to mention the good emotional landmines can really shake your peaches. So, tell the other folks you're mentoring to look out for the good ones too.

That's all for now. I'm making sure I'm still eating right and doing my exercises and other therapy. I started carving mini totem type poles to help keep my hands busy. I was smoking too much, so hope this will help. My sleep disorder still flares up now and then, but it's less frequent.

Oh, one last thing, the girl is having bad dreams. I can hear her fussing at night, and I don't know what to do. I decided I wouldn't leave her alone in the dark, and so I quietly peek in a few times. Each time she was still sleeping, but fussing pretty hard, so I surreptitiously tucked her back in each time without waking her. I gave her a cool lava lamp for a nightlight, and I have even put a bell on her nightstand so she can ring for me in the night if things get bad. So far, she hasn't.

It's a new level of heartbreak to hear her at night and not being able to do anything, but having the puppy there helps. Boudicca whimpers a bit, but burrows into the blankets next to Mei. I hope that provides some comfort to the kid. Mei doesn't seem to remember much about her nightmares in the morning, then again, she still shuts me out, I guess there's nothing to do but keep a good face on this and wait, huh?

I'll let you know if they continue or get worse. I'm looking for a good child counselor. If you know anyone or have pointers for finding a good one, I would appreciate it.

Thanks, man.

Your favorite bullet magnet.

The Big Man hit send, then wondered if being honest about his worries and anxieties made him sound weak and whiney to the Chaplain. He decided he didn't care. Saving the little girl is what's most important, not his ego. At least that's what he tried to convince himself. It wasn't easy going from being one of the best at what he did to being a rookie at a completely new situation.

He puffed on his cigar and pondered. It sucked to feel helpless, and it was causing his own sleep disorder problems to recur. He'd have to be extra cognizant and proactive in taking care of his own recovery issues, too. Tomorrow he'd send a note to Johnny Boy. Johnny said he heard new kinds of therapy have been successful. The Big Man was interested in what was going on. He'd had outstanding success outside of the military to get help from private doctors to recover from his TBIs(traumatic brain injuries) and some of his spinal injuries. New treatments for military or veterans were becoming available. He'd reach out and network to find out the details. In the meantime, he'd continue with the light kettle bell work outs, juru/katas, and yoga routines the old wrestler suggested. Maybe he'd find a personal trainer or a pool and do water workouts.

He needed to keep trying; to keep putting in the work. Onward and upward....

Chapter 18

The Big Man

The Big Man woke up early the next morning, and after using the bathroom, donned his workout clothes and headed to his gym in his garage. As he walked into the living room, he noticed his cell phone flashing a voicemail alert. Normally, he wouldn't let his phone distract him from his morning workout, but he noticed the "unread text" alert icon was lit up as well. He picked up the phone and checked the text.

"Check your voicemail" From the Chaplain.

The Big Man punched in the voicemail code. After a pause, the Chaplain's deep, soul singer's voice came on.

"Hello to my favorite bullet catcher, IED dodger, and all-around bad man."

The Big Man smiled at hearing his friend's voice. Even though it was early in the day in Chaplain's time zone, the Big Man could hear the ever-present sincerity in the voice.

"Okay, my friend, this message is going to be long and a bit hurried, because as usual, I'm on the run, and this may be a bit scattered, but I wanted to reach out to you directly. Read your email last night. We have a lot to discuss in a short amount of time, so here goes..."

"First off, you're on the right track. Children want boundaries and expectations. Chores, standards, and education are good things, and "gentle forward pressure" is a great term, because you set the pace."

The Chaplain took a deep breath. "Just make sure you temper your forward pressure with understanding, kindness, prudence, and flexibility. I know you will, but I had to say it. I recommend you look into the classical liberal education model tailored down to her needs; arts, math, science, languages, problem solving, and logic. Look online and drop me a line if you have more questions."

"Part Two. Yes, sooner or later, many parents have the feelings you described, so I would say they're appropriate for your situation. I suggest you acknowledge them so you can deal with them appropriately and not get bogged down with them. I also think her reactions to her auntie and grandpa aren't unusual. Keep me posted, and we'll discuss it if we need to."

"Part Three, the final part." Again, the Chaplain took a deep breath. "Listen here, little brother, you have to stop holding yourself back. You don't have to be reckless or bombastic, but certainly don't need permission to be the awesome Big Brother the little girl needs. If you need evidence of my faith in you, remember I wouldn't have wasted my time coaching you and getting you all that volunteer time at the hospital and church daycares, especially if I thought you would harm that child, or any other child. Remember, this was your momma's dying wish."

The Big Man's breath came in a gasp, and his stomach clenched.

The Chaplain pushed on.

"You are her best and only hope for her to become a good human being. You set the pace, you set the example. So be her protector, her leader, her teacher, and her biggest fan. You know, a big brother. Keep expressing and showing affection. She needs you and you need her."

"Oh Yes!" the Chaplain exclaimed with a chuckle. "One last thing, your face. You have to soften that mean mug of yours. Seriously, I know you Marines "keep your bearing" behind a poker face of fierceness, but you need to find a way to show warmth and caring in your face, at least to her. She's a lost little kid you're trying to charm, not a Taliban fighter you're trying to instill terror in."

The Chaplain's voice was full of merriment as he continued. "And don't try to pass off your basilisk's grin for a smile. You'll stunt the child's growth."

The Big Man was caught off guard by the Chaplain's unexpected but accurate suggestion. His first instinct was fiery denial, but he took a breath and realized his friend was right. This was something he needed to fix and was glad the Chaplain pointed it out.

"Well, I have to go," the Chaplain said, then paused and chuckled into the phone. "Sorry this conversation was so rushed. Kind of like a coach talking to a boxer between rounds. I always like hearing from you, you big gorilla, so stay in touch, and like the Irish say, "May God hold you in the palm of his hand."

The call ended and the Big Man hit save, then shut the phone off. He'd been holding his breath, so now took a few deep breaths. So much to think about. He didn't miss the hospital, but really missed the Chaplain. A few more deep breaths and he was back to normal.

Smiling? Really? Little things just kept popping up. How in the world was he going to do that? He headed into the garage gym; he'd think and workout at the same time. He had things to plan, and maybe filtering them through sweat and pain would bring clarity.

Chapter 19

Mei Mei

As Mei thought back on those first few days, she focused on getting the sequence of events right. So much of what happened during the remainder of her childhood, spent in Brother's care, had their foundations based on what Brother had planned out in those early days.

Over the next few weeks, Mei and the Big man settled into a routine. Mei still thought of him as "The Big Man" and not her "Brother." She still wasn't exactly sure what him being her "Brother" meant, but saw how things were much different in her new life. She also saw how the Big Man was different that anyone she'd known, including the Curley's. She still felt unsure what was really going on, or what the Big Man might be up to, so she still (mostly) kept her guard up.

One night at the dinner table, Mei was reaching for something and accidentally knocked her drinking glass over with the back of her hand. The juice spilled out across the table. She recoiled in horror from the mini disaster and immediately looked at the Big Man.

Instead of yelling at her, he looked at the mini flood spreading across the table and just said, "oops." Then he mopped at the flood with his napkin. Even more shocking, he chuckled and said, "man the pumps!" as if it was all a big joke. He looked over at Mei. "It's okay, kiddo, no harm no foul," he said, then pointed to the counter. "Grab the paper towels and the dish towel and let's see if we can stem the tide here."

Mei stiffly did as he'd directed, and together they cleaned up the mess. She moved robotically, holding her breath, tummy clenching, while she waited for the storm to break from the Big Man, but nothing happened.

Sitting back down to the table, he said, "ya know..."

Here it comes, she thought.

"If you think I need to do a better job at washing the dinner table, you could just say something instead of being dramatic. I'm a pretty good listener." He grinned at her and winked.

Mei was so mistaken about her expectations, she fell to tears. She just couldn't stop herself. What did he mean by trying to be funny about a big spill at the table? Why didn't he know this was a bad thing for her to have done?

"Oh, hey kiddo." The Big Man's voice came out like a soothing rumble, and Mei felt his hand gently rubbing her back.

He hunched down next to her chair. "I didn't mean to upset you."

"No!" Mei choked out. "I spilled it, not you, and..." she choked on her words. "I ... I ruined dinner!"

"Says who?" the Big Man asked. His voice sounded genuine. "You spilled some juice, so what? You didn't mean to, and we cleaned it up. What's the problem?"

Mei heard the understanding in his voice.

He reached over and patted her arm.

Oh, oh damn! she thought.

"You were thinking what would've happened back at the other place, weren't you?" he asked.

She froze for a moment; her tummy was clenching. Then she nodded.

He nodded back in acknowledgement, and a cool stillness came over him. "Well, you aren't there anymore. You're here with me now, and it's a different world."

He reached over to the table and picked up a clean paper towel, crumpled it up and smoothed it out to remove the rough scratchy stiffness, then dabbed the tears from her face.

"There we go," he said, and handed her the paper towel. "I'll let you blow your own nose." He winked when Mei looked up at him and nodded.

"Okay, let's try to get back to dinner and see if we can get some fuel in us for tomorrow's adventure."

"What's tomorrow's adventure?" she asked.

"Dunno, the Big Man said, "but I think we'll be able to manage whatever comes our way."

Mei nodded, and a picked at the rest of her dinner, chatting with the Big Man. When she went to bed for the night, she realized, for the first time, she hadn't minded him touching her.

Chapter 20

Mei Mei

The Big Man acted odd in other ways. He wore a tough look on his face that made him look stern, when he was actually nice and often funny. Mei found it funny that he liked to cuss. She could tell he tried not to cuss when she was around, but occasionally would slip and let rip with a ton of bad words. The very odd part of his cussing wasn't the bad words; but so bad they were funny, at least to Mei. Most of the time she struggled not to giggle when the Big Man cut loose. Besides, she could tell he wasn't trying to be mean to her or make her feel bad. It was just his way of venting.

Another funny thing about the Big Man was, after a week or so, it became clear he was a singing man. He knew tons of songs of different kinds and seemed to know all the words to at least half of what was playing on the radio or computer stereo.

Mei would often hear him singing at the other end of the house or out in the yard. One time she was watching him clean the kitchen, and he was having a ball, belting out a song while he put dishes away. When he saw her watching him, he stopped and smiled.

"I like to sing," he said. "I was really into music when I was a kid, and my brother and a couple of us had a band." He paused in thought. "We weren't very good, but we had a lot of fun. Then when I was in the Marines, one of my jobs was to sneak around quietly, so I didn't get to sing as much." He nodded. "So now that I'm out, I do what I like."

"I know you're shy, but you can sing." Then he started into a song...

"And you can dance if you want to,
you can leave your friends behind
Because your friends don't dance and if they don't dance,

118

They're no friends of mine...."
Mei shook her head and left, leaving the Big Man to his lyrics.

Chapter 21

Mei Mei

The differences in being with the Big Man continue popping up. For example, he encouraged Mei's participation with everything they did. He asked her lots of questions, and also encouraged her to ask him anything in return, and when she stayed quiet, he would keep talking to her. He always talked to her as if she was a grown person. Mei liked that.

The Big Man made lots of time for Mei to play on her own; around the house, in her room, and in the yard. Even when she was at Auntie's or Pop's, he'd tell her to "go play." She loved taking her stuffed rabbit or one of her dolls and wander around Auntie's Garden. She would imagine she was in a magic kingdom of a faraway land where she was safe and could learn magic. When Mei played at Pop's, she was in a different faraway land with its own kind of magic. In Auntie's kingdom, Mei learned how to plant and grow and watch animals. In Pop's kingdom, Mei learned how to do mechanical things and how to be brave.

Mei continued to read every day. Sometimes she'd read to herself, sometimes read aloud to the Big Man or Auntie or Pop, sometimes the Big Man read to her. She quickly improved her reading skills. She finished her Pippi Longstocking book, and the Big Man helped her get another book when they went on an adventure to the library. She got to look at lots of books, and the Big Man got her a library card so she could check out books for herself.

The Big Man liked to read a lot. When he read, he would often use a pen to underline passages in the book, or write notes on the page. Mei freaked out the first time she saw him, and when the Big Man noticed Mei's discomfort, he motioned for her to come sit with him and discuss it.

"I only write in the books I own," he said, and I make notes so I can remember the passages which inspired me. When I'm done reading, I write a little synopsis (he explained what that meant) because that helps me remember what I read. If I want to remember what the book was about, I can scan the report, and from there, can dig up one of the notes I made. All of this helps me get the most learning I can from what I'm reading."

Soon Mei was doing the same.

Chapter 22

Mei Mei

Despite things going so well with the Big Man, sometimes memories of the 'bad place' popped up, and she felt scared, lonely, ashamed, helpless, and sick to her stomach all at once.

If this happened when she was around the Big Man, she would sit or stand close to him. Even though she still wasn't completely sure of him, she felt safer than with anyone else. As time passed, she realized she liked it when he would put his big arm around her or pat her back. Or her favorite—he would scratch the back of her neck with his fingertips. She'd feel safe and better in a minute or two.

If he wasn't around, or Mei was having one of her "worried spells" about liking him too much, Missy Boudicca was her next best good friend. Mei would hug Boudicca around the big pup's big neck, and sometimes tell the ever-growing puppy her secrets. Boudicca would thump her mighty tail and lean up against Mei, nuzzling her big head against Mei's little body.

The worst times were at night when the bad dreams came. Mei loved her bed and her room, and her blue lava lamp serving as a night light. But sometimes, she'd wake up crying from the bad dreams and her bed would be all messed up. She didn't want to ring the bell and wake the Big Man, but after the bad dreams woke her up, she couldn't bear being alone.

Reluctantly, the first few times anyway, she'd ring the bell next to her bed, and soon the Big Man would burst into her room, wearing gym trunks and an old t-shirt, his eyes fierce with concern. He'd quickly assess the situation then would sit on the edge of her bed and take her into his arms. He'd rock her gently until she calmed down. He was warm and strong, and Mei would fall asleep curled up on him.

One time, when the dreams were particularly bad, Mei accidentally wet the bed. She felt ashamed, and wouldn't have rung the bell, but felt so upset. The Big Man came in and, as usual, hugged her tight. He sent her with a change of pajamas to the bathroom to shower and clean up. When she returned, he'd changed the sheets, then dried and remade the bed. He kissed her forehead and tucked her under the crisp, clean sheets. After he pulled up the covers and got her settled, he rubbed her back and hummed in his deep voice until she fell asleep.

The next morning, she woke up to find he'd put Boudicca up on the bed, and the big pup was curled up snug next to her, snoring big puppy snores. When Mei looked over the side of her bed, it surprised her to find the Big Man curled up and asleep on the floor, wrapped up in a blanket and wearing his giant bathrobe.

Mei was embarrassed she'd caused so much fuss, but the Big Man woke up and carried on as if nothing had happened. Later, when he was making breakfast and noticed Mei was quiet, he gave her a quick scratch on the back of her neck.

"It's a new day, Mei Mei," he said, "let's go do some things!"

He sure seemed to know how to make things better. Mei just wished she knew how to tell whether he was pretending.

Even though Mei still didn't like talking much to the Big Man, he continued to try to help her grow in all kinds of ways.

One day he hung a big dry-erase whiteboard on the wall near the kitchen next to the wall phone, then used it to write a weekly schedule. He'd note what groceries to buy and chores he wanted done. At dinner, he'd often have Mei read out loud the to do list for the following day. They'd discuss how they would accomplish the tasks. Sometimes, he would ask Mei to tell him what she thought they should do.

"Since we're going to go help Auntie dig in her garden, what kind of clothes do you think you should wear?" he would ask. It became clearer to her he wasn't trying to trick her, but to include her in what was going on in her life.

The Big Man also wrote emergency numbers and their home address on the whiteboard. Then he taught Mei how to call for help, and what kind—police, ambulance, or firefighter. He also had a small cell phone in a holder next to the wall phone, with a bunch of numbers programmed into it, but wanted her to memorize the emergency numbers.

Chapter 23

The Big Man

How's my favorite Miracle Man?

Just a rundown of the past few weeks. Things are a bit better. To be honest, that's like saying a fever patient is doing better when their temperature has stopped climbing, but they still have a fever.

The good stuff; Mei is eating better. The nutrition guidelines the doctor sent are easy to follow, and although she isn't eating a lot, she already looks better. Her skin looks better, her eyes are clearer, and the listless, shell-shocked look she had when I first saw her is gone.

The not so good; I was doing laundry, and when I went to put clothes away in her room, I accidentally found some food she'd hidden. I know what that means for a kid who has suffered the kind of abuse she has, so thought it best to leave it alone and not say anything.

I'm still collecting my retirement, VA pension, and investments, so don't need to rush off to find a job right away, if I stick to my budget. I've gotten us into a domestic routine to give Mei some structure.

I have to say, domestic life can be a fucking bore! Holy shit! No wonder housewives are so desperate. I must be feeling better, because I'm getting antsy. I need to find a way to get a little action in my life or I'll go crazy. Sigh! I've started pushing my exercise and recovery routine and am back with my Master's program, mostly online. With Mei here to fuss over, I have something to do. I know what I'm doing is important, but I want to push my recovery work harder so I can go do....??? Someday I'll figure it out. Maybe I can find a gym with a trainer who can work with me or at least has a pool.

As dull as the routine can be, it's helping Mei. Just recently, I heard her talking to herself while she's playing, and she talks with Boudicca a lot too. We're interacting more. Sometimes she looks me in the face, and occasionally we even talk. She's still very guarded, so I'm careful not to push, and yes, I've tried to keep my face friendly when I talk with her.

Okay, as you know, I write my notes out longhand, then voice to text email to you. I hadn't finished this report when this happened...

The Big Man was abruptly woken up in the dark hours of the night. Before he was fully aware of what woke him, he'd exploded from under the covers and was standing in a crouch next to his bed with his hand on the door of the safe sitting next to the bed. He paused to let his brain catch up with reflexes. What was it? A bell....? MEI! He jumped up from his crouch, grabbed a pair of trunks he had next to his bed for emergencies, then walked into them as he opened his door and went to Mei's room, doing a full scan on the way.

He opened her bedroom door and continued to scan and assess. In the glow of the lava lamp, Mei sat huddled on her bed, clutching the bell and crying. Boudicca sat next to her, whimpering and nuzzling, but wasn't having much success at getting past Mei's defensive posture.

In his best "soothing the wounded" voice, he began talking as he approached the bed. "Hey, Mei Mei," he said, then reached out and stroked her back. Her back muscles felt as tight as a drum. "You're okay now, sweetie. I got you. Your big brother is here," he said, then gently took the bell from her and put it back on the bedside table. He picked her up despite her minor objections. Yep. She'd wet herself and the bed. Poor kid. The Big Man wrapped his big arms around her and held her, then rocked her while he hummed and talked to her. Boudicca leaned over and offered a wet puppy nuzzle.

It took a while, but the sobs subsided to whimpers. Then the Big Man felt Mei unclench her body as she calmed down. He got up with Mei in his arms and walked over to the dresser. Setting her down, he got a clean pair of pajamas out and gave them to her. "Mei, I need you to be a big girl and take a quick shower and put on these pajamas, then come back here."

Mei nodded and zombie-walked to the bathroom, with Boudicca following.

The Big Man got fresh sheets and blankets from the closet in the hallway, then returned to Mei's room and remade the bed. He finished just as Mei came back in. He swept her up in a hug, tucked her into bed, then kissed her forehead.

As he got up to leave, Mei said, "don't go."

"Okay, sweetie, I won't."

She settled back into the covers and rolled over. The Big Man sat with her and stroked her back as he hummed a few tunes. After three or four songs, when he was sure Mei was asleep, he got up.

Mei rolled around, and still asleep, reached out a hand. He reached down and held her hand for a minute, then got up and retrieved another blanket and pillow from the closet. He returned to the bed and wrapped her up in the blanket, then laid down next to the bed.

The floor felt hard. Between the hard floor and jumping from the bed when Mei rang the bell, he knew his wounds would cause him pain the next day. He answered his own thoughts. "Fuck it. This was a test, and I'm going to ace it, because the kid needs me." It took longer to fall asleep than he expected, but he managed.

Chapter 24

The Big Man

Mei adored Boudicca, even when the big puppy knocked over the trash and made a mess in the kitchen. One night, the Big Man had Mei sleep in one of his old t-shirts instead of her pajamas, then the next day, used the t-shirt to rub the puppy down. Then they put the crumpled shirt in Boudicca's bed. "That way, she'll know your scent and feel better," he said.

Sometimes the Big Man called Boudicca funny names like, "big girl" or "flappy face," and the pup responded. She usually followed Mei around the house (even into the bathroom if Mei allowed) and followed her into the yard when Mei went outside to play. Sometimes Boudicca would lean up against Mei in her friendly way and end up accidentally tripping Mei, but Mei liked that. Usually, Boudicca was so happy whenever Mei or the Big Man walked into the room, the happy pup immediately start thumping her big tail on the floor.

As much as she followed and fussed at Mei, Boudicca loved the Big Man most of all, and he clearly loved her back. Often, Mei would hear him talking to Boudicca as if she was a person, and when the Big Man took a nap on the couch, he let her get up on the couch to snuggle. It wasn't unusual for Mei to come in from playing and find them dozing on the sofa. As Boudicca grew, the couch soon became quite crowded.

Over time, Boudicca's tail became grew into a weapon. If she wagged her tail when she was laying down it made a serious "Tha-wump!" each time it hit the floor. The big man said that when she got bigger, they'd have to be careful where they put things on the end tables or Boudicca would end up knocking them off.

Boudicca would snore when she slept In fact, she would snore so loudly, that Mei could hear her all the way in her room when the big pup was in the living room One strict rule that the big man had (and Mei learned to agree with) was that Boudicca only ate her own food If she ate people food, the big pup's gas would drive Mei and the big man out of the room!!

If the big man wasn't around, or Mei was having one of her "worried spells" Missy Boudicca was her best good friend Mei would hug Boudicca around the big pup's big neck and sometimes tell her secrets. Boudicca would thump her mighty tail and lean up against Mei, nuzzling her big head against Mei's little body.

"She loves you and is worried when you're not okay," The Big Man had said. "Mastiffs are soft-hearted and they love people."

"I love her, too!" Mei said, hugging the big dog's neck.

"Good," the Big Man said. "Me, too."

Chapter 25

The Big Man

The routine of the days turned into weeks. Mei felt better about her new life (maybe the "fever" of the patient was down to 103 or 102.5???), but there was still no real "breakthrough moment." Perhaps there never would be. Maybe Mei was a long-term "patient," with baby steps and minor victories. So that's what the Big Man planned for.

The Big Man's ability to mentally compartmentalize his emotions proved to be invaluable. If he'd dwelled on anything out of his direct control, such as Mei's past, the lawsuit with foster care, or his own disabilities, he'd already would've had a full-blown meltdown. As it was, the time between his feeling of anxiety and outrage to acknowledge and manage them grew less over time, and he felt proud.

Mei had a few more nightmare episodes where she had to ring the bell for him to come, but fortunately none as bad as the big episode. The Chaplain had suggested the Big Man log the episodes on a timeline, so when he found a good child counselor, he could report the events accurately.

To the Big Man's relief, Mei had really warmed up to Boudicca. Watching the two play in the yard together, and hearing Mei share her secrets with the big puppy, inspired hope. Mei would wipe off Boudicca's drools and read to the puppy as she stroked her fur. If Mei Mei could form a bond with Boudicca, he felt hopeful of forming a bond with Mei.

In the meantime, the Big Man had continued his campaign for Mei's future by including her in as much of the day-to-day activities around the house. Besides chores and light exercise, he got creative in his efforts to include her. For example, the inspiration (where he got it from he had no idea) to hang the dry erase whiteboard with a schedule and notes.

Mei's reluctance to interact with him was fading. She still wouldn't initiate a conversation, but would respond to him, and was making eye contact more often than not. The Big Man considered those victories in his campaign.

Chapter 26

The Big Man

The Big Man was selective about teaching Mei things from his military training. He had no intention of militarizing her; after all, she wasn't a Marine. Still, he could teach her useful skills to improve her life.

The first one he taught her was Kim's Game, aka keep in memory. This wasn't a military skill per se, but a great memory and learning life type hack that strengthened the practitioner's practical memory and recall. As young as she was, if she could learn this skill, it would bear untold returns. The Big Man had a friend who became a lawyer after leaving the military who used the techniques from Kim's Game to graduate at the top of his law school class.

"Do you know how helpful it is to have to read something only once?" his pal had said. "It's stored in your memory for whenever you need it."

The Big Man felt sure this skill would serve Mei Mei well. He used flash cards for live memory practice and taught her to sketch what she recalled. He called it her "Mind Picture." And she took to Mind Pictures like a fish to water. She seemed to have a gift for observation and details, and was proficient at drawing what she saw. Even if her drawing was still at the level of a little kid, it was clear what she was trying to represent, and the drawing would improve with practice.

The next skill wasn't a military skill, but the Big Man heard of it as an urban legend when he was in the hospital, and when he discussed it with the Chaplain and psychiatrist, to his surprise, he found merit with the concept.

The story was, a famous musician met a little boy on a movie set and found out the little boy struggled with anxiety and fear. So the musician shared his own fears, and when things got bad, he'd put on an invisible mask. The mask didn't make the fear disappear, but would make him feel braver. The little boy tried it, and it helped him through some tough times in life.

Kudos to the musician, the Big Man thought. He was already a fan of the musician's music. Now he liked and respected him as a person.

After the Big Man met Mei Mei and saw fear had become her constant companion, he recalled the story of the mask, and taught it to her. He had to help her manage her fear. Education, ethics, action, and bravery seemed to be the keys to help her transcend from victim to victor.

Not all his ideas on Mei's life education were easy ones. He struggled with whether to teach her how to fight. After much thought, he decided if his goal was to raise her to become a whole person who would one day take a full agency for herself, sooner or later she'd have to fight for it. Preferably she'd learn to avoid, outwit, and or out maneuver her adversaries, but if it came down to physical conflict, he'd prepare her as best as possible. In Iraq and Afghanistan, he'd seen first-hand what happened to women who couldn't or wouldn't fight for themselves. Ugly memories.

The Big Man decided he didn't care what anyone thought. His sister, her life, her happiness and future mattered, and all needed to be protected. The naysayers' opinions didn't matter. Fuck 'em. Besides, he rationalized, he would be her mentor in how to behave, and influence her uses of force and ethics.

So, Mei's training began.

The Big Man had written down all of this in his notes, but rather than transcribe them into an email, he called the Chaplain directly.

He missed his friend.

Chapter 27

Mei Mei

The Big Man had been hurt when he was wounded in the war, and Mei was pretty sure more than once. Besides his scars, his body sometimes creaked and made weird popping noises when he moved. The results weren't always the same. Sometimes the popping noise made him clench his teeth, and his face became pale. He would stop and breathe deep for a few minutes until he could move again. Other times his face would relax, and he would sigh like a weight had been lifted. Often, he ignored it and kept doing whatever he was doing.

He exercised every day, always starting with pushups, especially when he seemed on edge. He said it helped him. Sometimes Mei thought of what it would be like to sit on his broad back, horsey style, while he did his pushups. At first, he could do only twenty-five pushups, but increased it to one-hundred after just a few weeks.

They visited the local YMCA where he took water therapy classes with a coach named Leeanne. She showed him how to change up his other workouts as he started getting stronger. As with most things, he included Mei in his workouts.

"No one who loves you wants you to be weak," he told her. "Anyone who wants you to be weak is someone you shouldn't trust. The people in your life should want you to be the strongest, fastest, smartest, best Mei you can be. And part of that is making your body into the best it can be. Your body is the greatest machine you'll ever use. Let's train it to do amazing things."

The Big Man taught Mei to yoga stretch and the proper form to lift weights of different kinds, especially kettlebells. He got small kettlebells for Mei and watched her closely as she swung them around. Using the kettlebells was harder than it looked, but Mei enjoyed doing it.

The Big Man's injuries weren't just physical. In Afghanistan, Iraq, and other places he had seen and done much. True to himself, he took the direct approach with Mei. He sat her down and told her he had PTSD and explained the condition.

"They call it Post Traumatic Stress Disorder," Brother said. "It's not a mental illness and I'm not crazy." He smiled. "It's a biological defense mechanism. It really is a kind of super power, because PTSD can help people survive terrible circumstances. Don't get me wrong, its not something you really want to have and there are probably better ways to cope with bad circumstances, but I went to war so many times, my brain and body taught itself how to act and think along with my training in order to survive and win in battle. Now, I am learning to teach my brain and body it's no longer at war. I also need to think like a big brother and how to be a good person."

"So, how do you do that?"

"Well, it's a process. I need a sleep schedule, so usually go to bed right after you, and I have a machine to help me breathe better when I sleep. Then I get up at the same time every morning. Staying well-rested helps. Sometimes I have bad dreams, so you might hear me fussing at night, but it's nothing to worry about. They're just dreams, and I usually don't remember them in the morning. Okay, so if you need me during the night, just ring that bell, okay?"

Mei nodded.

"Okay, let's see, what else?" The Big Man thought a moment. "I get antsy and frustrated sometimes, and that's why you see me doing push-ups or taking a quick walk. And sometimes I'm grumpy," he said sadly. "But keep in mind, it has nothing to do with you, and I certainly don't mean to worry you. In fact, this is why I'm telling you all of this. You're a smart girl and you deserve to know, so you don't worry."

He thought for a minute, then continued. "I get the blues now and then, but I'm seeing a special doctor, Dr. Tom. He's very good at helping me sort things out. I'll introduce you to him sometime. I also talk with other people who've been through the same thing, and it really helps, so even if I don't feel great, I know it won't last forever, and I can go back to being the old me. I have other issues, like needing to watch what I eat so I don't get too heavy while my bones heal. It's tough because I love to eat. But that kind of stuff is normal. Everyone has their own challenges. I'm no different."

Mei nodded. Then, without thinking, surprised herself by asking, "Is there anything I can do to help you?"

The Big Man's scarred and battered face broke into one of his big, warm smiles. "You already are helping, Mei Mei, just by being here and being my little sister."

Mei cocked her head and frowned.

The Big Man nodded. "It's true. Lot of people have similar issues, because they get out of balance when they return from a war, and leave the military because they think they no longer have a purpose to their life. So, I'm lucky, because I have you!" He squeezed Mei. "You make my life better, Mei Mei. Thank you!"

Mei shocked herself by tearing up. She never thought anyone would be glad she was there, let alone make their life better. Certainly not a giant like the Big Man. She wasn't sure she believed him and retreated into herself.

The Big Man saw her tears and said gently, "hey now, don't you worry, I'll discipline and bawl you out, and make you act right." He laughed. "And generally, get on your case. It'll make you mad sometimes, but never, ever doubt that I love you."

This was so much for Mei to understand. No one had even been this direct with her. It made her feel uncomfortable and glad at the same time. What was she supposed to do? What was she supposed to think?

The Big Man also taught Mei more "important things" he said she'd need to know. He taught her what he called "Kim's Game." He would place several things on a table in front of her, let her look at them, then put something over them, then ask her what was there, what she could tell him about each thing, and how they were laid out. He also taught her to freeze moments in time, so they became snapshots in her mind.

He showed her what he meant one day when they sat down on the back porch. He drew his own Mind Picture with a pencil on a big pad of paper. The picture showed Boudicca lying on her back in the backyard. He concentrated for a short time, then scratched away on the pad. He never looked up to see what Boudicca was doing or what she looked like.

After a few minutes, still without looking up, he handed the pad over to Mei. "Here, check my work."

The picture showed Boudicca laying in the grass just like she'd been. She lay on her back in the same place in the yard, the same distance from where the Big Man and Mei were sitting on the porch, and the Big Man even included a few small but important details, like the clumps of grass when he'd mowed the lawn and Boudicca's rumpled fur. The picture also showed the right trees and bushes in the background. It wasn't perfect like a cartoon drawing, but was very good.

"Keep it," the Big Man said, when Mei tried to hand him the pad. "That's the starting place for you. It will show what you want is possible, what you can do, and show you how to take mind pictures and draw them better than I can. For this to be of value, Mei Mei, you need to remember your pictures in honest detail. If you get the picture accurate, you can save it in your mind and pull it up later and look at it again. As you learn more, practice as hard as you can, get older, mature, and have experiences of your own, you can look back at the saved picture and learn new things from the same moment in time. But it works only if you're accurate. Being accurate is hard; colors, distances, assumptions, emotions, sounds, lighting, all of it can blur the accuracy of your mind's picture, so you have to practice to be good, and to make it work for you."

And so Mei did. At first, she practiced on simple things, like Boudicca playing, or an apple on the kitchen table. As time passed and Mei improved at "Kim's Game," the Big Man added times and dates to the game. Still, taking mind pictures at home was best because then she could check her memory by taking a photo with the Big Man's phone and seeing if what she remembered matched up. Or she could measure distances she'd guessed by counting steps. She felt frustrated at first, but the Big Man patiently helped her practice almost every day, and she improved over time. Later on, when she improved at taking mind pictures of still things at home, she practiced on people and events away from home; people at the grocery store, the neighbor's cars, the time of day the mail came. It was hard sometimes, but the exercise eventually became a habit.

When they drove someplace, Mei really enjoyed locating where they were by remembering the street names, turns they took, landmarks, and counting miles, or the time it took to drive on each part of the road. At first, she did it to make the Big Man happy, but the more she practiced, the more she could remember, and the more she enjoyed having and improving the skill. She considered it as her superpower.

The Big Man also taught Mei to challenge herself and ask questions like, Why? What is the next question? How? How can I do this? What happens when I look at this from another point of view? What are we trying to accomplish? How did this event or situation come increase her understanding and awareness of the events and her environment?

"Mei Mei, you're not helpless," the Big Man would say. "Even though you might not get the answer, you understand at the time. Keep trying. You'll get better."

The Big Man taught her another very special thing, just for her. He knew she was very shy and often afraid, so taught her about her mask. "I understand Mei Mei, you're shy and little, and afraid of a lot of things. But I also see you becoming braver every day. Every bit of bravery helps you get better and stronger."

Mei nodded. "It's hard to do."

"I know, baby sister, I know," he said. "In my life, I've been afraid a lot, of many things, but I don't let fear stop me from doing what I need to do."

"Really?" Mei asked skeptically. "But you're big and strong, and you can fight."

"So what?" the Big Man said. "I still have fear, just like anyone else."

Mei looked puzzled. She never considered a strong giant like him could be afraid of anything.

"Here's some truth about fear, Mei Mei." He paused for a moment. "Fears are personal. What scares you might not bother me, and vice versa. And fears come and go, and that's okay, too. The most important thing is that fear is a good thing, especially when you learn to manage it."

"A good thing?" Mei asked. "No way! I don't like being afraid."

"You're not really supposed to. Fear can keep you alert, keep you safe, and can keep you motivated. But you need to manage fear so it doesn't take over your life."

"How do I do that?" Mei asked.

"Educating yourself is a big help. Learn as much as you can about what you're afraid of, how it works, its weaknesses, and what you can do to reduce your fear. But if something is happening fast and you don't have time to study it, you need to put your mask on."

"What?" Mei asked. "A mask?"

"Yes. I have a magic mask I put on when things get too hard."

"It's invisible, but I always have it, even when no one can see it. I wear it here at home, when I was away at war, when it's dark, when it's daylight. I always have it and it always works."

The Big Man raised his left hand and drew it slowly in front of his face from top to bottom, as if pulling down a curtain. He smiled and took a big breath, then let it out. "There, I feel better and I'm not afraid. The mask is like a shield that blocks the jolts of fear, or at least makes them smaller. They don't bother me, and certainly can't stop me. Are you ready for your own mask?"

Mei nodded in wonder. Was this a trick?

"Okay, I'll make it right now, and show you how to put it on so you'll always have it."

Mei nodded again.

The Big Man rubbed his hands together for a minute, then started gently waving his hands near her. He then reached over and took Mei's hands in his big hands, and raised both sets of hands above her forehead. His hands were so close she could feel the warmth of them. In a quiet but deep voice full of love and strength, he said, 'mask,' as he drew their hands downward in front of her face.

Mei thought she felt a soft jolt that sent a shiver down her spine, but immediately felt the mask in place! It really was like looking through a mask! No one could see her face or the fear on it. Maybe it couldn't find her. And she felt better ... braver ... less worried. She smiled.

The Big Man smiled when he recognized Mei's expression. "Try it out. Think on something that used to scare you before you got your mask."

Mei knew immediately what to think. She knew what scared her most in the world. She took a breath and thought of ... the bad house...the bad times...and them. She hated to think about any of it because it upset her so much. Now, through the shield of the mask, they didn't frighten her, as if the fear they sent at her couldn't find her. She wasn't small; she wasn't helpless. Her stomach didn't hurt, her hands didn't shake, her legs weren't weak. They couldn't reach her, and the thoughts that reached her just disgusted her, and most of all, made her mad. With the fear gone, she felt stronger, braver, and just.... better.

Mei looked at her brother. "Oh, it's good!" she said.

"Yeah, it is," the Big Man said. "Odd thing," he continued, grinning, "sometimes the mask seems to go away, but if it does, you just reach up like I just showed you, focus your mind, and pull it back down. It will always be there and be stronger than ever." He chuckled. "It'll even work if you forget to put it on. It just feels better when it's on." He cautioned "You have to practice with it. Like everything else, it takes work for it to best help you."

Mei beamed at the Big Man (her Brother?) through her new mask. Had she just thought of him as her brother, at least a little? She'd been trying to keep space between them, but sometimes it felt good to hold his hand when they went to the store, or sit next to him when he read aloud to her. She really enjoyed riding on his big shoulders. He never yelled or made her feel small, and no one had ever taught her about using a mask to defend her from fear thoughts. It seemed as though everyone wanted her to be afraid of them all the time. Everything was so new and different here, and she wasn't sure what to think.

Whatever was going on, Mei knew it was too soon to tell. Better to stay as safe as she could.

Chapter 28

Mei Mei

One day, after being with the Big Man for almost a month, they were eating lunch on the back porch. "Your birthday is coming up. What do you want to do for it?" he asked.

Mei stopped eating the chicken leg she'd been nibbling on and looked at the Big Man with a puzzled look. "My birthday is coming?"

"Yeah, it's a week from this Saturday. You're going to be the big eight."

"Oh." Mei paused. She hadn't really thought of it. In fact, she hadn't really "had a birthday" since mommy and daddy had died. She'd gotten used to not being important enough to "have a birthday," so she locked it away and stopped thinking about it. She didn't even feel sad about it anymore. It was just one of those things about which she felt blank inside.

The Big Man interrupted her thoughts. "It's your big day, and your first one here with me, so let's have some fun. I'm kinda new to this sort of thing, but pretty sure the protocol for this event is you get to have a say in what you want for your big day."

When the Big Man used the words "kinda new" together, it showed Mei he was new to something. She had to admit when he said, "social convention," it not only meant he was new to something, but he was going to still try to do good at it. Mei looked at him quizzically. "Like what?" She was getting used to the fact the Big Man was sincere when he asked her a question. He wasn't trying to trap her with words, he was trying to find out something important.

The Big Man was taken aback. "Like, what kind of cake do you want? What kind of ice cream do you want? What do you want to have for your birthday dinner? What do you want to do?"

Mei picked up a piece of cheese while she thought. "I don't know." She took a breath. "I didn't get birthdays before I came here, so I don't know what to do."

The Big Man's face clouded for a second, but he quickly regained his composure. "I understand. Let's start with, what kind of cake do you want?"

"I don't know. I'm trying to decide if I want a cake because it's chocolate or vanilla, or maybe because the frosting is a pretty color."

The Big Man opened his mouth to speak but paused and thought about what Mei said. He nodded. "Good point. Sometimes a cake looks good but doesn't taste good, or at least as good as you'd hoped." He snickered. "Los of things are like that. But let's not overthink it. I want to get what you want, and even I don't know what's possible, let's plan a trip to the store and see what they can do."

"Sounds good."

"Oh yeah, ice cream," he said, then sipped at his iced tea.

"Ice cream?"

He nodded and put his glass down. "Ice cream is important, so we'd better add a trip to the ice cream shop to the list of our preparations to check out what kinds are best for the occasion."

"Really?" She felt embarrassed but excited to be the center of this new kind of attention.

"Oh God, yes," the Big Man insisted. "Ice cream is a singular treat and a thing of beauty for the senses, and when done for such an important event.... no...no... it must be done correctly!"

He was working himself up into one of his silly, cheerful, excitements, and Mei couldn't help but be amused.

"Now," he began his happy rapid fire talking to himself routine. "Normally you'd tell me what you want for your dinner, who you want to come, and what you want to do. However, we're on short notice, so I don't think we could get a dinosaur cloned in time for you to have dinosaur rides." He rolled his eyes and looked up. "I'm not sure how the winds will be on your birthday, so a hot-air balloon race might be out." He looked back at her. "I don't know what boy band singer you like, so if you want that little Jesse the beaver, or whatever his little twerp's name is, I'll have to see if he's in the country or overseas." He looked up in thought. "And if I can brew chloroform in enough time ..." His eyed snapped back down and looked directly at Mei. "And you, young lady, are too young to have a Chippendale's squad dancing for you, so that's out!"

"What?" Mei sputtered "Dinosaur rides?"

"Yeah," the Big Man said. "Definitely not enough time to clone anything that flies, so if anything, it will have to be a ground type runner, and a small one, I'm sorry to say."

"What?" Mei said, pressing her lips together and making fists out of frustration at Brother's weird and rapid fire dialog.

"Well excuse me, Missy" he said in his funny act face and voice, "there isn't enough time to clone and grow a T Rex or Brontosaurus in two little weeks, maybe we can swing a Velociraptor in time, but only if you make up your mind today, and even then it'll only be able to race with a small fry your size on it."

I don't want to ride a veloci-whatever on my birthday!" Mei said.

The Big Man nodded and bobbed his index finger. "Velociraptor, and I don't blame you. They can be a bit," he paused, "bitey."

"A bitey dinosaur?"

"Velociraptor," he repeated. "Yeah, and they're antsy too, kinda like Jack Russell terriers, but Velociraptors aren't as looney."

"No!" Mei said firmly. "And the singer isn't, "Jessie the beaver, and why would you need to brew chloroform?"

"You seriously don't think that little twerp is tough enough to take a blackjack upside his head, do you?" The Big Man continued in his rapid pace. "You may like his singing, but you have to figure he's probably made of glass."

Mei threw up her hands. "What?"

"Well, I'm sure he won't come willingly, and probably won't just let me stuff him into the back of the truck and drive him here for your birthday without making a fuss, do you? And I'm sure not going to let him sit up front with me. That boy would start yapping, and I'd end up stuffing him into the glove box, which would probably ruin the trip here, and he might not be ready to sing for you when I fished him out of the glove box. So, chloroform is the solution. Singer for you, quiet trip for me."

Mei opened her mouth and blinked. "No!"

"You sure?" the Big Man asked with sincerity.

"Yes!"

"Okay. Just saying."

"No!" she shouted.

They sat quietly for a minute.

"What's a Chippendale dancer squad?" Mei asked.

The Big Man snorted the iced tea he'd been sipping. "Yeah," he said deliberately. "I probably shouldn't have brought that up. Why don't we let that one rest for a bit?"

Mei sensed something, so she pushed on. "How long should we let that one rest?"

The Big Man gave up trying to drink his tea and set his glass down. "About thirteen years or so will do."

"Maybe I'll ask Auntie," Mei threatened.

He snorted. "Yeah, you do that."

"I will."

He gave her a thumbs up and finally sipped a drink of tea.

Ultimately, they decided to invite Auntie, Pop, and Miss Janice over for pizza, cake, and ice cream.

Chapter 29

Mei Mei

The Big Man, true to form, turned the trip to the ice cream shop into an adventure. In the later morning on a nice day in late spring, they drove the truck to the ice cream shop in town. The store had just opened when the Big Man, holding Mei's hand, opened a glass door with a tinkling bell. Cheerful music was playing, and they were the only customers in the shop. They approached the long glass counter and stopped to look at the rows and rows of multicolored tubs of ice cream lined up behind the glass.

Mei was just tall enough to see them without help.

"Hello," said a young man from behind the counter. "I'll be right with you."

"No rush" the Big Man said. "We're just looking for right now." He looked down at Mei. "Well, kiddo, let's see what they have to offer." They walked the length of the counter, looking at the different flavors. When they got to the far end of the counter, they stopped.

"Do you know what kind you would like?" he asked.

Mei shook her head. She hadn't eaten ice cream in a long time, but was eager to try some.

"Well, let's take a look," he said. "Why don't you read the names aloud for me? It's a fun way to practice your reading."

Mei didn't really want to read out loud in front of the man working behind the counter, but when she glanced at him, he gave her a genuine smile and a thumbs up. "Okay."

They strolled back down the counter for another look. This time, Mei read the names of each of the flavors out loud. Most names she could sound out all by herself, but with a few of the fancy names, the Big Man needed to help her. He was as patient as ever and nodded encouragement while she sounded out the words.

Some people came in and got ice cream while Mei was reading to the Big Man. She felt a bit worried she wouldn't get ice cream, but he calmly kept her on task, and she knew he wouldn't let her stop until the job he'd given her was done.

The young man behind the counter helped each of the customers, scooping up ice cream onto cones and making milk shakes. It took a while, but when Mei and the Big Man reached the end, he patted her on the back. "Good job. You're making progress with your reading. Now this particular ice cream parlor will let us sample a small taste of the ice cream before we buy, but I'm going to limit it to three samples each, so we don't take advantage of the store."

Mei's heart raced. Three samples of ice cream! Thoughts raced through her mind. What did she want to try? How would she know which to get?

The Big Man noticed her anxiety. "Okay," he said soothingly, "calm yourself. I can see you working yourself up, so let me teach you about making decisions under stress. Now take a breath. I can see you're worried about which flavor to choose. Right?"

Mei nodded and tried standing on her tiptoes to see further down the rows.

"Alright, now hold still."

Mei eased down to her feet. He hunched down next to her, which was what he did when he wanted her to understand something. He gestured to the glass counter.

"Here's the good news. There's plenty of ice cream, and it's not going anywhere."

She had no idea what he meant.

"So, there's no need to get freaked out or rush your choice. Now more good news. This situation is what I call "a no lose choice," meaning, no matter what you pick, it'll be great. Now, let's pick some samples, and as you pick out what you want to try, I want you to think of two questions. The first one is which flavor do I want for an ice cream cone today?"

Mei's heart leaped.

"And what flavor do I want to go with my birthday cake at my party? It can be the same as the cone you get today or different. It's your choice. Do you understand?"

Mei nodded. "I think so."

"Okay good. Now I've talked long enough, so let's get to sampling."

Mei looked up and down the row until she saw a fruit flavor she couldn't resist. She asked the young man for a sample and remembered to say please and thank you. The Big Man was big on manners.

The young man handed her a tiny scoop and Mei thanked him. It tasted amazing! So good!

The Big Man asked the young man for a sample of another flavor.

Mei put her tiny scoop into the trash, and looked for a moment, and chose a flavor with chocolate chips.

To her surprise, the Big Man was ordering a whole cone.

"What are you getting?" she asked.

"Oh, it's just one of my ridiculous favorite flavors that's hard to find anywhere else."

The young man behind the counter handed the Big Man a waffle cone with a giant scoop of black ice cream on top!

"What's that?" Mei asked with total fascination.

"This, my baby sister, is the most amazing and rare black licorice ice cream," he said in his showman voice.

"Really?"

"Yeah! Want to try some?"

"Oh, yes!" she said and stepped forward.

"Cool! Not everyone likes black licorice."

It tasted great! "That's what I want for my cone!" Mei said.

"Are you sure? You don't have to like something just because I do."

"Nope, I like it all on my own"

"Alrighty then, go nuts."

Mei and the Big Man sat at a table in the ice cream shop eating their ice cream cones. It didn't take long to see how the black from the ice cream cone got everywhere. They wore black ice cream smiles and stuck out their blue-black tongues at each other, causing them both to giggle.

They chatted, and as much as Mei like the black licorice ice cream, she decided it wouldn't go with her birthday chocolate cake, so she got the tasty fruit ice cream for her party.

When he was paying for the ice cream to take home with them, Mei saw the Big Man slip money to the young man working behind the counter.

"Thanks for your patience today," the Big Man said.

"Wow," the young man said. "Thanks, but I can't accept."

"Yes, you can," the Big Man said. "You were patient with us while I tried to teach the girl life skills, and you do good work." He smiled. "So please take yes for an answer."

"Okay. Thank you."

"You bet. I'm sure we'll be back."

"Good," the young man said.

Mei waved goodbye, and they left.

Another big day out with the Big Man.

Chapter 30

Mei Mei

On the morning of her eighth birthday, Mei woke up to a knocking on her bedroom door.

"Are you up, Mei Mei?" the Big Man asked through the door. Unless she rang the bell next to her bed to signal an emergency, he never entered without her consent.

"Yes," she said, still groggy with sleep. She rolled over and faced the door with just her head peeking out of the covers over her stuffed rabbit.

"Can I come in?"

She felt tempted to say no just to be a brat, but that would be mean. "Yes."

The doorknob turned, and the door swung open. A scramble of happy puppy feet sounded as Boudicca scampered across the door and jumped up on the bed.

Mei got excited when she saw the Big Man come in, carrying a tray.

He sang, "happy Birthday to you...happy birthday to you...."

Mei craned her neck for a better look at what he was carrying and saw a giant plate loaded with pancakes shaped like cats! She couldn't have hoped for more. When she tried for a better look, Boudicca bowled her over and held her down with puppy kisses and slobbers.

"Boo!" Mei said, trying to sound stern, but could only giggle at the big puppy. She tried to withdraw under her blankets, but Boudicca burrowed under the covers after her.

"Okay," the Big Man said after a minute. "Come on, flappy face, it's time for the birthday girl to eat her birthday breakfast."

It took some time to get the big puppy settled enough so Mei could come out from under the covers and sit up.

The Big Man balanced the tray on the edge of her nightstand, eased her clock and lava lamp over, then slid the tray onto the nightstand more securely.

Mei scooted over and looked at all the food on the tray. Included with the cat-shaped pancakes was strawberries, whipped cream, pieces of bacon, and a small bottle of orange juice without pulp.

The Big Man handed her a fork and slid the pancakes over to her. They still felt warm, loaded with syrup and butter. Mei cut away at the cat cakes and started eating.

"Good?" he asked.

She nodded, although felt a bit embarrassed at how thrilled she felt about the breakfast. She didn't know what to say, so kept eating.

The Big Man grabbed a fork, speared a strawberry, then slid it through the whipped cream and began eating.

Mei snuck a look up.

The Big Man smiled at her and winked.

Mei blushed and resumed eating.

"Did I get enough syrup on your cat cakes?" he asked.

Mei nodded. She wanted to continue eating, but made herself stop. She just couldn't look up at the Big Man, but took a breath. "Thank you."

"Oh," he said, with raised eyebrows. "You're sure welcome," he said with genuine warmth.

They ate in silence, with Boudicca watching intently the entire time.

When they finished, the Big Man gave Boudicca the command to follow, picked up the tray, then headed down the hall. Before he left, he leaned over and kissed Mei on the top of her head. "Happy Birthday. We're going to have a great day," he said, then walked out with Boudicca following.

Mei got up, made her bed, laid out her favorite sun dress, put the lava lamp and clock back to their correct places, then went down the hall to the bathroom. She got ready, spending extra time on her hair, making it extra nice for her special day.

When she went out to the kitchen, the Big Man was just finished the morning dishes and wiping down the counter. He looked up when Mei came in. "You look great!"

Mei blushed again. "I tried to make my hair like Miss Tracy showed me."

"Well, you did her proud," he said, then pulled his phone out of his pocket.

"Do you mind?" he asked.

Mei shook her head, and he took some pictures, posing Boudicca next to her. "Smile and say bacon."

Mei was surprised at her giggle, and Boudicca thumped her tail enthusiastically at the mention of the word bacon.

"You're supposed to say cheese," she said.

"You're right. Let's do it again."

"Ready?"

Mei nodded.

"Say cheese...y bacon!" he said.

Mei gasped in exasperation as the Big Man snapped a picture.

He put his phone down and gestured at the kitchen table.

Mei looked and saw a gift sitting on the kitchen table. He'd wrapped it in ducks and balloons wrapping paper and tied a big bow tied around it.

"What's that?"

"Well, from where I'm standing, it looks a lot like a birthday present. Do you know anyone who's having a birthday? Maybe you should take a look and see if you can figure out who it might be for."

Mei shot the Big Man an exasperated scowl but walked over to the table.

The gift didn't have a card, but up close, she could see "Mei" written next to the bow. She looked back at the Big Man.

"It says Mei."

"Well then, I suppose you should open it," he said with a smile of encouragement.

Mei pulled the present toward herself and unwrapped it. She pulled off the wrapping and found a big shiny box with pretty words and pictures of fairies and magical animals dancing in front of a cottage in a forest.

Mei's head was spinning from the amazing breakfast, the gift, and the party later in the day. A wave of emotion pushed up from her chest, and her breath was heavy.

The Big Man's voice snapped Mei back to attention. "What do the words say? Go on, read them out loud."

Mei cleared her throat and sounded the words out in her head; first once, then twice. Then out loud she read, "Mrs. Fox's magical fairy adventures."

"Good. What is it? A game? A book? Turn the box over and see if it tells you on the back."

She followed his instructions and took her time reading the writing on the back. She read the words from right to left and from top to bottom, just like he'd showed her. As she read, she looked at the pictures.

"It's an adventure and crafts set. It has a book and magic craft projects. Wow! Looks like you'll have a lot of fun with that."

Mei looked up in wonder. "Yes...I think I will." She thought for a minute. "And thank you."

The Big Man smiled. "You bet. I'm glad you liked it. Finding a gift was tricky, since we just got you all set up with dolls and stuff when you got here. Tell you what, I need to prep the ingredients for the pizzas before we run an errand or two, so why don't you open up the Fox Box there and take a look while I do all of that?"

Mei nodded, then sat down at one of chairs at the table and opened up her amazing gift. She took the book out and looked it over. It was brand new, just for her. She couldn't remember getting such a new and magnificent book. Her Pippi Longstocking book had been new to her (and she really liked it), but wasn't brand new like this. This Mrs. Fox book was so new, its binding was stiff when she opened it and the smell of new book wafted up to her nose. The pages were colorful and glossy when she turned them, each one full of writing and pictures.

As she continued turning the pages, Mei looked over the big words in the titles of the chapters, as well as the pictures. She sounded them out. The Big Man's coaching was quickly improving her reading skills. She no longer needed to sound the words out loud anymore, but the Big Man said it was fine if she did.

She soon became so lost in reading the story and looking at the craft projects, she didn't hear the Big Man working in the kitchen right next to her.

Chapter 31

Mei Mei

A while later, the Big Man interrupted Mei's gift exploration. "We have errands to run before the party. Why don't you go take a quick nap? It'll be a long day for you."

Mei looked up from her reading. Somehow, Mrs. Fox's book and fairy extravaganza had spread across the kitchen table. She'd been reading it for hours and wasn't sure when or how it happened.

The Big Man noticed her anxiety and smiled. "It's okay, birthday girl. It can stay there for now. Why don't you take Boudicca and lay down for a bit?"

Mei didn't want to, but also didn't want a fuss with the Big Man on her birthday So, she got up from the table and called for Boudicca. The puppy jumped up from where she was lying and trotted over to Mei.

Mei ran for her bedroom, and Boudicca barked and chased after her. Mei raced down the hallway, into her room, and jumped up on her bed with Boudicca climbing up after her. She laid down and endured a few sloppy puppy kisses until her four-legged pal laid down and snuggled next to her. She petted Boudicca and talked to her about the book she had read, and how excited she felt about the party. Boudicca was a good listener.

Mei didn't fall asleep, but must have dozed, because she woke up when the Big Man knocked on the door.

"Hey Mei, why don't you get up and we can go?"

Mei went to the bathroom and put on her sandals, then patted Boudicca goodbye. She and the Big Man loaded up in the truck and headed out. He let Mei put the truck's stereo on to the station of her choice. She didn't know what she wanted to listen to, but it was fun pushing the station buttons at random with impunity. The Big Man didn't say a word as she flipped back and forth.

They went to the grocery store and bought some things, then went to the Farmer's Market. Mei chose a light lunch of chicken kabobs on a stick, and strawberry lemonade from the food trucks.

As they ate, the Big Man said, "I had you lie down early because we have another stop before we go home and prepare for the party."

Mei was curious and looked a question at the Big Man, but didn't say anything

"Are you cool with a surprise stop on the way home?"

Mei's mind raced. A surprise? What could it be? A birthday thing? What was the Big Man doing? Her tummy churned, but only slightly. She nodded her assent.

They finished eating, cleaned up, then left, touring the market on the way out. Before they left the grounds, the Big Man stopped by a plant and flower stand. He talked to the owner, who seemed to know him. The woman gave the Big Man a cardboard box, and then he paid her, said thanks, and they walked out to the truck. He didn't mention what was in the box, so Mei paid it no mind. The day was pleasant, and she was enjoying it.

They loaded up and drove on down the road. Mei played more with the stereo, but still got no reaction from the Big Man, so she settled on a fun sounding song.

He pulled into the salon he'd taken Mei to when she first came to his house. Mei was curious but didn't ask. They got out, and he took out the cardboard box he bought at the Farmer's Market, took Mei's hand, and they went up to the fancy glass door.

"I'm told it's common for ladies to have their hair done on their birthday," he said almost uncertainly, "so this is another part of your big day."

Mei felt stunned. She never thought she'd be able to come back to the salon! She didn't know what to say, so just nodded.

The Big Man nodded back, and they went inside.

The pretty lady at the counter welcomed them both by name with a big smile. "Hello! Is this our special birthday appointment?"

The Big Man returned her smile with his best. "She sure is."

"Oh good, I'll take you back. Miss Traci is just about ready for our birthday girl."

They followed the pretty lady back to Miss Traci's station. Miss Traci was there and looked prettier and more glamorous than ever.

"Well, look at my beautiful people!" she said, then walked over, hunched down, and reached for Mei. "Can I get a hug from the beautiful birthday girl?"

Mei sensed Miss Traci's genuine excitement and couldn't resist, so hugged her. Miss Traci felt warm and safe, and her perfume smelled amazing and exotic. When they separated, Miss Traci said, "I love your dress! And your hairdo is very pretty! Did you do it yourself?"

"Yes, Miss Traci," Mei said, smiling.

"Good girl! I knew you could do it! But then you had the best teacher!"

Mei nodded, still smiling. "I did."

Miss Traci stood and faced the Big Man. "I won't ask you for a hug. I'm just getting one." She hugged him warmly.

He hugged her back as best as possible while holding onto the box he'd brought from the truck. "Hello, Miss Traci," he said, and handed her the box.

"Is this it?" she asked.

"Yes, just like you suggested."

"Good. I like a man who can follow directions."

"It helps when those directions come from an experienced lady who knows her mind. Amateurs can get a bit...skittish."

Miss Traci's eyes flashed "Oh yes? You have a lot of experience with this, do you?"

The Big Man shrugged. "Not as much as I'd like, but probably more than I deserve."

"I'll bet," Miss Traci said, and cocked her head. "Now go do whatever you do, while Miss Mei Mei and I make magic."

"Yes ma'am. I'll go and make magic with whomever, just like you said."

"That's not what I said!" Miss Traci retorted.

"Are you sure?" he asked, with a bad man smile. "Maybe you need to improve your skills at giving directions."

"Here's a direction for you," Miss Traci yelled. "Out!"

The Big Man chuckled. "Will do," he said, then leaned down and kissed Mei on her forehead. "I'll be back in a bit. Miss Traci is going to fix up your hair extra special."

Mei nodded, and the Big Man turned and left the salon. Although she knew he wasn't leaving her forever, she felt an odd sensation at seeing him walk away.

After he left, Miss Traci chuckled. "That big gorilla." She turned to Mei. "Let's get started. Hop up in the chair!"

Mei nodded and walked over and climbed into the big salon chair.

Miss Traci went to work.

Chapter 32

Mei Mei

Mei liked many things about Miss Traci. Her looks, her kindness, her skills at making Mei look pretty. But what she liked most was the way Miss Traci didn't talk down to her as if she was a child. She wasn't like teachers or caseworker ladies or other adults in that way, and Mei appreciated it. She was like the Big Man in a way, and although Mei didn't understand what that meant, she locked it into her mind so she could think on it later.

Miss Traci talked with Mei as she washed, dried, and trimmed just a bit of Mei's hair. "Not too much." she said. "Your hair is looking so much better now than when you first came here. It looks like your Brother is taking good care of you."

Mei reluctantly nodded. "He's trying."

"Good," Miss Traci said, then looked directly at Mei. "Are you trying too?"

Mei looked down. "Yes," she said quietly, "but it's hard sometimes."

"Yes, it is, sweetie, but you need to keep trying, okay?"

"I will."

"There's my girl," Miss Traci said. She turned the salon chair around so Mei faced the big mirror behind her, then hunched down next to her and both looked at the mirror.

"It's a lot of work, but you're going to be okay," Miss Traci said, then put her arm around Mei, and squeezed, then stood. "Now your Brother had an idea about your hair I agreed with."

"What?"

Miss Traci walked over to where she set the cardboard box, then opened it up and lifted out a beautiful circlet of summer flowers and ribbons.

"These are real flowers your Brother had arranged just for you." She walked over and pinned the circlet on Mei's head.

Mei was amazed and eager to see what they looked like on her head, but held still while Miss Traci worked.

After some time, Miss Traci stepped back. "Oh my, you look extra special good!" She moved so Mei could see how she looked in the mirror.

Mei took a moment to take in her reflection. Then she closed her eyes, took a breath, and looked again, because even though she'd just looked at herself, this time she focused on her image. It surprised her how much she'd changed in the last month, and the flowers in her hair were nothing short of amazing.

Miss Traci came back with other salon ladies and a few of the customers. They all cheered and complimented her hair, the flowers, and her dress. Mei felt a wave of pride lift her up and raise a smile on her face. They fussed and chatted before the pretty lady from the front counter clapped her hands and started singing. "Happy Birthday to you..." All the ladies sang along, then clapped and cheered for Mei, who was flushing with happiness and considerable embarrassment.

They just finished when the Big Man walked up to the cheerful scene. "Oh, wow!" he said with a big, cheerful grin. You look amazing!"

Mei smiled. "Thank you," she mumbled.

"Miss Traci, you're an artist," he said. "Mei looks so good, she could fit in with the Summer Court of Faeries."

"Oh yeah, Big Man?" Miss Traci said. "You best be careful. I could be a Leanan sídhe."

"And here I was thinking you were a nymph," he said, with a quarter bow. "My apologies."

Miss Tracie rolled her eyes and shook her head. "Mei Mei, please take this big beast out of here before I have to chase him out with a broom."

Mei smiled and hopped down from the salon chair, then turned to Miss Traci. "Thank you for the beautiful hairdo and flowers."

Miss Traci hunched down to look Mei in the eye. "Thank you, sweet girl. You're one of my favorite people, and you're going to do big things. I want you to look good when you do them. Now give me a birthday hug and go on now."

They hugged and Mei walked over and took the Big Man's hand and they walked to the front of the salon. He paid the bill, and they said their goodbyes to the pretty lady at the front counter, then left.

Chapter 33

Mei Mei

When Mei and the Big Man arrived, he asked Mei to change clothes while he unloaded the truck. "We're going to build monster pizzas, and they can get messy when we add flour and sauce and other condiments."

Mei hurried into her room, and being careful with her hair, changed clothes. Then she went to the kitchen, where she found the Big Man setting out the ingredients and a mixing bowl.

"Hey, birthday girl! You ready to make pizza?"

Mei nodded.

"Good, come on."

They spent the rest of the afternoon making pizzas, starting with the dough. The Big Man read the instructions and measured out the ingredients, while Mei put them into the mixing bowl. They mixed it by hand before putting it into a big electric mixer.

The Big Man let Mei push the button to turn on the mixer. The mixer was loud, but Mei was fascinated to watch it mix the dough. When it was done, the Big Man took the dough out and set it aside to rise.

"I think we'll cheat and used canned pizza sauce this time, but it should still be good."

Mei nodded.

"Besides, we need to chop up all the toppings," he said.

Mei was fascinated with the entire process.

The Big Man cleaned up the mixer and brought out another machine he called a food processer. "I have to do most of the next part because of the cutting involved, but I'll find something for you to do."

And he did! He cut up different kinds of cheese and put them into the food processor, then allowed Mei to push the start button after showing her how it worked and how to be safe. The processor groaned loudly and grated the cheese up in no time! After the cheese, the Big Man and Mei cut up pepperoni and the rest of the condiments! Mei loved working the food processor.

By the time they finished cutting, the dough was ready.

"Okay," he said. "There are two kinds of pizzas, round and square. Some people like one kind, some people like the other." He grinned. "I like both."

Mei nodded.

"However, it's your birthday, so you can pick what kind you want."

Mei thought for a moment. "Can I have one of each?"

The Big Man nodded. "Good call."

They put down flour and rolled the dough out. She enjoyed it but found the rolling pin trickier to operate than she expected.

The Big Man joked with her while they tried to get the shapes right. Eventually, they did, more or less. They added the sauce, cheese, and other condiments.

When they finished, the pizzas didn't look restaurant made, but still looked tasty.

The Big Man told Mei to pose next to the pizzas, and he snapped a photo. She didn't mind. Actually, he'd been taking photos of Mei all day on the sly, at breakfast, at the salon, making the pizzas. She could tell it meant a lot to him, yet it didn't feel creepy.

"Wow! Look at the time," the Big Man said. "Our company will be here anytime. Why don't you get cleaned up, put your nice dress back on, and I'll warm up the oven and clean up in here?"

Mei nodded and trotted off.

Chapter 34

Mei Mei

Mei had cleaned up, touched up her hair, and was carefully putting her summer dress back on when she heard the front doorbell ring. The Big Man answered the door, Boudicca yapping at his heels.

Mei suddenly felt butterflies in her stomach. Only this time they felt different, not uncomfortable when she was upset. She heard cheerful voices, so took a deep breath and looked at herself in the mirror before heading down the hall.

Miss Janice and Pop were in the living room petting Boudicca. When they looked up and saw Mei, they stopped and looked at her with smiles reaching their eyes.

"Wow Mei!" Miss Janice said, "you look great!"

"Yes, you do," Pop agreed.

Mei blushed.

"Mei, would you mind if I took your picture with Pop and Miss Janice?" the Big Man asked.

Mei shook her head, and they stood together while he took pictures. They were almost done when Auntie walked in carrying a package. She patted Boudicca on the head with her free hand and stopped in front of Mei. She looked Mei over and nodded. "It's a good thing you're pretty and can dress yourself. If it was all on your brother..." She held her hands up in surrender. "I don't want to even think about it."

Pop and Miss Janice laughed.

"Hey now," the Big Man said.

Auntie waved him off. "Yeah, yeah."

Mei smiled. She knew Auntie loved the Big Man, but it was funny how she teased him.

Auntie smiled at Mei. "I heard you made pizza today?"

Mei smiled and nodded.

"Well, let's go see."

They went into the kitchen. They talked until the pizzas were done, then went out to eat at the table on the back porch.

Mei didn't talk much, and it was odd being the center of attention, but she liked it more than she thought.

After eating, the Big Man came out with a big pink box open at the top.

Mei recognized it as the box from the bakery with her cake inside. Sure enough, when the Big Man lifted the top, there it was; a round chocolate cake with purple frosting, just like she'd asked for but didn't think she would get. Candles crowned the top, and across the face, frosted calligraphy spelled out her name. Overall, it was amazing! And it was just for her.

The Big Man lit the candles, and they all sang Happy Birthday to Mei (three times in one day!). She blew out the candles and everyone clapped. As the Big Man cut the cake, Auntie took out the fruit ice cream from the freezer and brought it out to the porch.

They dished out the ice cream and ate. The purple frosting on the cake was a source of amusement, especially when Pop dropped some in his beard. Soon everyone looked like they were wearing purple lip gloss.

Then came time for presents. Mei was getting better at talking and eating around people. Even celebrating a birthday in front of everyone wasn't terrifying, but people buying her presents? Mei had already received the Mrs. Fox's book and craft set, and everyone had admired it. Pop had even picked up the new book and thumbed through a few pages. She got cat pancakes and a day at the salon. She felt uneasy because of all this. Excitement and anxiety swirled around in her stomach, which was full of pizza, cake and ice cream. She took a breath and steadied herself. It will be okay.

First up, Auntie handed Mei a box in wrapping paper. When Mei opened it, she found a pail Auntie had painted purple, with 'Mei Mei,' bunnies and flowers around the outside. The work gloves and trowel were inside the pail. Her own gardening tools! Auntie topped off the present with her own potted lilac plant!

Mei felt thrilled. "Thank you, Auntie! I can't wait to plant this and get my tools dirty!"

"Atta girl! Tools are meant to be used. Just make sure you take care of them."

Mei nodded solemnly. "Yes, Auntie."

Miss Janice's present came next. Mei opened it to find a package of fancy coloring pencils and a pencil sharpener. "Oh, nice!" Mei said, her eyes open wide. "These are the grown-up ones! Thank you."

Miss Janice liked to hug, so Mei obliged.

Next, Pop told Mei to reach into a big brown paper sack he brought. Mei drew out a long leather belt with pouches stitched.

"Here," Pop said, and wrapped the belt over her left shoulder, down across her body to a buckle at her right hip, then back across her back diagonally to her left shoulder. The pouches lined up in front. Up close, Mei saw writing and little pictures on the pouches. It was neat, but she still didn't know what it was.

"Okay, watch me carefully," Pop said. He showed Mei how to pop the top of a pouch open. She noticed the pouch was more like a little armored box. In each box, stored in a slotted holder, was a throwing star, just like she'd practiced throwing at the target by the barn! The way the slots held each star, Mei could draw it out without cutting her fingers.

She must have had quite an expression on her face, because Pop smiled. "Now this is a big girl gift, and I expect you to always be safe and smart with this rig."

Mei nodded, then looked up at Pop and pounced on him with a fierce hug. She caught him off guard, and they almost tipped the chair. They laughed at the near miss.

The Big Man was last, and Mei suddenly felt uneasy again. He brought out two packages and set them on the table, then picked up one and held it out.

Mei reached over and took it tentatively. Purple wrapping paper covered the box. Mei sat down in her chair and opened it to find a pair of binoculars and a case. Her first thought wasn't a gracious one. Doesn't he know I'm an eight-year-old girl? she thought, but said nothing, and kept her reaction from showing on her face.

"Pick them up and look through them," the Big Man said. He pointed across the yard to a stand of trees in a field. "Look over there."

Mei did, hesitantly. When she held up the binoculars, the faraway trees jumped at her! She snapped her head back, then looked at the trees over the top of the binoculars. They were far away again. She looked down through the binoculars, and they came closer. Interesting. She looked at other objects. They looked blurry at first, but when she held the binoculars steady, they came into focus. Interesting.

The Big Man reached over and showed her how to adjust the binoculars to bring objects close in focus, then back out again. Mei thought she might change her mind about the present from the Big Man.

She put them back in the box and looked at them one last time. "Interesting," she said, aloud this time, and looked up at the Big Man. "Thank you."

"You're welcome. I'll show you other cool things you can do with those." He handed her the final unopened box, covered with the same purple wrapping paper.

Mei tore open the package and found a long, thin box. Inside was a knife handle sticking out of a sheath. She set the box on the table and picked up the sheath, then drew out the knife. It was a throwing knife! Her very own weapon! She held it by the grip and looked with awe at the heavy, elliptical throwing blade. It was balanced for throwing and sharp only at the tip. The sheath was black leather with loops.

Mei looked at the knife for a moment in silence. She turned it over in her hand, then turned it around, slid it into the sheath, then back out. She was all alone with her new knife. She heard something in the distance, and when she looked up, she felt as though she was waking from a dream. Everyone's eyes focused on her.

"Is it okay?" the Big Man asked.

Mei looked down at the knife, then back at him. She nodded at him with sincerity. "Oh, yes," she said, then slid the knife into the sheath and put it down. She stepped back and looked at it.

"I'm pretty sure the sheath will fit onto your cross belt, so when you take the field, you'll have all your cutlery with you," the Big Man said. "Tomorrow we'll set up a throwing range with a target."

Mei nodded again. She felt thrilled with the knife and was interested in the binoculars, but wasn't sure she could hug the Big Man just yet. She didn't know why; she just couldn't.

Everyone talked and had a good time. The Big Man cleaned up the food and plates and still had time to smoke a cigar with Pop. The two men stood away from the porch blowing big clouds of blue-black smoke and talking. Auntie and Miss Janice got into Mrs. Fox's craft box with Mei and they enjoyed examining the contents. Mei read a page aloud from Mrs. Fox's book and asked questions about the crafts.

Too soon, it was time for everyone to go home and for Mei to go to bed. She picked up her things and put them away. The Big

Man thought Mei's new belt and weapons needed hung up on a special peg in the closet in the TV room for safekeeping.

Mei wasn't sure she wanted to be parted with her new tools. "What if monsters attack me in my room?"

"Then you'll have to ring the bell and I'll come sort them out. You're not trained enough to go to war yet, kiddo. You'll need lots of practice and show me you're mature enough to be ready for that."

Mei wasn't thrilled, but knew the Big Man had made his mind up. "Can Auntie tuck me in tonight?"

"Ask her," he said. "If she's cool with it, then say good night, go brush your teeth and wash up, put your jammies on, then come get your auntie."

Mei spun and looked at Auntie. Before she spoke, Auntie said, "yeah, sure, go get ready for bed."

Mei raced off to get ready. She hung her flower circlet on a coat hook in her room and turned on the lava lamp. Later, after she'd washed, brushed, and changed, she came back and stood in her pajamas in the doorway to the backyard. "I'm ready, Auntie."

"Oh, yeah?"

"Yes."

"Aren't you forgetting something?" Auntie asked.

"What?"

Auntie walked over, hunched down, and in a quiet voice, said, "you need to give your big brother a special thank you for a great birthday. He worked hard to make today special for you, and he deserves to be thanked for it."

Mei felt embarrassed. She hadn't thought of all of things the Big Man had done for her. She hung her head.

Auntie put a finger under Mei's chin and lifted her head up. "No, my niece, stand up straight, go be my big girl and do the right thing. You don't have to hug, but you do need to show your gratitude."

Mei nodded and trotted over to where the Big Man was sitting, and without waiting, reached up and hugged him fiercely around his big neck. "Thank you for today. It was my best birthday ever."

The Big Man awkwardly hugged her and patted her back. "You're sure welcome, Mei Mei," he said, his voice cracking.

They let go and looked at each other. Then slowly, as if rehearsed, they nodded at each other, and after a few seconds, broke into grins.

The Big Man chuckled. "Go on, go to bed now."

Mei smiled again and raced off to bed with Boudicca and Auntie following.

Her special day had been magical.

Chapter 35

The Big Man

After everyone had left and The Big Man had the house to himself he sat down at his laptop and wrote an email to the the Chaplain.

Hi, Sky Pilot!

Your favorite crayon cruncher here. I managed to make Mei Mei's first birthday a good one. Please tell Miss Elaine her suggestion of cat-shaped pancakes was a big hit, and so was your idea about pizza, but I had to one up you, and so Mei and I made pizza from scratch. I called my big sister and got her nana's old recipe. It came out pretty good. That girl is vicious with the garlic, though. I'll need to keep an eye on her in the future.

I must humble brag but having the salon braid flowers in her hair was definitely a winner. Check out the pictures I attached to this email. The food, playing, and sunshine are doing her a world of good.

Side note—what's with the prices at the salon? Are they all this expensive? I swear, if that salon lady wants to rob me, she should just put a pistol to my head and tell me to empty my pockets! Anyway, as much as it cost, it was worth it.

Mei is slowly coming out of her shell and talking with me a bit more. Her reticence is more like shyness now, so I sass her a bit now and then with outrageous dad type jokes. I've also been pushing her a bit more by throwing couch pillows at her for fun. She's not quite ready to throw the pillow back, but doesn't seem to mind too much. She looks at me a lot through her side eye.

Anyway, the birthday went great. I'm proud of my people and their thoughtfulness in picking out special gifts for Mei. And yes, I decided to buy her the throwing knife, but insisted for safety's sake she throw only at the target we set up in the backyard, and only

171

when I'm watching. I have to say, she's at it every day. It's funny to watch her set up her dolls and stuffed animals as an audience or a royal court of some kind and practice over and over again with them watching. I don't think she's a natural, but she's determined. When she hits the target, she cheers as though she just hit a home run, but then buckles down and continues to practice.

The best part of the birthday was at the end, when she surprised me by hugging me of her own volition.

More small wins.

Onto other things. I reached out to Dr. Tom. He's a great old guy, not at all what I expected. I met with him in person, then followed up with a phone call. He sure can talk with a guy without making them feel like a freak. So anyway, he's pretty sure I had my PTSD under control for a long time, but now I'm wrestling with the kind of separation-from-the-service type anxiety many guys get after leaving the military. Mine is a bit more acute because of my length of service, my abrupt departure after being wounded, and my high adrenaline type career track. Dr. Tom is pretty sure taking on Mei is a good thing. It taxes my skill set in new directions and gives me someone to care about and be responsible for. So I'm going to take Mei to meet with him informally so he can see how we interact. Oh! He also recommended a colleague of his to help Mei; a Dr. Amy Nguyen. He says she's brilliant, so I'm crossing my fingers.

No word from the attorney on the lawsuit. She said the state would fuss around a bit, then probably settle after the prerequisite amount of puffery. It's too soon to say, and I'd like to see every one of the mutts responsible chain-dragged through the streets, but we'll probably have to settle for money. Sigh. Well, if there's money, I'll add it to Mei's trust where I put her inheritance and social security money. Speaking of money, I am good for now. With my retirement, VA pension, and investments (thank God my sister bullied me into investing; she threatened me with a baseball bat) I started investing when I received the inheritance and re-enlistment bonuses; I have enough money for the both of us. I don't need Mei's.

School is going well. I'm still anxious, but still carving and I joined a gym. They have kids' classes. I considered enrolling Mei, and I met with a trainer named Leigh Ann, who's an Air Force vet. She's good at injury recovery training and various forms of other physical torture, but it's time to take the next step.

Yes, my birthday was two days ago, a few days before Mei's, but I don't care about that. It was more important for Mei to have a real birthday with her family around. I'll have more, but I appreciate the card and kind words from both of you.

Please tell Miss Elaine I miss her cooking. No one prepares Jamaican chicken curry like an Island Lady.

I'll call again soon.

Cheers!

Chapter 36

Mei Mei

A week after Mei's birthday, the Big Man took her to a place called the 'VA,' to see Doctor Tom. He worked at a big hospital with doctors and specialists to help veterans like the Big Man.

"Doctor Tom has helped me deal with my bad dreams," the Big Man said. "I think he might help us with yours."

The first time they visited the VA, Mei wasn't sure how they were helping anyone. The buildings, grounds, even people, had a gloomy, creepy feel.

"Stay close to me and don't talk to anyone unless you check with me first, okay?" the Big Man had said as they got out of the truck. "Doctor Tom and his staff are good, but we don't trust everyone here. Do you remember the passwords and the signals I taught you?"

Mei nodded. The Big Man had taught Mei ways they could say words to each other, so she'd be able to tell what kind of person he was introducing her to. He also taught her to understand and use sly hand signals only they knew, to communicate with each other out in public without words. Mei liked it. It was like a fun game and made her feel as though she was included in a secret. The signals were useful because they gave her a way to ask the Big Man questions without getting embarrassed in public.

They had walked across the VA hospital campus to go to Doctor Tom's office. The buildings were old and run-down. Instead of cool shade, the tall trees between and around the buildings made everything gloomy. Both the workers and the veterans, hoping for help, looked unhappy or upset. She was glad the Big Man was there with her.

Doctor Tom's office area was a happy change from the outside. The entire office area was scrubbed and painted. Nice pictures hung on the wall, and Mei had a view of the lake out of a big window.

The lady behind the counter didn't look very nice until she spoke. The Big Man checked in and used the code words to let Mei know the lady behind the counter was okay. Somehow, although she didn't smile much, Mei knew this lady was a good person. Mei had learned, even if someone didn't smile, they could still be a good person, like Auntie, a good person who looked stern but actually smiled and laughed often.

They sat on the chairs in the office and waited. After a minute, Mei got up and looked out the window at the lake. The skies were gray, but the lake looked nice. Ducks were swimming around near the shore. People were rowing boats across the lake in what appeared to be a race.

A tall, thin, well-dressed man wearing glasses walked into the room. The Big Man got up, wearing a genuine smile. This had to be Doctor Tom.

"Hey now!" Doctor Tom said. He looked taller than the Big Man.

"Hey now!" the Big Man said, then took Mei's hand and approached the doctor. The Big Man and doctor shook hands as if they were old friends.

The Big Man introduced Mei to Doctor Tom, who, to Mei's surprise, extended his hand. "Hello, Miss," Dr. Tom said.

"Hello, Doctor Tom," Mei said. She tried shaking his hand, but it didn't go well. Her hands felt lost in Dr. Tom's much bigger hands. He didn't seem to mind.

"Please come in," Dr. Tom said, and they all went into his office.

Mei wasn't sure what to expect, but was happy Dr. Tom talked to her as if she was a grownup, just like the Big Man. Dr. Tom showed Mei around his office. It looked comfortable and clean, but didn't smell of chemicals like a regular doctor's office. They looked out of the windows, at Dr. Tom's fish tank, then sat down at a big table.

Dr. Tom brought out a big piece of paper and crayons, and they all started drawing and coloring. Dr. Tom was a talented artist; he could draw and color better than most people. Mei colored well, but not as good as she'd wanted. The Big Man wasn't good at either, but seemed happy scribbling away.

The time passed quickly and Mei enjoyed herself. Dr. Tom and the Big Man talked a lot but included Mei. Dr. Tom spoke to Mei and the Big Man formally, but friendly.

Finally, they picked up all the crayons and rolled up the big paper.

"Miss Mei," Dr. Tom asked in his formal way, "do you mind if I keep this?"

Mei thought she would get the big paper, but didn't mind. "No, Doctor Tom, you can have it."

"Thank you, Miss. I appreciate the gift of your time and your art. Perhaps one day we'll get to work on it again."

"I'd like that, Doctor Tom."

They went out to the waiting room, shook hands, and said goodbye to Dr. Tom. The Big Man walked Mei over to the stern lady at the desk.

She looked up from answering the phone. "Hey, big guy," she said kindly, "you ready to make another appointment?"

"You bet, Ms. Carrie."

She clicked on her computer, then gave him a day and time.

"Got it," he said and logged the information into his phone. "I'll see you then."

"Hold on," Ms. Carrie said, looking to make sure no one was around. "You got a minute?"

The Big Man looked at her and he frowned. "Sure."

Mei felt curious about what was going on.

Ms. Carrie hit a button on her phone, then reached into her desk and pulled out a folder. She got up and walked over and stood next to the Big Man. She looked him up and down. He grinned at her, but she shut him down.

"Cool your jets there, Don Juan. This isn't anything scandalous."

He showed his palms. "Perish the thought," he said in mock sincerity.

"Get back on the clock," Ms. Carrie said.

Mei didn't know what that meant, but the Big Man immediately dropped his goofy grin and narrowed his eyes. "What's up?"

Ms. Carrie looked at him, then pointedly at Mei, then back at him.

Ms. Carrie shrugged. "A couple of days after your last visit, a guy came into the office and asked about you."

Although the Big Man didn't move a muscle, Mei could sense a change in him. He went completely still, almost frozen. His hand holding Mei's hand got cooler. Normally, his hands felt warm. This was weird.

The Big Man's voice was likewise devoid of its typical warmth. "Oh, yeah?"

Ms. Carrie nodded. "Yeah, he did, but I could tell he didn't actually know you."

"How so?"

"He said your name wrong. He used the name on your records, not the one you use, and certainly not 'brother,' or what you're going by these days." She took a breath. "He said you and he were old army buddies."

Mei started to say the Big Man was in the Marines, not the Army, but he squeezed her hand to signal her to say nothing.

However, Ms. Carrie had seen Mei move, and she looked at her. "Yeah, kiddo, I know," then looked back at the Big Man.

"I told him I didn't know you and asked him what this was about. He was pretty slick and didn't give me much, but he didn't read like a hunter or a cop, more like a private investigator."

The Big Man nodded. "That could be any number of things. Okay, thanks."

"Hold on," she said. "After I figured he wouldn't give me any information about him, I brushed him off, but called the campus cops. Big Wayne rousted him after he caught him trying to get info about you from the prosthetics dept." She smiled and handed the folder to the Big Man. "So, ultimately, Big Wayne got his ID, picture, and license plate number."

The Big Man broke his stillness. "My girl!" he said, and held his hand up.

Ms. Carrie's face brightened, and she slapped his hand. "I'm pretty sure he won't be hard to find. He was young and arrogant."

"This is much appreciated," the Big Man said. "Dinner is on me. Big Wayne too."

Ms. Carrie shook her head. "No need," she said, then showed her palm as the Big Man puffed out his chest. "Don't be a jerk, and take "yes" for an answer."

The Big Man sighed, looked down, and nodded. "Okay," he said, then looked Ms. Carrie in the eye. "Thank you."

She broke her stern face for just a second and gave him a friendly wink. "You're welcome. Now get outta here. I have work to do."

"Yes, ma'am."

Ms. Carrie looked at Mei. "Take care of the big guy for me, okay?"

"Yes, Ms. Carrie." Mei was puzzled. It seemed that a lot of ladies wanted her to look after the Big Man.

Mei felt worried as she and the Big Man walked back to the truck. "Is someone looking for us?"

"Maybe, but don't worry. It could be any number of things. Could be my VA claim. Someone might want me to recommend an old teammate for a medal, or maybe they have the wrong guy."

Mei wished she could have believed the Big Man, but he'd already taught her how to read people so well, and she knew he was lying. Not to be mean, but it made her sad, and felt her trust in him slip.

Chapter 37

The Big Man

The Big Man followed up on Dr. Tom's suggestions and took Mei to meet a mental health doctor. He took her to meet Dr. April, making it clear on the ride over that Dr. April was Mei's doctor, and she could tell her anything. She could share what made her happy, sad, or caused concern. She could tell Dr. April about her bad dreams. However, the Big Man said Mei didn't have to tell Dr. April anything if she chose.

Mei nodded and said nothing. She wasn't sure she would say anything.

However, her resolve flew out the window when she met Dr. April. She liked her right away. Dr. April was a small lady with jet black hair and wore a necklace with big colorful beads. She didn't look like a regular doctor, but Mei could tell she was sincere and wouldn't mistreat her.

Dr. April asked Mei a few questions, but instead of sitting around, they went for a walk outside. Mei liked that. Outside of Dr. April's office was a small park with a pond, a walking path, and benches.

Mei mostly just answered Dr. April's questions, but she talked about Auntie and Pop and Boudicca.

"You have a puppy?"

Mei nodded enthusiastically. "She's a big puppy. She's an English Massive, and the Big Man said she's going to grow into a giant walking huggy bear!"

"That's so great! I love puppies and big dogs! Maybe your brother will bring her the next time you visit."

Mei jerked her head back. "You want to meet her?"

"Oh yes! I can't think of a better way to spend time than with a special girl and giant puppy."

Mei stopped talking and looked off into space.

"Mei," Dr. April asked. "What's wrong?"

Mei thought for a moment, then said carefully, "the Big Man, I mean, my brother, says that too."

"What does he say?"

"He says things like you said, like he can't think of a better time than a great day with a special girl and giant puppy." She took a breath. "Do you think he means it? For real?" As she spoke, she searched the doctor's face; looking deep for the truth.

Dr. April gave Mei a sincere but sad look. "Oh yes, yes, he does. I'm certain your big brother loves you very much. I talk to lots of young people and their parents, and can say without a doubt, not all of them are nice or tell the truth." She took a small breath. "So I'm sure he means it."

Mei thought for a moment, then nodded. "Okay. He's really different, and I didn't know."

Dr. April smiled. "He's different for sure, but he's still good. If you're not sure, you can watch what he does. And you can ask me, or your Auntie or God Pop, whomever you feel comfortable talking to."

"If Boudicca comes with me, I have to bring a towel, because sometimes Boudicca gets the drools."

Dr. April chuckled and made a funny face. "Puppy drools!"

Mei perked back up. "Yes! She slings them out of her flappy face, and they can go anywhere, even high on the wall over my head!"

"No!"

"Yes!" Mei insisted. "And her tail can knock things off the end table when her behind gets high enough, like when she gets on the sofa! The Big Man says we'll need to clean more when she gets bigger."

The next time Mei visited Dr. April, Boudicca came too.

Mei knew when the Big Man was struggling with his PTSD. Normally, life at home had become a routine of exercising, playing, doing chores, reading, and running errands, all mapped out on the big whiteboard next to the kitchen. Once in a while, when he was struggling, he would change everything up, but in a funny way. He'd go on a cooking tear, mixing up spices, pickling eggs, making cheese or bread, then they'd leave on a shopping adventure. They'd drive to grocery stores, spice shops, and other stores to buy odd pans, or whatever he needed to complete his culinary quest, because ordering online would take too much time.

When they found what they were looking for, they'd get home and spend the day turning the kitchen into a big happy mess of an experiment. The house would smell of baking bread, spices, coffees, teas, fruit infused waters, or simmering soups. Often, their experiments would turn out good, resulting in a ton of food. If practical, he'd store most of what they made. If there was still too much, he made gift packages to donate to needy people.

Because of the Big Man's spur-of-the-moment adventures, the kitchen shelves and cupboards became full of cooking utensils, and his spice collection grew into a smelling library, with every spice from all-spice to zaatar.

Chapter 38

Mei Mei

Sometimes people from the case worker agency came by. Usually, it was a man and woman together. They would talk to both the Big Man and Mei, then, usually the woman would ask Mei to show her the bedroom while the Big Man and the man from the agency talked.

Mei showed the woman her lava lamp, her growing collection of stuffed animals and dolls, the giant fairy wings she could tie on and wear, and the glowing art her and the Big Man painted on her bedroom walls. When she turned off the light switch, the dark room came alive with stars, clouds, trees, and animals.

The woman would ask Mei questions about how she liked living with the Big Man. Did she like the food? Did he ever yell at her? Was everything okay? Sometimes the woman and Mei would go out in the backyard to see where Mei played.

A couple of times, the lady and the man sat with Mei in the living room and asked her questions about the bad place. Mei didn't like talking about the bad place. Sometimes she'd get upset, but the Big Man figured out having Boudicca sit next to her on the sofa helped curb her emotions.

Even if she was upset, Mei always told the truth, which seemed to make the lady happy, because she would write in her notebook. After a while of living with the Big Man and getting to know him better, Mei noticed he often seemed tense when these people came by. He never said anything to Mei, but she could see it in his face and how he moved.

Chapter 39

The Big Man

Before it happened, the Big Man wasn't sure why he felt apprehensive about taking Mei Mei out to the VA to meet Dr. Tom. He could say he was ashamed of how nasty the buildings and the campus of the VA were or some other excuse, but that wouldn't be true. He felt on edge because so much was riding on a positive meeting between Dr. Tom and Mei Mei. Overthinking the matter increased the pressure on himself. He really liked Dr. Tom and considered him more of a confidant than a regular shrink. The Big Man admired Dr. Tom because he was not only a veteran himself, but genuinely cared for his vets and treated them more than just a paycheck. Dr. Tom and Chaplain were a lot alike in that way.

The Big Man took a breath and fought to control his blooming anxiety. It had been a while since the snakes of his bad thoughts tried to slither out of their baskets. He focused on his mental strength. It would be okay. He had trusted Dr. Tom with his background and candidly discussed his secrets and unspoken fell deeds. The Big Man had likewise been very open with Dr. Tom about adopting Mei, and his fears about his suitability as a parent. As part of those discussions, the Big Man's dad shared Mei's background, including case files with Dr. Tom.

"It's all up to me, Doc," the Big Man had said. "No pressure."

"If you're willing to put in the work, I'm sure you'll find a way," was Dr. Tom's reply.

The meeting went great. Dr. Tom had set out crayons and spent the meeting coloring with Mei as the three of them chatted pleasantly. At one point during the meeting, Dr. Tom had given the Big Man a surreptitious nod to indicate all was well.

The Big Man was nearly floating with relief when they left Dr. Tom's office. The euphoria lasted nearly five minutes, and came to a screeching halt when Ms. Carrie told him someone was making inquiries about him. The words echoed in his mind.

"He was pretty slick and didn't give me much, but he didn't read like a cop, more like a private investigator."

Boom.

Fortunately, the VA campus police officer, Big Wayne, had obtained information about the man and gave it to him on the sly. Sure enough, the man was a licensed private investigator. That told the Big Man whatever was going on concerned Mei. So at least the Big Man wasn't completely in the dark and had a place to start.

The Big Man always casually scanned his surroundings out of habit. Now he ramped up his scans and reran the counter terrorist training curriculum in his mind. It was still there.

Unfortunately, Mei Mei had spotted the subtle but deliberate change in his demeanor and asked him what was going on. Caught off guard, he fumbled in the moment and ended up lying to her. DAMN! He felt as though he'd broken a trust with her. Even worse, he was sure she knew he was lying. FUCK! How do I fix this?

He mentally refocused. He had to concentrate on safety now, feelings later. He just wondered whether fessing up to her would fix it. Once again, he found himself alone and in the dark. He'd been there before, but it never got easier.

A bright spot for the Big Man was meeting Dr. April. Dr. Tom had referred and introduced them. With the Big Man's permission, Dr. Tom had prepped Dr. April by providing her with the background, case files, and professional opinion on both Mei Mei and the Big Man. Dr. April and the Big Man interviewed over the phone before meeting in person.

To the Big Man's surprise, Dr. April was a tiny but attractive Asian woman. She was also quite accomplished and put the Big Man at ease with her balance of professionalism and easy common parlance. The Big Man felt comfortable being frank and safe enough with her to share his concerns and plans.

"The both of you sound like special people to work with," Dr. April had told him. "I'm happy to see how I can help both of you succeed."

The Big man nodded as relief washed over him. "Thank you, Doctor." He didn't know what else to say, so he and the doctor began making plans.

Chapter 40

Mei Mei

Mei noticed little things changing around the house with the Big Man. Pop and Pop's son (and the Big Man's brother) Michael came over and helped the Big Man make a place for the truck around behind the house. They also built a small fence around the perimeter, with a closable gate across the driveway.

"It's so Boudicca can play in the front yard," the Big Man had said when Mei asked. He dug wide flower beds along the fence lines and put small flower and clover plants in the wide dirt flower beds. Auntie brought over big wind chimes and she and Mei hung them up along the outside of the house. Mei liked how these chimes made big, deep ringing sounds instead of little tinkle-y sounds from little chimes.

A few days later, the Big Man's friend Don came over and put up more lights around the outside of the house and cameras the Big Man could monitor with his phone. They also put up alarms around the driveway and yard that flashed a laser beam. Anyone crossing in front would automatically ring the doorbell. In no time, the yard looked different from when Mei first arrived.

Mei knew all the digging and building put a strain on the Big Man. He walked more stiffly and slowly than normal, but still exercised and stretched every day. He also continued doing things just for Mei. One day, he rolled a big black and white coloring print poster out on the kitchen table for Mei to color. He lifted a brown paper shopping bag onto the table, then reached in and pulled out big multi packs of colored markers and. "Would you like to color with me?"

Mei nodded excitedly. Then she and the Big Man colored together.

"Should we use markers? Crayons? Or both?" the Big Man asked.

"Crayons," she said.

"Good choice," the Big Man said, then put the markers back in the bag. The poster showed a big, enchanted forest with elves and dwarves, unicorns, and other magic things throughout.

Mei hesitated.

"What's wrong, Mei?"

When she didn't answer, Big Man said patiently, "it's okay, sweetie. What's bothering you?"

Should she tell him? Would he understand? Mei took a breath. "It's a nice poster, and I don't want to mess it up."

"You mean you're worried about coloring outside of the lines?"

Mei nodded. "Or using the wrong color."

"I understand your concern, but this is a practice poster."

Mei cocked her head and wrinkled her brow.

"When I got hurt, I hurt my arm and hand, here and here," The Big Man said, pointing to the scars. "Part of my rehabilitation is to color, and I'm not very good at it, so was hoping you liked to color. That would help me."

"Oh, yeah?"

"Sure," he said, then pushed the crayon box over to her. "Come on, let's give it our best shot."

Mei looked the poster over. She planned where she wanted the colors, then picked out a green crayon and colored the trees behind the unicorn. The Big Man took a crayon and started coloring on the other side of the poster.

They spent the afternoon coloring. Sometimes they talked; other times were quiet. The project turned out to be the first of many posters, and even more opportunity to talk.

A couple of times, the Big Man and Mei worked together on art projects, creating a mess with a paper mâché pinata meant to be a unicorn, but ended up looking like "a rhinoceros that had a rough life." They filled it with candy and took it over to a cookout at Pop's. Many people attended, so they hung it up and had fun taking turns whacking at it while blindfolded. Miss Joyce ended up breaking it open, and the candy poured out.

Another fun activity was washing and drying old jars and painting the insides with glow in the dark paint. When Mei took them into her room and shut the lights off, the jars glowed! It was so great; she made many more. She and the Big Man put them up outside and gave some to Auntie and Pop. Auntie had been thrilled with the bat box Mei and Pop made, so Mei did more things for her. She wasn't sure what to do for Pop, but thought about it.

A couple of the projects didn't turn out very well, but the Big Man supported her effort. "Well, we tried, but still had fun."

Mei realized she had fun doing stuff with the Big Man, because he didn't get mad or sad when things didn't go his way. He still made sure Mei had plenty of time to play in the house and outside by herself. He said it was important for her to use her imagination, and to be alone with her thoughts. Besides, he said, he and Boudicca were always nearby if she needed them.

Mei didn't always play alone. The Big Man often played with Mei outside in the backyard, encouraging her to do physical things. Mei enjoyed this. He took time to stretch and warm up, and then they'd set up makeshift goals and kick a soccer ball back and forth. Boudicca loved getting in the way when they played. The growing puppy would bark at and chase the ball, which Mei found funny.

Sometimes they threw a frisbee back and forth. The Big Man always threw easy to give Mei a good chance to catch it.

Sometimes they held pillow fights in the living room. Mei wasn't sure she wanted to at first, but the Big Man could be so funny, and despite herself, Mei couldn't stop herself from picking up a sofa pillow and swatting away at him. Like most things they did, he never played too rough to prevent Mei from bopping him with a pillow.

A couple of days after Mei and the Big Man visited the VA, packages were delivered to their house. When he saw the packages, the Big Man pumped his fist and said, "yeah!" before carrying them in and opening them in the living room.

Mei watched him taking things out of the box for a minute, and when she couldn't figure out what he was doing, asked, "what did you get?"

He looked up and smiled. "It's a drone. It's like a remote-controlled plane."

"You know how to fly it?"

"Yes, when I served in the Marines, I was on a team that tested a couple of different types of drones out in the field."

"Oh. So, what does it do?"

"This one flies and takes pictures and videos." He held up a big part of the machine. "See this part?"

Mei nodded.

"This is the camera, and this part over here is where you put on a holder so you can carry small things and do a flying delivery." He looked up. "I thought it would be neat to take it out to Pop's and fly it over the farm. I bet we can shoot some great video of the farms and the animals, even map out the place using coordinates. Those are measuring points on a map to help you find your way."

"Can we take videos of Auntie's gardens too?" Mei asked.

"You bet! I'll have to put it all together and test it out here; fly it around to make sure I get the controls and camera right."

"Aren't you worried it will it fly away?"

"Nope, it's got a homing signal, so it comes back even if the controls stop working."

Mei watched with fascination over the next few hours as the Big Man unpacked, then assembled the drone. She sat off to the side and petted Boudicca so she didn't get in the way of him working on the drone, the remote system, and the camera. He systematically read the instruction books and then tested all the features to make sure they worked and he could operate them correctly. As he worked, he chatted with Mei and explained what he was doing. He even admitted when he didn't know something or made a mistake. Mei never would have imagined something like this could be so interesting.

When it was all correctly assembled and tested, the Big Man cleaned up the mess and parked the drone in the spare bedroom, which served as his office. "We'll check the weather for tomorrow, and if it looks good, we'll test it out. I'm curious to see how well the camera works."

The next day, the weather was nice, so they packed a picnic lunch, loaded the drone into the truck, and drove to Pop's farm. They set up in an open pasture and tested the drone. Mei thought they would jump into flying the drone, but the Big Man told her what each test would tell them about the drone.

"It's important to take each step easy and be deliberate. That way, we can get the most out of the machine's performance. This is a good lesson for you, Mei Mei. Whenever you're learning something new, break it down into steps. It makes things easier to learn, and if something goes wrong, it's easier to start over." He snapped his fingers. "Now, just because you're going step by step doesn't necessarily mean you're going slowly. You can proceed at a quicker pace with fewer mistakes."

Mei just held onto her bunny and kept watching without saying anything. The drone was fascinating. She'd seen planes and helicopters, of course, but the drone was like a robot bug with four propellers. The entire project became more exciting when the Big Man started flying the drone.

He started off with slow easy turns, followed by a few swoops, then guided it around the pasture. He told Mei to stand close to him so she could see how the controls worked. They flew the drone all around the pasture, past the orchard, over the barn, and over Pop's house. As soon as the drone's battery ran low, the Big Man flew the drone back to where they stood and landed it.

They ate lunch in the pasture, talked with Pop for a bit, then returned home. When the Big Man hooked the drone's camera to his computer, Mei was surprised at the video they recorded! The picture of her and the Big Man standing near the truck showed from a bird's-eye view, but there they were! The other pictures looked great too, but the video footage was the best.

The Big Man had activated the camera when the drone took off, and Mei felt an odd sensation of flying while she watched the movie theater quality video. The drone climbed in the air, then circled the pasture. Mei now understood what people meant when they said "bird's-eye view." The video looked like real life, and as she watched, she felt a few more moments of disorientation as she learned to see things like a bird as the drone flew.

She loved it! In fact, the video made her want to learn to fly, but fly what? A plane, a helicopter? Too noisy. Maybe a big hot-air balloon? Could she do mind pictures from a flight? She needed to think more about this, but felt sure she wanted to get higher up. Maybe climbing a tree? But would it be the same?

The Big Man interrupted her thoughts. "Are you okay, Mei?"

She nodded, but said nothing. She needed to keep special thoughts like these to herself. She liked the Big Man enough these days, but her thoughts were too important to share. "Can I see the video again? I want to try a mind picture."

"Sure." The Big Man reset the video, then got up and let her sit in his chair. He hit play then left, leaving Mei to enjoy the video and her own thoughts about flying. She felt something about flying she really liked and needed to think about it more.

Chapter 41

The Big Man

The Big Man continued his dual campaign to win Mei over and give love and joy to the rest of her childhood. His latest gambit was to keep them busy with fun cooking and art projects. He would email his sister-in-law for kid friendly activities, choose one of her suggestions, then write his plans on the whiteboard and engage Mei Mei. They'd spend part of a day doing the actual project; pickling eggs, doing an art thing, fixing up Mei's room, or baking bread. The Big Man had a weak spot for fresh bread, so much so, he uploaded a carb/calorie calculator app on his phone so he didn't violate his eating plan. He made veggie and fruit smoothies for breakfast and lunch mostly for himself. He still needed to bulk up for his fitness goals, but could tell his anxiety was pushing the limit. Chunking up by overeating would only make it worse. He caught himself stress shopping, and his spice rack and libraries were growing.

Overall, each project became a small win. Mei participated with a quiet but growing enthusiasm. The Big Man discovered a funny thing. Sometimes the projects that didn't turn out were still fun, and they were glad they tried them. Like when the soup they tried to make from scratch didn't turn out well at all, he got an inspiration and used it as a learning experience. Instead of crying about a loss or throwing a fit, he would try to diffuse the tension with a cheerful jest or calm words. When it was obvious they couldn't save the soup, he quoted a line from Star Trek. "I'm not going to win this one, am I, Chief?"

"No, sir."

Then he tossed out the soup and they made sandwiches instead. And the paper mâché unicorn they tried to make looked, well, bad, so he cut open the top and filled it with candy. The unicorn disaster turned into a fun pinata.

He also set up a target and coached Mei on how to improve her knife-throwing. She practiced every day and was getting consistent hits with it.

The Big Man took what he felt was his biggest chance so far in his interaction with Mei. He had continued teaching her how to fight, mostly how to spot and get out of the way of an attack, how to keep her balance, and move to generate power. He still let her punch him with gloves on, and she learned to pack quite a wallop for her size. But all the teaching and interaction was still clinical. She listened, asked and answered questions, but remained emotionally distant, as though their relationship had plateaued. The Chaplain said this was normal and to continue, but the Big Man felt the need to 'push the envelope.'

So, using the pillows from the sofa, he started a pillow fight. He was scrupulously gentle when he lobbed a pillow at her while she watched a cartoon. Plop!

She looked up at him in surprise.

He grinned and tossed another pillow. It landed next to Mei and cartwheeled past. Before Mei could decide what to think, he laughed and cheerfully yelled, "come get me, small fry! Kill!"

Lost in the moment, Mei grabbed a pillow and charged at him.

He feigned terror and back pedaled. "Yikes! It's the tiny terror!" He pretended to block Mei's wild waist high pillow swings, then turned enough to allow one to swat his behind.

"Aaah! Critical hit! You wounded me in the butt! Now I have a giant crack in my butt! I think it's a fatal hit! Call a doctor or I'm gonna die!" He pretended to faint and flopped onto the sofa.

Mei had looked as if she was going to smile, but then clamped down and swung her pillow as hard as possible. She windmilled at him until she was out of breath and the Big Man was roundly thumped.

They had fun for a time, but the Big Man felt disappointed when the brawl ended.

Mei calmed down and went back into her shell as if the fight had never happened.

Sigh.

Chapter 42

The Big Man

In the back of his mind, the Big Man's paranoia lingered. To make matters worse, if he felt concerned about his paranoia, the next visit from the Department of Child Services didn't calm his concerns. They called and wanted an almost immediate visit with Mei. Normally he'd receive an email and letter setting a visit date for the following weeks, or even a month. This time they called on a Monday and wanted to come the next day, and instead of the usual field caseworker, they were sending an investigating manager. The lack of preliminary documentation, the abruptness of the timeline, and the change of the investigator's rank set off his inner alarm.

He made a phone appointment with his attorney, and she agreed; the actions by Child Services were irregular. They agreed to proceed with the visit, but the Big Man should closely monitor everything.

"In fact," the attorney said, "are you familiar with nanny cams?"

"I've heard of them."

"Well, you might get one and record the meeting."

"Do you think that's necessary?"

"I'm not sure, but it can't hurt," the attorney said.

The Big Man thanked her and hung up. He had considerable surveillance/counter surveillance training from his work around embassies, so was familiar with the process. It seems more of his training and experience from his misspent youth would again prove valuable. He sighed, then went to his desk and pulled out a pad of paper.

Time to build a game plan.

Due to the urgency of the Child Services visit, the Big Man bought and installed basic nanny cams he bought locally, rather than the high-tech cams he'd used before. He ordered more improved counter surveillance equipment for later, but what he had would work in the short term. He installed the nanny cams on the sly while Mei was out playing in the yard. He felt odd about installing these in his own home but had no choice. After the meeting, he would take them down. The other measures he was planning would become a permanent fixture. It wasn't about the odds of something happening, but rather the stakes if something did happen. He didn't know what to expect from Child Services, but whatever it was, they didn't know who they were dealing with. He still wasn't sure how to include Mei in what was going on, but a course of action was brewing.

Chapter 43

The Big Man

The meeting finished with no specific issues, but the Big Man's instincts wouldn't allow him to let his guard down. Something was in the air, but he didn't have enough information to form a concrete decision. A man and a woman from Child Services came at the scheduled time, both wearing their fake smiles. They were clearly surprised to see the Big Man's size, scars, and demeanor, and although not visibly nervous, he sensed their tension.

After the standard greetings and introductions, the Big Man asked, "before we get going, can you tell me why you're here?"

"Just a routine visit," the woman investigator answered.

"Oh, yeah?" the Big Man asked. "Normally, they send a regular field investigator."

"We're short staffed," the male investigator said.

"Hmmm, is that why this meeting was scheduled so quickly? Normally I get a letter, an email, and a call scheduling a home visit weeks in advance, so I'm curious. Why the change?"

"Well, we had an opening in our schedule, so we called as soon as we knew," the male investigator said.

"Well then, it's fortunate that we could fit you in on your abrupt schedule. Or should I say, both of your management type's schedules," the Big Man said flatly.

"Yes, it is," the male investigator said, with a strain to his voice.

"Well, since we're all here now, let's begin," The Big Man said.

He gave them a quick tour of the living room, kitchen, and Mei's room, and then they all sat in the living room. Mei sat next to him when they asked her questions and answered with truth and bravado.

An amusing moment occurred when the male investigator asked the Big Man if he'd really called the director of Child Services to confirm their identities and email picture identifications to the Big Man's attorney?

"Yes, I did, doesn't everyone?"

"No, they don't," the woman investigator said.

"So, you mean to say people let random strangers into their homes and around vulnerable children without confirming their identities?"

The male investigator shifted in his chair. "Well, no."

"That sounds like lack of due diligence on behalf of the guardians," the Big Man stated in a neutral tone.

The investigators hemmed and hawed for a moment, then continued with more questions. Soon enough, they were done and were preparing to leave.

"When will your notes be ready?" the Big Man asked. "I'd like a copy sent to my attorney's office."

The woman investigator raised her eyebrows. "We don't normally share our notes."

"Oh, I see. Okay."

Just as the investigators relaxed, the Big Man spoke again. "So, when my attorney files a Freedom of Information Act request with your director's office, how soon can she expect your compliance?" He paused. "Oh, never mind, she'll know all the rules on that sort of thing. That's why she gets paid the big bucks."

Both investigators narrowed their eyes and tightened their jaws in unison as if rehearsed. "Well, that's fine," the male investigator stammered. "That's your right to do so."

"Yes, it is. Good day. I'll see you out," he said, then walked the investigators to their car. He couldn't help but notice a deputy's cruiser parked down the block. He looked back at the investigators, who noticed his reaction to their backup. They then hurried into their car and drove off.

Curiouser and curiouser.

The Big Man channeled his paranoia and anxiety into setting up and shoring his home security. He could have kicked himself for not doing it sooner. He had put in fire alarms and CO2 detectors. Why didn't he do security stuff then? Too much on his mind? Didn't want to admit he'd need security here in rural suburbia?

Well, it was time to remedy that mistake and reinforce the home defenses. He checked his finances, called friends, then began his plan. First, he put up better fencing around the entire yard with privacy screening around the backyard. Next, with the help of his brother Michael, Pop, loads of gravel, and a tractor, they ran a driveway extension around the house so he could park behind the house and out of sight. Pop found a closable wrought iron driveway gate online, and installed it with a friend's help. Unfortunately, the gate wasn't powered, but they could still close it.

Working out at the gym doesn't prepare the body for everything. Still, it felt good to work on a project, and even if the labor caused aches, he still enjoyed the effort. He finished by reinforcing the doors, door frames, bracing the windows with dowel blocks, and putting hurricane film on his windows.

Chapter 44

Mei Mei

After a few weeks with the Big Man, he and Mei started going to the local YMCA twice a week. He did lots of special exercises in the pool and he also did injury recovery workouts with a physical therapist/trainer. Summer was drawing near, and since the Big Man didn't need to rush to find a regular job. They spent lots of time together.

Mei joined by practicing yoga, taking swimming lessons, and occasionally the Big Man's trainer showed her how to do kettlebell exercises for kids, making sure she did them correctly at home. Mei also took jujitsu classes, one of the few things the Big Man insisted upon.

The Big Man brought up the topic a few days before Mei's birthday, while they were sitting on the back porch. She'd been playing with her dolls and he'd been carving on a post when he told her about his latest plans for her.

Mei wasn't sure she liked the idea. "But you're already teaching me how to fight." She liked the fight training, but that was just her and him, not in public with people she didn't know. So, she decided to test him.

Patient as ever, he said, "this is a unique style of fighting. It will also teach you more than fighting."

"Like what?"

"You'll see."

"But I'll be the smallest one there."

"Most likely," the Big Man said, seemingly without a care. "So what?"

Mei gaped in surprise.

The Big Man looked up from what he was doing and chuckled.

"Do you think monsters and bad guys come only in your size? Or do you think monsters and bad guys will wait for you to grow up so you'll have a better chance of beating them?"

Mei sat stunned while he returned to his carving.

"Look here, Mei Mei, trouble always comes, and it's best to train for it and be as ready as you can. And you'd better figure on being smaller and outnumbered."

He stopped carving and flicked a splinter away. "But you can be more determined, better trained, faster, mentally stronger, better educated, and put in more work than anyone else. Those are the things a smaller and outnumbered person can do to win. And as a girl, you just might be better at planning than a boy."

Mei sat in stunned silence. She could be better at fighting because she was a girl? That was crazy!

"Why do you think we practice with flash cards? Or mind pictures? Or practice punching and doing your chores? It's all part of doing the work. And it's not just about fighting. You apply the same principles with your schoolwork, your studies, whatever you do. Now go play," he said, and resumed carving.

The Big Man got Mei a work out uniform called a GI to wear in class, changed his schedule to coincide with his therapy sessions with her jujitsu, and off she went. Sensei Ben taught jujitsu in one of the smaller training rooms (called a dojo) at the YMCA.

Sure enough, Mei was the smallest person in class, and didn't know anyone. At first, she felt nervous, so she would pull her mask on when she went onto the mat. However, the situation improved because Sensei Ben was patient, and taught both kids and adults. Mei learned the basics; how to fall and roll, basic moves, and how the courtesies of class bowing, shaking hands, and tapping out were important for getting along with others and having what Sensei Ben called 'a healthy class.'

Mei liked the other kids in class, and although didn't consider them friends, were nice and didn't hurt her when they trained. At first, she felt awkward grabbing and wrestling with people she didn't know, but her first big challenge came when Sensei Ben told her she wasn't aggressive enough.

Sensei Ben gave Mei and Robby, a boy in class, extra one-on-one time to help them harness their aggression and focus it properly. Sensei Ben would take Robby and Mei over onto another mat, while the other students practiced other moves. He got into a kneeling position so he was close to their height. Starting with Robby, Sensei Ben had them practice running at him at full speed, then slamming into him with a hugging tackle. Sensei Ben was big and strong , but wasn't mean. He encouraged Robby to run and slam into him again and again. At first, Robby was scared of hurting Ben, but Sensei Ben had Robby come at him again and again without ever raising his voice.

Mei noticed Robby slowly catching on. As the speed of his runs increased and tackles became stronger, Robby became more confident and determined.

Suddenly, it clicked for Mei. Sensei Ben was teaching Robby how to be aggressive the same way the Big Man showed Mei how to punch! She now knew what to do. She looked up as Robby made a furious run at Sensei Ben and crashed into him with a loud thump.

"Yes!" Sensei Ben barked, and the students and other instructors watching cheered and clapped. Robby started crying, not because he felt afraid, more because he was no longer afraid.

"Are you alright, Robby?"

"Yes, Sensei," Robby said, and sniffed.

"Good! Now, you know what to do, right?"

"Yes, Sensei."

"It's going to take more practice, but you're on your way now."

Sensei Ben and Robby bowed, and Robby walked off the mat.

"Okay, Mei Mei," Sensei Ben said. "Come on."

Mei bowed and walked onto the mat. Even though this running and tackling was new, she knew what to do and felt a rush! She faced Sensei Ben and bowed. He returned the bow.

"Come on, Mei, come hit me!"

Mei took a breath and dropped her mask in place, then shot forward like a rocket straight into Sensei Ben. She launched into him so hard, her teeth chomped together, but she slammed into him hard enough to tip him over backwards! She was pretty sure Sensei Ben went over because she'd surprised him, but it was still cool!

"Wooo Hoo! Now that's a hit!"

The class members cheered for Mei, which fired her up even more.

"Can I do it again, Sensei Ben?" Mei asked, extending a hand to help him up (like good sports should).

"Well, yes, you can, Mei. Just let me get set this time. You're quite the little cannonball, aren't you? Why weren't you this aggressive before?"

"I didn't know what you meant until I saw you and Robby do it, Sensei,"

"Okay, well, now you know, so do it again!"

Mei rushed at Sensei Ben several more times until Sensei Ben stopped her. "You got the basic aggression down. Now you just need to practice it and learn to apply it with your techniques."

Mei nodded and bowed to Sensei Ben, then walked to the edge of the mat and bowed. When she lifted her head, she saw the Big Man standing across the dojo, smiling at her.

Chapter 45

Mei Mei

When it came to actual grappling, Mei began getting rough and wrestling with the other kids, even though she was the smallest one in class. She practiced her aggression and her basic moves, even at home.

She was challenged to get a "lock" on one of the bigger kids, and over time, once she started grappling with an opponent, she competed ferociously. Mostly she lost and had to "tap out," because the moves seemed complicated. The Big Man insisted this was normal while learning. She wasn't so sure, then after a few classes, one or two little things clicked for her, and she understood how to move! She'd been "rolling" with a girl a year older than her when Mei figured out how to apply an armlock. The bigger girl had to tap out!

Mei felt proud of her first win, but shook hands with her opponent. Respect of fellow students was important. But no matter who lost or won, Sensei Ben taught his students to be careful, use the proper techniques, and be good sports. Mei wondered if the other kids sometimes let her win just to be nice, but hoped they didn't.

A few weeks into training, a bigger and older boy accidentally smashed Mei in the face with an elbow when they were rolling on the mat. Although the hit stunned her and she felt blood trickle from her nose, she felt more surprised than hurt. She ignored the pain and blood and kept pressing her attack, but Sensei Ben stopped the match.

The boy, Jason, saw what he'd done and, to Mei's surprise, started crying.

"I'm sorry, Mei," he bawled.

Mei felt sorry for Jason and teared up herself. "It's okay, buddy," she said, and added a line she'd heard from the Big Man. "You didn't mean to, and I'm still pretty."

On hearing that, Sensei Ben laughed, but Jason still felt upset. When Sensei Ben stopped Mei's nose from bleeding and checked to make sure she wasn't badly hurt, Mei went and put an arm around the bigger boy.

"I know you didn't mean it, and I'm not mad. Don't be mad at yourself."

Jason nodded "Okay."

She patted him on the shoulder and smiled. "Maybe I'll tap you out some time, but don't you dare let me. That will make me mad for real, okay?"

Jason wiped his face. "Okay Mei," he said, forcing a smile.

"That's the spirit, you guys!" Sensei Ben said.

Mei loved it.

Later, the Big Man saw Mei's nose and puffy black eye.

"Well, now," he said, hands on hips. "You got your first war wounds!" He winked at Sensei Ben. "Did you get some licks in?"

Mei shrugged. "It was an accident. Jason didn't mean it, but I was trying really hard, and we just got carried away."

"Good, and yes, that happens. And you didn't die from it, did you?"

"No. We shook hands and said we'd try again next time."

"Good girl, Mei!" He and Sensei Ben then talked a bit as Jason sheepishly walked by with his mom.

"Jason!" The Big Man said.

Jason stopped and his eyes bulged.

The Big Man reached over and put his hand on Jason's shoulder. "It's okay, little brother. Accidents happen, so don't let it bother you. Mei's becoming a feisty little monster."

Jason smiled awkwardly. "Yes, she is, but I still didn't mean it."

"We all know you didn't mean it. Have yourself a great day." Brother looked at Jason's mom and said politely. "He's a good boy, ma'am."

Jason's mom smiled. "Thank you. Your... sister is a great kid, too."

"She's the best," the Big Man said proudly.

Mei blushed.

Chapter 46

Mei Mei

Besides everything else in Mei's new life, going to the YMCA became part of the routine. The exercises and Jujitsu made her feel tired at first, but then bigger and stronger, and she liked the feeling. She also felt pleased she wasn't as afraid of things as she used to be. The dark no longer scared her, and although she still had nightmares, they came less frequently and weren't as vivid. The thoughts of the bad place lingered, but no longer paralyzed her.

Mei wondered if these new feelings meant she was becoming more brave. She was sure the Big Man was responsible for her new feelings. He was warm, kind, and steady to her. He was driven and loved to teach her things. Finally, even though he'd been hurt in the war and covered with scars, he was still big and strong, thanks primarily to his exercise routine.

He always seemed as if he knew what he was doing, and she felt safe with him. She knew he kept things from her, but somehow, she knew he did it to protect her. Is this what a brother was? Mei wasn't sure. She knew brothers were related by mother and father, but the Big Man wasn't like any brother of the kids in her jujitsu class. Whatever he was, he was special. She just didn't know how everything worked. Yet.

Chapter 47

Mei Mei

The destructive storms that came into Mei and Brother's life didn't come under dark clouds, nor announce themselves with booming thunder or flashing lightning. Instead, they arrived with a ring of the doorbell.

It happened one day when Auntie came over to spend time with Mei. The Big Man was getting ready to run errands at his school and was walking out the door when the alarm sounded, alerting them someone was pulling into the driveway. Boudicca started barking; not happy, but loud and threatening.

The Big Man shushed Boudicca and looked out the window. He froze in place.

Mei had never seen someone go from moving to absolute stillness so quickly.

In a calm and almost soothing voice, he said, "there are two cars in the driveway. One is a sheriff's deputy car."

"Oh, really?" Auntie asked in a calm voice that sounded forced. "Whatever did you get up to?" She got up and walked to look out into the backyard.

Mei popped up from the chair. "What?"

The Big Man turned around and narrowed his eyes at Auntie. "Really?" Then he gave Mei a hand signal.

Mei froze in place.

"Take Boudicca and go to safe place number two and wait," he said. He'd taught Mei safety drills, like fire drills and other emergency drills, so she wouldn't be scared and would know what to do.

She grabbed Boudicca by her collar and walked down the hall and stood next to her bedroom door.

The doorbell rang again.

"The cameras are on," Auntie said.

"Thank you," the Big Man said.

Mei craned her head to listen. Her heart was pounding, and she tried holding her breath so she could hear better. She kept holding Boudicca's collar and petted her big head so the big puppy wouldn't fuss.

She heard the door open.

"Hello."

She heard a man talking, but couldn't make out the words.

"Stop," the Big Man said, in a no-nonsense tone Mei had never heard before. "Who are you?"

The man replied.

"No, sir, before we go any farther, you're on my property, you knocked on my door, and didn't even have the good manners to return my greeting, so now you can show me some identification, or I'll have that deputy arrest you with necessary force, for trespassing. And yes, you're being recorded."

The man replied.

"Okay, so that's a name, now the identification," the Big Man said, still in a commanding voice.

The man replied.

"Last warning before I call the deputy."

The man showed his identification.

"Okay, now that we've finally determined you are who you say you are, how can I help you?"

The man told him.

"Uh huh," the Big Man replied. "And who sent this? Uh, huh." He paused for a long moment. "Okay. Now get off my land."

Mei heard the door close.

"Well, now, the game is afoot."

"Is it what you thought?" Auntie asked.

"Yeah. Mei, you can come out now."

Mei let go of Boudicca's collar and they both went to the living room. The Big Man was looking over papers; Auntie leaning against a kitchen counter watching him. He looked up when Mei walked in.

"Mei, you did good with that. You followed my orders and didn't panic. Well done."

"What's going on?" Mei asked, more than a little worried. The situation felt weird and sinister. The Big Man and Auntie acted serious in a way Mei had never seen.

The Big Man's face lit up, and he smiled. "It's okay, Mei Mei. Let's have a seat at the kitchen table. I could use some iced tea. How about you?"

Mei nodded.

The Big Man turned to Auntie. "What can I get you?"

"Seltzer water for me."

Mei and Auntie sat at the table while he got the drinks. He grabbed ginger cookies and set everything at the table, then sat down. Mei took a cookie and passed them to Auntie.

The Big Man looked at Mei. He looked as tense as a coiled spring, and was clearly struggling to keep himself under control.

"They're legal papers, but they're pretty complicated, so I don't know what they mean exactly. I have to talk to our lawyer, so I can understand what's going on and figure out the right thing to do."

"Is it about me?" Mei asked. Something in his face indicated they concerned her.

"Yes, they are."

"What do they mean?"

The Big Man's face suddenly snapped forward. It was only maybe half an inch, but his eyes were blazing, and it startled Mei.

"Girl, didn't I just say I didn't know, and I had to talk with the lawyer?"

Too stunned to speak, Mei nodded in reply.

The Big Man forced an exhale through clenched teeth. "Okay," he said, and waved a hand. "Go play."

Mei's face flushed with anger and shame. She didn't like being treated like that and felt betrayed. She ran out of the room and left the Big Man and Auntie to discuss the papers.

"Oh, damn it," Mei heard the Big Man say. "Mei, wait up."

Mei didn't care. She went into her room, slammed the door, then set the lock. For the first time, she was actually mad at the Big Man, and didn't think her anger would soon pass. Her mind spun, and she laid down on her bed. What this the mean monster side of the Big Man that she hadn't seen? Maybe he was hiding behind the good guy she'd warmed up to. Had she been tricked.... again?

Mei heard the front door close, then thought she heard the truck start up and drive off. So, what was going to happen next?

Mei jumped when Auntie knocked on the door. She'd forgotten she was still here.

"Mei," Auntie said in just above a whisper. "Open the door." Auntie's voice didn't sound mean or aggressive, but Mei could tell Auntie meant business.

Mei got up and opened the door. Auntie stood there waiting as if nothing was wrong.

"Go wash your face, then we'll make lunch and talk," Auntie said, then turned and walked down the hall.

Mei followed along and turned into the bathroom. She cleaned up, washed her face, then went into the kitchen.

Auntie was slicing cheese. She looked up when Mei walked in.

"I'm thinking grilled cheese sounded good today. What about you?"

Mei nodded.

"Good. Grab the butter from the fridge and point out where the bread knife is, and we'll get going."

Mei complied, stiffly at first, but relaxed as Auntie talked normally with her. They cooked the grilled cheese, then put the sandwiches on plates and went out onto the back deck. Boudicca came out and sat in front of Mei, drooling at the sight of the cheese. Mei made the pup lie down so they could eat undisturbed.

Even though the sandwiches tasted delicious, Mei munched with little enthusiasm.

"Your brother may be a big gorilla, but he can sure make excellent bread," Annie said matter-of-factly.

Mei nodded.

"Do you want to know where he learned to make bread like this?"

Mei shook her head.

"My mom taught him a long time ago."

"Really?" Mei asked. She didn't know why, but this sounded interesting.

"Yep," Auntie said. "She taught him when he was a boy. He was young, but smart for his age."

Mei couldn't imagine the Big Man as a boy, without scars or tattoos.

Auntie must have noticed the puzzled look on Mei's face. She chuckled. "Yeah, your giant brother was a little pain in the neck pee wee once upon a time."

Mei smiled at the term 'pee wee.' It sounded funny, even funnier when used to describe the Big Man.

"I don't know if you know this, but my mom adopted your brother when he was a little baby."

"Really?" Mei asked, listening intently.

"Yeah. I was older than him, so I was like his big sister."

"What was he like as a boy?"

Auntie smiled. "Pretty much like a bratty little brother, making messes, getting into things, making a racket, and being a pain in my neck."

Mei giggled.

"When mom passed away, I was grown up and out on my own, so mom had arranged for Pop to adopt him into his family. It was tough on your brother, but he kept going. Mom had told him what she expected of him, how to act right, and carry on when she was gone."

"I didn't know that," Mei said.

"It's okay," Auntie said. "Your brother never complained, he just manned up and lived his life as best as he could, just like mom expected. Mom didn't tolerate people who wallowed in their problems or made excuses. She was always proud of him, even when she was whipping his butt into line."

"I think I like your mom," Mei said.

"She was something else," Auntie said, with a slight crack in her voice. "Now let's feed the dog before she starts a riot." Auntie looked at Mei. "He's really sorry he snapped at you."

Mei stopped eating and listened.

"He knows it was wrong, and I'm sure he'll talk to you about it in his own way." Auntie continued in her matter of fact, no nonsense tone. "He loves you a lot."

Mei looked up in surprise. She knew the Big Man was trying to be nice to her, and he'd taught her a lot and they did lots of good stuff together, but somehow, she still hadn't realized what it all meant. "Really?"

"Yep," Auntie said, "he really does. And the thought of losing you to a bunch of trash who didn't care about you and taking your money really makes him, well, all of us, mad."

Mei frowned. "Is that what those papers were about?"

"I can't go into all of it right now, but..." Auntie's face turned fierce... "just keep in mind, if those trashy creatures really wanted what was best for you, things could have, no, should have been done much differently, and you and your brother wouldn't have had it so rough. But he and the rest of us did the best we could with what we had to work with."

Mei wasn't sure what to make of this. What had been going on she didn't know about? She needed to try to figure it out.

Auntie shook her head and relaxed the look on her face. "Okay, that's a topic for another time, so let's get back to today."

Mei nodded agreement, then asked, "things are rough on your brother?"

Auntie shushed her by holding up her hand. "Adult things, not for you to worry about. But, despite the burden he carries, he's handling it well. Today was a rotten surprise that caught him off guard."

"Oh, yeah?" she asked.

"Sure kiddo, think about it. Without warning and before he had time to react, your brother was blown up and crippled, forcing him to leave the Marines. He spent a long time in the hospital and had a hard time recovering, then needed to figure out what to do since he no longer could be a Marine. He needed to find somewhere to live, then on top of all that, he found out he was someone's big brother and parent. Someone he didn't know and who didn't know him."

"That's a lot."

"Most people would have fallen apart and handled it horribly, but look around. See the nice house, nice yard, the best dog, and the good life you have? He's trying real hard and succeeding. He doesn't want anyone to feel sorry for him. He'll be just fine. Today was just an unpleasant episode. We'd have reason to worry if he yelled and freaked out all the time. Does that make sense?"

Mei nodded. What Auntie said fit with what she knew about the Big Man.

"So, that brings us back to today," Auntie said. "Now you have an idea of what's going on, so you know it's okay to shake it off and keep on going. Right?"

Mei wasn't sure, but slowly nodded. Auntie had a knack for explaining things.

"Okay."

"Good. Now let's clean up the kitchen and then we can think of a funny prank to play on your brother to cheer him up!"

"What?" Mei asked, and giggled, despite still being mad at the Big Man. "Oh, absolutely!"

Chapter 48

Mei Mei

Despite Auntie's talk, Mei's anger at the Big Man lingered. She wasn't sure why, but she carried her resentment and used it like a shield and retreated behind it every time the Big Man tried to make amends for snapping at her. She felt betrayed by him. They'd been having a fun time together, and she had started to think of him as more of a "brother" than just "the Big Man," but now wasn't so sure.

One day after jujitsu class, Mei got tired of sitting in her usual spot while she waited for the Big Man to finish his workout session. For whatever reason, she decided to explore the YMCA building. It was enormous with lots of rooms and classes, so she wandered around. She walked from gym to gym and watched the classes until she found herself at the climbing wall.

The climbing wall was a giant wall two stories high, with hand and foot holds. People usually tied ropes to themselves and scaled the wall, as though practicing for climbing up the sides of a mountain. She'd passed it several times, but this was the first time she stopped to look closely.

Mei stood in awe of the wall. Due to its vastness, she needed so step back to see to the top. Something was tickling at her brain as she looked it over. Could she get up on top and see far? Would it be like the video from the drone? She knew she was in a building, but felt the urge to see from the top. The wall didn't scare her, and she wasn't even wearing her mask. She took a few more minutes and looked over the ledge the climbers used for the handholds and footholds. She saw something there, but didn't understand what it was. No one was around for her to ask, so she used some of the think tricks the Big Man had taught her.

Then it clicked. The drone, the view from the top. Would it be as good as flying? The handholds and footholds carved a path up the side of the wall to the top. She had to know! She flushed with the excitement of figuring it out all by herself and felt a sudden and irresistible urge to climb to the top of the wall. With the aid of the handholds and footholds, how hard could it be?

Mei figured if she was fast enough, she could get up and down the wall with no one knowing. So she went over to the wall, and without thinking, dropped her gym bag, pulled her mask on, grabbed a handhold, and started to climb.

She felt tentative at first. She tested her reach and made sure her feet wouldn't slip on the footholds and levered herself up. It was easy! She kept climbing, bracing with her legs as she reached higher and higher, pulling herself closer to the top. She was moving along with a head of steam when she heard someone yell, "you can't climb on that!"

She ignored the voice and kept climbing.

"Hey, little girl! You need to come down right now!"

She pressed on without hesitation. Her arms and legs burned with the strain, but she didn't care. She might get in trouble later, but wasn't going to quit now. She'd climbed too far to turn back.

"Come down, this instant!"

She pushed on, reaching with her arms, and holding with her legs. Soon she heard other voices yelling at her to come down. Their yells fell on deaf ears.

Then, she heard the Big Man's unmistakable voice cut thru the other voices.

"Well, fuck me!" he said.

Mei was sweating and straining to keep climbing, concentrating hard now, trying not to focus on her fatigue, determined to reach the top. After the exercise and jujitsu, her arms and legs were much stronger than ever, but her strength was tested. Far away, through her concentration, she heard the Big Man shushing everyone. It became quieter. She looked up. She was almost there!

Then her foot slipped.

Mei dropped for what felt like a mile, but was actually only two or three inches. Her dangling foot placed extra strain on her hands and arms, but she surprised herself by not panicking or even feeling scared. She hung on tightly and reached out with her foot, found the foothold, then set into it and pushed up. Instantly, she felt the strain on her arms go away. Her hands felt exhausted now. The slip sapped her strength, something she couldn't afford.

From below, Mei heard a thump, felt a vibration on the wall below, and heard grunting. Someone else was coming up the wall. She pushed harder, wanting to be the first to reach the top. Worry crept into her mind as her hand slipped. She hadn't realized how tired she was from jujitsu. Maybe she should've waited to climb before jujitsu class, but it was too late now.

Her body shifted, and she felt herself slip again. She heard people gasp and start yelling below her. She kept cool and, quick as lightning, grabbed a closer handhold and locked herself in place. She steadied herself, took a breath, pushed the worries from her mind, and continued the climb. What else could she do? She could hear the other person gaining on her, but was getting near the top.

Her hands burned, but it was just a bit further. Tired or not, she was going to beat them to the top!

She felt slightly surprised when she heard growling, grunting, and a familiar "click" and "pop" of bones and joints. She chanced a look down. The Big Man was coming for her! Despite the strain and fatigue, she was glad it was him. Did he really care that much? She shook the question from her mind and focused on the top of the wall.

A couple of hard pulls, and she reached the top. She heard the Big Man grunting close behind her. She carefully glanced below, and saw him pulling his big muscular body up the wall, coming fast. He looked up, face twisted, red, and sweating.

"Go! Go! Go!" he roared. "Dig deep and pull hard!"

Shocked into action, Mei instantly knew what he wanted her to do. She felt a burst of strength and scampered up until she pulled herself over the top of the wall, then flopped down on her back, waving her tired hands. A few seconds later, the Big Man heaved himself up next to her.

They both were out of breath. As soon as Mei caught her breath, she clenched her fists and yelled in triumph. She couldn't help it and had to peer over the side. Whoa! She was really high up! It was like looking down through the drone camera. A crowd gathered at the bottom of the wall looked up at her, pointing and waving, as though they'd spotted a UFO.

The Big Man caught his breath. "Are you okay?" he asked in a calm voice.

"Yes!" Mei laughed exultantly, still flapping her hands, which had started to sting.

"Okay, good."

Mei looked at him. He was in bad shape. The climb had cost him, but Mei felt sure he did it to see she made it. Her mind raced as she tried to sort it out.

The Big Man took a deep breath, then looked Mei in the face. His normally warm, kind eyes were flashing. "Missy, girl, you're in deep kimchi..."

Oh boy, was he mad! Mei didn't know what kimchi was, but felt pretty sure she didn't want to be in it, let alone in it deep. "I know."

"No," he corrected. "you think you know, but you really don't. We're going to take the stairs down."

"Maybe I want to climb back down," Mei teased.

"I didn't ask you, did I?" he hissed fiercely thru clenched teeth.

Oops, this was bad. She'd never seen him this mad before.

"No, Brother," she said, hanging her head.

"Then do it!" he commanded.

Before they climbed down the stairs, Mei stood up and looked from the top of the wall again. She had climbed the wall, was in trouble for sure, so felt she'd earned a last look from the top. The view wasn't great, but she took a mind picture, anyway. Then she followed the Big Man down the stairs.

A crowd waited at the bottom when Mei and the Big Man emerged from the side door at the base of the wall. Mei saw Sensei Ben, the Big Man's trainer Leigh Ann, and the gym manager among the crowd. Mei realized she'd messed up. Big time.

The Big Man calmly gathered up all their gear sprawled across the floor.

Chapter 49

Mei Mei

They all went to the gym's admin office, and the Big Man and the YMCA manager went into her office. The Big Man made Mei stand in a corner outside the office. Her heart had dropped into her shoes. She listened hard and thought she heard their voices, but they weren't yelling. That was good, wasn't it?

She continued to stand in the corner. Her entire body felt tired. Her limbs were singing to her, but not a pleasant song. Despite her aches and exhaustion, she was thinking about what happened at the wall. She had climbed it all by herself! Well, not exactly. If the Big Man hadn't climbed up after her and helped her to the very top, would she have made it? Or would she have fallen?

Mei wasn't sure what to think about what the Big Man had done. Thoughts and ideas came crashing in on her all at once. She made herself slow down and take some deep breaths, then did the "think" things he'd taught her to help sort out her feelings and troubles.

She calmed down and thought back through the events. She loved climbing the wall, but didn't get permission, and that was bad. She was in trouble, and she guessed the Big Man was too because of what she'd done. She didn't like that thought but hung onto it. Her next thought was knowing she should've worn safety gear, and took a lesson on how to climb the wall. She might have (and almost did) critically hurt herself by slipping off the wall.

Her thoughts kept coming back to the Big Man, and confused her. She felt surprisingly happy he'd climbed up after her, but felt ashamed her actions caused him to come after her. Even with all his hard work to recover from his war wounds and injuries, he was still too hurt to be climbing up tall walls after misbehaving little girls.

Mei let the thoughts swish past her until one shocked her. The Big Man climbed after her and saved her from falling despite being hurt, feeling tired, and fearing heights. A lump formed in her throat. She remembered Mr. Curley telling her, her brother was a hero, and heroes helped people.

Is that what had really happened? Is that what he'd just done? For her? Is that what the Big Man was? A hero? Is that what heroes did? Was he more than just the Big Man? Was he her hero?

She struggled to keep her thoughts from spinning. Even when she tried hard to do her "think" trick, her thoughts still tried to control her mind, so she concentrated on breathing and remaining calm. She felt sorry she'd caused so much of a fuss. Why hadn't she just asked if she could climb the stupid wall?

After a time, the door opened, and the Big Man came out. Without speaking, he snapped his fingers and Mei turned around. Not good. Wordlessly, he held out his hand. She took it and they left the building and got into the truck. He sat very still, looking ahead in total silence.

Mei couldn't bear the silence. "I," she started, but his hand moved so fast, she couldn't see it until it snapped up between them. But instead of striking her, his hand froze in midair, index finger pointed up. "Not a word. I'm in a place and can't speak just yet. I need to think."

Mei felt crestfallen, and they drove all the way home in silence.

When they got into the house, the Big Man pointed down the hall without looking at her and said, "room." Then he went to his shelf and opened a box of cigars, took one out along with a cutter and lighter, then went out to the back porch.

Mei went to her room and climbed onto her bed. She buried her face into her pillow and cried as quietly as she could, like she'd done so many times at the bad place. Her worries came like a flood. Was the Big Man going to send her back? What would she do if he did? Would he believe she was sorry? As the cloud of emotional exhaustion descended, her mind shrouded in a cloud of worry and bad thoughts.

She tried to nap while waiting for the Big Man, but kept waking up with starts and fits as she wandered in and out of dark dreams. Through her open window, she could hear him doing push-ups on the porch while Boudicca barked. She thought that she could smell the smoke from his cigar.

Her mind still in a fog, she drifted off into another uneasy doze. She awoke again, this time to the sound of the back door opening. She heard Boudicca scramble across the floor as the door closed, then heard the Big Man snap his fingers. "Boo! Go get Mei!"

Mei tensed all over. She could tell he was still mad. She turned on her side to face away from the door and willed herself to be small. She could hear Boudicca gallop down the hallway to her room, then collide against the closed door. Boudicca sniffed and whined at the door.

Soon the Big Man opened the door. "Go get her up, Boudicca!"

Boudicca bounded to Mei's bedside. Mei pretended to be asleep, but Boudicca climbed onto the bed, then on top of Mei and put her soggy, mushy, mastiff face into Mei's face and sniffed.

"Get up, Mei," the Big Man said calmly. "Go to the bathroom and wash your face, then come to the living room." He turned to the pup. "Come on, Boo!" Boudicca stopped mashing Mei's face, hopped to the floor, and followed the Big Man as they walked back down the hall.

Mei went to the bathroom, took care of her business, then washed her face as instructed. She looked at herself in the mirror. Not the same girl who came here a short time ago. Was she going to be the throw away kid she'd been? She didn't want to think the Big Man would get rid of her, but wasn't sure. She took a breath, put on her mask, and headed down the hall.

Instead of a snarling ogre, the Big Man was calmly sitting on the sofa when Mei cautiously walked in. He looked up, then held his arms out.

Mei's mask fell off, and she burst into tears, then leaped into his arms. He stood up, lifting her with him, then rocked back and forth while he held her. He smelled like cigars, soap, and the balm he put on his muscles when they hurt. She remembered these smells from the first day she saw him. Now she knew where the smells came from.

"Okay, okay," he said soothingly as he continued to rock her. "We both had quite a day. Hey!" he said in mock protest, "are you besnotting my shirt—again?"

Mei snorted despite herself. "Maybe a little."

The Big Man smiled. "You call that a little?" he groused and pointed to the growing stain. "Look at that streak! I bet you don't have anything left in your sinuses." He tilted Mei's head back and tried to peer up her nose.

"Gross!!" Mei said.

"Tell me about it. I'm coated!"

"Are not!" she objected, then looked at his shirt. "Well..."

"Well, never mind. Let's get to it." He sat Mei on the sofa and sat next to her.

She didn't mind him so close.

"I don't know the right way to do this, so I'll just say it the best way I can. You scared the ever-loving shit out of me today! I haven't been scared like that in a long time, and it caught me by surprise." He took a breath. "Whatever possessed you to climb that wall?"

Should she trust him with her fascination with heights? "I don't really know," she said carefully. "I'd never seen anything like that before, and when I did, something just came over me. Ever since I saw that drone video, I've wanted to see things from high up."

"Okay," the Big Man nodded. "Did it occur to you it was dangerous? That you should've asked first? Used safety gear? That it was a stupid thing to do?"

"Well, I didn't think of the danger. Somehow, I just knew I could do it."

"Uh, huh. You didn't think there's a reason for all the rules, helmets, ropes, and harnesses hanging on the wall?"

"Well..."

"Yes, you did, but you wanted to take a run at it before anyone could stop you, so you kamikazed your way up the wall."

"Yes," Mei said with a tinge of defiance.

"That's selfish, and your selfishness put you in danger." His brows drew together. "And that's why you're in the most trouble." He reached over, took her gently by the chin, and turned her head to look him in the eyes.

"I should've said this sooner. I know you don't like me very much, but I love you. You mean a great deal to me, and you're important to me." Sadness showed in his big, brown eyes. "If something happened to you, I don't know if I could bear it."

Her heart leaped into the back of her throat, and she fought to keep her tears in.

"It's not okay for you to hurt yourself or put yourself in danger. Ever. Not. Okay. Ever."

Mei felt shocked. He didn't think she liked him? Her mind reeled as she tried to understand that thought.

"In the future, if you get the urge to do something stupid, just ask me. I've done lots of stupid things, and you know what? Believe it or not, you can do stupid things safely."

That was another twist. This talk wasn't going like she expected. "Really?" she asked. "You've done stupid things?"

His face broke into a laugh that lasted a few seconds. "Sure. Climbing, flying planes, parachuting, riding horses, all kinds of things."

"Well," Mei said, then the words tumbled out. "I'm really sorry I scared you, because I did a dumb thing, but I'm not sorry I did it and I want to do it again!"

The Big Man grimaced and gritted his teeth. "I was afraid of that. Well, at least you're not lying to me." He cocked a brow and shook a finger. "However, young lady, you're still in the doghouse, missy spider monkey."

She repeated the words over in her mind. Spider Monkey... she liked that name.

"Pay attention!" the Big Man snapped. "Restriction, extra chores, and more. You're grounded from the gym for a month." He lifted his chin and pursed his lips. "After that, if you don't do any more stupid things, we'll see about getting you lessons on climbing the wall."

"Really?"

"Yes, but, as I said, after your punishment is over, you also owe letters of apology to the manager at the gym, and to Sensei Ben as well. He was worried, too."

"Oh, I didn't think about that part."

"No kidding," the Big Man said more as a statement than a question.

"You have people that care about you now. Pop, Auntie, Sensei Ben, and even Boudicca. If you insist on doing stupid things, you owe it to us to do them safely."

"They care about me because of you, right?"

"No, I only introduced you. They care about you because of you. If you were a little brat, they wouldn't care about you."

"Really?"

"Yes!" he said. "Okay, this is the second part." He let out a breath. "I didn't know how to tell you this, so I'm going to say it straight."

"What..."

"Hold on Mei, let me speak." He sighed. "When your mom and dad died in the wreck, your dad died first, and your mom, well, our mom, held on for a few more days. From what I understand, it looked as though she would be okay, but then took a turn for the worse and never recovered. She stayed awake long enough to have an attorney change her and your dad's will. For whatever reason, she listed me as next of kin, which means she wanted us to be together." He gazed softly at her. "Believe me when I say I'm not sorry at all, but I sure was surprised." He paused to gather his thoughts. "It took the attorney time to find me. First, he tried to locate me in Afghanistan, then Iraq, then finally found me in the hospital. I was really busted up, and it took me a long time to heal well enough to get out, get discharged, get set up here, and get you."

"Lately, some of your dad's people decided I shouldn't be your parent, and they're using legal actions to try to take you away." He took a deep breath. "And it seems like you don't enjoy being here very much, so maybe you'd be better off with them. It doesn't have to be a big fight."

"No!" Mei shouted.

The Big Man's eyes snapped open wide, and he leaned back in surprise.

A wave of feelings boiled up in her and tears tugged at the corners of her eyes. "I don't want to go!"

"Stop!" He held up his hands in a defensive gesture. "I said they're trying. I didn't say they were succeeding. My attorney doesn't believe they have a case." His features stiffened, and he looked at Mei with narrowed eyes. "Unless you get hurt doing something stupid."

"Oh," Mei said, as it sunk in.

"Yeah, oh," he said, rolling his eyes. "But before we go any farther, I'll ask you this. Do you like being here, and do you want me to be your parent? It's okay if you say no. I'll always be your brother, but it doesn't seem that you like being here." The Big Man's voice got hoarse. "I know I'm not much of a parent type figure, or at least one you're used to, and I won't ever be, well...mom."

To Mei's surprise, he looked embarrassed and sad.

"Maybe you need more; more than I can give."

Mei looked up at him with saucer eyes, her lips squeezed together.

"Think on it as long as you like."

Mei sat still and stared out into space. Then she closed her eyes and summoned the mind tricks the Big Man had taught her.

She let the thoughts of the past few weeks spent in her brother's company pass through her mind. All they did, all he tried to teach her, all the care he put into what he did on her behalf. She thought again, step by step, until she figured out answers for herself. Maybe she was too little to articulate what she thought, but had to try.

She opened her eyes and locked eyes with the Big Man. "You came for me," she said calmly manner. "Twice."

He frowned.

Mei repeated, "you came for me. You were hurt bad and in the hospital, but you got out before you healed up and you came for me."

The Big Man clenched his jaw and sucked a breath through clenched teeth. "Yes, but I..."

Mei held up her hand, and to her surprise, he stopped talking.

Gathering up all her courage, she said, "I'm in trouble, but I'll still say what I have to say." She cocked her head. "You were still hurt. You came as soon as you could, but you were still hurt when you left the hospital."

"Yes," he said, and swallowed hard. "It still took a long time to get you." He bowed his head and took a breath. "Too long." He turned his hands in his lap. "If I'd gotten there sooner..."

Mei raised her hand again, but slowly. "No one else came any faster, and if the others wanted me so bad, why didn't they come for me when you were in the hospital? Maybe I could have stayed with them instead of the bad place, and maybe things would have been different, the important kind of different. Instead, I was thrown away. Thrown away like garbage, like I didn't matter." Mei heard his teeth grind and saw his fists clench.

"I can't say why they didn't do what they should have done," he growled.

Mei nodded. "And you came for me again today. You saw I was in trouble on the wall, and you climbed up after me faster than most people could run the same distance." She smiled. "And you didn't put on any safety gear either."

The Big Man grinned sheepishly, then silently held his hands palms up in a "Whaddya going to do?" gesture.

"And you hurt yourself again when you came for me today."

He nodded his big head. "The next few days are going to be ... special, but I'd do it all again." He gave her a serious glance. "All of it. Not just the wall."

And she knew he meant it.

Mei took a deep breath. "Maybe I haven't been fair to you. I thought you were waiting until you could surprise me with a mean trick or something. That's what they did at the bad place. Pretend to be nice, then trick you and treat you mean. Or maybe you wanted to give me away to someone else. But now I don't think you're like that, but couldn't tell for sure if you were real. So, all I could do was wait and watch. And now I know." She paused. "Talking with Auntie helps too."

Suddenly, everything fell into place. Her fears, how the Big Man treated her, doing her hair, teaching her, parenting her, Auntie, Pop, Boudicca, the other people.

"The other people, I didn't matter to them until they thought they could get money. They don't care about me. They didn't come get me. They didn't give me a name, a new name for a new me. But you did." She jumped up and pounced on the Big Man, then wrapped her arms around his big neck and squeezed. "How could I go anywhere else?"

Caught off guard, he hugged her back awkwardly. "Well, now, hmm, that's good," he said, struggling for the right words. He held her at arm's reach. "But you're still in trouble there, Missy spider monkey."

"Okay," she said with a grin.

"I mean it!" he said jovially. "I'm scared to death of heights, and here I am chasing some freaky tot up a frickin' man-made cliff, so someone, meaning you, has to own it."

"You're afraid of heights?"

"Hell, yeah!" he said. "I had to put my mask on before I started up after you."

Mei stopped and looked into his eyes, searching for the lie. "But you're not afraid of anything!" she said. "And what about all the climbing and stuff you did in the Marines?"

"Look, Mei Mei, I'm in fact afraid of heights, but I learned I can't let fear stop me from doing what needs to be done."

"Wow!" She still couldn't believe he, of all people, was afraid of anything, even the wall. He tore up the wall after her faster than she thought possible.

"Mei," he said, "after punishment is over, I think you should go back and take some classes on how to climb the wall."

"Really?" Mei asked. "But you don't like the wall or heights."

"What does that have to do with anything?"

"Well…"

"Look," he said, "you don't have to like everything I like, and you'll certainly find things you're better at than I am. It's my job to help you find those things, and help you to improve even more."

Mei's shoulders sagged. "I'll never be better than you.

"Oh yes, you bloody well will! One day, I want you to be better than me at everything you do! That's a parent's job. So, I'm going to give you plenty of opportunity to learn as much as you can. That way, when you grow up, you'll find your own way." He patted a huge hand on her knee. "Now, that's enough for now," he said as he stood. "Let's feed Boudicca and make our own dinner."

Mei wrapped her arms around his thick neck and snuggled close. He felt safe. He felt big and strong. He smelled good. He was her brother.

Her brother; her very own brother.

"You're my Brother now, I am not leaving. If they take me away I will escape and come back. If they take you away, I will come find you, just like you came and found me." she said, her voice catching in her throat.

He just nodded.

Chapter 50

The Big Man

The Big Man had enrolled Mei and himself for classes at the local gym. Getting out of the house with regularity would do them both good. His trainer, Leigh Ann, was an Air Force Vet and understood recovery work. So, she pushed him to maximum effort in the pool, stretching, or pumping weights. The process was painful, but speeding recovery was worth it. Despite the pain, he was starting to feel good.

The Big Man enrolled Mei in basic swimming classes and she took to them with no apprehension. Later on, he also had enrolled her in the gym's Jujitsu class for kids after he had gone and observed the class. After watching the class for an hour or so, the Big Man had been impressed with the instructor, Sensei Ben, and how well he ran the class.

Sensei Ben obviously loved jujitsu and was proficient. He wanted the kids to learn and enjoy it too, and he and his junior instructors didn't compromise on safety or discipline. So when Mei Mei and a little boy crashed into each other, the Big Man wasn't worried. In fact, he felt proud of how Mei handled the matter. She didn't fall apart and was a good sport. The little boy felt upset he hurt someone, so the Big Man made sure the boy and his mom knew everything was okay.

The Big Man was feeling good, school was going well, Mei Mei was doing well at home with her mind picture studies, and at the gym, so naturally, the shit storm hit. The day after he sent his "good news" email to the Chaplain, he was getting ready to attend an in-person study group meeting at the college when he was startled by the doorbell. Fuck! He immediately directed Auntie and Mei into their places of safety, then began his high speed situational processing. He'd set up his house with fences and signs to discourage casual visits. His friends knew not to just drop by without calling or texting. No one was bashing in the door. So, this wasn't likely a direct attack on the home.

He had Auntie confirm the security cameras were operating and Mei was in her room. Auntie had not warned him trouble was at his door, so the Big Man calmed his breathing, made sure his concealed pistol was close by, and checked the door cameras. A gray looking man stood on his porch, and a sheriff's deputy parked across the street in a clearly marked car.

Maybe not a direct attack on his home, but an attack of some sort. He opened the door.

Chapter 51

Brother

The unwanted visitor was a process server delivering legal paperwork confirming that the Big Man and Mei were under attack.

The Big Man signed for the paperwork, escorted the process server off his land, waved at the deputy, (really?) and opened the document folder. He speed scanned the documents, and learned it wasn't just any attack, but the worst kind.

As he read the documents, the truth dawned on him. Before he could acknowledge and compartmentalize what he was feeling on a visceral level, poison black hate tendrils slithered from the corners of his vision.

Mei's dad had a distant family, and they'd filed a motion with the court to take custody of her. The Big Man recalled what he knew about them, and it wasn't good. According to the attorney who handled Mei's estate, to his credit, her dad had tried to break away from a generational toxic family shit show. Off the record, the attorney mentioned that most of Mei's dad's relatives were trash. "The kind Jerry Springer wouldn't let on his show," he'd warned. "They're a cunning pack of vermin though, the kind with a long history of welfare scams, insurance frauds, 'stay with me' babies, and false accusations. I must warn you, they've also been implicated but never convicted of, serious crimes. They know how to slide out of trouble with a slap on the wrist, while their victims pay the price. They're smart, violent, and think the rules of society apply only to other people, so I advise you to avoid them at all costs and hope they forget about your little sister."

This suggested why Mei's (and the Big Man's) mom had fought so hard with her last bit of life to make sure Mei came to live with him and not them. Now, here they were. They probably figured out Mei had an inheritance and social security. Not a great deal of money in the grand scheme of things, but to them, a free fortune for the taking. They probably wouldn't be dissuaded by the Big Man putting all of Mei's money into a trust and living off his money. No, their kind wouldn't care, they only took, never gave.

The thoughts stoked the Big Man's internal rage furnace. He struggled to keep calm, then called the all-clear to Auntie and Mei. He put on his own mask to buy time to process his thoughts by sitting at the table and drinking.

Poor Mei. She knew something wasn't right. She stood there and looked at him with questioning eyes. He didn't know what to say. She must have figured this had something to do with her. He felt bad for her, more hatred for them. His feelings were conflicting, and he wasn't managing them well.

Naturally, that is when Mei started asking questions. The Big Man tried to quiet her with platitudes. Even at eight years old, Mei knew there was more going on than he'd say. She asked again, and to his own shame, the Big Man snapped at her.

Fuck!

The look of pain and betrayal from his baby sister was more than he could bear, but he made it worse. "Go play," he ordered.

Mei ran to her room.

Hot tears of hate and shame filled his eyes. He clenched his teeth and stepped towards Mei's room when a lifeline reached out. Auntie's hand gently but firmly reached out and grabbed his shoulder. "Don't," she said, nodding with understanding. "Go out for a bit. I've got this."

Not trusting his voice, the Big Man nodded and wiped his eyes. "It's bad."

"I know, but so are you little brother, so are you. We'll see to this. You just need to leave for a while and give her space." Then, with a smile, she scolded him with one of their mom's favorite warnings. "Now you stand up straight like a man."

Despite it all, that made him smile. "Okay."

"Now get outta here. Go think."

"Thank you, Auntie."

"Out!"

Chapter 52

Brother

Mei and the Big Man made peace, but it was clear she was still mad at him. She withdrew to a place she'd been a few weeks ago; engaged less and keeping more to herself. She had a session with Dr. Amy. who confirmed what the Big Man suspected. Yes, Mei Mei was mad. Yes, she felt betrayed. And yes, it would take time for that to change.

There wasn't anything he could do but continue life as best he could, but the double punch of the court case and Mei's withdrawal made him doubt whether he could ever win Mei over. If he could, what would that look like? If he couldn't, was he really her best choice? Had he failed a dying mom's last wish? Oh, man. The dark thoughts really put him in a bad place, which compounded the problem by aggravating his sleep disorder.

It was time to reach out for help, which was a concept that he had struggled with for a long time, before understanding how necessary it was to get "ok" with asking for help. Brother could no longer afford to let his ego stop him from doing what he needed to do to be the most effective protector that he could be for Mei. He called the attorney, the Chaplain, and Dr. Tom to put everything into place for the big fight over Mei. But to what end? He wasn't big on self-pity, but needed to be realistic. Was he really what was best for her? Sure, he'd tried hard, but was this the right step to get to the best outcome for his little sister? He'd fight for Mei with everything he had, but he had doubts about his ability to win a court fight. He could just see himself up against the judge.

"Hey, your honor, I'm the best worse choice for this little kid, so how about cutting me a break?"

The blues were back and trying to get a death grip on him. So it had already been a tough week when after his workout session at the gym with Leigh Ann, he went to pick up Mei from jujitsu class and she wasn't there. He looked around. No Mei. DONT PANIC! He ordered himself. "THINK CLEARLY!" Maybe she went to the bathroom. He looked around for a girl or a lady he could ask to check for Mei in the ladies' room, when he spotted one of the assistant jujitsu instructors, a thin teenage boy. "Have you seen Mei?"

"Yeah, she had her gear and was walking that way a minute ago," the teen said, pointing down the hallway towards the weight room and the climbing wall.

"Thanks, man," the Big Man said and hastened in that direction. He thought Mei would be in the weight room, so was shocked to his core when he glanced at the climbing wall and in a moment frozen in time, spotted Mei! Thoughts bombarded his mind.

Why is she climbing? Does she know what she's doing? She's not wearing safety gear. Man! She's going strong. I hate heights. Holy Shit!

Out loud, he said, "well, fuck me!"

People had gathered around and started yelling, but that only spurred Mei to keep climbing. She ascended with steady speed and confidence. Then her foot slipped, and the Big Man knew she wasn't wearing the right shoes! The crowd hushed, and the Big Man heard her grunt in frustration. She was high enough that a fall would be...bad. She regained her footing and continued her climb, but with less confidence.

The Big Man knew he had to save her. In the past, he'd learned to keep his fear in check, and as much as he hated climbing, was experienced. Dropping his gym bag, he kicked off his shoes and tore his socks off, then pushed through the crowd and sprang on the wall as high as he could. He caught a handhold and pulled himself up, then reached with his other hand. Burning pain radiated from his low back and down his hips into his legs. Man! He'd just finished a brutal kettlebell workout and was already tired! Nevertheless, he pulled and locked and levered and strained. Time slowed to a crawl. He couldn't hear the crowd below. He ignored the fatigue, cramping pain and focused on maintaining technique.

Mei had slowed, she was getting tired.

A quick assessment showed the Big Man the fastest way out of danger was to press on upward. He was almost even with Mei when he heard a scrape and a gasp and saw her foot slip off. She squeaked in fear. If she locked up, she would fall.

The Big Man reached into his military skills toolbox and pulled out a favorite weapon of the Marine Senior Non-Commissioned Officer. The command voice. For over two hundred years, US Marines NCO's used it to cut through the cacophony of war, issue commands, inspire confidence, and win against all odds.

"Mei! Don't stop. Dig in and climb! We're almost there!"

His deep voice seemed to lift the little girl upward as she madly scrambled the last few feet.

"Dig deep and pull hard!" He pressed on. The next lift caused a lightning bolt of pain to slash down his back, through his buttocks, and into his thigh. This time it was he who slipped. Clenching extra hard with his hands, he held fast and gained his footing, then pulled upward.

Mei was nearly at the top, and she looked back down to find the Big Man.

"Don't look! Go! Go! Up! Up!" he said. He tried to ignore the itchy trickle of sweat running into his eyes, as well as fight against the muscle fatigue from his hour-long kettlebell workout. Still, he pressed on until he heard a change in the noises from above. He looked up. Mei had pulled herself up over the ledge to the top.

"Thank God!" he said and kept pulling. When he finally felt the top, his back spasmed, and both feet slipped from the holds.

Using the last of his brute force, he pulled his cramping body over the ledge to see a grinning Mei Mei.

The little shit was grinning? He wanted to choke her.

Chapter 53

The Big Man

The next few minutes were a pain blur. The Big Man's spikes in pain in his back and legs were off the charts, but he wouldn't show weakness or vulnerability in public. He fought off pain activated shock, made himself relax, and then got up. As he and Mei walked down the stairs, he remembered speaking to her, but wasn't sure what he said.

His mind was foggy, but he kept his bearings, while inward he felt sure the agency would use this as a reason to prove he was unfit to keep custody of Mei. Fuck! To make matters worse, she wouldn't stop grinning! She was reveling in her belligerence and her win, with no idea of the future repercussions her actions might cause for both of them.

The Big Man resisted the urge to kick her backside up over the top of her head. He shot her a ferocious look, but it didn't produce the desired effect. Instead of being contrite, she kept smirking, which aggravated him to no end.

The crowd was waiting at the bottom of the stairs along with the managers of the gym. The Big Man knew he'd need to deal with them, eat smoke, and hope for the best. He put his own mask on and prepared to face the music.

He made Mei stand in the corner, facing the wall, while he met with the general manager and facility's functionaries in an impromptu meeting. He had to endure his pain and embarrassment, let the storm settle, while wearing a sincere look of contrition on his face. After all, they were right. Mei Mei was way out of line, broke rules, and put herself in danger. Now he hoped he could salvage something from this mess.

Using honest regret and a little verbal judo, he calmed everyone down, communicated his apologies, presented his needs for a place for physical therapy, gain understanding of Mei's status as an orphan, and propose a solution. Leigh Ann and Sensei Ben both came and spoke on behalf of Mei Mei and the Big Man. In the end, Mei was limited to watching the Big Man exercise, but was banned from using the facilities for a month. She also needed to write apology letters to everyone involved.

The Big Man knew not everyone was happy with the outcome, but the director was a softy, and her word was law. Overall, he still felt embarrassed.

He didn't trust himself to speak, so snapped his fingers. Mei fell in with him and they left the building and got into the truck. She tried to talk, but he shut her down, and they went home. When they arrived, he sent her to her room and took some of his rarely used painkillers, grabbed ice packs, balm, his cigar kit, and went out to the back porch.

Chapter 54

The Big Man

The Big Man's body was a furnace of pain. To add to the "fun," he was also dealing with a post adrenaline crash and an anxiety spike. The muscle relaxer and pain killer hadn't taken effect yet, so things were spinning. Fortunately, he'd been here before. He set down his stuff, and ignoring the pain, performed a pseudo-yoga stretch. After a few moves to assess his status, he dropped and did pushups; easy and steady, assessing his body as he exercised.

He felt the drugs working, so went back into the kitchen, downed a glass of water, refilled the glass, then came back out to the porch. He relaxed in his comfy chair, then prepped and lit a cigar. Time to settle down, think, rub balm on his aches, and ride out the pain.

The cramping and pain spikes rolled in and out. Some were severe enough to overcome the pain meds. The Big Man grit his teeth. He really wanted to drown himself in high-grade Irish whiskey, the golden-brown lighting igniting fires in his chest and freeing the monsters he'd locked away, but he knew better. That approach was wrong and diverted attention from the problems at hand. He dismissed the selfish thoughts, puffed on his cigar and concentrated, using his logic exercises to resolve the problem facing him.

He sat and smoked three cigars while pondering the situation. Eventually, thanks to the meds, ice packs, and generous doses of balm, his pain decreased from spikes to a dull roar. He mentally untangled the entire situation as best he could, arranged outcomes from best to worst, and then rested. Checking the time, he knew he'd done everything he could. Now it was time to face the future.

He hoisted himself to his feet, pain shooting, finding new and tender places to stab its hot daggers into. He moved, albeit unsteadily and went into the house. He gathered up Boudicca and headed to Mei's room. Her bedroom door was open, but she was facing away from him.

He used Boudicca to get her up and out to the living room. At his suggestion, she washed her face in the bathroom, so when she came out, her face was clean, although it was obvious her whole body was wound up tighter than a tripwire.

The Big Man did what fathers and father figures have done throughout time when their daughters are in extreme distress. He held out his arms. He wasn't sure what he expected her to do. Maybe she'd withdraw in defiance; throw a fit; run to her room and slam the door. The ball was in her court, and he prepared himself for the outcome by assuming the worst.

Mei charged into his arms as though fired from a cannon. Her tiny body wracked and heaved with heartbreaking sobs.

Chapter 55

The Big Man

"Okay, okay," he said soothingly as he rocked her. "We both had quite a day."

Even in a life with more than its share of all-or-nothing moments, the next few minutes were agony for the Big Man. He drew upon every emotional control technique he'd ever learned in training, and then hammered into his reflex memory via the fiery hell of combat. He needed to stay focused and calm when all he really wanted to do was make whatever concessions he needed to stop his baby sister's hurting.

But in the deep and coldly logical part of his mind, he knew he couldn't take the easy way out. He recalled the old cliché. If he took the easy way out, it might make things temporarily better, but most likely would eventually make things worse. It had to be here and now. Damn, this was hard! However, Mei Mei was still a little kid. He didn't need to be cruel when he talked to her, and if he was deliberate and honest, maybe he could pull off a win for both of them. His mind spun for a moment, so he took a moment to relax, remember what he'd planned to say, and ease into the conversation.

He spent the next several moments feeling as though he was walking a tightrope; high in the air and stretched across a canyon. Rain fell. Darkness came. But being who he was, the Big Man walked out on that tightrope because of what was waiting at the other end. Still, one slip and he'd lose it all.

The Big Man tempered the truth with tact, but told Mei everything. His history, her history, his faults, his fears. If they wanted to succeed as a family, she couldn't be along just for the ride. She needed to choose to be an active partner. She might not think that's fair, but still needed to make the choice.

And she made her choice; in her own words and in her own way.

"You're my Brother now."

When he heard those words, a giant weight of toxic uncertainty he didn't realize he was carrying fell off his chest. A power plant had now replaced the weight of that burden. A nuclear power plant kicking into overdrive, fueled with righteous fury and burning love. The Big Man had never been so sure of the direction of his path.

He stopped what he was doing and swore at the commitment from every father who had loved his family and home. The message was the same in every language and throughout all time.

"For those I love, I will do great and terrible things."

Now it was a matter of planning how to do those 'great things' so he could avoid the 'terrible things.'

Chapter 56

Mei Mei

Mei smiled when she thought of that first summer with Brother. He set a busy pace with learning, chores, and adventures almost every day. So much to do, so much to see, so much to learn and accomplish. He knew Mei had lost so much, so he worked hard to give more back to her and guide her on the right path.

"We're going to pack so much living, learning, hard work, and fun into the time we have together," he'd said with a smile. "We'll remember it forever, no matter what happens! Then he uttered one of his favorite phrases in Latin. 'Dum Viva Vivamous! (While We Live!)'

Interestingly, despite the busy pace, he never made her feel rushed or ignored. For all of the jujitsu and swimming lessons, and the other lessons in chores, manners, and playing "Kim's Game," Brother made sure Mei enjoyed her days. Working barefoot with Auntie in her flower gardens; working with Pop, learning to ride and care for horses; climbing trees out on his farm, or working in his shop. She also enjoyed lazy days of playing unsupervised in the backyard with her toys, sitting, sketching on her drawing pad, and reading books while Boudicca snoozed next to her.

Brother was always busy, but Mei knew he enjoyed it. He was using funds from his GI Bill and VA Benefits to attend college, and although many classes were online, he'd still need to go to the local college a couple times a week for class projects and research. He'd started taking classes when he was in the hospital and with his ambition, mastery of "think" things, Kim's Game, and his natural intelligence, he was taking more classes than most students, and placing high in all of them.

"Most of my courses aren't very hard. I have a pretty good memory," he said. "Some are good, some are stupid, but I need to earn a few college degrees to achieve the legitimacy to impress certain people."

"What people do you mean?" Mei asked.

"In this case, I mean the courts and your schoolteachers. I already have more academic training than most post-graduate students, but these people don't value that kind of education, so I play the game, while still being me."

"But I enjoy learning things, and I'm learning to understand non-veteran people. My GI Bill and another Veteran program will pay for schooling I don't want to go to waste. And," he snickered, "I admit it'll be a joy to show my academic degrees when people dismiss me as a big dumb Marine thug."

Brother managed his busy schedule by staying regimented in his day-to-day life. He went to bed shortly after Mei and he would awake before she did. He was still trying hard to rebuild himself after his injuries, so stuck to his workout routine. Additionally, he would often do mind type exercises to keep his brain sharp. After, he would wake Mei up and prepare breakfast. Sometimes he'd also do Mei's hair if she was struggling with it, but that happened less and less as time passed, because Mei was getting better at grooming her own hair.

Sometimes Mei could tell Brother had a bad night due mostly to pain, but on those nights, he worked hard to stay even-tempered. His therapy was doing light chores around the house and taking Mei to spend some extra time at Auntie's while he rested. She really enjoyed going to Auntie's but felt guilty having a good time when he felt bad. She mentioned this to Auntie while they were both busy painting a small flower bed on a big piece of plywood with different colors and shapes.

"Oh, it's okay, kiddo," Auntie said. "Your brother is doing everything he can to get better, and besides, even at his beat down lowest, he's still better than most." She laughed. "I don't tell that to the big lug though, he might get too big for his britches."

Mei nodded. She sure hoped so.

Chapter 57

Mei Mei

Brother's college wasn't his only priority. He needed to buy groceries, wash clothes, clean the house, mow the lawn, and cook the meals. As if this wasn't enough, he had to deal with the legal battle over Mei. She felt the fuss was all her fault, despite Brother insisting that wasn't the case.

For example, after the man from the courts delivered the papers to the house, Brother did what he called "court" or "legal" work. He shopped around and interviewed several attorneys until he found the right one to help him fight for Mei. Then he hired another attorney to help him with 'Mei related stuff.' Meeting with the attorney created more paperwork for Brother, and he worked at his computer more than ever. Obvious to Mei and everyone around Brother, he wasn't enjoying the process.

He was so busy, he started taking his laptop with him almost everywhere they went; taking Mei to the park to play, and over to Auntie's. He'd position himself to work on the computer and watch Mei at the same time.

"It's as if I have another class for school," he sarcastically joked to one of his friends. Then he'd breath deep and exhale. "But it's worth it." Then he snorted with a wicked smile and said, mostly to himself, "these mutts don't know who they're dealing with."

For a reason Mei didn't understand, more people from the court wanted to meet with and talk to her. They were like the caseworker people. The first-person Mei met was an average sized pudgy man with a tired face. They met in his office while Brother waited outside.

The pudgy man wasn't too bad, and his questions weren't unusual or mean. He asked Mei about living with Brother, what they ate for dinner, whether Brother was ever mean to her, and what happened when she was bad. The same questions other people from the adoption place asked her after she'd moved in. The pudgy man smiled when Mei told him about Boudicca, saying he liked dogs too. He chuckled when Mei told him about the big puppy's drools and snoring. He agreed shoveling up after Boudicca was icky but necessary. Mei was sure he meant well for her, and looked more overworked than anything.

The bad person came soon enough.

Chapter 58

Mei Mei

The lady Mei called the 'court lady' that came to the house to meet Mei was another matter. She reminded Mei of the people from her days at the "bad place." Not the people who did the bad things, but the people who weren't supposed to let the bad things happen to her, but didn't care if they did.

From the moment the court lady knocked on the front door and conducted a 'home visit,' Mei put on her mask. She couldn't say how she knew, but she suspected the court lady was wearing a mask of her own. From her actions and words, Mei was sure the court lady's mask wasn't there to protect, but rather to hide something; perhaps something bad.

When the court lady came into the house, she all but ignored Brother's greeting. She didn't shake hands, accept an offer of coffee or tea, and never made eye contact with Brother. Instead, she dismissed him and looked around the living room as though inspecting a dirty kitchen, and nobody else was in the room. She even quietly talked to herself, jotting notes in a large black notebook.

The situation turned even more weird when the court lady turned and saw Mei, who'd been standing there the whole time. Instead of greeting her, she looked Mei over as if Mei were an object, not a person. Then she locked eyes with Mei.

"So, this is the girl," the court lady said in a flat voice, a statement rather than a question.

"Her name is Mei," Brother said coolly.

"That's not the name in my file," she said with an undertone of smugness, still fixated on Mei.

"Then your file is incorrect," Brother said levelly. Mei heard something creep into his voice. "It makes me wonder what else you have wrong."

Mei saw the court lady's eyes flare, then she flashed a manufactured smile at Brother. "No, I'm sure I have it right."

"You're welcome to be as sure as you like," Brother paused while meeting her gaze, "but you're still wrong. And in this house, when speaking to my sister, please address her correctly. It's wise to show professionalism when representing your agency. Don't you think?"

"Are you trying to be rude, sir?"

"Quite the contrary. I abhor rudeness, especially in a professional setting, and especially in the presence of a vulnerable minor who the courts have entrusted into my care."

"That's the matter I'm here to determine," she said, her voice thick with smugness.

"In fact, you're not," Brother said calmly. "You're here to investigate a very narrow set of facts, facts already confirmed by one of your agency's, shall we say, more experienced counterparts?"

The court lady drew a breath to retort, but Brother jumped in before she could speak.

"I'm sure if your findings differed from what were already found, you might have a hard time explaining the discrepancies to your agency and the court. Furthermore, I notice you're taking your own notes rather than using a department issued digital camera for your investigation. That concerns me."

"What are you saying?"

"It should be clear to you what I'm saying. Your method is against agency policy, isn't it?"

The court lady opened her mouth to speak, but once again, Brother beat her to the punch.

"Which most likely means, for whatever reason, you want your opinion to be reported as fact, rather than the truth. However, we shouldn't worry. I have my own report in progress." Brother held up his phone and then pointed over to his laptop sitting on the end table.

"If I were you, I'd be concerned about the validity of my report, especially when the color video and audio portion of my report show all the date stamps clearly visible." He looked at the court lady and winked. "Plus, the current live stream my attorney is watching right now."

The court lady's mask slipped, and Mei could see her face had gone pale, and the skin on her neck was flushed with red. She tried to compose herself and begin to speak, but Brother cut her off again.

"Or," Brother continued smoothly, "we can return to the task at hand, be professional, and still part as friends. What do you say?"

The court lady stiffened. "That would be fine," she said coldly.

"Good. Please continue."

The court lady conducted her business quickly. She glanced at the kitchen and jotted her notes. She asked to see Mei's room, but with just her and Mei present.

Mei looked at Brother, who nodded and then slyly gave her a hand signal. It meant he was 'on guard,' and she should 'be careful' when speaking to the court lady.

Mei nodded and led the court lady down the hall to her room without touching her or speaking. Mei paused when the court lady stopped and looked into the bathroom, then followed Mei to her room. Once again, the court lady acted as if she was the only one there, jotting notes and muttering under her breath.

When they got to Mei's room, Boudicca was up on Mei's bed. The big pup looked up and started thumping her tail in her usual cheerful way. The court lady gasped and furiously continued writing in her notebook.

"Is that dog supposed to be in her?" she asked Mei.

"It's okay if she is," Mei said. "That's just Boudicca. Sometimes she sleeps with me."

"Really? Has it had its shots?"

"Yes, she has," Mei said deliberately. "See her dog tags on her collar?" She was going to say more, but sensed she should stop talking.

The court lady looked around the room. She jotted more notes on Mei's toys, dolls, books, stuffed animals, and the tie-on fairy wings Brother bought her at the Farmer's Market. She looked over at Mei's lava lamp on her dresser, and paid extra attention to the posters on the walls, especially the ones Mei and Brother colored together.

The court lady smiled to herself then walked out of the bedroom and to the living room without speaking to Mei.

Mei trotted after her and got to the living room as the court lady was walking towards the front door.

Brother stood across the room and made no effort to stop her. He cleared his throat. "Excuse me, miss. I'd like a copy of your report and notes."

"I'll see if you do," she snapped.

"Oh, I do," Brother said. "Your agency senior, my attorney, and the court commissioner all assured me you would give me a copy before you left here."

The court lady gritted her teeth and tossed her head forward with a jerk. "I will submit my complete report to the court."

"I would prefer my paperwork today, before your go."

"No," the court lady said stubbornly.

"I'm afraid I must insist."

"I will not."

Brother sighed. "I'm continuing to record this interaction and will present a copy to your agency and the court, with my request for administrative action." He waved his hand in a dismissive gesture. "In the meantime, you may immediately get out of my home, and off my land, you wretched creature."

The court lady was so mad, she was shaking, then suddenly, got still. To Mei's surprise and discomfort, the court lady smiled, but not a pleasant smile.

"See you in court, sir," she hissed.

Brother gave his dismissive smile. "Just like you'd planned all along, right?" He waved his hand. "Go."

The court lady swiftly walked out to her car, got in, and drove away quickly.

"Well, now," Brother said after she'd pulled away. "What a nasty bit of trash she was."

"She was bad all the way through, I could tell," Mei said.

"Yep."

"Will she cause trouble?"

"She'll try, but that was her plan before she even got here."

"But you got the video."

"Yes, I do," he said, and snickered. "All of it."

"What?"

Brother help up his hand, then walked over to his laptop and clicked some keys. He was quiet a minute, then clicked more keys and closed his laptop. When he looked over at Mei, he wore a giant alligator grin with a wicked look in his eyes. "If you look on the shelf in your bedroom, you'll find a new vase."

Mei cocked her head.

"There's a cam in there that recorded everything you and she said and did. I just put it in there this morning. "Let's get it out of there. I'm not spying on you and never will, but in this case, we needed to play dirty to counter her dirty tricks." He got a faraway look in his eyes, as though he was remembering something, and in a weird voice, sang the words: "Quis custodiet ipsos custodes?" then chuckled and shook his head.

"What does that mean?" Mei asked.

He thought for a moment. "It's a phrase in Latin, written on a sign in formal script on the wall of one of my old reconnaissance team buildings. It's an old scholar's question that means 'who watches the watchers?' And written on the sign under the formally scripted question is a skull. In blood-red letters, it says, 'we do,' USMC Force Recon. That slag has no idea who she's dealing with. My attorney warned me this particular lady was known for lying about people, so I took precautions. If she would have played fair, so would I."

Mei tried to take a mind picture of the moment, certain something important had just happened.

Brother winked and walked out of the living room. Over his shoulder, he said, "let's get that camera out of your room, then we can go outside and play."

Mei just shook her head in wonder. Her Brother was ahead of the bad people, and she was glad.

Chapter 59

Mei Mei

Once in a while, Brother would pack a lunch and drive Mei out to the park or hike through the woods behind Pop's farm. They'd spend the morning playing in the outdoors or flying Brother's drone (When Mei tried, it crashed into the weeds on takeoff.) Then they would eat what Brother packed, and Mei would often nap with Boudicca on a big blanket Brother spread on the ground. Usually, Brother worked on his college courses, and sometimes Mei woke up to find him dozing next to her.

One of Mei's favorite memories from that late spring/early summer was when she and Brother took time from his schedule to spend a few days planting apple trees on Pop's farm.

"It's a little late to be planting, but should be okay," Pop said. "This isn't a commercial apple tree farm. I'm just adding a little extra to the place."

So, for two days, they planted trees.

The planting was quite an event. Pop already had a full-grown orchard near the house, so for the new orchard, he chose a field on the far side of the farm. Using his tractor, he dug rows of holes, while Mei and Brother followed along and dug deeper to put in a baby tree. It was a lot of work, but Mei enjoyed it. She enjoyed learning new things, digging in the dirt, and, most of all, sharing responsibility with Brother and Pop.

Each day during the apple tree planting, Brother did something cool for lunch. One day, he built a campfire between the rows of holes and cooked cans of stew by setting the opened cans in the coals of the fire. When the stew was ready, he lifted out the cans with pliers to let them cool. Then he took out a loaf of homemade bread he'd baked the night before, tore pieces off to share with Mei and Pop. They ate the stew right out of the cans with one big spoon, then passed the cans around and dipped the bread to sop up the leftovers.

The next day, Brother brought the rest of the bread, a hunk of cheese, and a small ham. They ate as they did the day before, tearing off pieces of bread and cutting ham and cheese with their pocketknives.

Mei thought this was odd. She was used to eating sandwiches on sliced bread, but decided she enjoyed eating this way too.

After two days, they'd planted several rows of baby apple trees. Pop showed Mei how to scoop fertilizer around the base of each one and mix it in with the dirt. Finally, Pop and Brother ran water lines down the rows to hydrate the new trees.

Mei didn't work as much as Brother and Pop, but appreciated being included in the project.

Chapter 60

Mei Mei

As they spent more time together, Mei found out more about Brother by watching his day to day routine. He sang a lot, and sometimes when he was working on his college courses, he'd talk to himself. He stayed busy. He had eccentric projects, especially if he and Mei were watching a movie or just hanging out. For example, he'd learned basic sewing from Pop's wife, Miss Janice, so he stitched, by hand, two mountain man shirts for himself, one made from cloth, one from buckskin. He wore them while working around the yard or at Pop's farm.

Another odd project was carving his own totem poles. They were about the height of fence posts and about the same size around as a baseball bat. He'd bought a stack of white ash posts, and would trim them in Pop's wood shop. Then, when they'd visit Pop, Brother would stack them on the back porch out of the weather. Often he'd take one out and burn words and symbols onto them using his own wood burner. The words were Latin or Gaelic; the symbols represented animals. He'd rub cigar ash on the symbols to highlight, and add iron nails from Pop's forge, nailing a piece of silver to it for good measure. After he'd finished, he'd take the pole back to Pop's shop and coat it in bee's wax. Finally, he'd put them in the yard around the fence and plant clover seeds around their base for decoration. He happily worked away on them, never saying what they were for.

Other times, Mei would read to him as he whittled and carved, or he'd roll out a big canvas cloth in the living room and whittle on the totem poles while they watched a movie.

They didn't watch TV often, but occasionally watched movies or DVDs of old cartoons. Brother was careful about what Mei watched. He liked a space cowboy series called Firefly. He and Mei would sing the theme song and use the language for the show. For example, instead of saying 'good,' Brother would say 'shiny.' Or they would share lines from the show. Mei liked the show even when Brother skipped the parts where characters were having sex or something was 'a bit rough.' He would say, 'not for you, not now. Someday, not today.' Mei thought it was funny to see him a bit off balance.

Another show they liked to watch was about a town full of fun mad scientists who invented things. Brother thought it was a fun show and would explain what was going on. So, after a while, Mei liked the show too.

Chapter 61

Mei Mei

When her punishment for misusing the climbing wall was over, Mei took climbing classes! Her climbing instructor, Mr. Rob, said she was a natural. He showed her the proper way to put on safety gear, how to work with other people, and techniques for not just climbing, but traversing the face of the wall. She wanted to take more advanced classes, but Mr. Rob told her she needed to work on the basics. She told Mr. Rob Brother had called her Spider Monkey, and Mr. Rob thought that was funny, and accurate.

Mei also mentioned to Mr. Rob that even though Brother feared heights, he'd climbed in the Marines and climbed the wall to get her. Mr. Rob nodded and said he'd met Brother and talked with him. Mr. Rob also said he'd been in the Army and taught many soldiers how to climb, saying most people were afraid of heights and shouldn't be ashamed. Mr. Rob said everyone was afraid of something, but brave people face their fear and do what was necessary, like rescuing little girls who climbed up a wall without training or safety gear.

"Oh, yes," Mei said. "My Auntie told me Brother was very brave and earned medals for bravery."

Mr. Rob nodded. "I believe it. Sounds just like him."

"Do you know him?"

"No, but I could tell."

"Did you get medals too?"

"Well, Mei," Mr. Rob said with a smile, "that's not a polite question, so I'll decline to answer. No offense taken."

"Oh. Sorry, Mr. Rob."

"No worries, Spider Monkey. You didn't know, but now you do, so let's pick up the gear."

"Okay," Mei said and started coiling a rope. She turned and looked at him. "I bet you did. I can just tell."

Mr. Rob snorted. "Get busy, you impertinent little snot!"

Mei appreciated Mr. Rob talking to her as though she was a person and not a little kid, even when he was gruff, just like Brother did.

The dark cloud of the custody battle lingered in the background. Brother still had to meet with attorneys, and legal papers kept coming in the mail. Brother sat down and discussed it with Mei, telling her he was doing everything he could, but some things were out of his control. "So, instead of worrying about it, we're getting on with our lives."

"What if I have to go away?"

"What if you get to stay and they never come back?" Brother asked with a warm smile. "Mei, Mei, try not to worry about what your enemy will do. Think about what you'll do to them. Be the aggressor, stay ahead of them, and stay on the attack." He paused. "Be smart about it, do your homework, but always figure out how you'll hit them to keep them off balance."

Mei couldn't imagine being big enough to hit people and keep them off balance, but she listened to Brother and tried to learn what he was teaching.

Chapter 62

Mei Mei

As much as Mei liked going to the gym, she liked her time best with Auntie and Pop, for different reasons.

When she went to Auntie's, if the weather was pleasant, the first thing she'd do was take off her shoes and socks. She loved the feel of dirt, grass, and mud on her bare feet. No matter how many times she stepped on a sticker or stubbed her toe, it was worth it. She just had to be careful to avoid racoon or rabbit poo. Lots of critters lived in Auntie's garden.

Mei would also strap on her butterfly wings and zoom around Auntie's gardens and yard. She loved wearing the wings, but sometimes they weren't practical, like when she wanted to climb a tree, the wings would hang up in the branches.

Auntie bought Mei a big sun hat to wear on hot days. Auntie rarely wore a hat, but always had work gloves in her pocket. She usually wore an untucked, unbuttoned work shirt with the sleeves rolled up. One day Mei and Auntie were getting food out for the raccoons, when Auntie's shirt blew back in the breeze. Mei noticed Auntie wore a pistol in a holster on her belt, and asked her about it.

"It's just another tool. Women need to be willing and able to defend themselves. This was my mother's pistol. She was a great lady, and having it reminds me of her, how much she taught me, including how to take care of myself."

"I think I like your mom."

"She was something else. Now let's feed the critters before they riot."

Auntie's yard had magnificent trees for climbing, and Mei would scamper up the tallest tree she could find at every opportunity. She didn't even need to put her mask on. Sometimes the squirrels would chatter, and once Mei swore they were tossing peanut shells at her when she was climbing. No matter how challenging the climb, it was always worth it to get a view from above. It made her feel like a drone.

Like Brother and Pop, Auntie always talked to Mei like a person. They talked while they planted, weeded, watered, and trimmed in Auntie's gardens and greenhouses. The gardens were huge and so overgrown in places they resembled a jungle. But there was beauty everywhere in Auntie's yard.

Auntie knew lots of stuff besides plants, had her own workshop, and fixed many things. She had her own saws, drills, and wiring and plumbing tools. Most of it was too big for Mei to handle, but Auntie showed her how the tools worked at every opportunity.

Auntie painted and did art on concrete, like stepping stones with colored pebbles, flower pots, flower pot stands, and birdbaths. Mei loved it when she and Auntie made wood forms in Auntie's shop, then poured concrete to form them to their liking. A concrete project was always drying, waiting for Auntie's finishing touches. One time, Auntie had Mei put her hands into one of the concrete forms so her prints would stay in them when it dried. It was cool!

Auntie made stained glass art and hung random windows of colored glass set by themselves in her garden where they would catch the sunlight. Sometimes Mei would find their colorful shadows stretched across the ground. She'd lie in the middle of the pool of colors, and bathe in the light while gazing at the sky, wondering what it would be like to fly.

The first time Auntie came across Mei bathing in the colors, staring at the sky, and humming a song, she said, "what are you doing, kiddo?"

"I'm soaking in the colored light and smelling the garden."

"Really? Why?"

"I like how the colors look and wanted to see how they feel."

"Oh, okay. Um, how do they feel?"

"This one mostly feels red and blue, with some green." She stretched her feet out. "I'm too short to reach the orange shadow."

Auntie chuckled, then put down what she was carrying and laid down next to Mei. "Never thought of doing this."

"I like it. Do you?"

"Well, it's new. I've been blue before, but not red or green."

They gazed up at the sky for a bit.

"Auntie?"

"Yes, kiddo."

"I like being here."

"I enjoy having you here, kiddo. You're a good worker and good company."

"Good."

Chapter 63

Mei Mei

Mei would often practice her mind pictures while bathing in the colors. Brother had told her mind pictures were good for attaching fond memories to remember later on.

Mei would imagine the stained-glass window in its frame hanging from a tree limb. She would color in the tree, the sky, then the colors of the glass. She would listen hard and remember the sounds around her; squirrels chattering, Auntie digging in the nearby flower beds, birds chirping, Brother singing a tune as he worked in the garden. She would concentrate on the feel of laying in the grass and dirt, the sun shining on her, the smells around her; the dirt, plants, fertilizer Auntie used on the flower beds, the smell of her brother's cigar. She would dig deep into herself and think how good she felt laying there, safe, happy, and belonging to loving and caring people.

She'd lock the event in her mind to remember. Sometimes, while away from the garden, she'd sit down with her sketchpad, think about the event, and draw it from memory. Mei wasn't a skilled artist, but was improving.

Many times, Brother was there, and Auntie showed him things, too. She bossed him around a lot, but he didn't seem to mind. She did it in a nice way.

Sometimes Brother would work on his college courses on Auntie's porch while she and Mei worked.

Auntie planned a project to build a big greenhouse, but being Auntie, she wanted to build it her way, it would be big, with lots of shelves, a tool rack, electric plug-ins, fans, and stained-glass windows. She was always working on it, improving her ideas, and, like her other projects, making it in her style. As time passed, Mei could see the greenhouse taking form according to Auntie's plan.

Mei also enjoyed going to Pop's house, where she found so much to do and learn.

Farms need lots of work to function, so Pop was always busy, and Mei happily tagged along with him, usually wearing her butterfly wings and sun hat. Pop did most of the work himself. Mei couldn't help much because she was too small, but liked to observe Pop. Occasionally, she did help, like when Pop dropped a wrench while working on a truck, she crawled under and got it. She was also good at running and getting things or relaying questions to Pop's wife, Miss Janice, or Michael, one of Pop's sons who lived with his family in a house on Pop's farm. She also swept the floors in Pop's shop and the barn with the horses, at least as best she could.

On the days Mei visited Pop's, at least once a day, she and Pop would practice throwing knives. Pop coached Mei, and she improved. At home, Brother had set up a knife target in the backyard, and every day, Mei practiced with him. She enjoyed wearing her leather belt with the pouches and drawing and throwing her knife.

Brother was great at throwing axes and tomahawks, even though he didn't practice as much as Mei.

At first Mei worried whether she and Brother would get in trouble by the 'court lady,' or other agents if they saw them throwing knives.

Brother wasn't worried. "I think court lady has enough to answer for with her conduct at the house. As for the other guys, I heard they're having too many troubles of their own to worry about us."

"What do you mean?"

"What I mean is, as far as the custody drama, you just have to hold fast for now while the courts decide. In the meantime, we'll enjoy our time together. Make sense?"

Mei nodded.

Chapter 64

Mei Mei

Mei felt surprised to find out Pop was an artist. He could draw, carve, and paint. Her and Pop working in his shop was one of her favorite activities. He'd show her how to use an old pencil to draw pictures on wood, then burn into the wood with a wood burner. They practiced pictures and words on scrap boards. She found it difficult at first, and scorched her hand twice, but kept trying. Pop showed her how to sand a board smooth to make it nice to draw and burn. They'd finish by applying a coat of varnish or stain to make it attractive. They made a sign for Mei's bedroom door that said, 'Mei's room,' with a picture of Mei and Boudicca as stick figures.

When Pop's work was serious, Mei would help Miss Janice, mostly in her vegetable garden, which Mei enjoyed just as much. Mei helped Miss Janice more than Pop since she'd performed similar tasks with Auntie, such as digging, planting, watering, and weeding. Mei would gather eggs from the chickens, but didn't like that as much, because chickens smelled, and more than once a mean rooster chased her out of the chicken coop.

Sometimes Mei would take a book and find a place to take her shoes off. Although the farm wasn't as barefoot friendly as Auntie's garden, she'd curl up and read. Those times alone were fun. Sometimes Pop would find Mei napping in the sun with her book or sketch pad, exhausted from a hard day's work.

Pop's farm had fields to explore, animals to feed, and places to climb! Mei climbed trees, ladders, and fences at every opportunity. She still had no fear of heights, and most tall things just seemed to call her to climb to the top for a bird's-eye view.

Pop always warned her, "don't break your neck."

"I won't, Pop!" she assured him.

She was careful when she climbed, but one day she raced up a tree without looking, and almost climbed into a yellow jacket's nest! She'd climbed several feet up when she saw it, only about three feet from where she hung onto a branch. The yellow and black bees were buzzing in and out of the nest, but hadn't noticed her yet. Terror bolted through her body for a second, but she surprised herself by not panicking, then deliberately climbed back down without angering the insects.

When she was safely at the bottom, she trotted away and then sat down. Her head was spinning, and she felt scared sick, but soon it went away. She felt good. She didn't panic! Yes, she felt scared, but willed the feeling away and saved herself!

She sprawled back in the grass and gazed at the sky. Thoughts bounced around in her mind; the biggest one an image of Brother with a giant grin on his big scarred face, cheering her on with one of his favorite sayings; "So much. Yes! So much Win!"

A new feeling washed over Mei.

Pride!

Chapter 65

Mei Mei

Even with all the climbing, gardening, and knife throwing Mei did with Pop, she liked it best when he taught her to ride horses. Mei loved climbing up and sitting on the back of Pop's gelding. With Pop leading the horse by the bridle, she felt over fifteen feet tall riding around the corral. She could see for miles! She was so little, the horse probably didn't notice her, but Mei loved it. She wished she was bigger and stronger and could help Pop get the chores done faster, so she had more time to ride. In fact, she finally asked for a chores list from Pop so she could guarantee as much riding time as possible.

"I want to ride a lot, Pop, but I know the rules. TANSTAAFL!"

Pop and Brother roared with laughter.

"Okay, you little mercenary," Pop said. "Let me see what I can do. I may not always be able to give you rides, but we can come to an understanding."

Pop, Miss Janice, Michael, and Brother had used the phrase quite often, and Mei asked what it meant.

"It means 'there ain't no such thing as a free lunch,'" Brother said. "Everything costs something. It's an important rule of economics and life. If you want something, you must pay for it, either with money or by working for it. If someone offers you something for nothing, be very careful. They're either not very smart or up to something."

Chapter 66

Mei Mei

That summer became the happiest of Mei's life. The learning, the companionship, the sense of having a family, was overwhelming. Returning home from the farm or garden, tired out, with dirty feet, grubby clothes, sunburn, often with newfound wisdom, was the best thing ever. Even when Mei did something to earn time in the corner, she took it all in stride.

Brother was full of surprises. Like a couple of days after Mei had visited the tired round man, Brother wrote 'Dinner' on the whiteboard in the kitchen. "I have a new learning adventure for us."

Mei wondered what was going on. They'd eaten a lot of dinners together, so what was so special with this one?

"You'll see," was all Brother had said.

When the day got close, they went to the grocery store. Brother bought a load of groceries. That afternoon, he brought out the expensive dishes and silverware, and they washed them together. After that, they baked a cake. Mei felt fascinated with the care Brother put into the cake. He frosted it and put strawberries on top to decorate it.

He explained while they worked in the kitchen. "I realized I don't have very good manners and very few formal ones, so I thought we'd have a fancy dinner, and that would be a fun way to learn, even if there's a lot of preparation and fuss."

The next day was the dinner day. Together Brother and Mei watched a video on how to set the table formally with candles and cloth napkins. They copied the video and sat as closely as possible. Brother made a couple of different kinds of fancy foods, then had Mei put on a suitable dress and shoes, while he dressed in a shirt, slacks, and a tie.

They had both finished dressing when Auntie, Pop, and Miss Janice arrived for dinner, all dressed nicely. Pop had even gotten a fresh haircut and trimmed his beard and mustache.

Brother showed Mei good table manners and courtesies and how to take care of guests. Which fork to use, how to drink from glasses, and how to act extra polite, addressing as Mr., Mrs., or Miss., all of which Brother included in his training. Also, perhaps most importantly, no cussing was allowed. That wasn't easy for Brother. He liked to cuss.

The dinner was a big hit, and Mei felt fascinated she could learn while eating dinner.

A week or so later, she noticed a recent note on the whiteboard. 'Tea Time.'

The day before 'Tea Time,' they bought another load of groceries, and that afternoon Brother again brought out the expensive dishes and silverware for them to wash and prepare.

"It's good to practice manners," he said. "It's a British tradition and a good way to meet new people. Manners are important skills and knowing how and when to use them is just as important."

When the afternoon for 'Tea Time' arrived, some of Brother's friends from college and one of his professors, Mr. White, came over.

For the tea, Brother and Mei had made little sandwiches of all different kinds and cut off the crusts. Brother also made scones, bought cookies from a bakery, fancy teas from the grocery store and made another fancy cake. He brushed Boudicca, and both he and Mei once again dressed nicely.

Mei had fun meeting Brother's classmates. Many were veterans like Brother, and some had actually attended a 'tea' in England. They enjoyed discussing their current school projects. They complimented Brother and Mei for their efforts.

Brother slowly expanded their circle of friends by hosting cookouts on the back porch, which usually involved plenty of food, cigars, alcoholic drinks for the grownups, and loud, cheerful laugher. Brother enjoyed cooking and frequently experimented with different recipes. Most were homemade and prepared from scratch, like tacos and curry. However, Brother worried about his weight from all the cooking, so he remained diligent to his food intake.

Not all Brother's cooking adventures were winners. Once, they had a stew disaster that resulted in Brother cussing and Mei giggling at his exasperation.

"I followed the damned recipe, I swear!" he said as they munched on sandwiches later.

Once he tried making a jar of kimchi, a pickled Korean style cabbage. Somehow, he didn't fasten the lid on the kimchi pot properly, and when it fermented, the jar farted pickle juice! Kimchi odors permeated the kitchen. The result meant significant cleanup, running a fan and opening windows to air out the kitchen.

Chapter 67

Mei Mei

Two of Brother's close friends were Mr. White and Mr. Norris, professors from grad school, both intelligent and kind men, who often attended the cookouts Brother hosted in the backyard. Like Brother, both enjoyed smoking cigars. Both loved to teach people without making them feel dumb for not knowing something.

Mr. White described himself as a rover when he was younger, and a world traveler. Currently, besides teaching college economics, he was an author and freelance writer with a photographic memory. He also taught martial arts and was a fencing master with the Polish saber. Like Brother, Mr. White was a single father. His son, George, was a brilliant, dark-haired, hulking boy, four years older than Mei. George was deceptively strong, clever, and perceptive about people. George and Brother hit it off and chatted during the cookouts. Brother talked with George like he was an adult, same as he did with Mei Mei or anyone else.

Mr. White's other child was a girl named Judyta, two years older than Mei. Judyta was a thin, high-energy, ring-tailed terror who, as Brother said, lived her young life like the riff of a rock and roll band, asking no quarter and giving none in return. Judyta wanted to conquer the world, or at least make it bend to her indomitable will. She insisted on using her proper Polish name and dared anyone to challenge her. She tried to climb everything, eat anything, and fight anyone about anything. Like her father and older brother, she was also brilliant. Best of all to Mei, despite Judyta's high energy living, she was kind and protective of people she liked, yet civil to people she didn't like. The minor exception was her brother, and the two fought constantly.

Mei's friendship with Judyta was another life-changing experience. When the two met for the first time, Judyta immediately gave Mei a big hug and showered her with friendship and positive energy. At first, Mei was almost overwhelmed with Judyta's onslaught, but over time became friends. Judyta didn't let Mei withdraw into her shell and would happily take Mei's hand and drag her out into the world. They quickly became crime partners and climbed trees, raced about the house and yard, did projects out of Mrs. Fox's book, and laughed hysterically. As mismatched as they were in age and personalities, they spent as much time together as possible.

Sometimes, when Mr. White was teaching or correcting papers, Judyta and George spent the day with Brother and Mei. Judyta and Mei usually went to Mei's room to pursue more craft adventures with the esteemed Mrs. Fox

The first time Mr. White dropped off the kids, Brother and George looked at each other in awkward silence, until Brother said, "I have to do some lifts. Would you come and spot me, so I don't break my neck?"

George shrugged. "Sure."

"Thanks man, that would be a big help. After I'm done, do you want to hit the bag with me a bit?" He punched George lightly on the arm. "I bet you pack a punch!"

George grinned and nodded. "Yeah, I do.. Dad's been teaching me."

"Right on," Brother said, and they headed to the gym in the garage.

On one visit, Judyta, always ready for devilish play, had brought her backpack. When they went to Mei's room, Judyta gave Mei a wicked smile, opened the pack and pulled out two big Nerf dart guns.

She smiled. "Let's go shoot the boys."

Mei could see Judyta's coiled spring energy, and Mei wasn't sure why, but plunking the boys with darts seemed like a great idea. She smiled back.

Judyta reached for a Nerf gun. "Oh yes, yes, indeedy do!" she said, like Brother said sometimes. "This one is George's. It'll be fun popping him with his own gun!"

"How do I work this?" Mei asked.

Judyta gave her a quick demonstration of how to load and shoot. The dart guns would fire several times before reloading. The young pistoleras loaded their guns, grabbed a pocketful of extra foam darts, and headed out.

"They should be in the garage, working out," Judyta whispered as they crept down the hall. They passed Boudicca snoozing on the sofa, and when they reached the garage door, they heard music playing.

Judyta reached out, grabbed the doorknob, then looked at Mei. "Are you ready?"

Mei held her dart gun with both hands and nodded excitedly. Her heart was racing! This was going to be fun.

Judyta slowly turned the doorknob and then quickly flung the door open and charged in. Mei rushed in, hot on her heels, gun up, ready to launch foam mayhem. The lights were on and music was playing, but the guys weren't there.

"Where?" Judyta said, but Brother's voice boomed behind them. "Light 'em up, Georgie boy!"

The would-be assassins were startled out of their minds. "Eek!" Judyta chirped over the music, then spun around, looking for the voice. At the same time, Mei shrieked and flailed around with her gun.

Nerf darts flew out and hit them from the open doorway, while another volley flew across the gym and hit them from another direction.

"Havoc!!!" George roared from where he was hiding.

The girls tried ducking the flying darts, and Judyta returned fire, but it was too late. They were done for. Darts bounced off them.

"Okay! Okay!" Judyta shouted over the music, while Mei swung her pistol in Brother's direction.

Judyta caught her hand. "Stop, Mei. We're busted and dusted."

George shut off the music and he and Brother laughed as they walked over. They high-fived each other. "Two tangos neutralized," Brother said, still laughing.

"How did you know?" Judyta asked.

"And where did you get dart guns?" Mei demanded.

"I had intel delivered via a local asset who told me insurgents were going to attack my COP with ruthless cunning and determination, so I and my fellow coalition member," Brother pointed to George, "planned and executed a textbook counter ambush."

"Wait," Judyta said. "Dad! It was dad who ratted us out!"

"Not fair!" Mei shouted.

"I cannot confirm nor deny my source," Brother said. "And what's this 'fair' you speak of?"

"If you find yourself..."

Whap! Mei zapped Brother with the dart gun while he was in mid-sentence.

"Their guns are empty, Judyta! SHOOT! SHOOT!!!" Mei yelled.

"AAAAHHH!" Judyta howled, as she whipped up her gun and blazed away, first at a surprised Brother, then at a stunned George.

Like a brush fire blazing to a full-scale bonfire, the ensuing dart gun melee quickly grew to all-out war in the house, out in the yard, around the side of the house and back through the front door with darts whizzing everywhere, ambushes, frontal assaults, counterattacks, and hasty retreats. When ammo ran out or reloads were too slow, they threw pillows or used them in hand-to-hand combat.

They bumped into things, tripped over, knocked over, and ran smack into the walls. No quarter was given; none was asked for. The only rule was Boudicca was off limits, but everyone agreed to that, anyway. On one of the temporary truces, Brother wound an old white T-shirt around Boudicca's middle and used a marker to color a red cross on the front.

"Boudicca is our doctor," he said as the kids cheered. "She gives loves, and her kisses are healing."

Boudicca thumped her tail in agreement.

"Game on!"

When Mr. White came by a few hours later to pick up his offspring, he was stunned at the bedlam. "Dear God," he said, "what in the..."

"Words can't describe."

"Sorry, Steve," Brother said, and limped over to greet the professor. "I guess we got carried away, but we bonded and had a good time."

"I guess so," Mr. White said.

"Yeah, dad!" Judyta said. "And you told the boys that were were going to attack them, and our cunning ambush turned into a fight! This could have been over quickly, but nooooooo."

"True" Mr. White said. "but I thought I'd teach you a lesson in treachery. For example," he drew a Nerf gun from the satchel he wore over his shoulder and plunked Judyta!

"AaaaGH!" Judyta shrieked in surprise and outrage.

Mei stood with her mouth open.

George laughed at his sister's plight until a dart from Mr. White skipped off George's head.

Everyone scrambled for arms and ammo, and the war resumed with a renewed liveliness lasting into the late afternoon, when everyone was finally spent with exhaustion from running, gunning, and laughing.

Such was Mei's life when her new friend Judyta was around.

Chapter 68

Mei Mei

Brother's other close friend was Mr. Norris, a retired Air force combat fighter pilot. His children were grown and gone from home, and he seemed quieter than Mr. White.

However, like Mr. White, Mr. Norris was brilliant and fascinated with learning, and spent years traveling the world. Brother said Mr. Norris was different because he came from a working-class background, and loved working with his hands. And like Mr. White, Mr. Norris loved to learn for learning's sake and teach others without making them feel stupid for asking questions, or not understanding right away. He was also a champion pistol shot, and despite not looking the part, taught hand-to-hand combat.

One time during college, a mugger had mistaken Mr. Norris's calm, kind demeanor as weakness, and learned a just, if painful, lesson. With that event, combined with Brother and Mr. Norris's shared love of the works of Robert Heinlein, Brother nicknamed him 'Prof' Norris. 'Prof' seemed rather pleased with the sobriquet (Mei was learning lots of new words) and used it often.

Like Mr. White, Prof often challenged Brother intellectually, always in the spirit of helping a good guy get better. Over time, the relationship between Mr. White, Prof, and Brother grew from student, to mentor, to friends, to equals. Often, Prof or Mr. White consulted with Brother, or hung out and talked like pals. They swapped books and articles, and often argued good-naturedly while smoking cigars on the back porch.

Chapter 69

Mei Mei

Even though the summer was mostly a happy time for Mei, it wasn't always a fairytale. Sometimes she felt cranky or stubborn, and argued too much, or didn't do all of her chores. Other times she just didnt want to do things like clean Boudicca's slobber streaks off the walls and furniture. At those times, Brother was patient with her, but she still ended up in the corner a few times, followed by her apology and a consolation hug from Brother.

One day after morning chores, Brother said, "You should try drawing your mind pictures, but only the ones you want to share."

Mei nodded, but felt apprehensive.

Brother noticed. "What's wrong?"

"I've tried, but don't think I can draw good enough," she said.

"Don't worry about it. Just keep the picture clear in your mind and draw it the best you can. Drawing well takes lots of practice, lots of work, and many mistakes....but its worth it."

"Okay."

"Well, why don't you get the big sketch pad and pencils and join me here? I have work to do, but we can have quiet time after."

His suggestion sounded good, and she recalled a great mind picture she wanted to revisit, so got her things and set up her drawing equipment next to Brother. She looked at the paper, then thought of a mind picture from camping. She took a minute to determine where on the paper her picture would fit, then picked up a pencil and started.

Fifteen minutes later, she growled and scribbled over what she'd drawn, then threw the pencil down in frustration. As she crossed her arms and sat back in her chair, she felt Brother's eyes on her. Without moving her head, she looked at him out of the corners of her eyes.

Brother impassively looked at her through his cigar smoke. Calmly, he said, "what's the fuss?"

"I can't make my hands draw the picture I see in my mind."

"I'm not surprised. Your mind skills are much sharper than your hand skills."

Mei was caught off guard by what he said. He always acted calm and reasonable when she fussed, and sometime it made her angry. She glared at him. "So, I can't do it?" she asked.

"Not with that attitude."

Mei felt herself clenching up.

"The question you need to ask yourself in these situations is, how can I do this?"

Caught off guard again, Mei relaxed. "What?"

"Say it with me," Brother said. "How can I do this? Emphasis on the word 'how.' How can I do this? Ask it like a question, not a cussy command."

"But I...," Mei started, winding up for a fit.

Brother snapped his fingers, and they cracked like a gunshot, startling Mei. He held his palm out and raised his eyebrows. "Take a breath and ask yourself the question, please."

Mei sucked in a mouthful of air, then asked out loud, "how can I do this?"

"Good," Brother said. "Now focus on the question. How can I draw the mind picture I see on this paper?"

"How can I draw the mind picture I see on this paper?" Mei repeated out loud.

"Yes!" Brother said with a broad smile. "How? What can I do? When you feel like throwing a fit and quitting, don't give in to the temptation. Instead, focus on answering your question and solving the problem." He took a puff from his cigar. "Now, to the problem-solving part. Try to come up with three ways to solve your problem, and since you've shown me you want to be the kind of person who solves problems, I'm more than happy to help with suggestions you might want to consider."

Mei, distracted, forgot her building fit and nodded.

"You can map out what you want on the paper and where you want it to go. Here." Brother scooted over and flipped the pad to a clean sheet of paper. "First way, you can write the words instead of pictures on the paper, like this." He wrote the words 'Mei Mei,' 'Boudicca,' and 'Judyta,' in the center of the paper, then wrote 'Campfire,' below. Above, he wrote 'Truck.' He sat back. "See? There's my mind picture of you and Judyta. playing with Boudicca at the campsite."

"But it wasn't like that," Mei said.

"Ah ha!" Brother said with a smile. "This is my mind picture, not yours. Here's another way you can draw it." He leaned in, flipped the page to a blank page, and instead of words, drew stick figures. "Now, you can break down each picture, and instead of a stick figure, you can concentrate on each person, the dog, the truck, and the campfire. Then you'll know what part of the picture you need to work on; you, Boudicca, Judyta, the campfire, or the truck." He leaned back. "A third way is to cut out pictures of each person and glue them to the page."

"That's weird."

"True, but at least it forces you to think of solutions to your problem instead of throwing a fit and quitting. Some solutions are better than others. Most require thinking, planning, and work, but they're there if you look for them. If you keep this mindset and practice it, you should be able to find a solution, but don't sit around crying about it, and never quit. Things might not come easy, and you might need to work harder than other people, but so what? You can do much more than you think by using your new problem-solving skills. So, Finnegan, begin again," he said, then flipped over to a new page and handed the pencil to Mei.

She looked at the paper and started drawing. She thought she'd try mapping her mind picture out using stick figures by drawing people in the places she remembered. When she drew the stick figures, she posed them like the people in her mind picture; their posture, which direction they were looking, and what they were doing. When she did that, she remembered what they were doing and the expressions on their faces when she took the mind picture. Then she drew details around them; tables, vehicles, chairs, food, whatever she pictured. Then she added the scenery; trees, sky, grass, smoke from the bonfire, and people in the background.

Mei became happily lost in the process, stopping only to change pencils or close her eyes to consult her mind picture. When she completed the picture with the stick figures, she took her big eraser, and one character at a time, erased and redrew the stick figure as a fully sketched person. The process was time consuming and messy. Several times, she resisted the urge to throw a fit. Instead, she considered each problem and asked herself, 'how' to fix it or do it better. She stayed focused on her tasks. When she sat back, Brother was gone, and she realized her hand hurt from drawing so much, and she needed to use the bathroom. She looked over the picture and sighed in despair. She hated it! It looked terrible! She felt embarrassed and mad she'd wasted so much time on it! She felt so mad, she wanted to throw a real fit and trash the picture, kick over the table, and cuss out Brother! Unfortunately, for her impeding tantrum, her need to use the bathroom took precedence, so she dropped the pencil and stomped into the house and down to the bathroom.

Mei used the bathroom, then washed up and splashed water on her face. She'd calmed down, but felt depressed. She dried off with a towel and walked back outside, then froze when she saw Brother standing next to the table. He was holding up her picture and looking it over.

Mei's heart dropped to her feet. Brother would probably yell at her for doing such a bad job and wasting all that time. She couldn't move or think of an excuse, and felt so upset at the dumb picture, after everything else she now did so easily. She must have accidentally made a noise because Brother looked up. But to her surprise, rather than exploding, he simply nodded.

"This is pretty good," he said, looking back at the picture.

Mei's mouth dropped. "What?"

"Yeah, it is. I can see people I know, in a place I was at, during a time I was there. It's rough, but I can tell who the people are by how they're standing. And look here." He pointed to the picture. "I can tell by her hair, her stance, and that wicked grin, that's Judyta." He pointed to another part of the picture. "I think that's the time you two were laughing at each other's jokes, right?"

Mei was surprised. "Yes."

"Okay," Brother said, then nodded again. "I mean, sure, you have lots of room to improve, but you're on the right path. As far as problem solving, you did what you were taught, and you put in the work. Right?"

"Uhm, yeah."

"Well, it shows," he said, and put the picture down. "Good job. Keep this picture as a memento of where you started, because if you keep going in this direction, keep practicing, and putting in the work, you'll get better, until one day your mind pictures will match what you see in your mind. You like drawing, don't you?"

"Yes."

"That's good, then you won't mind working hard at it."

Mei nodded.

Brother walked past her and patted her shoulder, then went into the house.

Mei went over to the picture and looked it over.

"Mei?" Brother called from the house.

"Yes, Brother?"

"Are you looking at your picture?"

"Yes, I am."

"Good. Look hard at it."

"I am."

"Look really hard."

"I am."

"I looked all over your picture, and saw no reason for you to be as mad as you were a minute ago, and certainly no reason to throw a fit. Do you?"

Mei pursed her lips. "No, I don't."

"I'll teach you how to keep your temper in check. Now pick up your stuff and come in for dinner."

Chapter 70

Mei Mei

After dinner, Mei took her throwing knife to practice at the target in the backyard.

Brother had his struggles. Sometimes his pain would flare up enough to interrupt his sleep. He'd become cranky and uncharacteristically frustrated. He never showed anger at Mei directly, but sometimes she felt uncomfortable around him. Mei was more scared for him than of him, mostly because she didn't know what to do to help him.

He'd reassure her. "It's okay, Mei Mei. I'm not made of glass, and neither are you, and despite everything we've been through, we don't ever feel sorry for ourselves. Sometimes bad thoughts need to work their way out in a safe release." So whenever they could get away, Brother would take them camping. When Mei first came to live with him, she wasn't sure she wanted to go camping. But Brother, with his usual patience, eased her fears.

They started by camping in the backyard. Brother would build a campfire and they'd cook dinner over it. Then he'd read to her out of a book she picked out. She'd snuggle into a sleeping bag, and Boudicca would snuggle up next to her. They'd look up at the stars and listen to Brother's deep voice. He'd sleep in a pile of quilts or big, thick Scottish or Mexican wool blankets, because most sleeping bags were too small. Late in the night, she'd hear him snoring. Usually Boudicca would be snoring next to him, but Mei didn't mind. It was new and odd, but fun.

She did enjoy being tucked into her blankets and looking up at the stars. The deep, starry sky was a little scary, but also wondrous. She'd look up and wonder what was out there, what it would be like to fly that high and look down at the Earth. Would she be able to see Brother and Boudicca from space? Eventually, Mei brought her binoculars to get a better look at the night sky.

In the mornings, Brother cooked breakfast over the fire, and showed Mei how to put out the fire using a fire extinguisher or dirt and water. She'd begun to like camping and loved looking up at the sky, but only when she was next to the campfire with Brother nearby. He noticed Mei's fear of the dark and he came up with a plan.

When they were still camping in the backyard, Brother would wait for it to get dark and let the campfire burn down low. He'd then teach Mei how to walk around in the dark, although it wasn't pitch black since the embers from the fire gave off light. But Mei learned how to let her eyes adjust to the night and how to walk carefully so she didn't trip. It got easier and easier each time until Brother had her lead him around instead of him leading her around. Neat!

Later on, after they got used to camping in the yard, they'd load the truck and go camping away from home. Boudicca didn't go with them because it was her job to watch the house. Sometimes they'd go to a campground or a wilderness area, but always next to a river or lake.

Mei loved taking a mind picture of Brother reading her a story next to a campfire, and could remember the smell of the wood smoke and brother's cigar, and the sound of his voice with the river rushing in the background.

While they were camping, Brother taught her how to go to the bathroom in the woods and keep clean by washing in a river. For fun, he used wood ash and dirt to paint her face like a savage warrior, to throw rocks and spears, how to creep through the woods without making a sound, and how to find and watch animals in the woods. It surprised Mei to see so many rabbits, deer, and birds.

Brother taught her what to do if she got lost and how to light the campfire using flint and steel, matches, or a lighter. How to cook hot dogs and marshmallows, potatoes wrapped in tinfoil, and canned food over the fire. He made her a leather 'possibles' bag, which is like a duffle bag, just like the mountain man scouts used. He showed her how to pack emergency things so she could find them in the dark. Mei liked it so much she wore it often, even when they weren't camping.

Best of all, he taught her how not to be afraid of the dark. "Most people are afraid of the dark, but if you can learn to conquer that fear by making friends with it, you'll have the advantage over most people. Put your mask on and learn to use your surroundings and be careful, the same as when you climb."

He taught her how to hide in the shadows, to move around quietly in strange places, and how to use the moonlight's reflections to see things she didn't know were there.

Mei thought it all was neat! And so much better than being afraid. And she never grew tired of looking up at the stars at night and imagining flying around in space.

"I know we're really active and I'm loading you up with lots of new things and information," Brother said, "but life is a banquet, so take big bites. And when school starts in the fall, we'll need to slow down and establish a different routine."

Mei didn't mind. She liked it all. "Can Judyta, George, and Mr. White come camping with us sometime?"

"I think that would be a fine idea," Brother said. "I enjoy their company."

"Me too."

Chapter 71

Brother

After the day court papers were delivered, and the day Mei climbed the wall at the YMCA, aka the "Day of the wall" Brother made some hard and deliberate decisions, the first of which was they wouldn't sit and wait for something to happen. He acknowledged the possibility he may lose Mei, and if so, needed to prepare her for a life without him. He had put gentle forward pressure on her to encourage her to grow out of her shell, so now he needed to put more pressure on himself to lead.

The first thing Brother did was research, investigate, interview, and hire a competent private investigator of his own. He needed to know more about the people trying to take Mei away. He had a great deal of experience at reconnaissance and surveillance, but he lacked the expertise for this kind of work, and time was of the essence. Brother hired Jaime a high quality private investigator, to help him, and although his services didn't come cheap, he had experience in getting information Brother and his attorney could use in court. Brother also paid Jaime to help Brother protect himself from an unwanted investigation by the other team.

Taking every step to prepare for the court case, Brother could turn his attention to Mei. Based on his experience at war and being away from home, he decided the best way to protect her heart and soul was to armor her with memories of love and good times. So he packed as much love, learning, and fun, into the time they had left.

He summed it up with a Latin phrase, 'Dum Viva Vivamous!' which he thought was better than the Marine Corps' version of the same idea. 'Full Throttle and Fuck It!'

Brother sat down with a calendar and planned out the remaining eight weeks of summer. He needed to work around his school schedule and maintain his physical rehab routines, but that still left lots of time to accomplish epic things.

Of course, as soon as he planned out their schedule, unforeseen events popped up to interfere. They needed to deal with legal issues, meetings with the attorney and Guardians ad litem, reports from the PI, and his own legwork.

Brother hired Doctor Amy to keep meeting with Mei, including (after her expulsion was over) observing her during her swimming and Jujitsu classes, as well as obtaining physical health progress reports from the doctor and dentist. The list was endless, but important for him to document everything.

Thank God the Chaplain had warned him that someday, someone would want to get into his business with Mei. He needed to keep current and accurate records. In a short amount of time, Brother provided his attorney with a ton of valuable information, above and beyond what the court normally asked for. The holy man had once again saved the day.

His attorney provided valuable behind-the-scenes information on who the Guardian ad Litem would be, and the next investigators from Child Services, and how to prepare in each case. Fortunately, in this case, the Guardian ad Litem was an old school professional. He was concerned with what was best for the child and treated all parties involved fairly and equally.

"No worries there," the attorney said. "Just be honest and be yourselves."

On the other hand, the attorney warned, the Child Services Investigator was the type of bureaucratic pit viper whose job was to get promotions and power within her agency, and she didn't care how many coworkers, parents, and children she stepped on along the way.

So, Brother prepared accordingly. Ultimately, the attorney was right, and Brother was glad he made the right decisions. He arranged with the PI to see what he could find out about the Child Services Investigator. Brother also set up an internal surveillance inside his home for the meeting, complete with audio and video.

A final touch was adding a manually activated electronics scrambler to confound any wireless surveillance gear the investigator might try to sneak into his house during the meeting.

Before the meeting, Brother was concerned he was becoming paranoid. However, less than a minute after the Child Services Investigator arrived at his home, Brother thought he might not be paranoid enough. After the meeting, he gave all surveillance information and the private investigator's report to the attorney to prepare for their defense.

When the Chaplain read that part of Brother's report, he'd laughed so hard, he needed to call and talk to Brother directly.

"You're a wicked and fiendish man," the Chaplain laughed. "Please don't spare a single detail."

Chapter 72

Brother

Fortunately, Brother kept most of the drama from the court cases out of Mei's notice, and over the next month and a half, they spent a lot of time together learning and exploring. He kept Mei working on her reading, doing art, exercising, and working hard on her Mind Pictures.

They had a pleasant week helping Pop with late apple tree planting, and weekly gardening visits to Auntie's. Brother splurged and arranged Mei a kiddie climbing class at the gym where she could learn to climb the wall correctly, using the safety equipment. He wasn't sure what triggered Mei's love of climbing, but that little imp would use any excuse to 'go vertical,' and not just on the climbing wall. She'd scamper up on top of anything; barn roofs, ladders, every tree at Auntie's and Pop's. Brother would turn his back for a second, and there she'd go, up the side of a tree with her binoculars strapped around her side and butterfly wings tied to her back. As someone who hated heights, he shuddered, but climbing lit a fire in Mei, and it wouldn't be right for him to squash that fire, so he gritted his teeth and watched.

He enjoyed seeing Mei act like a busy little tornado. She did chores at Pop's, rode horses, helped Miss Janice, got chased by chickens, and built things in the shop with Pop. At Auntie's, she gardened, helped build shelves, and anything else Auntie let her. She was always dirty, often sunburned, and game for anything. Sometimes Brother would slow down things, and they'd just go to a park, where Mei played and Brother did schoolwork.

Since Mei had become comfortable playing savage outside, Brother added other learning events to her schedule. He hosted a formal dinner where they dressed up and practiced good table manners. When the dinner went well, Brother planned an English

Style High Tea. He and Mei watched a video online of what to do, then they cooked a bunch of food, and invited Brother's friends from grad school over for relaxing fun. It was a lot of work, but beneficial for them to try new things.

In a pleasant surprise, and for a reason known only to her, Judyta, Mr. White's daughter, immediately adopted Mei. It amazed Brother at how fast Mei transitioned from introvert to an outgoing maniac when Judyta was around.

Brother felt more than grateful for the budding friendship between the two families. The friendship between Mei and Judyta was worth more than gold, and Mr. White's good-natured, logic-based arguments pushed Brother to stretch more of his learning muscles. Plus, with Steve being a single dad, family events and get-togethers came easy.

Chapter 73

Brother

Life didn't always go smoothly. Mei was still a little kid and she would occasionally act up. Sometimes it was normal growing up stuff, but she also liked to push her boundaries, telling Brother she wanted to stay up late, or refusing to do her chores. Sigh. Pushing boundaries was fine, but Brother couldn't allow blatant mutiny. So now and then, he reluctantly made Mei stand in the corner or grounded her from doing something for a couple of days. He tried to remain open to understanding why she did what she did, but often she popped off at the worst of times, adding to his frustration. That girl!

Still, they accomplished a lot. They continued to practice with mind pictures, reading, and whatever Brother thought she needed to work on.

Chapter 74

Mei Mei

Looking back, Mei understood the Ceilidh(pronounced Kay-Lee), and everything that happened during those few amazing days resulted from Brother's clever orchestrations. A planner by nature, he hated leaving important things to chance. The Ceilidh was a brilliant opportunity for Brother to orchestrate a dress rehearsal for Mei to put together everything she'd learned since living with him, and try them out in a place she felt safe and autonomous.

But as everyone knows, the best plans don't always lead to favorable results.

The summer days with Brother passed quickly. Around the Fourth of July, Mei heard about an event coming at the end of summer. At first, she paid little attention. After all, she was enjoying a busy but satisfying summer. However, Brother and Pop kept discussing the event while Mei was around. Finally, one day Pop and Brother started talking about the upcoming 'Ceilidh' (Kay lee) scheduled to be held on Pop's farm. Pop had a special fenced area next to an orchard he kept groomed and landscaped like a private park that he sometimes rented it out for weddings or special events.

Apparently, this year the Ceilidh was going to be bigger and more important because some influential people planned to attend after missing several years. Brother was one of those influential people.

Mei found all this out one day while at Pop's farm when she wandered into a discussion between Pop and Brother. Pop acted uncharacteristically animated, although not mad at Brother.

"It's the way it is," Pop said. "We're all proud of you."

"I don't like being in the spotlight, Pop."

"We've all missed you, were worried about you, and everyone wants to see you. And there's the Mei situation."

"Well, yeah, she's the important part. Me? Not so much."

"Will you please shut up!" Pop said. "The entire clan was always behind you, and you've always been in our thoughts. People were always asking about what you were doing and where you were. It's time to let them know you're back and doing well."

Brother sighed. "I don't really have a say in this, do I?"

"If you don't play along, it's like turning your back on us," Pop said.

Brother shook his head in defeat. "Shit. Okay, fine."

"Oh, stop it," Pop said, chuckling. "You're acting as if you're standing blindfolded before a firing squad."

"What's going on?" Mei asked.

"She doesn't know?" Pop asked.

"I haven't told her," Brother said.

"Well?" Pop asked and raised his hands.

"Okay, Mei, have a seat," Brother said, and lifted her to a rare clean spot on a workbench. "This will take some explaining, so here goes. Pop is proud to be an American but has Scottish ancestry."

Pop nodded in agreement.

"Anyway, in ancient times, Scottish people were related to each other by clans. Those are communities of people, both closely and distantly related. They had the same or similar names. Anyway, in ancient Scotland, clansmen banded together in these communities to thrive and for protection. Each clan had a chief as leader. To be a member of a clan, you can be born into it, marry into it, or adopted by it as a child, or on rare occasions, you could be brought into a clan because you had a skill they needed. Once you were part of the clan, you had people to help you, feed you, and fight with you against others. Now it wasn't a free ride. You had to obey the clan chief and help other members of the clan in need. Ancient

Scotland was a tough and lawless place. Most of these traditions aren't followed anymore, but Pop revived a few of the old ways and made them work for a loose community of people for modern times.

We have a loose bunch of people who are family, by blood or by choice, who appreciate belonging to a community. We like Scottish heritage, traditions, food, all kinds of music, and history, but we're not all necessarily Scottish by blood. You'll see lots of ethnicities in our clan. We try to help people in need and celebrate wedding, achievements, and new children. And sometimes we kick people out of the clan, but only if they've done really bad things.

Anyway, at the end of each summer, Pop holds a clan gathering, and Ceilidh, which is like a big reunion, party, and fair all rolled together. We offer lots of food, music, athletics, and dancing. It's a ton of fun! In this area, Pop is the unofficial chief of his clan. He adopted me when I was a kid, so even if I'm not Scottish, I have people. This year, we want to adopt you into our clan."

Mei gaped. "Really? Am I Scottish?"

"I don't know, maybe. It really doesn't matter."

Mei cocked her head. "For real?"

"Oh, yes!" Pop said happily. "But this year we also want to celebrate your brother coming home and his service to our country, and that's what he's being all pissy about."

"Yes! You should, Brother!" Mei said. "You can show your medals and tell us what you did in the war!"

"Oh, God!" Brother groaned. "No, not you too!"

Pop looked at Mei. "Yes, your brother needs to remember he should be proud of all the things he's accomplished."

"Yes!" Mei clapped her hands.

"But..." Brother said.

Pop cut him off. "That's it. It's done."

"Crap," Brother said.

Chapter 75

Mei Mei

Even with everything else going on, the more Mei heard about the Ceilidh, the more excited she became. She had a feeling this would be something big. She felt wanted when Pop spent more time with her throwing knives and encouraging her to practice more on her own. Miss Janice took time to measure Mei for a new dress to wear to 'the main ceremony.'

Mei asked Brother what he was doing when he opened storage trunks and sealed boxes he'd stored away. He said he was double checking to make sure his uniform and kilts still fit properly, and all the accessories were ready. Mei felt a little weirded out at the sight of Brother wearing a kilt, but he looked kind of cool for a Brother.

However, when he put on his Marine uniform, she saw a completely different Brother. He became all business, and energy flowed around him. He acted deliberately and with what Auntie said was 'purpose.' Mei finally realized the rumors of her big, patient, funny, and kind- hearted Brother being a war hero could be true.

Chapter 76

Mei Mei

At the farm, Pop put together a team to plan and execute getting the preparations just right. As the big day approached, Pop and Brother took turns mowing the field where the celebration would be held. Pop, Brother, Michael and friends dug fire pits and set up spits for cooking, set up tables and benches, put up awnings, and stacked cords of firewood for campfires. They set up a covered stage at one end of the field. Brother's friend, Don, wired the lights, speakers, and a microphone. Josh, another one of Brother's friends, set up and leveled a big wooden dance floor. Outside a nearby barn, Pop and Brother assembled temporary showers and wash areas, complete with sinks, benches, and privacy curtains. Mei and Judyta, who visited the farm often, helped by being "gofers" and running errands.

A week before the big event, Pop announced to everyone working on the Ceilidh, "looks like the weather will cooperate this year. No rain, and not too hot."

Everyone cheered.

Chapter 77

Mei Mei

A few days before the Ceilidh, Mei and Brother were working in the front yard when a sheriff's cruiser pulled into the driveway. Mei didn't know what was happening, and her anxiety twisted her stomach into knots. Brother acted cool as ice. Back creaking, he stood up from the flower bed he was working on and brushed off his hands. He reached into his pocket and pulled out a key fob, hit a button, then put it back into his pocket. He winked at Mei and gestured for her to remain calm.

The deputy got out of his cruiser and walked over to Brother. "Are you ....?" and asked if Brother was Brother, using Brother's real name.

Brother responded politely "That's me, deputy, how can I help you?" Brother answered politely.

The deputy asked Brother if he knew the people trying to take Mei away.

"Yes, I know them," Brother said.

"They've made accusations against you," the deputy said in a professional manner.

"Oh?"

"Yes, they have. Do you mind if I ask you some questions?"

Brother replied politely. "Yes, sir, I do mind."

The deputy locked eyes with Brother.

Mei swallowed hard at Brother's response to the deputy.

"Why is that?" the deputy asked.

"I'm locked in a custody dispute with them, and don't trust that they're operating in any more good faith with you than they are with me."

"So, there are bad feelings between you and them?"

Brother said flatly. "No disrespect to you and your duties, sir, but I'm done speaking on the matter."

"Would you like to come down to the Sherriff's office and answer some questions there?"

Brother continued in his flat tone. "No, sir, I wouldn't. However, if it's necessary, please make an appointment and I'll come down with my attorney if she thinks it's prudent for me to do so."

The deputy nodded. "And who is your attorney?"

Brother gave the deputy her name.

The deputy pulled out a notepad and wrote the name down, then looked up. "Thank you for your time. Have a nice day."

"And you too, sir."

The deputy got into the cruiser and typed on the dashboard computer, then spoke into his radio, backed out of the driveway, and left the property.

Brother turned back to Mei, noticed the look on her face, then walked over and scooped her into his arms.

Mei felt rattled and hugged him tight, then pressed her forehead against his. "What's going on?"

"I'm not exactly sure. He's just a man doing a job, but I think our opposition is starting to question their life choices about now."

Mei didn't know what that meant, but trusted Brother. Why can't those people just leave us alone?

Brother lifted her in the air. His body barely creaked anymore when he did. "Hey," he said cheerfully, "it's still a nice day, so let's finish playing in the yard, then we'll get creative in the kitchen for dinner."

Mei smiled and nodded.

"All right!" he said and swung her gently back to the ground.

Brother's carefree charm made her feel better the rest of the day, but that night, even though she was exhausted from another busy day with Brother, she thought hard about the deputy's visit. Why was he there? What did he think Brother did? What were the fiends (that's how she thought of her dad's relatives now) up to?

Then again, did Brother do something he couldn't tell Mei about? She was surprised to find herself hoping Brother was retaliating on the fiends. She enjoyed her life here and wanted to see what would happen next. She drifted off to sleep, wondering how she could help.

Chapter 78

Brother

Brother started packing for the Ceilidh days before it arrived. On the morning of the big day, they packed the truck and a little tow trailer with their camping gear, food, clothes, then headed to Pops.

Brother looked at Mei and Boudicca crowded into the passenger side of the truck. "My girls are growing up. I'll need another vehicle before too long."

Mei reached down at her feet and petted Boudicca's head. "I like it this way."

Brother chuckled. "We all do, but you and big girl are going to outgrow that seat."

Mei smiled and kept petting.

Brother took a deep breath to suggest he was about to talk about something tough but important. Mei listened hard, because she appreciated him trying hard to do the right thing for her.

"I really think we'll have fun this weekend. It's the end of our first summer together. We've come a long way in a short time."

Mei smiled and nodded. He was right, and it was good, but she couldn't stop worrying about the court case and the police visit. "I'm happy too, but I'm worried about what's going to happen."

"Happen with what? Oh, the court case?" He glanced at her, then looked back at the road.

Mei nodded.

"Well, we've done all we can for now, so I want us to take a break from worrying. Let's relax and just have fun this weekend. How does that sound?"

"I think that's a good plan," Mei said.

"Right on!"

Chapter 79

Mei Mei

When they arrived at Pop's farm, they noticed more vehicles and people than Mei had ever seen at the farm before. Brother and Mei pulled up next to Pop's house, and since the front door was already open, carried plastic tubs with their nice clothes inside. The house was bustling, so Brother and Mei said quick 'hellos,' stashed the tubs in a back room, then returned to the truck.

The set-up crew had clearly been hard at work, setting up barbeques and outdoor ovens, putting garbage cans in place, and lined up port-o-potties along the back fence.

Brother pulled all the way onto the Ceilidh field, but instead of going to where everyone else was setting up tents and trailers, he drove far across the field and parked near the far fence bordering the orchard.

They got out and set up their camp. Brother unhooked the trailer and set it in place. He said they planned to use the trailer for storage and the bed of the truck as a sleeping area, and a spot beside the truck for Boudicca.

"I like seeing everyone," Brother said, "but sometimes I get 'peopled out' and need space."

Together they dug a small fire pit between the truck and the fence and lined it with rocks, adding a cooking spit and rack. A table and a bench and coolers completed the setup. Brother showed Mei where her clothes were and where to find the food and drinks. "Okay, like we talked about before, this should be a fun event for everyone. Prof is coming, and maybe Mr. White with your partners in crime, so have fun and run amok. I'll probably be distracted catching up with friends, but I'll be around if you need me. If it's an emergency, you can get me or Pop or one of my brothers. Do you remember the hand signals I taught you for 'all is well' and, 'I need you, but not an emergency?'"

"Yes, like this," Mei said and showed him.

"Good. If it's an emergency, don't stand on ceremony, just shout out. Do you know where the bathrooms are?"

"Yes."

"Okay, you can eat the food here at the campsite if you get hungry, or can eat off the big tables. Just make sure you drink two bottles of water each day."

"Okay."

"And anytime you want quiet time, you can take a nap in the truck or trailer."

"Okay."

"Do I need to mention you don't drink any alcohol?"

"No, I don't like it." Mei had tried sipping Brother's beer and other alcohol drinks, and didn't like the taste.

"Okay, final point. You should be fine here, but if anyone gives you the creeps or makes you feel uncomfortable, walk away from them, then come get me or Pop. Got it?"

"Yes." Mei felt safe from that advice.

He took a breath. "As a kid, sometimes I acted like a jerk, and there might be people here who aren't ready to let the past be the past. They have no business bothering you with it, but if you hear anything unpleasant, just ignore them and move on. Okay?"

"You bet," She felt excited to take part in the whole Ceilidh business.

"Well, it'll be fun, but we never surrender our common sense or go outside our boundaries."

"Now, let's hide out for a bit and enjoy some downtime."

They hunkered down and relaxed in their little campsite. They chatted, played with Boudicca, snacked, read, and dozed. Brother braided Mei's hair, set up gear, and let other people set up their campsites. Mei liked Brother's choice of campsite. The truck and trailer created a noise and sight barrier, secluding their spot from everyone else.

When the afternoon ended, Brother got up and went to the trailer. He belted on his kilt (a black one, not the formal tartan one) and a dark green t-shirt. He brushed his hair, strapped a sporran over his belt, then slid a sheathed antler-handled dirk into his belt, and a sheathed sgian dubh into one of his kilt hose. Finally, he put on a leather vest, then stood and faced Mei. "Well, how do I look?"

"Oh, yeah," Mei said, but noticed his nervousness. She looked at his giant, scarred, tattooed, and muscled body, and wondered what he could be nervous about. "You look like you could rescue a lady from a monster!"

He grinned. "Thanks, Mei Mei."

While Brother finished dressing, Mei put on one of her favorite 'gypsy girl' dresses, complete with a silk scarf for a belt, covered by another belt of silver-colored beads and little bells. She topped it off by tying a brightly colored bandanna over her head. She finished dressing as Brother put a leash on Boudicca and slung a leather bag over his shoulder.

He took Mei's hand. "You look awesome! Let's see what's doing."

And they walked out into the evening.

Chapter 80

Mei Mei

Mei was surprised how many people came and set up at the main campsite. She saw more tents, trailers, and campers organized in rows. Campfires were burning, and barbeque grills cooking, all wafting faint cooking smoke smells in the summer evening breeze. People settled in their campsites with lots of joyful shouts and chatter.

As the trio walked down a row of campsites, a tall, kilted man stepped out. He wasn't as wide as Brother, but was taller, strong looking, and handsome, even sinister looking. Brother stopped, and without taking his eyes off the man, slipped Boudicca's leash to Mei, then snapped his fingers. Boudicca immediately sat.

The man approached, and to Mei's shock, reached over and pulled a cigar out of Brother's vest pocket and put it in his teeth. He stepped back smoothly, and without taking his eyes off Brother, produced and cracked a wooden match with his thumbnail, and lit the cigar. "I heard you were back," he said, and puffed the cigar to life.

"Aye, tis me, so it is," Brother said, in a weak attempt at a brogue accent.

"Still with that stupid accent?"

Boudicca started growling. Still keeping his eyes locked on the man, Brother reached down and petted Boudicca, then straightened up and stepped toward the man. "Your wife likes it, so she does."

"She's always had a weakness for ...weird things, lost causes, and... big dumb animals that have a problem not making messes in the house." He took a step toward Brother.

"Isn't that why she's still with you?" Brother asked, closing the gap between them.

The man stopped and puffed on his cigar. "I don't care why she stays, I'm just glad she does."

"You were always lucky like that. But I'm still the pretty one."

"Oh yeah, sure," the man scoffed.

"Tis true." Brother said. "I am so pretty that ladies give me gifts!" Brother said, then reached over, took the man's cigar, clenched it in his own teeth, and blew a cloud of blue-black smoke into the air.

"Well, then it's a good thing the clinic can clear them up for you!" the tall man said and roared with laughter.

Brother roared with laughter too, and then they charged each other and bumped chest to chest, followed by a powerful bear hug. They laughed and slapped each other on the back.

"Damn, it's good to see you!" the man said. "You got my notes when you were in the hospital?"

"Yeah, I did, thanks," Brother said. "And it's good to be back."

"I hear you're going by the name 'Brother' now."

"Yeah, but it's more like a title."

"Well, it fits," the man said, then pointed at Mei. "Is this her?"

Without waiting for an answer, the man stepped over and extended his hand. "Hello, Miss Mei Mei. My name is Arik. I'm your brother's big brother, so that makes me your brother too!" His expression was warm and friendly.

Mei's eyes widened. Another giant of a Brother? She shook the big man's hand. "Hello."

"This is Pop's other son," Brother said, "so he's Michael's brother too."

"It's true!" Arik said to Mei. "Can you imagine the trouble I had growing up with two little brothers like them to look after?"

Mei giggled.

"Your dress is very pretty, but not as pretty as you. Are you sure you're related to us?"

"I am now."

Arik chuckled warmly. "That's the spirit, wee girl!" He looked at Boudicca. "What a pup!" He reached down and petted Boudicca with both hands. "Look at that mushy face! I love her!"

Boudicca thumped her tail in appreciation.

Arik stood up. "You guys gotta come to the campsite with me, like right now."

"Yeah, sure," Brother said.

"Mei," Arik asked, "do you mind if I pick you up for a hug?"

Mei shrugged. "I guess so, if you're my real brother."

"That I am and always will be," Arik said, and scooped her up. "What a doll you are! Pop told us you're smart and brave too!"

"Well," Mei said shyly, "I'm learning to be."

"Well, that's all good stuff to learn, and never stop learning it," Arik said, then put Mei down gently. He took her by the hand and the three walked together down the row.

Chapter 81

Mei Mei

The evening was settling in as Mei, Brother, and Arik walked to Arik's campsite, waving hello to other people gathered around campfires. Arik stopped and pointed to a site at the end of the row, then hand-signaled to Brother, who grinned and signaled back. Arik squatted to eye-level with Mei.

"Do you mind playing along with me? It's a joke on my missus, but I promise, not a mean one."

Mei looked at Brother with raised eyebrows.

Brother nodded and gave her Boudicca's leash, then Mei turned and nodded at Arik.

Arik grinned, stood up, took Mei's hand, and they continued walking to the campsite. When Mei looked back for Brother, he'd slipped between the campsites and trotted around behind the row ahead of them.

They strolled to the edge of a campsite, where an attractive blonde woman was putting blankets on chairs. She turned as Arik led Mei and Boudicca into the edge of the firelight.

"Hey sweetie," Arik said.

"Hey," the blonde woman said. "Did you find him?" As the trio got closer, she frowned. "Who's the little gypsy?" she asked, then noticed Boudicca. "And cute pup. What's going on?"

Brother's deep voice rumbled from behind her. "You left me unsupervised, baby doll, and the family got bigger, but not by me, as you probably figured."

The blonde woman spun around, gasped, then broke into tears. She overhand slapped Brother on the chest. "Oh, you big bastard." She pounced on him, kissing his cheek and squeezing him around his neck. "We thought we lost you."

Embarrassed, Brother returned the hug, then picked her up and swung her in a circle. "Naaaw," he said, and set her down. "There ain't a bullet made, or a germ grown that's gonna kill me!"

"You're so full of it!" she said, wiping her eyes. She sniffed and then slapped him on his big arm. "I was so mad at you when you told us not to come to the hospital."

"I know, doll, but it was an ugly situation, and I was in a bad way."

"That's why we wanted to get to you... you big jerk!"

Brother took her hands in his. "I know. I was wrong and selfish, and I'm sorry. But I'm here now, and I have a kiddo and a dog!"

She turned to Mei and kneeled down until she was at the same eye level as Mei. "Hello, gypsy girl, my name is Sarah. I'm your brother's sister-in-law."

Mei held her hand. "Hello, Sarah, I'm Mei Mei. I think we're... sisters-in-law?"

Sarah smiled. "That's right! I'm glad you're here. I need help wrangling these two knuckleheads."

Mei narrowed her eyes. "Brother isn't a knucklehead. He's a very smart man!"

Brother and Arik roared with laughter.

Sarah nodded. "I think you're right, but when those two get together, they act like wild animals. But we love them anyway. Right?"

Mei nodded.

She took Mei's hand. "Come and sit by the fire, sister mine."

They gathered around the fire and talked about how Brother was feeling, how long Mei had lived with him, and how long it took Arik and Sarah to drive to Pop's. Arik put a big teakettle on the fire. Brother pulled out a big bundle wrapped in wax paper from his bag, and unwrapped fresh scones. He offered the bundle to Mei, who took one and passed it on. She bit into it and found it sweet to the taste; full of apricots and pineapple chunks. Amazing.

When the water came to a boil, Arik put on a hot mitt, took the kettle, and poured water into mugs holding tea bags. The tea smelled spicy and good. Arik handed her a mug. "Careful, honey, it's hot. And this tea is okay for you. It's a non-caffeinated spiced blend."

Mei held the warm cup and waited for the tea to cool, wondering what Arik meant by spiced. She found out when Brother dipped his scone into the tea and took a bite.

She followed suit. The liquid was still hot, but tasted good on the tea-softened scone with a spicy cinnamon flavor.

As time passed, Mei heard people talking at other campsites. The light from the campfire flickered off their faces. Brother, Arik, and Sarah's conversation revealed their close relationship, and how much they'd missed one another. They talked the deep kinds talk that people who are dear to each other, who haven't seen each other in a long time.

Mei sat on the ground and leaned up against Boudicca, drinking tea and listening. She noticed Brother's face softened as he spoke, like a weight had fallen away. He pulled out more cigars and gave another one to Arik. They cut off the ends and lit up, and more big blue clouds of smoke mixed with the wood smoke from the campfire.

Brother opened a bottle of Irish Whiskey from his bag. "Here's to the pure life," he said, and drank.

It surprised Mei when Brother handed the bottle to Sarah. Sarah took it. "I'll take a shot if you sing for us," she said with a smile.

"Yeah!" Arik yelled.

"Oh, come on... " Brother protested.

Sarah cut him off. "Nope! I want the old days, the rock and roll days, and I want them right here, right now. You owe me. You know they want to hear you sing again."

In a mock announcer's voice, Arik belted out, "the band is back together! For one weekend only!"

Mei sat up. "What do you mean?"

Sarah looked at Mei. "Your Brother didn't tell you?"

"Tell me what?"

"When we were kids, we had a band, and your brother sang! It's how Arik and I met. Your Brother brought me to practice and Arik was a bass player. We've been together ever since."

"Your brother was a good singer," Sarah said. "Not great, but good."

"My brother can do anything!" Mei insisted with pride. She knew he liked to sing, but didn't know he was a professional.

"Have you seen his handwriting?" Arik cut in with mock disdain.

"Oh yeah, that." Mei said.

"Hey," Brother said, "I'm sitting right here!"

Arik ignored Brother's protests. "Your brother's trying to get out of singing."

Brother pointed at Sarah, trying to divert the conversation. "She didn't drink."

Sarah stood up with her hands on her hips and stared at Brother. Then she spread her feet shoulder width apart and without breaking her stare at Brother switched her grip until she was holding the bottle by the neck. She raised it to her lips and tilted it up and took a long swig.

Arik and Brother clapped and shouted. "Brava! Brava!"

Sarah scrunched her face and forced out a breath. Tears formed in her eyes.

Brother laughed through the cigar clenched in his teeth. "Okay, bratty Sarah. What do you want to hear?"

"We're going to sing a lot of the Celtic stuff this weekend, and it's a new day. I want a song about hope."

Brother reached over and took the bottle from Sarah. He gulped the gold brown liquid, but unlike Sarah, didn't make a face. He puffed on his cigar then cleared his throat. Standing in the campfire's light, he started humming low and deep, then nodded. He held out his hand and Arik slapped it.

"'I, I'm a one-way motorway'"
"'I'm the one that drives away'"
"'Then follows you back home'"
"'I, I'm a streetlight shining'"
"'I'm a wild light blinding bright'"
"'Burning off alone'"
"'It's times like these you learn to live again'"
"'It's times like these you give and give again'"
"'It's times like these you learn to love again'"
"'It's times like these time and time again.'"

He smiled and winked at Mei. She giggled.

"'I, I'm a new day rising'"
"'I'm a brand-new sky'"
"'To hang the stars upon tonight'"
"'I am a little divided'"
"'Do I stay or run away'"
"'And leave it all behind?'"

His head snapped back around. Sarah and Arik joined in.

"'It's times like these you learn to live again'"
"'It's times like these you give and give again'"
"'It's times like these you learn to love again'"
"'It's times like these time and time again.'"

Brother abruptly stood up, took Sarah by the hand, and pulled her into a swing dance hold. They held up their opposite hands.

"'It's times like these you learn to live again'"
"'It's times like these you give and give again'"
"'It's times like these you learn to love again'"
"'It's times like these time and time again.'"

Everyone sang the final chorus.

"'It's times like these you learn to live again'"
"'It's times like these you give and give again'"
"'It's times like these you learn to love again'"
'It's times like these time and time again.'"

Mei jumped up and clapped.

Arik and Sarah piled into Brother with a big hug, laughing and slapping him on the back. Even people from other campsites cheered.

Mei was surprised. She'd heard Brother sing around the house and when they rode in the truck, but this was different.

They all sat down around the fire, laughing.

Arik slapped Brother's shoulder and looked him in the eye. "Damn! It's good to hear you again."

"Thanks man," Brother said. "I've been gone so long, I thought I'd forgotten what I wanted to be. But I'm starting to remember."

Mei got up, sat next to Brother, then leaned against him. Boudicca followed. Without a word, Brother wrapped his big arm around her and pulled her in tight.

Arik offered the bottle of whiskey to Brother, who raised his hand. "I'm good for now. The next few days will be busy, and I can't drink like I used to."

"I got you," Arik said. "Hey, Pop said we're going to adopt Mei into our clan."

Brother beamed. "Yeah. She's one of us. Pop's making it official."

"I'm so glad to have another girl around, Mei," Sarah said sincerely. "We have lots of boys already, and we love them and all, but another great girl will keep balance."

Mei didn't know what to say, so just nodded.

They talked until night came. They ate from Arik and Sarah's cooler, and lots of people dropped by the campfire to say hello.

"Hey guys," Brother said. "We're going to get bedded in for the night. I need to stay on my sleep schedule if I want to make it through the whole Ceilidh." He stood, picked up Mei and took Boudicca's leash.

Arik and Sarah stood. "Gotcha," he said. "We need to finish setting up here."

"Need a hand?" Brother asked.

"No, we're okay. You two have a good night," Arik said and hugged Brother and Mei. "Mei, I'm glad you're my new sister. We'll have fun this weekend."

Sarah kissed Brother and Mei on their cheeks. "It's going to be fun this weekend. Have a good night."

Brother carried Mei to their camp, but circled around the row of tents instead of walking down the row. They stopped by the port-o-potty on the way. When they got back to their campsite, Brother set Mei down and handed her a little flashlight. "Go put on your nightshirt and sleep shorts." Then he lit a fire in the circle of stones.

After Mei changed, she brushed her teeth and got out her sleeping bag.

Brother saw her. "I was going to sleep in the bed of the truck under the stars," he said. "I brought a futon mattress and blankets. Where do you want to sleep? The trailer? Next to the fire with Boudicca?"

"Can I sleep in the truck with you?"

"Uhm, are you sure?"

She nodded.

Brother paused for a moment. "Okay, we can try, but with my sleep troubles, I might need to move you to the trailer during the night. It won't be your fault, okay?"

"Okay."

"Alright, give me a minute to set up."

Brother got a thin futon mattress from the trailer and rolled it out in the bed of the truck, then got a stack of quilts, pillows, and wool blankets. He rolled Mei's sleeping bag and pillow out on the futon. "Okay, climb in and get settled."

Mei scampered up into the bed of the truck and snuggled into her sleeping bag. She gazed through the clouds at the stars. She listened to Brother change into his trunks and a tank top. He packed all his gear and put it into the trailer. Mei felt the bed of the truck shift as he climbed into the truck.

"Are you still up?" he asked.

"Yes, I'm watching the stars."

"Oh yeah, that's great." He got under his blankets and settled in. "Good night, Mei Mei."

"Good night, Brother."

Boudicca started whining from the end of the truck.

"What the... ?" Brother said. "Boo! Shush!"

But the big pup continued to whine, then started barking.

Brother sat up. "Aargh! That Dog! Shush!"

"What's wrong?" Mei asked.

"Boudicca the bratty dog, thinks she needs to be up here," Brother said.

"Why can't she?"

"She snores! And kicks! And farts! She's a farty dog!"

Mei laughed. "She does not!"

"Yes, she does!"

"Well, maybe sometimes," Mei admitted.

Boudicca chuffed at their conversation.

"Shut up, dog!" Brother said.

But Boudicca wouldn't surrender. She put her paws on the tailgate and scratched the metal.

Brother cussed. "Okay, damn you. Up." He slapped the blankets.

Boudicca scrambled up into the bed of the truck, stepping over Brother and Mei with her big puppy paws, causing Brother to grunt and cuss, and Mei to giggle.

The big pup burrowed between them and thumped her tail.

"I'm going to kick her royal backside right off this planet," Brother said. "Hey! Get your nose out of my armpit before you become the first flappy face mastiff maniac in outer space!"

Mei giggled, then grunted as the dog squeezed up against her.

"Are you okay?" Brother asked.

"Yeah," Mei said. "She's a bed hog!"

"Yes, she is, but she'll keep you warm tonight."

They all fidgeted to get comfortable, and soon settled down. The stars shone brightly through the clouds. Night sounds surrounded them, but with Brother and Boudicca close, Mei found them pleasant, and loved looking up at the night sky. Despite the cramped space with the three of them, Mei felt comfy and happy.

However, as happy and excited as she was, her sleep was interrupted when the court fight seeped into her thoughts like inky black liquid nastiness. She had no idea why this was happening now. She sure loved Brother now, had always loved Boudicca, and didn't want to lose them. She tried some brain exercises Dr. Amy had taught her to make the black thoughts go away. Unfortunately, as soon as she stopped concentrating, the black thoughts returned. Why now? she thought. It's a good time. I don't want to think of bad things now.

Sleep wouldn't come, and it sounded as though Brother was struggling too.

"You okay Mei?"

"Yeah," she said, "just excited about tomorrow, mostly."

"Mostly?" Brother asked.

"Yeah, mostly. You told me not to worry about the custody fight, but I can't help it. I don't want to go. I know you can't tell me everything that's going on, but can't you tell me *how* it's going? Are we fighting back? Are we winning? Not knowing is the worst."

Brother reached over with his giant arm and gently squeezed her.

She scooted next to him until she felt his comforting mass.

"Well," he said, "it's hard to say with certainty, but the fight is definitely going on. My attorney thinks it's going well for us. The fiends are making mistakes which aren't helping their case."

"Like what?" Mei asked with new hope.

"I can't say just yet. But this fight isn't going the way they'd hoped. Will it be enough?" he said rhetorically. "Nothing is certain in these kinds of fights, but we'll keep on living our lives and fighting the best we can. I can't promise the courts will be fair, especially to people like us, but no matter what happens, I'll always be your Big Brother, and will always love you and be on your side. I know you'll be a spectacular success no matter where you're living or what you're doing. You got me?"

His words weren't what she wanted to hear, but she still found them comforting. Brother never lied to her.

"Yes," she said.

"Good," he said. "Now, if I sing, will it help you go to sleep?"

"Yes, please! I like your singing. You should do it more often."

He chuckled softly. "Okay."

He started humming, his deep voice rumbling next to her. Boudicca squirmed and snuggled next to them.

"'When the night has come'"
"'And the land is dark'"
"'And the moon is the only light we'll see'"
"'No, I won't be afraid'"
"'Oh, I won't be afraid'"
"'Just as long as you stand'"
"'Stand by me'"
"'So darlin', darlin''"
"'Stand by me, oh, stand by me'"
"'Oh, stand, stand by me'"
"'Stand by me.'"
Mei was fast asleep before he finished the song.

Chapter 82

Mei Mei

The next morning, Mei heard and then felt Brother and Boudicca get out of the truck, but drifted back to sleep for a while longer. Later, she woke to see the early morning sky. She stretched and sat up, then peered over the side of the truck. Brother had fed and given water to Boudicca and was building a fire.

He looked up. "Morning."

Mei waved.

"Did you sleep okay?"

Mei smiled and nodded sleepily.

Brother nodded. "Me too, I'm happy to say. Come down. We can warm up together."

Mei grabbed one of the tartan blankets and climbed out of the truck. Barefoot, she skipped to where Brother was beginning his stretching routine.

"Don't you have to go to the bathroom?"

Mei shook her head. After a minute, she put down the blanket and followed Brother's stretches, as he moved fluidly from one stretch to the next. After stretching, he started calisthenics, with Mei happily following along. She couldn't do as many as Brother, but was happy she could do more than when she started.

Brother finished the workout with one-hundred pushups without stopping. He got to his feet, covered in sweat.

"You should probably head over to the port-o-potty," he said. "By the time you come back, the water will be hot enough to wash. Then we can eat and get ready for today." He paused and smiled. "It's going to be a great day."

Mei wrapped up in the blanket again, slipped on her shoes and walked to the port-o-potty. It was a pleasant morning. People stirred in their campsites. When she finished, she washed up, then headed back to camp.

Brother had a fire going, and with his eyes closed, was carefully shaving with his straight razor over a bowl of hot water he'd poured from a kettle. He opened one eye and saw Mei peering around the side of the truck. He paused. "I'm almost done here, then I'll start breakfast. There's water here for you to take a sponge bath. You can stand by the trailer and put up the curtain for privacy."

Mei grabbed her clothing bag and a bowl of hot water, then went over to the trailer. She cleaned up and dressed in a sleeveless dark t-shirt and knee-length leather and wool skirt, Miss Joyce had made for her, and a pair of high moccasins. Mei did her hair (which was getting long now) and finished getting dressed. She came out from behind the privacy curtain as Brother was putting food onto plates. She took a plate then squatted down next to the fire and ate.

Brother put a glass of water next to her. "Drink lots of water today, Mei Mei. It's important to stay hydrated."

"How much water should I drink?"

"Good question! That glass, plus two more bottles today should be enough. If that skirt gets too hot, don't be afraid to change into shorts."

Mei nodded.

They finished breakfast in silence, then Brother cleaned the dishes and Mei made the beds in the truck. Brother put on his kilt and slipped off his trunks.

Mei giggled at his squirming.

Brother smiled back. "Yeah, yeah, I know," he said, but took care to look good. He assembled his gear, including a dirk and a sgian dubh. He wore a black tank top that showed off his muscles, scars, and tattoos. He waved Mei over, opened a gear bag, and took out her knife on her birthday belt. He buckled it on her, then drew out a long dark green silk scarf. He wrapped it around her waist like a sash over the belted knife, but the knife's grip stuck above the sash so Mei could reach it with either hand.

Then Brother took out a smaller dark silk bandanna and tied it around her head. Reaching into his gear bag, he pulled out a leather wrist bracelet with a silver coin sewn into it. Mei held out her left hand and Brother tied it on. The bracelet was wide on Mei's wrist. He pulled out another bracelet, similar to the first one, but with an iron coin sewn into it. He tied it to her other wrist. Mei wrapped her scarf with the silver coins and bells around her waist.

Brother looked her over and nodded, then rubbed sunscreen on her face, neck, and arms. Finally, he took out a compact and gently painted black and blue and red swirls and stripes on her face, neck, arms, and legs.

The ceremony seemed a bit odd but comforting. They didn't speak, but when it was done, Mei felt strong, powerful, and fierce all at once!

Brother read her expression and smiled with understanding at her feelings. "Do I need to explain the conduct I expect out of you whilst you're armed?" he asked.

"No, Brother," Mei said.

"Good."

They were standing in the lee of the truck, strapping on the last of Mei's gear, when a loud booming groaning horn sounded. She knew it wasn't a car horn, but used to call people to action. Its loud drone sounded again, long and loud. Mei opened her mouth to speak, but Brother held up a hand. A third drone sounded, longer and louder.

"It has begun," Brother said. He acted uncharacteristically excited, and his skin seemed to buzz with energy.

People on the campsite grounds clapped and cheered, then a roaring war cry challenge echoed across the field, followed by one from the campground, and a third from by stage.

Grinning, Brother stood up straight, planted his feet, threw his head back and cut loose his own roaring challenge, startling Mei. She swore she felt the ground shake! A group of women at another campsite, not to be outdone by noisy guys, yelled high pitched screams.

Someone else started the drones and fired up a set of bagpipes, the skirl adding to the cacophony and sending chills down Mei's back.

Boudicca came over and leaned on Mei like she did when she was uncertain. Mei patted her head, and the big pup wagged her bullwhip tail.

Brother walked over to Mei. "Are you ready?"

Mei nodded and picked up Boudicca's leash, then they walked around the shelter of the truck and camper, onto the field in plain sight of everyone at the Ceilidh.

Chapter 83

Mei Mei

The morning sun illuminated the field sun as the trio sauntered along. People were coming and going like they would at a fair. Mei stopped and looked long and carefully around the entire field, then took a mind picture. When she finished, she took Brother's hand, and without a word, pulled him forward.

Brother nodded his understanding and led Mei and Boudicca in a slow stroll around the grounds, keeping them at a distance from the activity.

Mei felt sure Brother's slow pace was giving her time to observe as much as she could, and for the people to see him. They walked past the main stage where girls in pretty dresses were dancing a complicated but graceful leaping style to a bagpiper. Brother smiled and waved at the piper when the dancer's set was finished. The piper waved back with a big grin.

"That's Scott," Brother said. "He teaches bagpipes, and he's good. He attended a bagpipe school in Scotland."

Mei frowned. "There's a school for bagpipes?" She couldn't imagine such a place.

"Sure is. I know it's hard to believe, but there are schools for just about everything."

Mei pondered on that.

They passed a row of tables where people were setting up coolers, drinks, and food near a big, unlit bonfire with a giant pile of wood surrounded by a ring of stones. Kids with painted faces ran around, yelling and laughing, waving various forms of wooden weaponry or chasing soccer balls and Frisbees.

Brother gestured to the kids. "You can go play with them if you want."

"Not yet. We have to meet Pop. I'm going for it."

329

He nodded, and they moved on. They walked to the horse pasture next to the Ceilidh field. The horses had been moved and various athletic events were in progress. A growing crowd of people watched a group of big, strong, kilted men and a few women competing to see who could throw heavy things the furthest.

"Did you ever do that?" Mei asked.

"When I was a kid, I did a little bit," Brother said, "but I wasn't as good as those guys. I'll bet Arik is over there."

Across the pasture, Mei saw Pop dressed in a kilt, standing with a group of men, throwing knives at wooden targets. Mei tugged Brother's hand and nodded her head.

Brother lightly squeezed her hand, and they headed toward Pop. As they passed the athletes, Mei noticed a few waved and shouted happy greetings (and insults) at Brother as they went by.

Brother waved back.

When Pop saw Brother and Mei approaching, he grinned. "The prodigal son has returned!" He gave Brother a bear hug. "And he did us the honor of making our clan bigger, better, braver, smarter, fiercer, and most certainly, prettier than ever!"

Mei flushed and smiled at Pop.

Pop squatted and scooped up Mei, and they hugged each other. He was a tough man but very huggable.

Pop whispered in Mei's ear, "want to help me whip these guys at throwing blades?" He pulled his head back so Mei could see him wink.

"Yes," she said, then Pop put her down and turned to the big pup. "Oh yes, here's the star of the show." He petted Boudicca's big head and the pup leaned against him, whipping her tail happily.

Brother shook hands and clapped the group of men on the shoulders. They talked with him and petted Boudicca. Then Pop ushered everyone back to the target line. "C'mon lads, let's choose teams and get to it."

A cheerful-looking guy with a big gray beard said, "I suppose you're going to hide behind your commando son at this little contest?"

"I'll sit this one out, Don," Brother said. "It's too early in the morning to make a grown man cry."

The men crowed and laughed. Don chuckled good naturedly and shook his head in mock sadness. "I wish you'd be kind enough to tell my wife that."

"What?" Brother said in mock horror. "No sir! I didn't fight overseas to return home and die at the hands of an irate wife. Especially one that's not mine."

Don nodded. "You got yourself some smarts while you were away."

"We all thought you'd be done in by an irate husband," another man said with a laugh.

"You'd think they'd appreciate me helping them with the heavy lifting," Brother retorted, "but nope, no sir, no thanks at all!"

The group laughed.

Pop put his hand on Mei's shoulder. "I'll stand with my girl here."

Mei felt an unexpected pride in Pop's words and comfort from his hand on her shoulder. She straightened and held her head high.

"Why do I think this girl is a ringer?" the man next to Don said.

"Would I do that to you?" Pop asked.

"If it was for a bet, I wouldn't put it past you to send away to Japan for a wee ninja, just to get my goat."

They all picked up a throwing knife from a bucket and lined up in front of the target, except Mei, who, at a nod from Brother, drew her own knife. She felt tiny standing next to all the men and felt anxious.

As if reading her mind, Brother stepped up behind her and leaned over. "There's nothing to be worried about," he whispered. "In this type of contest, little can beat big. You've practiced all summer and have the skills."

Mei thought about it and knew he was right. Her confidence surged, and she knew she could hit the target.

"Take a breath," Brother said.

Mei inhaled and blew air out of her mouth. She felt calmer.

"Now put your mask on."

She reached up with her left hand and as she swiped on her mask, her doubt and anxiety disappeared. She could do it!

The men on the other teams threw their knives, and most stuck in the target. One didn't hit well and bounced away into the grass.

Mei's turn came, she put her hand on the exact spot on the handle to get the knife to turn in the air and hit point first, took aim, drew back, and smoothly let the knife fly. It stuck in the wood target with a plunk! Just like she had practiced!

"That a girl!" Pop cheered, then stuck his knife in the target with little effort. Mei looked around for Brother. He'd stepped back, but was watching her. He nodded, and even though he seemed calm, his eyes were bright and shining.

Mei smiled and nodded back, then turned and watched the competition. After everyone had thrown, they picked up their knives.

The participants moved further away for the next round and threw in turn. This time, one man threw too hard, and his knife skipped off the target, spun up into the air, and fell to the ground.

Mei stepped up and moved her hand on the handle to make up for the added distance. 'Plunk.' The knife stuck! She felt better at beating at least one adult!

The men applauded, teasing Pop he'd brought in a ringer and a ninja child.

Pop sailed his knife out and stuck it into the target. Plunk! The sound of hitting the target indicated Pop had put more effort into his throw.

The participants moved even further away the next round. Two men missed and were out of the competition.

Mei stepped to the line for her turn and realized this was the furthest she'd ever thrown. She made sure her form was right, her hand was right on the handle, then threw. The knife seemed to move in slow motion, a long and lazy flip that sailed on until it stuck in the target! Yes! She'd beaten two more adults!

Again, Pop hit his target.

The last five participants moved further away for the final round. Mei and Pop were the only full team still left in the game. As they walked to the line, Pop patted her on the back. "You've got this, Mei."

Mei wasn't sure. She turned and stepped toward Brother.

Brother held up his hand. "Stop," he said calmly, but with emphasis.

She stopped, and he came up and gently turned her until she faced the target. He squatted down next to her and focused on the target. She heard his back and knee creak and knew squatting was hurting him, although his face didn't show the pain. Instead, he radiated calm and confidence.

"Pop is right. You got this."

"It's so far."

"No, it's not, Mei Mei," he said in his calm, confident voice. "It's just a bit smaller."

Mei started to turn toward him, but Brother gently guided her back to face the target. "Look again. It's not farther, just smaller. If you were at the first line you threw from, you'd be able to hit a small target like that easily, wouldn't you?"

"Sure."

"So, hit the small target. Make sure your form is flawless and add just a whisper more of smooth force to get then knife to turn right while it's in flight. No problem." Brother got up and returned to his spot to watch Mei.

By now, all three other men had thrown. Two more were out, another one had hit the target on the outside.

Mei's turn came. Her mind raced from her Brother's words. At first, what he said was ridiculous. 'Just smaller.' The big dummy. Other, unkind thoughts raced through her mind for a moment, and she realized her mask must have slipped off. She put it back on, sucked in a long breath, then eyed the target.

It was just smaller. Watch your form. Place your hand in the right place one the grip of the knife to get it to turn right for the distance. All of her Brother's words from all of the practice sessions now made sense. Mei straightened up. She thought of throwing with perfect form. She set her feet. She squeezed the handle and drew back her hand, and positive thoughts flowed. Nobody was watching. No noise. No doubt. No mistakes. She whipped the knifed with the perfect amount of force.

If she thought the earlier throw moved in slow motion, this throw felt even slower. The knife left her hand in a higher arc, flipping once, then twice. It seemed to keep going and going, then begin to drop. She thought it was dropping too fast to make it to the target, but it hung in the air for a long breathtaking third flip, hit the target with a light plunk, and stuck in place!

The crowd roared! Where had they all come from? And when? She refocused and looked at the target. Her knife landed closer to the middle of the target than the other man!

Pop dropped his knife, picked her up and threw her in the air. Then he hugged her tight and danced in a circle. "I knew you could do it!"

Mei saw Brother standing with his arms crossed, slowly nodding. His eyes beamed with pride.

"Pop! Pop! Please put me down! You still have to throw!"

"Naw," Pop said. "You can win. It's okay by me!"

Mei drew up and froze. "Pop!" she said sternly, then reached down and picked up his knife and handed it to him, butt first. "We're a team. I did my part, now you have to do yours. And don't you dare miss. TANSTAAFL."

Pop stopped and looked at Mei then smiled and took the knife. He turned, and with authority, whipped the knife at the target. It struck the target in the middle.

Winner!

He turned to Mei, straightened, locked his heels and snapped her a perfect parade ground salute. Then he extended his hand. She shook it and they bowed their heads. He bent down and hugged her.

"There's my girl! I knew I was right to pick you to be on my team!"

Mei nodded. She didn't trust herself to speak. She turned and stood next to Pop, then they both walked over and shook hands with the other competitors, who continued teasing Pop about his 'ringer' and 'gypsy ninja.'

The crowd was clapping and wanted to congratulate Mei. She felt overwhelmed from so many wanting to say hello. Her anxiety boiled until Judyta blasted through the crowd. "You rock!" Judyta shouted and bear hugged Mei. "That was the coolest thing ever!" Even though Judyta was taller than Mei, she wasn't a big girl. Still, in her happy enthusiasm and wiry strength, she crushed Mei.

Mei felt overwhelmed and 'tapped out' on Judyta's shoulder with a rapid and firm slap. She knew when Judyta was wound up, you needed to get her attention.

Judyta let Mei go and held her at arm's length. "Mei Mei, that was awesome! You were sooooo cooool, like a Jedi knight, or a fighter pilot, or... I don't know, but that was AWESOME!"

Mei giggled at her friend's loud praise.

"Me and dad and my brother were watching from over there," Judyta said, waving a hand in the general direction of the main Ceilidh field. "We just got here. I was hoping to find you. We're going to run this place today!" Her rapid fire statements were blasting at Mei. She looked Mei up and down as though she had just noticed how Mei was dressed. "I love, love it," Judyta said in a calmer tone. She waved one hand up and down as though Mei were a new car on a game show. "Got anymore of that cool war paint?"

"I can ask Brother," Mei said, then realized she'd never thanked him. He'd slipped her mind in all her excitement. She held onto Judyta's hand. "I have to find Brother," she said, then looked around.

"This way, Mei!" Judyta said, and launched herself through the crowd, dragging Mei behind her. They waded through a crowd of spectators until they found Brother, Mr. White, and George.

"There she is," Mr. White said. "Excellent showing, Miss Mei."

George held his hand out and Mei fist bumped him. "Good job, Mei"

"Thank you, George," she said, then at last turned to look at Brother.

He stood erect with his hands on his hips, face blank, looking down at her.

Mei matched his stance by standing up straight and facing him head on. "It all worked, just like you said. It took me a minute to figure out the target and size idea, but my mask was perfect."

Brother nodded slowly, acknowledging Mei's confirmation of his teaching. Then his scarred face split into a grin and he leaned down until his face was level with hers. He raised his fists in front of him. "Yeaaaahhh!" he roared into Mei's face.

"Yeeeeaaahhh!" Mei roared back.

Gently, but with blinding speed, Brother snatched her up, and to her delight, lifted her over his head. Together they roared "Yeeeeeeeahhh!" and the entire White family roared with them.

Brother tossed Mei up, then caught her as she came down and squeezed her tight. "You were perfect, Mei Mei!" he said, then lifted her again and swung her around in a circle. "Perfect!" He stopped and set her down, but still held her hand. "You were so cool, and your form was just right. I was dying over here but wanted you to know you could do it."

"But I missed the center of the target."

"I don't give a fiddler's fuck about that!" Brother blurted out in exasperation, then calmly looked her in the eyes. "You learned to think clearly, manage your fear, and perform with skill under pressure. Everyone was watching. You're little, your competition was big, the target was far, and throwing knives requires skill. And you still did it! Now you know you can do difficult things when your competition is tough, and you feel afraid. It's important for you to know deep down in your heart and your bones you can. It will take more practice, more challenges, and making mistakes to get better, but you can do it, Mei Mei!" He hugged her again. "Alright," he said, then stood and wiped his eyes. "Go have some fun."

"Okay, Brother," Mei said "Can I paint Judyta?"

"If it's okay with her dad, sure. In fact, you should show Judyta where we're camped. The Whites are going to be our guests."

"Really?" Mei said, then jumped up and down clapping her hands. Judyta shrieked with joy and began jumping up and down with Mei.

"Okay, okay. Begone, young she-devils," Brother said. Then, in his narrator's voice, said, "the day goes on and I have my own affairs to see to."

As the girls turned to race off, Brother yelled, "drink water and eat something."

The girls raced across the field to the campsite, dodging people on the way. Back at camp, Mei found the face paint and soon had Judyta's face painted in crude, outrageous woad swirls and stripes. Heeding Brother's words, Mei drank water while Judyta redid her hair in wild ponytails and loose braids.

Judyta looked in the truck's mirror and smiled. "Yeah! Totally fierce! I wish I could have a knife too!"

Mei offered her water bottle to Judyta. "Maybe next time."

After the painted she-barbarians hydrated, they headed back out to the main field.

Chapter 84

Mei Mei

The fierce girls trotted along, talking happily until they heard more music. Not the creepy fun sounds of the bagpipers playing in groups or individual pipers playing for dancers, but coming from a stereo. They followed the music until they came to the source. Mei stopped and stared at what would become another turning point in her life.

People of all ages were dancing together as couples on the dance floor Pop and Michael had laid down. They swung around to the music, changed partners, and stepped together.

Mei was entranced. It wasn't the most exciting dancing she'd ever seen, but it looked like so much fun! The dancers seemed to be enjoying themselves a great deal, and Mei wanted to join them. When the music stopped, she took Judyta's hand and stepped to the dance floor.

A pleasant lady in a beautiful tartan dress welcomed Mei and Judyta to 'Scottish Country Dancing,' and paired them up with partners that knew the steps. They all walked through the steps a few times and then turned the music back on.

From the moment she stepped onto the dance floor, Mei was hooked. It felt a lot like stepping through a giant mask, but instead of feeling safe, she felt at home, in control, free to let loose and move! Like climbing, but better. She loved following the dance steps and getting lost in the music. By the smiling faces, everyone felt the same.

They danced several sets, and when they finished, Mei and her partner bowed to each other.

A smiling Judyta came over and grabbed Mei's hand. "This is so much fun!" she said, and Mei nodded enthusiastically. "Let's go eat and plot our next take over!"

Hand in hand, they raced off to the food tables. They waved as they passed Brother talking to Miss Janice, Sarah, and other people. A group milled around the tables, getting food and talking. An elderly, white-haired lady wearing an apron over a beautiful tartan dress saw the girls and encouraged them to eat. "Oh my," she said, "you girls need to eat and build your strength for whatever wars you're planning for today." She served them cheeseburgers and potato salad on paper plates. Mei tucked a bottle of water into her sash. She noticed people looking at her. The looks weren't mean, just the opposite. People glanced when they thought she wasn't looking, then looked away when she looked back at them. If Brother hadn't taught Mei how to spot it, she wouldn't have noticed. She noticed most of the people were looking at her rather than Judyta, although Judyta was dressed as outrageous as Mei.

Judyta was no dummy and noticed. Brassy as ever, she looked at the white-haired lady and said politely, but directly, "thank you for the food, ma'am, but can you tell us why they're staring at Mei?"

The white-haired lady smiled. "Sorry, girls, we didn't mean to alarm you." She turned and looked at Mei. "You are her. *The sister*."

Mei froze in place for a second.

"Your brother means a lot to us, and we heard about your coming into the clan and are... well, curious," the white-haired lady said. "Then, after your knife throwing competition, you've become a mysterious celebrity."

"Whooo hoo!" Judyta crowed, and socked Mei on the shoulder. "A celebrity! My girl!"

Mei felt flustered. "A mysterious celebrity?"

"Come on," Judyta said, "let's go eat before the paparazzi get here."

The white-haired lady chuckled and handed them small plastic containers. "Here girls, take some cake too."

The girls loaded their plates, then looked for a place to eat.

Do you mind if we go to the orchard for some privacy?" Mei asked.

"Nope," Judyta said, "That's a good idea, and totally worth the trip."

They took their food and headed toward the orchard. They passed Brother again, and this time he was talking to Michael, Don, and other people in a happy-looking group. Brother waved as Mei and Judyta passed. Pop had made the orchard off limits to everyone else, so the girls had it all to themselves. They walked the rows of trees until they found a comfy-looking spot in the sunlight next to a tree and sat down to eat.

The burgers and potato salads were tasty. Even though Judyta was often rowdy, they ate in silence. Mei shared her water with Judyta, who she knew wouldn't backwash. Despite all the energy they'd expended, they filled up quickly. When they set their plates aside, Mei asked, "are you going to eat your cake?"

"I'm pretty full right now, so I think I'll wait," Judyta said.

They stacked their plates next to the unopened cake containers, then stretched out on the grass under the shade of the tree. Even though lying on the grass wasn't as comfortable as the story books said, Mei thought it was still nice. She looked up through the branches and into the sky beyond. She thought about the knife throwing competition and the lessons she'd learned. A few minutes later, she heard Judyta breathing heavy. She'd dozed off and that was okay.

Mei felt satisfied just lying there and thinking. She replayed the entire event in her mind and put the lessons in order where and when they happened. She thought hard on how things looked in her memory, how they felt, and any smells she remembered.

After a bit, she grew tired of thinking about the competition, so thought about dancing. She loved it and wanted to do more. In fact, she knew dancing was definitely in her future. And more climbing. Speaking of which... she snapped out of her nap. Whew! Careful not to wake a sleeping Judyta, she got to her feet and walked over to the trunk of the apple tree. She walked around it, studied the trunk, the bark, and potential hand holds, looking for a path to climb.

She grinned, reached over, and started up the tree. God, she loved climbing! Experiencing so many of her joys in one day was beyond words. She climbed up, then perched on a branch. The branches in her tree and the next blocked her view, but she looked up to the sky through a small opening in the branches and leaves. When she looked down, if she craned her neck, she could see Judyta.

She climbed higher and got comfortable. Although her view didn't improve, she liked her spot. She rested her head against a branch and listened to the sounds of the orchard, and heard music and cheering from the Ceilidh field.

Mei was happy... very happy. She didn't know what the future offered, but for the first time she could remember, she looked forward to it. So many good things had happened since Brother came for her, and she didn't mind when unexpected tears of happiness formed in her eyes. She smiled as she processed the last few months. Brother, feeling safe, feeling important, feeling at home, learning new things, Boudicca, Auntie, Pop, Judyta, it felt very good. She hoped the courts wouldn't make her live with the fiends.

She sniffed as happy tears flowed and her nose ran. She leaned over, and a tear fell to the ground. It winked as it flitted in and out of the sunlight until it came to rest at the feet of Judyta, standing at the base of the tree.

"Mei?" Judyta asked. "What's wrong?"

Mei wiped her eyes. "Nothing, Judyta."

"I'm coming up to get you," Judyta said, then started to climb.

"No, don't," Mei said. I'm coming down." She scampered back down the tree, dismounting by hanging from the lowest branch and then dropping to a crouch at Judyta's feet. She stood, and saw the concern on the taller girl's face.

"Why are you crying, Mei?"

Mei pounced on Judyta and grabbed her in a happy bear hug, almost bowling them over. "Because I'm HAPPY!" Mei shouted as she squeezed her best friend. "So happy! And you are my best friend!"

The happy tears flew from Mei's eyes and she felt Judyta's tears soak her shoulder as Judyta cried with her. "Me too!" Judyta cried. "And you are too!"

The two girl-savages laughed, hugged, cried, and danced in place while holding hands. After a time, they sat down and opened the last containers and shared cake just like they shared secrets.

Mei told Judyta about the court case and the fiends.

"That sucks," Judyta said. "When my mom and dad split, it wasn't like that. Mom moved out and said George and me were going to stay with dad. No fighting. And I see her all the time."

Mei nodded. "That would be better for sure. But these jerks didn't even try to do something like that with Brother. It was all, 'Wham!' Suddenly, I'm supposed to go there. They didn't even try to see me or call when I was in the bad place and now expect me to believe they care? It's obvious they just want my inheritance."

"Yeah," Judyta said. "Greedy scum."

"I even asked Brother to give it to them if they'd leave me alone, but he said he wouldn't give them anything but broken hearts. Besides, he said it wouldn't be enough to suit them, because they wanted the money from the state, and would get it only if I lived with them."

"Those fuckers!" Judyta exclaimed, then settled down. "Well, they picked a fight with the wrong guy."

"What do you mean?"

"My dad says your Brother is one of the toughest and smartest people he's ever seen, so those fiends are in for a fight like they never imagined."

Mei was proud to hear someone as smart as Mr. White admired Brother. She nodded. "Thanks. Let's hope the court thinks I'm good by staying with Brother."

"They will," Judyta said, then patted Mei's arm. "But we can't do anything about it today, so let's have some fun!"

Mei smiled "Yes!"

Chapter 85

Mei Mei

They picked up their trash and headed back to the Ceilidh field to repaint their faces. As they approached, they saw Mr. White and Brother. Mr. White had spread sleeping bags around the fire pit and was arranging gear while chatting with Brother, who was lying on his back, smoking a cigar. Brother was shirtless, leaving his muscles, scars, and tattoos exposed. Fortunately, he had also exchanged his kilt for a pair of shorts. Boudicca was lying next to him. When the puppy saw the girls approach, her tail thumped on the ground.

"There they are," Mr. White said cheerfully. "Have you raided all the cattle and pillaged the shepherd boys?"

"Of course, father," Judyta said. "There's not a single case of purity left in the village. It's time to move on to greener pastures."

"Oh, dear," Mr. White mock groaned.

Brother snorted with laughter and coughed around his cigar. He took the cigar out of his mouth and looked up at Mei. Without a word, and without caring that Brother was shirtless, she pounced on him and hugged him.

"Hey! What? Whoa!" a startled Brother stammered, trying to keep his cigar from falling out of his mouth. Self-consciously, he gingerly wrapped an arm around Mei and tentatively patted her back. "What's wrong, Mei Mei?"

Mei sniffed. "Nothing. I'm just really happy."

Brother relaxed. "Really? Uhm, that's good." He paused and got his cigar under control. "I'm glad."

"Me too."

"I don't want to crush your happy," he said good-naturedly, "but you're be-snotting me a lot, and dropping boogers on my skin."

They broke out in laughter together, closely followed by Mr. White and Judyta, who'd been trying unsuccessfully not to intrude on the moment.

Mei clambered up the length of Brother's body until she reached his face, then turned his head to the side and kissed his cheek. "Judyta and I are plotting stuff together. After we repaint our faces, we have things to do, if you're okay with us running off."

"Are you drinking water?"

Mei nodded.

"Are you minding your manners?"

She nodded.

"Are you having fun?"

She answered yes with a wide grin.

"Alrighty then," Brother said. "Be back here around dusk if you don't see me out and about."

"Okay, I will."

"Okay, go get 'em", he said, then puffed on his cigar.

Mei hopped up and went over to the pack with the makeup.

Judyta received similar instructions from her father and joined Mei, stopping to pet Boudicca.

After a quick wipe with a handy towel, the young woad raiders repainted each other's faces. When they finished, they looked at each other, then at their father figures, and then dashed off, hand in hand.

"Where to, Mei Mei?" Judyta asked.

"Let's follow the sound of the music."

They soon found themselves back where they'd done the Scottish Highlands Dancing. Instead of the sedate cheerful tunes of rural Scotland, they heard a fast techno version of classic Irish music. Several young ladies were doing a faster and livelier version of the Irish step dancing.

They watched until the end of the song. The ladies noticed the woad raiders watching and waved them onto the dance floor. "C'mon!"

Without hesitation, they trotted over. Once again, when Mei stepped onto the dance floor, she felt free and energized. When the music started, the lady next to Mei said, "follow me," and stepped along.

Awkward and slow at first, Mei enjoyed trying to follow the steps. She noticed Judyta high-stepping and laughing with the other ladies in the group.

Judyta saw Mei looking over and laughed for her, and stomped harder.

Mei laughed and stomped harder right back.

They kept dancing thru the next song, lost in the sound and the motion. After the song ended, Mei and Judyta faced each other, panting and grinning. The group of ladies clapped. Someone turned the music down and they all grabbed drinks and chatted. The young ladies shared names and complimented Mei and Judyta, who felt fortunate to be included.

A tall lady looked past Mei and Judyta, then hunched down and spoke to the group. "Oh, here he comes!" she said, her face flushed.

"Who?" Judyta asked.

The group looked around and tried to see who 'he' was.

Mei didn't know who the lady was referring to, but listened to the conversation.

"Big and scary looking. Oh, my cousin said, killed... people. Look, and that kilt... He's coming this way...."

Mei maneuvered through the group until she saw the reason for the fuss.

Heading toward the dance floor, cigar clenched in his teeth, was Brother, dressed in his kilt, with Boudicca in tow.

Mei wondered, were the ladies fussing about Brother? The thought felt weird.

Brother stopped at the edge of the dance floor as Mei and Judyta broke through the crowd and ran to him. Mei screamed, 'Brother' with joy, and leaped at him. Judyta pounced on a wiggling Boudicca and hugged her fiercely.

Brother grabbed Mei in midair and tossed her up in the air with ease, laughing the entire time. He caught her in his big arms and brought her close.

Mei kissed his face, then reached up and took his cigar from his mouth, then pressed her forehead to his so she could look into his eyes.

"I was dancing," she said.

"I saw that. You were doing well."

"Thanks," she said, then half turned and pointed to the ladies. "They were nice enough to let me and Judyta join them and show us how."

"Oh?" He looked at the ladies, many of whom were now blushing. "Ladies," he said in his deep voice and bowed. "Thank you for including my baby sister. She's new to us, and I appreciate you treating her so well."

The young ladies broke out in a jumbled chorus of, "you are welcome, she's really good," and "I like your dog."

Still holding Mei, Brother did another half bow again. "Thanks again, ladies. We'll see you later." He took his cigar back from Mei and turned to leave.

"Hey, wait for me," Judyta said, then sprang at Brother and climbed up his body as if he was a giant oak tree. Brother stood patiently while she climbed and sat precariously balanced on his shoulder.

"Are you quite comfy, Miss Judyta?" Brother asked, cocking his head, and smiling.

"I'm good," Judyta said, then with mock graciousness, "carry on, good sir."

Brother's walk had turned into a lumber with the weight and awkward balance of the two raider girls, but he never broke stride.

People looked and cheered as they passed. The she-raiders waved back, and Judyta blew kisses as if she was the main attraction on a parade float. "Well, Mei and I decided we're sisters."

"Oh, yeah?" Brother asked.

"Yes, sir, sisters of choice," Judyta said, and Mei nodded. "And that means you're my brother, too."

"Is that so?"

"Yes. We agreed even though I think I'm getting the better deal, because while I get you, poor Mei only gets George."

Mei shrugged.

"Are you good with this?" Brother asked Mei.

"Yes," Mei said firmly. "Who knows? George might be good for something later on."

"I hope you got a good deal for trading me off."

"I didn't trade you away, silly. I simply gave Judyta permission to have you as a brother, and since she's often in trouble, she might need an extra one, especially one who was a Marine."

"Yes," Judyta said. "I have a brother, but he gets on my nerves all the time and I don't think he's as tough as you. And since you're Mei's brother, if anyone tries to fight you, they have to fight me too!"

"Well, now, isn't that something?" Brother said. "I guess that means we're all added to, not taken from."

Judyta squinched her face. "I think I agree, but need to be sure."

"Good girl," Brother said, and trudged along with his precious cargo. They finally came to a campsite where a group of familiar people were loading a long dinner table with tons of appetizing food.

Mr. White looked over and saw Judyta perched on Brother's shoulder. "Judyta!" he yelled. "Get down! Now!" Mr. White looked at Brother "I'm sorry. Please don't let that she-devil turn you into her pack animal."

Brother set Mei down, then lifted part two of the she-raider duo onto the ground. He stood up and slowly stretched his upper body one way, then another. "I'm afraid it's worse than that, Steve."

"Oh, dear," Mr. White said. "Did she talk you into selling your soul? Rustling cattle? Storming a castle? Driving a get-away car? Leading her mercenary army to free Ank Morpork? No? Let me pour a drink before I hear the answer." He scooped up a pint from a nearby table and took a deep drink, then took a deeper breath.

"Okay, what did Mademoiselle La Maupin do this time?"

Brother pointed at Mei. "Apparently thing one," he pointed at Judyta, "and thing two, decided they're sisters. I acknowledge this is like adding gasoline to dynamite, yet an idea I'm strangely comfortable with. However, I hasten to add, somehow, in the negotiation process, I've been annexed."

Judyta jumped in between both men and said in her best wheeler dealer sales pitch, "Brother! We're thinking that with me as another sister, you would neither be added to nor taken from!"

"Oh, really?" Brother said "So, this is all for my benefit?"

"Oh yes," Judyta said. "We think we can all use some help, and we're stronger and smarter together, but we're not sure we want just anyone. I hope that doesn't sound too mean."

Brother nodded. "It's okay, kiddo. I think I get what you mean, and think it's an idea to consider. Just not now, so you two eat dinner and have fun. There's more music and stuff tonight."

"Are you going to sing again?" Mei asked.

"Well, I..."

"Yes, he is!" a nearby lady yelled.

"Hey!" Brother protested.

But the smiling lady and others were not showing mercy.

Sarah appeared and joined in and yelled at Brother. "We want songs, we want them to be fun, and we want you to sing them!"

A chorus of 'Yeses' rained down on Brother.

"Okay, well maybe. It would be wrong of me to deny my fans, wouldn't it, Steve?"

Mr. White smiled and raised his drink in a salute. "My good sir, it would be positively bad manners."

"Well, that just won't do now, will it?" Brother asked in a stage voice.

"No sir, no indeed," Mr. White replied.

"Okay, then. I'll try to make Warren Zevon proud!"

Mei and Judyta clapped and jumped up and down. "We want you to sing a song for us!"

"Girls, I'm not sure I know how to sing anything you would like." Brother said, exasperated.

"You're our brother!" Mei shouted. "You can do it!!"

"Yes!" Judyta chimed in.

"Okay, okay," Brother surrendered. "I'll think of something but let's get you two fed. You're in for a treat. There are lots of good things to try."

Brother tied Boudicca's leash to a table, then they all went over to the big table and started picking out what they liked. Brother was right, they had lots to choose from. Getting food took longer than if they were at a restaurant, because lots of people wanted to say hello and introduce themselves. A few people congratulated Mei on her knife throwing win. It was a lot to take in, but everyone seemed sincere, so Mei didn't mind.

They sat and ate. Mei had followed Brother's choices in food selection and tried a chicken kabob on a skewer, a scoop of beans and rice dish, and a Filipino egg roll called lumpia. The kabob was barbeque and spicy goodness, the beans and rice were good, but the lumpia was the best of all.

"Did you like that?" Brother asked when he saw Mei enjoying the lumpia.

"Oh, yes."

"I love those things," Brother said. "I swear I could eat a dozen at a time, but I sure won't stay fit if I do. This Ceilidh is a great place to try different foods. The people in our clan like cooking and trying new things, and I love it. It's what you get when you have veterans, scholars, and world traveler types."

"Here's another life lesson you won't find in any college diversity book," Mr. White said. "Putting it bluntly, if one tribe of people meets a new tribe of people and the food is good and the people are attractive, there will be lines crossed."

An older man sitting nearby chuckled at Mr. White's statement, and in a Scottish brogue said, "aye, laddie. We Scots aren't stingy with our DNA!" Brother and Mr. White nodded in agreement and joined in the man's cheerful laughter.

Judyta scarfed a piece of pizza cooked in an outdoor oven and another lumpia. George had joined them and ate a ton of food loaded on his plate. Mr. White ate shakshuka, Naan bread, and big sausages and mashed potatoes called bangers and mash.

By the time they finished, it was dusk. They cleaned up, thanked the cooks, then headed over to Arik and Sarah's campsite. Along the way, Mei heard musical instruments, along with singing and laughing all around the Ceilidh field.

When they got to Arik's campsite, Michael, his girl, Pop, Miss Janice and a dozen others were setting up long benches and chairs all around the fire pit, except where three attractive young girls in their twenties were setting up with their own musical instruments.

When Brother saw the musicians, he stopped and smiled. "Oh, hey!" he said with surprise, and his face lit up with joy. He handed Boudicca's leash to Mei, then stepped over to the musicians.

When they saw him, their faces lit up. They stood up and rushed over and pounced on him with hugs and kisses.

Brother returned the hugs, then stepped back and laughed. He then scooped all three of them up in a giant awkward hug that turned into an enthusiastic staggering dance. The girls all laughed and squeeze him, trying not to fall over with all the clumsy kinetic enthusiasm. The watching crowd cheered, clapped, and made way for the mass hugging.

Two of the girls were clearly sisters; pretty, brunette, and blue eyed. The third girl wasn't related. She was taller, blue eyed, casually beautiful, with long curly honey brown hair.

They all parted, and Mei saw three sets of misty eyes, so she took a mind picture. Mei knew this was an important moment. She took in all the details she could and recited her remembering mantra. By the way the girls crowded Brother, they obviously knew him.

"I can't thank you enough for the music you sent to me when I was deployed," Brother said. "It really helped me and the guys get through difficult times."

"Aww, really? Oh!" the girls said, then continued to fuss over him.

"Oh, yeah, it did. My guys couldn't believe someone like me could have a trio of Irish, angelic voices on my side. In fact, once they found out I knew you, there were indecent Marine Corps type proposals offered to you. But I didn't think it was prudent to pass those kinds of comments along."

The girls blushed and giggled. "Oh, stop! You're teasing!"

"No, I'm not," Brother assured them. "Your music was so magical, a bunch of dirty bastard Marine gun fighters turned off their death metal and gangsta rap to listen. When we lost some guys and things got tough for us, we played your music and…" Brother's voice got hoarse, and he cleared his throat. "Well… you made things better for good guys you'll probably never meet. So, thank you."

Mei felt stunned. For the first time, Brother mentioned people who had died in the war. She held really still, because she knew she was witnessing something important.

Brother chuckled. "As a matter of fact, the guys made me promise I would spoil all of you and say thanks." He took a deep breath and let it out. "So, you'd better think about what you want for a spoil, because I gave my word."

All three girls choked up at his words.

"Oh hell," he said in uncomfortable exasperation, "I'm sorry to make you sad, but felt so surprised and happy to see you, I didn't think through what I should be saying."

"Oh, you big dummy," they said, and pounced on him again. When they separated, he pointed to Mei. "Hey, you have to meet someone." He turned and waved Mei over.

When Mei stepped forward, he gestured with an open palm up. "Ladies, this is my baby sister, Mei." Then he gestured to the youngest of the sisters. "This is Marla." Marla was obviously shy by nature, but smiled. "Hi Mei."

"Hello, Marla," Mei said.

Brother gestured at the older sister. "This is Audrey." Audrey was more outgoing than Marla, but wore the same friendly smile as her sister.

"Hello Mei," she said.

"Hello, Audrey," Mei said.

Brother turned to gesture at the last of the trio, but instead of waiting, the honey brown-haired girl stepped forward and held out her hand.

"Hello, Miss Mei. I'm Trinity."

Mei shook her hand. "Hello, Miss Trinity."

"Please Mei, just Trinity, and I love your war paint and hair. You look pretty and savage at the same time."

"Thanks, Trinity." She thought for a moment, then said, "I don't know what to say, except I'm sure your music is as beautiful as you are."

Brother beamed and looked over at Mr. White, who nodded approval at Mei's compliment and raised his glass in a salute.

"Well, now," Trinity said with mild surprise. "You have lovely manners; I wonder where you learned how to flatter so well." Her eyes flicked to Brother at the last part of her statement.

Brother adopted a 'who, me?' expression. "And are we going to have the joy of listening to you perform tonight?" he asked, attempting to divert attention away from him.

"You're not getting off the hook that easily, me laddo," Trinity said.

"So, no?" he asked, determined to slip out of the awkward situation. He turned to run and found himself face to face with Audrey, who said, "we told God Pop we'd perform for the big ceremony tomorrow night."

Brother turned and found himself boxed in on the other side by her grinning sister. Marla said, "you know, we sang for you, so it's only fair you sing for us."

The musicians and people in the crowd all cheered and hooted at Brother.

"Ugh!" Brother groaned and surrendered. "I've been getting beat up about singing all day! I haven't practiced in a long time, and wasn't that great to begin with!"

The musicians and the crowd hooted.

"Besides," he said, "this isn't America's got talent. "

Sarah interrupted, "Oh, look at him. He's trying to run!" She turned to the crowd. "Are we going to let him dishonor himself?"

"No!" the crowd shouted.

Arik, Michael, Pop, and Prof Norris, who Mei hadn't seen earlier, joined in with chanting and clapping. "Sing! Sing! Sing!," while Mei and Judyta stomped their feet.

Brother nodded in acceptance and looked at his people. "I won't forget this." He reached over to a table and plucked a bottle of Irish Whiskey. He popped the cap and took a shot straight out of the bottle, then set it back down. "So, what's it going to be? War song? Fun song?" He glanced at Trinity. "Dirty Bar song?"

"A bit early for dirty bar songs, boyo," Auntie said from the crowd.

Brother smiled and bowed in deference. Mei hadn't seen Auntie the whole day, but waved at her as others shouted suggestions.

Brother walked over to where Arik was messing with his guitar. He leaned down, and in a subdued voice, discussed something with Arik. When he stood up, they were both smiling.

Arik started a slow strum on his guitar, while Brother walked to the edge of the fire. He nodded at Arik and broke into a song. "I've always liked the message of hope in this song."

Brother started humming, low and deep, then bobbed his head. He started singing in a rich and smooth voice.

Mei looked around and noticed the surprise on the faces of those who had never heard him sing.

"'It used to seem to me that my life ran on too fast'"

"'And I had to take it slowly just to make the good parts last'"

"'But when you're born to run it's so hard to just slow down'"

"'So don't be surprised to see me back in that bright part of town.'"

He clapped, and the crowd joined in.

"'I'll be back in the high life again'"

"'All the doors I closed one time will open up again'"

"'I'll be back in the high life again'"

"'All the eyes that watched me once will smile and take me in.'"

Brother smiled a killer smile of joy and really pitched in as he snatched a whiskey bottle from Michael's hands. The crowd cheered louder and clapped harder.

"'And I'll drink and dance with one hand free'"

"'Let the world back into me and oh I'll be a sight to see'"

'Back in the high life again.'"

He took a shot from bottle and handed it back to Michael, then whipped around and held his hands out to Trinity.

"'You used to be the best to make life be life to me'"

"'And I hope that you're still out there and you're like you used to be'"

"'We'll have ourselves a time'"

"'And we'll dance 'til the morning sun'"

"'And we'll let the good times come in'"

"'And we won't stop 'til we're done.'"

More cheers sounded as Audrey and Marla jabbed cheerfully at a blushing and laughing Trinity.

"'We'll be back in the high life again'"

"'All the doors I closed one time will open up again'"

"'We'll be back in the high life again'"

"'All the eyes that watched us once will smile and take us in.'"

"Come on," Brother said to Trinity, and pulled her to her feet. He slipped his hand around her waist, and they started an easy moving swing dance, each with one hand free.

"'And we'll drink and dance with one hand free'"

"'And have the world so easily and oh we'll be a sight to see'"

"'Back in the high life again.'"

"'We'll be back in the high life again'"

"'All the doors I closed one time will open up again'"

"'We'll be back in the high life again'"

"'All the eyes that watched us once will smile and take us in'"

"'Back in the high life again.'"

When he finished singing, Brother dipped Trinity like a ballroom dancer. The crowd cheered and clapped. He then stood, they hugged tightly, and he kissed her on the cheek before they parted. He turned to the crowd, smiled and bowed, then walked over and scooped Mei up in his arms and hugged her tight.

Mei hugged him back. "You're really good, Brother of mine," she said into his ear.

"Thank you, Mei Mei."

Judyta bounced up, cheering and high-fiving Brother's free hand. Boudicca got up and leaned into Brother, mugging for attention.

Brother sat down on an open bench, with Mei next to him and Boudicca in front.

People walked by and patted his shoulder and told him, 'good job.'

Some folks sang a happy pub song and watched Trinity, Audrey, and Marla pull out their musical instruments.

When the pub song ended, the girls started tuning up.

Mei watched in fascination. The fluid way the musicians handled their instruments seemed magical.

Brother seemed to read Mei's mind. "They're exceptional," he said as he leaned in to speak privately. "You're in for a treat."

"How do you know them?" Mei asked.

"They've been playing music together since they were little. Audrey and Marla have an older brother, Christopher, who's a couple of years younger than me. When we were in high school, some guys beat him up for wearing his kilt and playing bagpipes. So, I stepped in and we had a proper scrum. We tuned up the lot of them, and even though Christopher took quite a beating, he hung in there and did the best he could. We cleaned him up and I got him and his pipes home in one piece."

"Arik and Michael heard about it, so we all put on our kilts and went back. By the time we got there, a bunch of them were hanging around, but we marched up and called them out. I'll be damned if little Christopher, beat to a pulp, didn't come running up at the last minute and stood with us. He could have stayed safe at home, but that wasn't his nature."

"So, the bad guys left you alone?"

Brother laughed. "Oh no, no indeed. It turned into a big brawl, and we were outnumbered. We almost got torn up."

"Oh, no!"

"It's okay, Mei Mei. We held tough, ate our pain, and fought harder and longer. See, the three of us had worked together so many times, we knew how to protect Christopher. We laid a beating on them they didn't soon forget. Unfortunately, it wasn't all one way. They beat on us pretty badly too, but we made them understand the error of their ways. They threatened us, and later we made a few of them into object lessons, and they finally left us alone. Anyhow, we became friends with Christopher, and that's how I met the girls. Years later, when I was in Afghanistan, they sent me a copy of songs they recorded in the studio. They were good."

"Now tell her what you really did for us!" Trinity interrupted. She had walked up while Brother was talking.

"What? It wasn't so much."

"Oh, shut up!" Trinity said, then sucked in a breath and looked at Mei. "Let me tell you who your brother is. The big gorilla was fighting a war thousands of miles away from home, and what does he do? What is he thinking of?"

"I..." Brother started.

Trinity held up her hand and shook her head.

"But..."

"Shush!" she cut him off again. "I mean it. This story is long overdue, and I don't know if we'll get another opportunity." Her tone made it clear Brother's protest landed on deaf ears. People in the crowd had leaned in to listen, and they giggled at Brother's discomfort. Trinity patted him on the head. "You just sit there and look pretty. Some people know this story, but I'm telling it again, here, and now." She looked at Mei. "Apparently, your brother met Mary Flynn, the famous singer from Ireland, the one that was on TV, while Mary was performing for the troops. So, he gave her the thumb drive of the three of us performing." She gestured to Audrey and Marla, who had walked up and stood next to her. "As well as our contact information. A few months later, Mary Flynn's manager called and invited us to play for her because she was doing a tour in the states. The meeting turned into an audition, and she took us on tour with her. Lots of doors opened for us after that, all because of him."

"You already sent me an autographed copy of the CD of your tour as a thank you, and it was great," Brother said. "So, we're done here, right?"

Audrey wagged her finger. "I swear, if you don't be quiet..."

Pop stepped up behind Brother and Mei and put a hand on Brother's shoulder. "Let the ladies say their peace, son. Besides, I'm curious, and bet everyone else is too."

The group uttered a chorus of 'yeses.'

Brother bowed his head but nodded acceptance.

Mei's mind was whirling, and she couldn't make sense of what was happening.

"Thank you, sir," Trinity said, "but that's not the complete story. We started playing with Mary Flynn and were getting along well as a group, learning how to play better than we ever thought we could, learning a ton about the music industry, traveling, and having the time of our lives. We became friends with Mary and her team, and one day she told me what really happened when she met your brother. It was at a base hospital. She'd been touring the hospital and visiting the wounded servicemen. It was hard to see, and Mary really wanted a cigarette. She'd quit smoking, but after seeing that, decided it would be okay to light up. So, she snuck out in a smoking area by herself, and met this," she held her fingers in air quotes, "giant, filthy, wounded, but still very charming U.S. Marine Yankee bastard. He walked into the smoking area and lit up a cigar while waiting for his turn to get patched up. Filthy, stinky, bloody, and bold as brass, he spots her and walks up to her, and..." She turned to the crowd. "And who does that sound like?"

"Well..." Brother started, trying to rally to his own defense, but a soft but firm hand reached up and covered his mouth. Little Marla wagged her finger. It reminded Mei of a cartoon of a bunny threatening a grizzly bear.

"Thank you, Marla," Trinity said. "Anyway, Mary said instead of hitting on her, the giant Marine surprised her by saying he knew who she was. Mary performed mostly for UK and Commonwealth troops. He asked about her music and thanked her for doing the tour for the U.S. troops. Mary made it a point to mention again to me how charming he was." She rolled her eyes and adopted a female lilt to her voice, mimicking an Irish woman.

"He stood downwind so his cigar smoke wouldn't blow on her, and turned his wounded side away so the bloody bandages didn't gross her out. He was so very polite." Trinity shook her head in frustration.

"Then, she said, he fished a case out of his pocket and asked her to listen to it. She said he was so enthusiastic and sincere, and the situation was so damned odd, she couldn't say no. She listened to it and was pleasantly surprised. So, she took our contact information. She was so taken with him, she broke her own rule and started to hug him, but couldn't because of his wounds, so she pulled his collar and kissed his filthy face.

Mary said the medical staff came out and ushered him into the hospital, then her tour liaison came and took her to the next stop. She was down the road when she realized she'd never got his name. But we knew who it was." Trinity choked up. "Mary showed me the case and the drive. It still had his dried blood on it. We all saw..."she trailed off "His Blood." She took a breath "What other wounded man in a war on the other side of the world would try to help the kid sisters of a friend way back here?"

Brother opened his mouth to speak, but Trinity spun and yanked up the left sleeve of his T-shirt, exposing a horrid waxy slash of a scar that crawled through his tattoos across his upper arm. Mei had seen it of course, but hearing part of the story behind it gave her chills. Nobody else had seen Brother's scars and seeing just one sent a hush over the crowd.

Embarrassed, Brother pulled away and tugged his sleeve down. "Tis but a flesh wound," he joked, but his joke fell flat. He tried again. "It isn't too bad. A round came in at an angle, skipped off my armor, and gave me a kiss goodbye. And I settled the guy who did it." Realizing what he'd just admitted to, he followed up with a more comments in rapid succession. "It itched more than anything. I just had to get it cleaned out to keep it from getting infected. No biggie."

Trinity looked at Mei, who had tears on her cheeks. "So that's what kind of man your brother is. And even when we're so frustrated with him we want to beat him with a stick, we're still proud to know him."

Judyta started clapping enthusiastically, and soon everyone joined her. Trinity pulled Brother to his feet, and in turn, each musician hugged him, looked him in the eyes and said, 'thank you.'

Brother hugged each one of them back and kissed each one on the cheek.

Mei wept with pride at her big brother. She'd never been so happy in her life. She tried hard to take the best mind pictures, hoping to remember it forever.

Judyta and George came over and stood with Mei and Brother. Judyta then pounced on Brother in a surprise warm hug, and George bumped fists with Brother.

Brother stood and looked around. "Well, how about some music? Just a few fun songs for tonight. The ladies have come a long way, and we all have a big day tomorrow."

Everyone agreed with his idea. The musicians took their spots and started playing.

Mei didn't recognize the Irish music, but the songs were fun, and the girls were talented. It sounded like a YouTube video. Everyone in the crowd clapped and sang along. They were done too soon, and the performance ended in thunderous applause.

To everyone's surprise, Mr. White stepped up to the fire and cleared his throat, then looked at his surprised children. "Your great grandparents taught me this song when I was a little boy." He turned to the crowd. "If you know it, please join in."

He started humming, then started his song in a clear and powerful voice.

"'Of all the money that e'er I had'"

"'I spent it in good company'""

"'And all the harm I've ever done'"

"'Alas it was to none but me'"

"'And all I've done for want of wit'"

"'To mem'ry now I can't recall'"

"'So fill to me the parting glass'"

"'Good night and joy be to you all.'"

Brother and Pop joined in.

"'So fill to me the parting glass'"

"'And drink a health whate'er befalls'"

"'And gently rise and softly call'"

"'Good night and joy be to you all.'"

The musicians stepped up and joined Mr. White.

"'Of all the comrades that e'er I had'"

"'They're sorry for my going away'"

"'And all the sweethearts that e'er I had'"

"'They'd wish me one more day to stay'"

"'But since it fell unto my lot'"

"'That I should rise and you should not'"

"'I gently rise and softly call'"

"'Good night and joy be to you all'"

"'Fill to me the parting glass'"

"'And drink a health whate'er befalls'"

"'And gently rise and softly call'"

"'Good night and joy be to you all'"

"'But since it fell unto my lot'"

"'That I should rise and you should not'"

"'I gently rise and softly call'"

"'Good night and joy be to you all'"

"'So fill to me the parting glass'"

"'And drink a health whate'er befalls'"

"'And gently rise and softly call'"

"'Good night and joy be to you all'"

"'Good night and joy be to you all.'""

The audience applauded and Mr. White bowed. Judyta jumped into her father's arms and hugged him hard. George wrapped his arms around both. The time for music had ended. After brief conversations with promises to meet the next day, people hugged, said goodnight, and headed to their campsites.

Mei took Brother's hand. She didn't want to let go, but Brother had many hugs to give and hands to shake. Most everyone patted Boudicca's big head as the big dog thumped her tail. A few grandmothers told Brother they were proud of him and what he'd become. He felt uncomfortable with the praise, but he awkwardly thanked them and bid them goodnight.

After most had left, Trinity and the sisters walked up to Brother. "We were planning on camping with you tonight if you'll have us."

"Uhm, sure," Brother said, and shrugged. "But I don't think it's the same fine accommodations big-time celebrities are used to when on the road."

"It's okay," Audrey said. "We thought it would be fun camping out under the stars, like we did in the old days."

"We brought sleeping bags and gear; we just need a place," Marla added.

"Well, come on, and welcome," Brother said, then paused. "There is one thing."

"Oh?"

"I have a favor," he said. "It's an epic thing, but I'd like you to do it tomorrow morning before breakfast, okay?"

Audrey narrowed her eyes. "Wait a minute."

"Yeah," Marla said. "We're going to need details."

Brother laughed. "Ladies, I promise you, it's nothing bad. In fact, I'd tell your parents at mass on Sunday without a concern."

"We're not Catholic, so try again," Trinity said.

"You know what I mean," Brother said. "Besides, have you ever heard of me making a promise to a lady, let alone three ladies, at the same time?"

"Mister man," Trinity said. "We're experienced campaigners and touring veterans, and never believe promises about tomorrow some lusty rogue makes just before bedtime."

"Peace, woman. I don't blame you." He looked around, then grinned. "What if I find a neutral party, tell them my plan, and let them make the call?"

The musicians conferred. "Yeah, sure," Audrey said.

Brother looked around and spotted Mrs. MacDuff, the retired music teacher. She was as formal and proper as they came. "Mrs. MacDuff, may I speak with you for a moment?"

"Sure thing, dear boy. Come on over."

Brother trotted over and chatted, gesturing towards the trio of suspicious musicians. He talked in hushed tones for a moment, then Mrs. MacDuff exploded with laughter.

"Oh, my!" she gasped between laughs. "That is indeed clever!" She looked over at the trio. "Ladies, there's nothing to fear. In fact, this clever young man will cheer your musician's hearts!"

Brother turned to the trio. "Does that ease your minds?"

"Yes, okay," Audrey said, but the look on her face still showed skepticism.

Brother thanked Mrs. MacDuff then came back over to Mei and Boudicca. "Let's get settled."

On the trip to the campsite, they showed the musicians the port-o-potties and made a pit stop. They got back to the campsite and found the Whites stoking the campfire and preparing their sleeping gear.

"I'll heat up the water for a quick wash up," Brother said. "I could use it, and Mei and Judyta are definitely in need of a rinse." He looked at George. "Do you mind helping the ladies get their gear and bring it back here?"

George grabbed a flashlight off a table. "Nope. I'm ready now."

"Thank you," Trinity said, and the group headed off into the night.

Mei changed into sleeping shorts and a t-shirt while Brother put an iron stand over the campfire and put a kettle full of water over it. They all brushed their teeth, rolled out sleeping bags, filled Boudicca's water dish, and got extra blankets. George and the musicians returned to the camp and settled in. Brother flashed George the thumbs up.

"Brother," Mei said, "can I sleep next to Judyta tonight?"

"Sure. Be careful Judyta, she snores."

"Do not!" Mei protested.

Brother chuckled, then poured warm water from the kettle into a washbasin. He gestured Mei over, scrubbed her face and arms with the washcloth, then wrung it out. Judyta dipped a washcloth of her own into the water and scrubbed.

Brother stepped into the darkness and returned to the firelight, bare-chested and wearing a pair of Marine cammie trousers cut off just below the cargo pockets. He hung up his kilt and put his other gear away.

Mei was used to seeing Brother with no shirt on, as well as the sight of his muscles, scars, and tattoos. Apparently, by the looks on everyone's faces, he was quite a sight. Judyta tried not to stare. Mr. White gave Brother a once over, then went back to his business, but the three musicians were clearly stunned. Mei was sure she could see the girls blushing in the light of the campfire.

Brother looked up from his washing and saw the musicians. "Oops. Sorry, ladies." He reached over to the bed of the truck, picked up a sleeveless flannel shirt, and put it on, covering up his real estate.

He showed the guests the privacy curtain, ice chest, stack of firewood, and how to lock their gear in the camp trailer. While the guests washed up and changed into their sleeping clothes, he went outside of the firelight and did an abbreviated version of his nightly stretching routine.

Mr. White went over and joined him and started doing what appeared as a kata of his own. Mei was interested. She thought only Brother did weird stuff like that. She also noticed Audrey and Marla had walked away from the group and were kneeling in prayer. Mei found it interesting to learn about everyone's private life and their various routines.

Everyone returned and gathered around the campfire about the same time Audrey, Marla, and George were petting Boudicca and talking among themselves.

"Are we ready to crash?" Brother asked. "I figured our guests can sleep in the bed of the truck. The rest of us will sleep around the campfire." He turned to the musicians. "I'm sorry ladies, but I have to take the futon mattress out for me, but have enough extra blankets to make it comfortable for you."

Everyone nodded and murmured okay. Brother rolled out a big canvas tarp on the ground near the campfire, then pulled the futon mattress out and laid it in the center of the tarp. Next, he laid out a stack of the soft wool blankets and pillows, then rolled out Mei's sleeping bag on one side of the futon. Judyta immediately scooted Mei's sleeping bag over and laid her sleeping bag next to Mei's on the edge of the tarp.

Brother looked at Mr. White. "Steve, just how much trouble am I in for?"

Mr. White looked at the two clean-faced she-raiders settling down and giggling to each other, then looked back at Brother. He held his hand to his chest, palm down. "About this deep."

"I'm not familiar with the protocols for this sort of event, so, is this okay?" Brother asked.

Mr. White smiled. "Not to worry, Little Brother, you're doing fine."

At this time, Boudicca decided all the comfiness on the ground was just what she wanted, and walked onto the blankets, sleeping bags, laughing little girls, and plopped down.

"Dog!" Brother yelled, "come on." He snapped his fingers. Instead of obeying, the big dog rolled over onto her back and stuck her paws in the air. Everyone chuckled at Brother's dilemma. Finally, Boudicca squished down between a giggling Mei and Judyta.

Brother raised his hands in surrender. "Well, that's about as good as it'll get tonight," he said, then did something odd. He stood up straight, bowed his head, closed his eyes, then stood still and quiet. After a minute, he opened his eyes, reached into a pocket of his trunks and put a piece of tape across the bridge of his nose. Then he removed his flannel shirt and crawled under his blankets.

Mei scooted next to him, and he put his big arm across her. This close, he felt big and strong, and she felt safe.

"Brother..."

"Yeah, Mei Mei, what's up?"

"Today was the best day of my whole life. Thank you."

He cleared his throat. "Well, you're sure welcome, my Mei Mei. You made me very proud today. But then again, you usually do."

They stayed quiet for a minute while Mei watched the stars and embers of the dying fire. She heard the girls in the truck talking and giggling as they moved around. Then, when Trinity walked up and put her sleeping bag down on the other side of Brother, Mei was surprised, even more when Audrey and Marla put their sleeping bags next to Trinity's. They all settled in, and Mei felt Brother go still for a minute. Then relax.

Mei drifted off to sleep listening to the sounds of the night, the campfire's occasional pop and crackle, and the breathing of the people she loved most in the world.

Chapter 86

Brother

On the first full day of the Ceilidh, Brother woke up earlier than Mei. He slid out of the bed of the truck without disturbing her. The usual aches were present, but overall, he felt good. He wasn't sure how he would do sleeping on a futon instead of on his bed with its special mattress, so this was a welcome surprise.

Leaving Mei and Boudicca to sleep in, Brother went to the port-o-potty, then returned and stretched, worked out, shaved, and cleaned up. By the time he finished, Mei was up and moving. They ate a quick breakfast and dressed in their Ceilidh finery, a fun mix of Celtic/gypsy/rogue accouterments sure to scandalize any of the groups.

He made a ritual of putting sunscreen and war paint on Mei, finishing by putting her sheathed throwing knife into the sash she wore at her waist. She planned to join Pop at the impromptu knife throwing competition this morning.

He stepped back and looked at his baby sister painted in her garb, standing proud in the morning sunshine. She looked amazing. Her eyes were wise beyond her years, but she'd lost the hollow-eyed, haunted look. He snapped photos with his cell phone for posterity.

As they stepped out onto the field, the ram's horn sounded; long and loud, echoing across the Ceilidh field. They'd been called to the blood! Cheering and shouts sounded from the field, raising goosebumps on Brother's skin. His heart pounded when he heard the second winding call! Now roars joined the other voices.

On the third blow of the horn, Brother stood up straight, threw his head back, raised his clenched fists, emitted a roar that started below his feet, through the earth and into memories of his past. It flowed through his feet, raced through his legs and groin, lifted his heart and rocketed up from his lungs into the sky! The volume could have split granite. A bagpipe started to skirl. Grinning, he walked over to Mei with his face alight. "Are you ready?"

"Yes," she said, and they joined hands and walked out into the day.

Brother and Mei headed for the knife throwing competition at the far end of the pasture past the highland athletics field. He guided them on a circuitous route to avoid most of the people and give him time to take everything in. He'd locked away this place in his memory while he was away, thinking only of it when life got difficult, and he hadn't been here in a long time. As he walked, many memories flooded back, and he felt relieved everyone was good, even the embarrassing ones.

Brother knew people were giving him second glances, but he respectfully avoided eye contact. No need to rush; he had plenty of time.

He gave Mei a quick tour, pointing out people, places, and activities of interest.

When they reached the knife target range, a group of men, mostly older and kilted, stood around joking with each other. In his wisdom, Pop had determined it was best to hold the knife throwing competition earlier in the day, before the heavy drinking started.

Pop broke out of the crowd and headed over. Some of the other men came over, and Brother recognized some of the faces. Most were grayer than when he'd last seen them, but he felt overcome with joy at the reunion. These were his people. The handshakes and good-natured kidding started. He felt at home again.

Teams were chosen, and everyone set up on a target. Mei stood next to Pop on the line. She looked so little among all the men, but Brother hadn't often seen the focus she wore on her face. She looked like a pilot or a sniper. He wasn't sure how she would do, but hoped at least she had fun.

When Mei's turn came, her movements were fluid and sure, and thunk! She stuck her first throw!

Fuck yes! Brother screamed to himself, while keeping a poker face. All her practice paid off.

The competitors who struck the target retrieved their knives and moved back twice as far, while those who missed were out of the competition.

Brother inched closer to see better and snap photos.

In the next round, Mei stuck her blade again, and Brother's excitement soared. Some more competitors missed and stepped off as the winners retrieved their blades and stepped back another double distance.

Brother noticed Mei looked a little troubled. She turned and moved toward him.

He held his hand up. "Stop!" He hunched down next to her and coached her.

"It's far," she said.

"No, it's not. It's just a smaller target and you can hit a smaller target. You've done it before. Mind your hand placement on the knife so you get it to turn right." He stepped back to the crowd and felt delighted to see the White family. He held a finger to his lips to preemptively shush Judyta as he walked over and joined them.

The other men started throwing, but when only one hit the target, Pop and Mei were the only two competitors remaining.

Mei stepped up. Brother saw her go through her internal processes as she stood up straight, took a good stance, and with perfect form, fueled with just a hint of extra effort, made her throw. The knife flew in a higher arc, turned once, then came down and hit the target!

Brother's roar of triumph split the air, followed by the rest of the crowd. He quickly composed himself and crossed his arms, trying to stay calm for Mei. Her knife rested closer to the center than the other competitor.

Pop scooped up Mei into his arms, and to Brother's surprise, Mei didn't freak out. Instead, she smiled at her grandfather, and said something Brother couldn't hear. Pop shook his head, but Mei's expression was insistent. She spoke again, and Pop nodded, then respectfully put her down. The grand old gent leaned over and picked up his knife, then quickly bent over and kissed Mei on her forehead. Then, in a blur of motion, he whipped his knife straight as an arrow into the center of the target. Bullseye!

As the crowd cheered, Pop faced his newest grandchild, snapped into a position of attention, and saluted the little girl.

Mei smiled, and Pop leaned down to hug her, and said something.

Mei nodded.

Unable to contain herself, Judyta flew past Brother and pounced on Mei. Soon, the girls were holding hands and jumping up and down. Brother marveled at the sincere affection Judyta heaped on Mei and felt a hand on his shoulder. He turned to see Steve and George.

"She's really come a long way in a short time," Steve said.

"Thanks, man" Brother said.

Steve chuckled. "You know her recovery is because of you, right?"

"Well..."

"Stop it," Steve said. "That's your work. Well done, sir. Keep going."

"Yeah, thanks, man."

Suddenly, Brother wished the Chaplain was here. He wanted his old pal to share this moment with him. Brother's mind picture skills weren't what they once were, but they were still good, so he locked the picture in his mind.

Judyta was pulling Mei through the crowd to Brother. They stopped in front of him, and Mei chattered away while she rode the wave of excitement. Brother talked with Mei for a few more excited minutes, both of them flying high on Mei's performance. Then Brother remembered the whole point of bringing Mei to the Ceilidh was to turn her loose. As if on cue, Mei and Judyta tore off at a run, hand in hand.

It just might be okay, Brother mused. He turned back to the gathering to accept handshakes and nods. He knew it was time for him to fulfill the reason he came to the Ceilidh.

Chapter 87

Brother

The morning flew by. Brother slowly toured the Ceilidh fields and greeted people from his past. He was almost embarrassed at the outpouring of sincere welcome he received from so many people; they shook his hand, hugged him, slapped his back, and he heard several stories, all beginning with, 'You remember that time?' If anyone drew more attention than Brother, it was Boudicca, and she ate up the pettings, tummy rubs, and kisses.

Brother tried to maneuver around to observe Mei's activities. Under Judyta's tutelage, Mei was a machine in motion. Both had painted their faces and arms, and Judyta was wearing a scarf and some of Mei's clothes. Several times they raced past Brother without seeing him, and that was okay. They were enjoying themselves, and Mei's face glowed like Brother had never seen before.

He became interested when Mei participated in the Scottish dancing. She was so absorbed in the music and motion, Brother was certain she'd found something to interest her more than climbing. He wondered whether she'd like gymnastics or acrobatics, and made a note to think about it later.

He held on for as long as he could, but by early afternoon, he was 'peopled out.' He felt guilty because everyone was so nice, but the constant attention from everyone was getting to him. He excused himself, then he and Boudicca beat a hasty retreat to the campsite for much needed and deserved solitude.

Brother took off his kilt, weapons, and boots, and slipped on a pair of trunks. He tossed down a blanket, and after removing his shirt, stretched out under the warm sunshine. After drinking her water, Boudicca laid down next to him, slobbering his face.

Ah, yes, siesta time.

Brother was roused from his doze when Steve and George came in carrying camping gear. He waved. The guys set up their gear while Boudicca supervised.

"Hey George, if you do me a favor, I'll do you one."

"What?" George asked.

"Well, I'd appreciate you taking Missy Boudicca for a walk. If you walked her past those Highland Dancer-girl cutie pies, you'll appreciate it."

"Okay," George said, but frowned.

"George, puppies draw girls your age faster than money," Steve said, "so your good pal here is setting you up for an opportunity to speak with a group of pretty young girls."

"Oh!" George said and bobbed his head.

"Do you have a kilt?" Brother asked.

"No."

"No worries, you look good enough, just go." Brother paused. "Wait up, George. If I can find one that fits, you want to sport a man's war skirt?"

"Uhm, sure."

"Okay, no promises, but I'll see what I can do."

"Thanks."

"Wait!"

"What?"

"What are you going to say to the girls?" Brother asked.

"Uh," George said, then shrugged.

"Steve, want me to help the boy?"

"By all means," Steve said.

Brother reached into his clothes and pulled out a cigar case. "George, listen up. Let me relieve you of a burden. You're not going to seduce any of those girls today. But it's a sunny day and you have an awesome puppy."

Brother clipped the end from a cigar and lit it, then puffed on it and lay it down.

"So, don't be a dope. Be nice. Take a breath. Relax. Offer to let them pet her. Tell them her name. If they ask, tell them she's an English Mastiff, about six months old. and she's your pal, then introduce yourself. Smile and just say, by the way, my name is George. What's yours? If they're a dancer, ask them if you and Missy B can come watch them dance. If not, just say thanks anyway. Maybe I'll see you later. You're out there to learn to talk to them and get attention for Boudicca. After all, she's your wingman." Brother puffed his cigar thoughtfully. "How am I doing, Steve?"

"I'd say you're spot on."

Brother looked up at George. "You got it, little brother?"

George took Boudicca's leash. "I think so."

"Good. Now I want you to talk to at least five girls around your age, and then tell me their names and something about them when you get back."

George frowned. "Like what?"

"I dunno. What color dress were they wearing? Were they Irish or Scottish? Do they have a clan? Do they wear glasses? Are they pretty or plain? Are they kind or were they too embarrassed to talk to you? Stuff like that."

"Okay."

"Go get them, killer!"

George and Boudicca headed off. Brother waited a minute, then looked over at Steve.

"Too much?"

"No, not at all. You probably made his day. He's at the age where he wants the advice, just not from me."

"Yeah, kids suck sometimes, but you're his dad, not me, so if you want me to enforce rules or avoid some topic, just say the word."

Steve snickered and then nodded.

"I think there's sunshine in a bottle around here if you would like."

"My good sir, I would very much like that."

Brother got up and retrieved a bottle of Irish whiskey from a duffle bag. He grabbed two glasses from a camp box, poured two fingers worth in each, and passed one to his friend.

Steve raised the glass in a toast.

"Slainte."

"Slainte," Brother replied and took a gulp. He put the bottle away and laid back down.

"This is nice," Steve said.

Brother started to answer when Mei and Judyta walked out of the apple orchard. Mei saw Brother and ran over and pounced on him in a hug. Bare-chested, Brother felt uncomfortable, but this was Mei's biggest expression of affection to date. Mei got up and sat down next to him. They chatted for a while as the girls reapplied their war paint before racing off together.

"Damn," Steve said.

"Indeed."

In the late afternoon, Brother got up, put on in his Celtic ensemble, then he and Steve wandered out. They were greeted with more welcomes and hugs. It felt nice to be remembered. They spotted George talking with a couple of kids his age, while Boudicca lounged on her back, and enjoyed a mom and her little boy rubbing her tummy.

"Is he taking a lunge at that mom?" Brother asked.

"Hey! That's my age bracket," Steve said in mild outrage after observing his son in action.

"Now, now, dad, I don't think he's trying to plant his castles in your sandbox. Probably just overcome and trying to be polite."

"Ugh!"

"If you're concerned your charms aren't what they used to be, I'll let you borrow the dog."

"Oh, do shut up," Steve said, with more than a little exasperation, then headed over to George.

Brother snickered, then saw Pop. He called him over, and they whispered among themselves. Pop nodded his head.

"Thanks, Pop," Brother said, then sauntered over to where George and Boudicca were holding court.

George was calmly chatting away while holding Boudicca's leash, and Steve was making headway with the mother of the little boy. Boudicca saw Brother and popped up and galumphed over to him, tugging George along behind.

Brother took the leash from George. "Thank you, sir. Okay, George, give me the rundown on the five."

George seemed excited about telling his story. "Okay, this was great! First there was a girl named Kaitlin, a brunette." He outlined more than the required five profiles to Brother, who noted the depth of George's descriptions. Steve joined them while George was talking.

"Okay, okay," Brother said after a minute. "Good job. Now you know more about talking to girls. Next time you can try talking to them without a puppy. Do you still want to kilt up?"

"I'll give it a try," George said.

"Okay, see my god pop over there? Go over and introduce yourself with a proper handshake, then tell him I sent you about a kilt."

Daunted, George looked over and saw Pop talking to some people.

Brother read the concern on the boy's face. "It's fine, go. Away knave!"

"Okay," George said then left.

"Stop!" Brother said, then reached over and put his hand on George's shoulder and pulled up. "Stand up straight, little brother. Make your dad proud."

George flushed but stood up tall.

"If it's okay, son, I'll join you," Steve said.

"Sure, dad," George said, and they went off together.

Brother looked down at Boudicca. "Let's go find Mei Mei and Judyta. I bet if we follow the music, we'll find both of them." He strolled through the crowd to the dance stage. It took him a minute to process the blasphemous, yet ridiculously fun music blasted from the stage speakers. Someone had recorded traditional Irish music to techno club tracks. Several young ladies in their mid-teens thru early twenties laughed and shuffle danced along with the tracks. Some wore Scottish highland dance dresses, some work skirts, all bedecked in various Celtic finery in a range of colors. It was quite a spectacle. This group of young ladies loved to dance for the joy of dancing. Sure enough, Mei and Judyta were right in the middle of it all.

Well, good for all of them, Brother mused, then without warning, a swirling wave of warm, indescribable emotions washed over him. The feelings he was having were so corny he almost wouldn't admit them to himself. At times like this, he felt proud he'd served and fought, so young ladies like these could enjoy their lives with happy abandon, oblivious to the evils girls their age lived with in other places in the world. Even the most jaundiced and cynical NCO would be proud of the happiness here, even if they would never openly admit it. When he was serving, it was easy, maybe necessary to hide behind a shield of cynicism and bad tempered contempt for everything, but there comes a time to turn it off. Back when he was in the hospital and found out that he was going to live, Brother had made a concious decision to keep being pragmatic but also greatful and appreciative. At first he took this path because he didnt want to be toxic around Mei Mei, but later on he found that he was also giving himself permission to let stuff go and be happy.

He snapped himself out of his reverie. "We're a weird bunch" he chided himself. He fished his camera out of his sporran and snapped photos of Mei Mei and Judyta dancing. The set ended, and the girls clapped. With the radar young women have, the pack of dancers had noticed Brother and Boudicca's approach and greeted him with giggles. Fortunately, Mei and Judyta burst out of the crowd.

Without warning or asking permission, Judyta climbed his body like a ladder and perched her bony behind on his shoulder.

For some reason, Brother let her. What the hell... Who runs Barter town? he mumbled to himself. Mei and Judyta lectured him on their plans as they headed to dinner. An embarassed Steve scolded Judyta, with little effect. So instead of making an issue about it, they ate dinner. While they were eating, George mentioned Pop set him up with one of Brother's old kilts. "I'll wear it tomorrow."

"Cool."

Before dinner was finished, somehow Brother reluctantly agreed to sing. When had he lost control of his own life? Was he paying for bad behaviors from long ago? Had he really been such a showoff when he was a kid?

After they finished dinner, they all went over to Arik and Sarah's campsite to spend time with loved ones. Throughout the campsite, people were lighting campfires, laughing, singing and carrying on. When they arrived at Arik's campsite, Brother got one of the bigger surprises he'd had in a long time. Considering the last few months, that was saying something.

Marla, Audra, and Trinity, known by their stage name as The Shaw Sisters, were setting up musical equipment by the campfire.

Damn! Without thinking, Brother handed Boudicca's leash off and stepped over. He was sure he said something, but couldn't remember what it was. He found himself in a crush of loveliness and euphoric happiness beyond anything he could've expected. He fought back tears of overwhelming joy as another heavy weight he didn't know he carried fell away. Brother stepped back and then reached out and hugged each one in turn. Then, partly from joy and partly to hide his misty eyes, he laughed his booming laugh.

The girls all laughed and jumped in for another mass hug.

He closed his eyes as the memory wheels spun. Overseas. The heat, crappy food, Taliban rockets, then the ethereal voices of the girls crossing oceans, deserts, and mountains reaching out, finding him and gifting him with solace and peace, even on his worst days. How could he ever explain? He let go of them and stepped back again. He'd wanted to express how much their music had meant to him and the guys out in the sticks in Afghanistan, but when he tried to articulate, the words sounded clumsy and stupid. He needed to buy time to get the words right, so he shut himself down and diverted the conversation to introductions. He felt distracted. The girls had grown up! He'd always thought of them as an old friend's kid sisters, but now. Audra and Marla were both attractive and shy, but Trinity... Damn! Her honey brown curls, elfin face, and the 'I dare you' look she gave him, not to mention her pheromones could jump start a truck. Easy there, killer.

Thinking about Trinity caused Brother to lose focus, but luckily, the topic of him singing popped back up and diverted his thoughts.

As much as he tried to put the slide and the glide on everyone, he couldn't see a way out and the crowd was going wild, so he might as well give them a show. He took a slug of whiskey while Arik warmed up on his guitar.

Brother started humming, low and deep. Then he started nodding his head as the song came on...

"'It used to seem to me that my life ran on too fast'"

"'And I had to take it slowly just to make the good parts last....'"

He clapped and played to the crowd, and they joined in. God, it felt good to sing again. He reached out and caught Trinity's hand, and pulled her into a dance in front of everyone, without missing a note. When he finished the song, he dipped Trinity, then pulled her up into a happy embrace. Everyone clapped and cheered. Brother hugged the pretty lady again and told her, 'thank you.' Then he went over to Mei and settled in as the girls played their instruments.

Mei asked about the girls, and Brother told her an abridged version about another of his misadventures as a teenager, and the time he spent in Afghanistan when the girls had sent him several songs they had recorded in the studio. He had almost finished when Trinity approached while Brother was explaining.

"Now tell her what you really did!" Trinity said.

Oh shit, no good deed goes unpunished. Brother tried to beg off, but Trinity wasn't having it.

"Oh, shut up!" she said.

Trinity then related the story of the odd circumstances of how Brother got the Shaw Sisters introduced to Mary Flynn, a recording deal and a place on a popular US tour.

Brother felt super embarrassed, but when he tried to speak up, he was kindly but immediately shut down. He might have walked away, but was stopped in place by Mei's look of admiration. Fuck. He could do nothing but endure his embarrassment. He wondered why it was so easy to ignore embarrassment about the stupid things he'd done, but the embarrassment of hearing about his good deeds was so excruciating? Generally speaking, he felt proud to help out, but just didn't want to hear about it later on.

Trinity finished her story, and the musicians hugged him again. Somehow, each one managed to press sincerity and gratitude into each hug.

It felt good... very good.

And then Judyta pounced on him with a ferocious hug of her own. Brother staggered in surprise. Then George fist bumped him, and he felt other hands pat him on the back. Finally, Mei squeezed his hand. Brother felt a wall melt inside him, and it was an effort to keep a cheerful face. He finally managed to redirect the attention. "Well, how about some music? Just a few fun songs for tonight."

Everyone agreed and settled to listen. God, those girls could play. Even performing next to a campfire in a pasture, they sounded as though they were being played on an MP3. Brother cuddled next to Mei with Boudicca at his feet. He closed his eyes and let the musicians' voices carry him into the night sky. They finished too soon, bowed to their audience, and everyone applauded.

Brother thought they'd finished for the night, but to his surprise, Steve stood up and launched into a great rendition of "The Parting Glass." He was good! Everyone who could, sang with him. An appropriate finish to a fun-filled night.

As everyone said goodbye and headed to their campsite, Brother, Arik, and George helped Trinity and the girls pack up their instruments.

Then Trinity and the girls dropped a bomb. "We were planning on camping with you tonight if you will have us."

Brother's libido lit up like a bonfire. Evil man thoughts launched and ricocheted around his brain. However, instead of howling at the moon, he stifled down his internal noise. "Uhm, sure."

The girls laughed, but it was clear the decision was made. At least they were kind enough to pretend his permission was needed.

"Well, come on, and welcome" Brother said. Then he paused. "There is one thing." He wasn't sure where he got the inspiration for the photo shoot, but there it was, and it was so eccentric and fun. How could he not try to pull it off? Now, how to convince the girls without ruining the surprise or freaking them out.

Then he saw Mrs. MacDuff.

Game on!

They headed back to the campsite and started getting ready for bed. Brother winked at George and asked if he'd help the musicians get their gear from the car. The lad understood and headed off to help. Good for him.

Brother stoked the fire and put water on to heat. He helped get Mei changed and settled in. Soon enough, George came back with the girls and their gear. Brother thought the bed of the truck might be a bit snug for the three performers, but comfortable enough with the extra blankets.

He wasn't surprised when Mei and Judyta wanted to crash next to each other. Everyone puttered around with their individual routines of cleaning up and settling in for bed. He decided to sleep near Mei and Judtya, so he pulled the futon mattress out of the truck and put it on top of a canvas tarp next to the fire. He put his blankets down, and immediately Boudicca claimed his bed as hers.

"Don't get comfortable there, you four-legged gangster."

Boudicca thumped her tail.

The water was warm enough to wash up, so he helped Mei scrub behind the privacy curtain. When she finished, Judyta took her turn.

Brother stepped off into the darkness to strip off his kilt and clothes and put on a pair of trunks. Shirtless, Brother walked back into the sphere of light from the campfire, and hung up his kilt and gear. If he was honest, he would have admitted he walked in shirtless on purpose because he wanted to thrill the musicians, especially Trinity. The silence that fell over the camp indicated he'd succeeded.

After a moment, Brother grabbed his sleeveless flannel shirt and pulled it on, then stepped away again and began his nightly stretching/juru routine. Steve joined him a moment later with a more traditional tai chi routine.

The musicians stepped away and prayed in private. Judyta and Mei curled up with Boudicca. Brother stoked the fire, then stepped back and looked around the campsite. He felt an incredible sense of affection. For the first time in a long time, he thought things might be okay, the fiends and their lawsuit be damned. He closed his eyes and sent a prayer of thanks to the Chaplain's God. It was the most hope he felt in a long time. He put a no snore strip on his nose, stripped off his shirt, then climbed into his blankets and got as comfortable as he could.

Still in her sleeping bag, Mei scooted next to him. He put his arm across her little body.

"Brother?"

"Yeah, Mei Mei, what's up?"

"Today was the best day of my whole life. Thank you."

Brother coughed softly. "Well, you are sure welcome, my Mei Mei. You made me very proud of you today. But then again, you usually do." He felt her smile. Brother was sure he would need to go see the shrink again to discuss his feelings. They were new and not natural. He lied to himself.

Brother was relaxing and starting to drop off to sleep when he heard giggles from the bed of the truck. He figured the musicians were just settling in. Then he heard movement from the truck. What the... ? He cracked an eye open.

The musicians were up and walking over, dragging their sleeping bags, pillows, and blankets with them. Trinity put her sleeping bag right next to him. Right next to him! Danger close!

The other musicians laid down on the other side of Trinity. They all fussed as they settled in, but soon quieted down.

Trinity was so close, Brother could smell her lavender and vanilla skin crème. Sleep would not come easy. It became much harder when Trinity snuggled her sleeping bag up to his broad back. Damn! He swore he heard her chuckle. Devil woman!

Chapter 88

Mei Mei

On the third day of the Ceilidh, Mei woke up with the sounds of morning. Birds chirping, a light breeze rustling its way through the trees of the orchard, Boudicca whimpering and growling.

Mei cracked open an eye and surveyed her immediate surroundings. Facing her, Brother was up and out of bed, and Boudicca lay against her, snoring contentedly. Mei rolled over, and like a cautious turtle peering out of her shell, she craned her neck out of her sleeping bag. Judyta was still dead asleep in her sleeping bag. Since she couldn't see much past Judyta, Mei laid her head back down and closed her eyes. She felt happy laying in her own sleeping bag, listening to the morning's sounds. When she listened past Boudicca's breathing, Mei heard people in the distance; opening and closing camper doors, talking, coughing, and moving about.

Without opening her eyes, Mei rolled around and reached out a hand and stroked the big dog's fur. Just like at home, Boudicca responded by thumping her tail against Mei's sleeping bag.

Despite feeling warm in her sleeping bag, Mei felt a chill in the air. She wiggled around again, and looking out, saw Brother stretching in the orchard.

Mei got up and wrapped herself in a short blanket and stepped into her shoes, then went to the port-o-potty, with Boudicca close behind. Before going in, Mei put Boudicca into a sit and commanded her to stay. When Mei came out, she found the big dog laying down and waving her puppy paws. Mei smiled, and Boudicca thumped her tail. After washing her hands, Mei commanded Boudicca to come, and they headed back.

Brother was still wearing his cut off trunks and sleeveless flannel shirt, stoking the campfire and talking softly to Marla when

Mei returned. Audrey was awake, but lay quietly in her sleeping bag, listening to Brother and Marla. Trinity was sitting up in her sleeping bag, looking at the growing fire. George and Mr. White hung out on their sleeping bags. Judyta was still dead to the world. Mei got back into her sleeping bag but sat up instead of laying down.

After putting the cooking rack over the fire, Brother put a pot of water on it. He saw Mei awake and walked to the truck, stopping to kiss her on the head. Trinity smiled at Mei and gestured for Mei to sit next to her.

Mei scooted over, still in her sleeping bag. Boudicca got up, went over to her water dish, and began slurping and sloshing. When she finished, the Mastiff walked back over and laid down next to Judyta, trailing slobber strings across the blankets. Everyone watching snickered.

Brother walked over with a small pack and eased himself down behind Mei. Without a word, he held up a brush and pointed to her hair.

Mei turned her back to him, then scooted closer.

Gently but firmly, Brother tamed Mei's 'bed head.' He brushed and detangled the best he could. Then he pulled her hair into a ponytail, banded it, and tied a silk bandanna over her hair, kerchief style. "There, we can paint you up before we head out for the day."

"Thank you," Mei said, then got up and went over to the food box. She rummaged around until she found a tea bag, then got a cup and headed back to the fire.

Brother looked over and noticed the lady musicians had been watching his salon work with fascination. He frowned. "Am I doing something wrong?"

They all adopted innocence on their faces. "No, not at all."

Brother frowned and held up his brush. "Would one of you like to be next?"

"Well, as long as you're offering," Trinity said before anyone else could answer. She scooted over to Brother and turned her back.

Brother looked at the happy tangles of Trinity's honey brown hair. He picked a spot, then brushed and detangled, trying to avoid pulling out her hair.

Mei thought the sight of a big scary looking guy like Brother fussing over a pretty little thing like Trinity looked odd, but Brother focused on his task. That was Brother's way; doing his best at whatever the job was. Mei continued watching. As he worked on Trinity's hair, he casually chatted with the musician, who, from her expression, was adoring the skill and attention Brother was giving her.

Mei was seeing a new side of Brother. She didn't know what she was seeing in his face and mannerism, but when he interacted with Trinity, he was ... what was it? More at ease? Relaxed? Casual? Sometimes Mei hated not knowing the right words, but she knew for sure, whatever Brother and Trinity were doing seemed like a good thing for both.

After working on it for a while, Brother pony-tailed and banded Trinity's hair. "Do you have a bandanna or something special you want me to put over it?"

Trinity looked like a drowsy cat. "Uhm, I might have something in my bag."

"Wait here," Brother said, then rummaged in his pack and pulled out a dark green bandanna and tied it around Trinity's hair. "There you go." Then, in a gesture familiar to Mei, Brother scratched from the back of Trinity's neck to between her shoulder blades. Mei thought it was odd. Trinity seemed to appreciate it, because her eyebrows went up and she gasped and shivered at the same time.

Brother looked over at Audrey and Marla and held up the brush. "You two want a turn?"

"No, I'm good. No thank you," they said in unison.

"Okay," he said, then sat back and stretched. "Mei Mei, will you get the da jit jow liniment out of my other pack, please? I feel achy this morning."

Mei nodded and headed over to the truck.

Trinity turned and looked at Brother. "Are you okay?" She seemed genuinely concerned.

"Oh yeah, just some aches. No big deal."

"Are you sure?"

"Oh yeah, one dab and I'll be good to go."

Mei brought the bottle over. She opened the cap and told Brother. "Take your shirt off and hold still."

Brother got up. "We should go over there."

Trinity put a hand on his knee. "Don't go on our account."

Brother blushed. "I don't want to gross you out, especially before breakfast. Speaking of which, we have to do that thing before breakfast."

"Stop it," Audrey said.

"Yes, stop it," Marla echoed.

"What?" Brother said. "You guys said last night you would do it."

Mei sensed Trinity was getting upset with Brother. She balled up her fist as if to slug him, but instead reached out and grabbed a handful of his shirt. She looked him in the eye and took a deep breath.

"Stop trying to dodge us," she said, very seriously. "If you want privacy, that's fine, but don't dare treat us as though we're stupid. We know you paid a price for your service. We read about you online." She released his shirt and put a hand on his arm. "Mary Flynn told us stories about the hospitals she toured in Afghanistan."

"We don't care about any stupid scars," Marla said. "We're just thankful you're here with us. Old friends, back together again. We just wish my brother could be here, but he couldn't get the time off."

From where he sat packing his gear, Mr. White spoke up. "My friend, it's wrong to treat brave, caring, and capable people as anything less. Like the ladies said, if you want privacy, we understand, but don't you feel ashamed."

George, standing next to Mr. White, gave Brother the thumbs up.

"Thanks, guys," Brother said with a nod. "I was never going to be a model before I joined up." He took off his shirt. Mei was used to seeing him shirtless, but for the others to see him shirtless in broad daylight was a sight to behold, especially if they hadn't seen it before. Mei poured out some medicine onto his back and rubbed it in. Since her hands weren't strong enough, she used her elbow to knead the knots out of his muscles, leaning in to exert appropriate pressure. After a couple of minutes, she felt the knot relax.

Brother's relief was quickly evident. After a few minutes, he stretched and stood up. "Much better! Thank you, Mei, and thank you everyone!"

Trinity and the sisters excused themselves to make a trip to the port-o-potty.

Brother looked over at Judyta, who was still sleeping. He looked at Mr. White. "Want her up?"

"It's about that time, isn't it?" Mr. White asked. "Judyta, wakey wakey!"

No response.

Louder, Mr. White said, "Judyta, time to get up!"

Judyta grumbled, then rolled over, eyes still closed.

Brother looked at Boudicca. In a stern, but not loud voice, he commanded,

"Boudicca. Up!" The big dog got up and looked at Brother. "Yes!" He pointed at Judyta. "Boudicca, wakey wakey!" Boudicca stepped over and snuffled her drooly mastiff flaps at Judyta's face. "Yes!" Brother said. "Kiss her face!"

Judyta fussed and finally woke up. "Aaargh!" she yelled, then burrowed into her sleeping bag. Undeterred and with tail wagging, Boudicca burrowed after her.

"Aaaallllllrrright!" Judyta yelled. "I'm up!" She sat up, opened the end of the sleeping bag, and with her tangled bed head hair, looked a happy Boudica in the face, who promptly muzzled the sleepy girl's face. Rather than reacting cranky, Judyta reached up and petted Boudicca's massive, happy face. "Hello dog."

Everyone chuckled. "Want me to come save you?" Mei asked.

"Nope," Judyta grunted. "I'm good."

"Mei, rescue your pal, and get that kaiju under control," Brother said, then prepped the wash table as Mei rounded up Boudicca. Mei watched him for a moment, and felt she knew what he was up to but didn't want to say anything and ruin the shock.

"Ladies and Gentlemen," Brother said, "I believe the water will soon boil and be ready for tea. We have an assortment to choose from, or if you'd rather have coffee, we can put on a pot." With his back to the group, he rummaged in a food box, then turned and put a big Dutch oven over the fire, without saying a word to indicate what he was doing.

The group collectively assented to tea, and Mei got out the tea bags and extra cups. After counting cups, Mei called to Brother, "we're a couple of cups short."

Brother was washing up in the washbasin. "Not to worry. How many do we need?"

"We have five cups and eight people," Mei said.

"Okay. You and I can share a cup, then the sisters perhaps, then the Whites, and Trinity."

"What about us?" Marla said, as the musicians returned to camp.

"We don't have enough cups for tea, so we need to share." Mei said.

Judyta piped up. "I'm not sharing a cup with George, so how about you and me, Mei?"

"Sure," Mei said.

Mr. White, who was arranging his sleeping gear, looked at his son. "George and I can share."

"Sure, dad."

"Marla and I can share," Audrey said.

"Good," Brother said, then sassed Trinity. "Then I won't have to share with Trinity. I hear she has cooties and likes to backwash into the cup."

"A girl must do what she must do to get her own space and her own caffeine," Trinity said. Everyone chuckled, then poured their tea.

Listening to Brother and Trinity verbally dueling and trying to one up each other was becoming a frequent occurrence in the short time they'd been together. Mei noticed Brother tried to be clever and funny when he teased the pretty lady, but didn't cuss or make mean comments. But he did tease Trinity by holding her mug just out of her reach for a moment before he gave it to her then retreated to the wash table.

"Why, you scoundrel!" Trinity said in mock outrage.

"Scoundrel?" Brother scoffed as he lathered a shaving brush in a mug. "Not bad," he said, then lathered his face with shaving soap. "Sounds like Han Solo. How about 'rogue?'" He wiggled his eyebrows. "That sounds more..." he snapped his fingers, "dashing."

Trinity fired back. "How about Masher? Sounds like a pervy guy from the 1920s who's awkward, unwashed, and grabby."

"Ouch. How about Scallywag?" Brother volleyed back, then paused and looked up. "No, sounds like a young kid like Tom Sawyer. Rake? No, sounds like a manual laborer."

"I have it. Bounder!" Trinity said.

"How Steampunk of you. If you're going Victorian on me, how about, 'Mollynogger.' That would be more accurate." Brother nodded and smiled, then adopted a terrible British accent. "I shan't deny I've done a bit of mollynogging when the opportunity presented itself. Or should I say *herself,* maybe *her selves?*" He winked at Trinity.

Trinity's face betrayed recognition of Brother's fancy word. "You're not even a little bit ashamed about your wicked exploits, are you?"

"Should I be? Don't you think fire breathing strumpets around the world appreciated kindness from a dashing young gentleman adventurer such as myself?" He continued matter-of-factly. "Besides, they were all paid in full, and I've passed all my blood tests, so no harm, no foul."

"Ohhhh, you!" Trinity spluttered in frustration, and the rest of the campers chuckled.

Brother boomed in a ring announcer's voice. "Ladies and Gentlemen, the contest was decided by TKO in the 7th round. Winner and still champion - BRROOTHER!"

Trinity scowled as everyone clapped and cheered.

"And now to continue my morning beautification," he said, then snapped a thick leather strap to the table and rolled it out. He opened a straight razor and stropped it on the belt. "Now I need to concentrate. No mirror."

Trinity stepped forward. "I'll be glad to take a razor to your face," she said with an evil smile.

"I think I'd rather have Boudicca do it." Then, in a low voice, he said, "I might never whistle again."

Trinity spoke in a growly scary voice, "Oooh, why so serious? Let's put a smile on that face."

"Whoa," Brother said, "that was fucking creepy right there." Then he mock shivered, and the crowd all clapped and cheered.

In her own ring announcer voice, Trinity said, "ladies and gentlemen. The rematch was stopped in the first round by TKO. Winner and new champion, Trrrinity!" She clasped her hands and held them over her head like a triumphant boxer.

Brother smiled and held up the razor in salute, then continued shaving.

Mei watched the crowd. Except for Mr. White, everyone watched closely, and unconsciously scrunched and shifted their faces, mirroring Brother's face as he shaved.

"How am I doing?" he asked.

Mei walked over and pointed out a few places.

Brother shaved the areas closer. "Thank you, Mei." He finished, then washed up and wiped his face. He cleaned the razor, rinsed it in alcohol, then gestured to his equipment. "Hey, Steve. Want to give it a shot?"

Mr. White nodded. "You know, if you don't mind, I think I will. It's been a while since I've used a straight razor. It might be fun to wake up the old skills."

"You know how to shave like that, dad?" George asked, impressed.

"Indeed I do, son. Indeed, I do."

Brother cleaned up the wash station, refilled the washbasin, and stropped the razor a few times on a leather belt. "All yours."

"Thank you, sir," Mr. White said, stepping up to the table.

Still standing by the table and one of the food boxes, Brother turned to the musicians. "Well, here's where I tell you my cunning plan from last night."

"Well, I for one, am intrigued," Audrey said.

The others nodded.

"I need you to get dressed in your daily wear, no shoes, and get Marla's fiddle and case and meet me over there by the orchard fence. George, can you help me? We need a table. Let's use the old picnic table over there."

Clearly inspired by his idea, Brother gathered up his pack and a grocery bag and headed over to the table. He stopped and looked at the rising sun from different angles. George helped him move the table over to the fence by the orchard. Brother fist bumped George and talked with him for a second. George blushed but nodded, then Brother punched him lightly on the shoulder.

As George trotted over to the campsite, he passed the musicians coming to meet Brother. Mei, Judyta, Boudicca, and a clean-shaven Mr. White watched the spectacle with interest. Brother fussed and grinned to himself the entire time.

"Okay, let's have you sit at the table," Brother said. He acted very animated and precise, and shushed all questions. He took a few minutes to pose the girls at the table while checking the light. Next, he laid a cloth over the table and arranged Marla's fiddle case exact. Finally, he set up a plate with scones and three glasses, one in front of each musician. He reached into the pack and pulled out a bottle of expensive Irish whiskey.

"Is he...?" Mr. White asked.

"What? What's he doing?" Judyta asked.

"Shh," Mr. White said kindly but firmly.

Brother poured whiskey into each musician's glass, then stepped back and pulled a digital camera from his pack and started taking pictures, checking the results on the monitor. He also snapped some pictures with his cell phone. He put his cell in his pocket and picked up the camera again, then took a breath. "I'm going to count down, and you all hold the glasses up in a toast, then drink while I take pictures."

"We don't drink very often" Audrey said. Marla started to speak but was interrupted when Mr. White laughed. He snorted as he fought to keep the laughter in.

"Okay now, boyo," Trinity said. "What's going on?"

"You don't see what we're doing?" Brother asked.

"No," Trinity said. The sisters shook their heads.

"I'm taking a picture of three young ladies drinking whiskey before breakfast!" Brother said, with a gigantic smile on his face.

Mr. White cut loose with a roar of laughter. George ran up, wearing one of Brother's spare kilts. It didn't fit perfectly, but where it didn't fit, George had it belted down. He looked at his father, who cracked up.

The girls sat stunned for a moment before breaking out in laughter. Brother took pictures of everything.

They picked up their glasses, toasted Brother, and drank. Then they raised their glasses again and elaborately toasted all the onlookers who gathered to see what was going on.

Boudicca wandered over to the table and coaxed a few pets from the laughing musicians. Brother took pictures of that as well.

Mei wasn't sure exactly what was happening, but it was quite a spectacle. The crowd cheered and clapped. Soon the glasses were empty.

Marla picked up her fiddle and played a quick tune.

After a time, Brother put down his camera and clapped and bowed to the musicians. "Okay, I think it would be prudent to eat breakfast after drinking whiskey on an empty stomach."

When the girls got up, they all hugged Brother, and he put his hand out to Marla. "Do you mind taking a picture with my pal, George?"

"Of course not," Marla said, then beckoned to the kilted lad. "Come here, me laddo."

Blushing and obviously smitten, George hurried over.

Brother took pictures of the two standing up next to the fence. Marla reached up and squeezed George's arm.

"You strong enough to hold me?"

Cotton-mouthed, George mumbled, "ye-ees."

"Are you ready?" Brother asked.

George nodded and put his arm across Marla's mid back, and she lightly jumped into him. George swung up his other arm and cradled her knees. They smiled for the camera as Brother clicked away., then George gently put Marla down.

"Thanks, big guy," Marla said, then gave him a sweet hug and headed over to the table with the girls.

George was thunderstruck. Brother and Mr. White walked over and slapped George on the back.

Chapter 89

Brother

They all returned to the campsite. The mood was cheerful. Everyone picked up their own things and hung them up to air out. Brother loaded the Dutch oven, put it over the fire, and placed coals inside. Then, he put the futon mattress back into the bed of the pickup. While everyone worked, the smell of cooking bread steamed up from the big black pot. Mei and Judyta put their 'raider gear' back on. They made sure Boudicca had food and water, then Mei rummaged in one of Brother's bags until she found the camouflage face paint.

"Hold on," Brother said. "You got a little pink from being out in the sun yesterday, so we need to put on more sunscreen today." Brother found the tube of sunscreen and applied it to any of Mei's skin exposed to the sun. He handed the tube to Judyta. "Here, kiddo, have your Pop see to your screen."

Then Brother painted Mei with camouflage paint. Thick, bold war stripes on her face and neck, smears of black, dark red, and pale blue blotched onto her arms and legs. "There," he said. "You're ready for the hunt." He smiled and then roared, "Raaaaah!" in Mei's face.

Instead of being upset, Mei yelled, "Raaaaah!" right back.

Brother smiled and hugged his sister, resting his forehead against hers. "I love you, Mei Mei. I'm glad you're here and sharing this with me."

Mei teared up and sniffed. "I never knew I could cry from being happy," she said, and wiped her eyes. "But it's okay."

"Yeah, it is," Brother said. "Let's see how the scones are doing." He got up and went over to the fire. Using a hook, he lifted the lid from the Dutch oven. Steamy bread aromas rolled out. He looked in. "Looks pretty good."

"Good!" Audrey said "I'm ready for some breakfast."

"Well, this is a warmup to tie us over for a bit," Brother said. "We'll eat more over at the food tables."

"Oh, so you mean there's going to be a second breakfast?" George asked, and everyone chuckled.

Brother laughed. "Yeah, a second breakfast. Oh, God, if only I could have that kind of metabolism again." He put the big cast-iron pot on a hot plate on the table and then scooped out the scones.

Everyone immediately grabbed a hot scone and juggled it until setting it down on the table, while waiting their turn at the butter and honey Mei set out.

They served more tea, and soon the scones were gone.

"What's everyone doing today?" Brother asked.

"We have a couple of sessions to sit in," Trinity said, speaking for the trio of musicians.

Mr. White held up two curved swords in their scabbards he'd retrieved from a case. "I'm giving a lecture on Scots in Poland and a demo on the Polish Saber, since so many Scots were exiled and went to live in Poland. George is going to help me." He handed a saber and belt to George, then belted on his own.

Judyta said, "Mei and I are going Rumspringa, but I want to wear my saber too, father."

"Do you think I can count on your cool head and discretion?" Mr. White asked.

"Oh yes, Daddy!" she said, then reached into a hidden pocket and pulled out a set of too-big-for-her brass knuckles. "I've had these this whole time on this trip, and I haven't slugged George once. Well, at least not while wearing these."

Brother choked on the coffee and ended up spitting it out.

Audrey and Trinity giggled.

"Hey!" Mr. White said. "Those are mine!"

Judyta furrowed her brow. "But I have them now, and I was a good daughter and wiped off your fingerprints."

Brother turned away and cracked up, then made eye contact with George. "This is my everyday life," George said.

Brother roared with laughter.

"Just you wait, bub!" Mr. White said to Brother. "This will be your life soon." He paused for a second to calm himself, then turned back to Judyta. "Why don't you come by the demo and we'll see then."

"Okay, daddy. What time and where?"

Mr. White told her.

Judyta smiled. "Mei and I are going to dance some more today."

"Take it easy, okay," Brother said. "It's going to be another great day, and we have the evening ceremony tonight. At about 2:30, you need to go to Pop's house to shower, fix your hair, and dress for the evening ceremony. I should be around to remind you, but if not," he looked at the sun, shielded his eyes and pointed, "when the sun is about there, head over."

"Are you going to wear your uniform tonight?" Mei asked?

"Uniform?" the girls asked.

"Oh, God," Brother said in exasperation. "Yes, I am."

"It's amazing," Mei said.

"Well," Trinity said, cocking an eyebrow, "Pop asked if we would play during the formal dance tonight. Now I'm glad we said yes. Right, girls?"

Audrey and Marla clasped their hands in mock rapture. "Squeeeee!" Then they fanned themselves. "Le Swooon!"

Brother groaned. "Really?"

Chuckling, Mr. White slapped Brother on the back as he walked past.

"Anyway, I'm going to finish getting ready, then head over for a second breakfast," Brother said. "Everyone is welcome to join me or not as they see fit." He looked over at Mei. "Mei, you're the exception. You come with me. You need to eat some scrambled eggs and maybe fresh fruit if they have it."

The people of the campsite were making their final preparations to set out for their various destinations when the war horn sounded. The deep and loud notes echoed across the fields. Like the day before, people cheered and applauded, then whooped war cries.

Brother stepped away from everyone, stood up straight, drew in a deep breath, threw his head back and let go with his challenging roar. Mei swore she could feel the ground shake. When he finished, Brother kind of collapsed in on himself, but was smiling. Other roars and war cries sounded back. Still smiling, Brother gestured everyone into a hasty group around him. He held up his hands, and speaking, counted down on his fingers, 3, 2, 1, then let out his war cry. Half a second later, everyone in the camp joined in.

The sound was incredible! Mei felt a shiver up her back and goosebumps sprang up on her arms. Brother stomped his feet and clapped his hands in a slow, hard cadence rolling like gunshots. Mr. White joined in, then everyone followed. George clashed the Dutch oven pot lid with a metal spoon. Then Brother raised his arms then dropped them, and everyone in the camp stopped to catch their breath. The horn in the distance stopped. and the last notes faded as a lone bagpiper tuned up and played.

Brother looked over at the group of his friends, then took Mei's hand. "Let's go." Then, in an unusually semi-formal voice, said, "you're all welcome to join Mei and I for breakfast. If not, please have a great day, and if you need anything, just let me know."

As a group, they all walked from around the vehicle barrier and into the open.

Chapter 90

Mei Mei

Mei, Brother, and their friends went to the big breakfast served at the cooking line. Lots of people attended. Just before they arrived, Brother pulled Mei aside. "Sweetie, there are going to be a ton of people wanting to talk with me." He rolled his eyes. "I'm not sure I want to talk to all of them, but I should try. They're good folks and many supported me with letters and care packages when I was overseas. But you don't have to talk. Be polite if someone asks you something, but if you want to run off with Judyta after breakfast, go ahead."

"I don't want to abandon you if you need me," Mei said.

He blushed and smiled. "Thank you, Mei Mei. That's nice and brave of you to offer. But just the same, go and have a good time." He patted her on the back, then they went and got into the breakfast line.

Mei chose cheesy scrambled eggs and apple slices. Brother chose a small bowl of oatmeal with fruit. He was right. People stopped to say hi and hug him before he even got his food.

After they found a place to sit, Brother became a target for well-wishers. Clearly the man of the hour, people mobbed him. Men shook his hand, grandmas hugged him, moms kissed his cheek and introduced him to kids, cousins, and friends. Everyone wanted to ask him how he was doing.

Brother appeared genuinely happy to see them as well. He answered their questions and asked a few of his own, but it was clear the people had good intentions.

Mei was finishing her food when Judyta bounded up, wearing a saber scabbard across her back. "Let's go, Mei!" They cleared Mei's dishes and ran off toward the sound of music.

They found the same older people Scottish country dancing on the dance floor as the day before. Without hesitating, they joined in. Even though the dancing was a different style than the day before, Mei loved it. The minute she stepped onto the dance floor, she lost herself in the music and the swirl of the steps. Everyone was smiling and having a good time, even the people who didn't dance well.

Time passed quickly, and Judyta and Mei danced several sets. Mei got to dance with Arik and Don, and spotted Brother dancing with Miss Janice. Finally, Judyta tapped Mei on the shoulder and pointed across the field. Mei bowed to her partner, a tall fellow with a long-braided ponytail and red tartan kilt, then ran along with Judyta to a crowd.

Mr. White was giving a class on the history of Scottish people in Poland. The gist of his presentation was, a long time ago, things were bad in Scotland, so a group of Scottish people went to Poland. Things were hard there, but the Scots were tough and smart, so eventually built lives for themselves. Many of them became soldiers and learned the saber. Mr. White was a good teacher who made it interesting. After his talk, he drew his saber and showed everyone its features and their names.

Then, he pointed to George, who drew his saber and performed a drill based on commands Mr. White issued in what Mei guessed was Polish. George was good! Normally, even though George was strong, he was bulky and slow when he moved. But not now. He cut the air with his saber with flashing speed and glided across the grass in a dance instead of his usual teenage boy lumber.

Mei cheered and thought she saw him smile.

When George finished, Mei turned to say something to Judyta, but Judyta bounded past her into the teaching area. She had removed the saber scabbard from her back and laid it down. She bowed to her father, then raised her saber. Mr. White and George clapped, but Judyta's expression of poise and concentration had replaced her normal impish expression. She slowly rotated her saber in continuous smooth cutting arcs, cutting and slicing the air.

Mr. White and George clapped harder and faster, and as they sped up, so did Judyta. When the crowd joined in applause, Judyta's movements became a blur! Her saber moved so fast it looked like a propeller! The saber snaked back and forth; the blade flashed in the sunlight just like in an action movie! The crowd applauded faster and faster, and Judyta kept pace. Then, abruptly, she snapped her arm around her body, so the blade flashed in front of her and then behind her in the same crisscross motion! She stepped lightly and danced with the sword. Then she executed a slow twirl, the blade whirling around her body. She made it look easy.

Mei felt afraid for, yet amazed and impressed with her adopted sister. But Judyta's expression never changed. Mei was sure the sword blade buzzed as Judyta twirled. Faster and faster it went until it looked as if Judyta was in a bubble of flashing silver, and then all at once, Judyta snapped the blade to a complete stop, locked out in front of her, ready to take on any challenger.

The crowd roared and cheered for her performance, Mei most of all. Afterwards, Mr. White continued his lecture to a growing crowd.

After a bit, Mei wondered what time it was. She asked a kilted man nearby for the time, then waved her hands to get Judyta's attention. She pointed in the direction of Pop's house, and Judyta waved. Mei blew her a kiss, then headed off to look for Brother.

Chapter 91

Brother

Brother awoke at the crack of dawn. He'd finally slept well, but it took a while to drop off to a deep sleep. Maybe because Trinity had snuggled her back and backside against him during the night. Unfortunately, she'd stayed in her sleeping bag. Sigh. He'd originally planned to keep the beautiful musician at arm's length, just chatting and playing word games with her, but she seemed to have her own agenda. Was she serious, or just playing chicken with him? He was puzzled, but he was also, well, *him*. At a certain point early in the night, he rolled over in his blankets and pulled her and her double sleeping bag into a spoon. He swore he heard her sigh.

His morning needs made him get up out of his blankets. The morning air felt brisk, but cold was never an issue. Boudicca thumped her tail when she saw him. He reached over Mei to pet the pup and stood. Damn! Pain in the form of cramps sprang to life. He silently eased himself into a stretch and worked out the worst of the pain. He then stoked the fire, loaded it with wood, and he slipped on his sleeveless flannel shirt as he went to the port-o-potty.

By the time he returned, the fire had grown nicely and people were stirring. He put more wood on the fire, then walked into the orchard for his stretching in privacy. He just couldn't get all the kinks out. He liked sleeping outdoors, but a hot shower would feel nice.

He saw Mei get up. She caught his eye then pointed to herself then the port-o-potty.

He nodded, and she took off with Boudicca trotting along beside her. They were a cute pair. He gave up hoping all the kinks and cramps would go away and settled for calming down the worst ones. He brushed his teeth, then walked back over to the campsite. The fire was crackling and throwing off a pleasant heat.

He put the kettle and a pot of water on to warm up. Most everyone was awake and seeing to their morning routines. The exception was Judyta, who was still out cold. Boudicca burrowed next to her and Mei, who was sitting in her sleeping bag. Brother walked by the truck and grabbed the morning pack and sat down behind Mei. He held up a hairbrush, and Mei scooted over so he could do her hair. He was much more skilled at taming 'bed head' than he'd been before, and it didn't take long to fix Mei up with a great ponytail bandanna combo. There! Salon ladies everywhere—beware! Brother and his fingers of doom are on the job, and the experience can be all yours for the right price. He smiled. If the guys on the team could only see him now. He scratched the back of Mei's neck and smiled at her shiver. He'd made progress. A few months ago, she wouldn't have let him touch her if she were on fire. Now she felt comfortable with physical affection.

Brother looked up to see an audience. The three musicians had been watching him with a combination of surprise and mild awe. He thought he would shock them for fun, so he asked if anyone of them wanted to be next, figuring they'd all decline.

Unfortunately, Trinity called his bluff, and before he knew it, she was sitting in Mei's place in front of him. Hoisted on his own petard, Brother set to work. He would do his best. After all, he had to uphold his reputation. As he worked, he tried to ignore Steve, who laughed at him out of the corner of his eye. Fink!

Taking the utmost care, Brother tamed the tangles of Trinity's curls, but it took a while. He wrestled her hair into a ponytail and tied it into place with a bandanna. The back of Trinity's neck was exposed, so he took the liberty of scratching it with his fingertips.

Trinity reacted with an adorable shiver and a set of goosebumps. Gotcha.

Shortly after finishing the salon stuff, like an old and unwelcome friend, his pain spiked again. He had Mei grab the liniment from his other bag. Another recent development with Mei was her willingness to rub the liniment on his back, and it wasn't even his idea. It happened one day a week or two ago while he was sitting in the living room contorting, trying to get a hard-to-reach spot on his back.

"I can get that for you if you want me to," Mei had said.

"You don't have to."

"I can get it. Give me the bottle."

"Okay," he said, then reluctantly handed her the bottle. If he hadn't been in such a hurt locker, he'd immediately run the scenario past the Chaplain, Dr. Tom, and Dr. Amy, and they'd all assure him everything was appropriate.

Since then, Mei had become adept at applying the liniment. Today, his anxiety was caused more from being shirtless in broad daylight, where everyone could see his scars. His peacocking last night was a brief pass and review, mostly in the shadows. Normally, he wore his scars and tattoos like badges of honor, but only around other Marines or men in the hospital with scars of their own. He didn't want to freak out his new friends. After all, how could they relate? The upside was, at least he would no longer need to worry about shadow dancing with Trinity. One clear look in daylight would probably send her off at a dead run.

He'd tried to put the slide and glide on the lot of them, making excuses and tossing out platitudes, but they weren't buying it. They made him sit down and let Mei take care of his back. Afterward, Brother felt thoroughly ashamed of doubting his friends. The comic relief came later when they woke Judyta up by siccing the flappy faced pup to wake her up with wet snuffles and sloppy mastiff kisses.

Watching Judyta wake up was something. She went from a dead sleep to waking up like an explosion. But once awake, she sat there calmly petting Boudicca.

The water was ready for tea, and they all played musical cups, with Brother and Trinity ending up sharing. He didn't mind, and seized the opportunity to verbally spar with the pretty musician. They cracked each other up and provided fun entertainment.

Brother then put on a demonstration on how to shave with a straight razor, and seemed to wow everyone except Mei, who'd seen him shave with a razor many times.

Everyone was dressing to prepare for the day. Brother dressed up in his kilt and t-shirt. He gave George a quick lesson in dressing in his old kilt. The boy looked as if he was having second thoughts, so Brother didn't pressure him. Brother sent George back to where the girls were dressing.

"Hey, ladies, it's time to do that thing I was talking about last night." He paused and thought for a few moments. "Okay, the double entendres make that statement sound horrible, but I need you to get dressed in your daily wear. No shoes and get Marla's fiddle and case and meet me over there by the orchard fence. George, can you help me get a table? We'll use the old picnic table over there."

The girls were game, so he set them up in a great photo shoot with their casual beauty glowing in the morning sunshine, sitting arranged with the violin and glasses of whiskey around the picnic table with the orchard in the background. Brother had set up a tripod mounted digital camera and began shooting pictures. He reposed and rearranged the sitting to make sure each musician was the featured subject of a couple of pictures, as well as great group pics.

Steve chuckled from behind Brother. It must have dawned on him what Brother was doing. Brother had the ladies toast at once and took a few more pictures, then all had a shot together.

The musicians were having a good time, but he could tell they were tired of him ducking questions, asking what he was doing.

"You don't see what we're doing?" he asked.

"No," Trinity said, and her sisters shook their heads.

"I'm taking a picture of three young ladies drinking whiskey before breakfast!"

Once the girls realized how far Brother had gone into Celtic music nerdom to pull this entire situation together, they applauded and cheered his aplomb. George came up wearing Brother's old kilt. Brother helped him straighten it as best he could, then thought he would hook up his little brother.

Brother put his hand out to Marla. "Do you mind taking a picture with my pal George?"

"Of course not," Marla said, then beckoned to the kilted lad. "Come here, me laddie boy."

George looked as if he could walk on clouds.

Brother took fun pics of Marla and George together, including a great one of George holding Marla in a cute cradle hold. The stars in George's eyes were priceless.

After they picked up and went back to camp, Brother put pre-prepped dough into the Dutch oven and put it in the fire to bake. Everyone packed up the sleeping gear and dressed for the day. They fed and watered Boudicca and Brother put sunscreen and war paint on Mei. "There," he said, "you're ready for the hunt." He smiled and then roared, "Raaaaah!" in Mei's face. Instead of being upset, she yelled "Raaaaah!" right back.

Brother smiled and hugged his sister for a few seconds. He felt proud of his baby sister and they'd come so far in such a short time.

He started getting emotional, so he shoved it down and diverted his attention. "Let's see how the scones are doing."

The scones were doughy, but otherwise hot and tasty. Really, they were a precursor to the second breakfast served over on the main side by the members of the Celtic Culinary Club. After eating their second breakfast, they discussed their plans for the day.

Steve and George were going to lecture and demo the saber. The musicians were going to sit in with session groups and play. Mei and Judyta were going 'rumspringa.'

Brother was stuck being the 'man of the hour.' Ugh.

He made plans to meet with Mei so they could go to Pops and get ready for the evening ceremonies. They were all finalizing their respective plans when the horn sounded, starting the day, and calling to the blood.

He sounded the first roar by himself. He stepped away from his friends, put his head back, took a deep breath, and let loose. His cry shook the ground and split the sky. Here I am. I stand between you and those that I love. Come if you dare.

He smiled and looked back at his friends as other roars and calls sounded across the Ceilidh. The looks of surprise on the White's faces reminded him he'd forgotten to tell them about the morning call, but the musicians were smiling as they prepared for the next call. Brother stomped his feet and clapped his hands, and everyone joined in.

The horn sounded again, and Brother counted down. Three, two, one, and let loose. The entire camp joined him a half second later. The sound beat against their bodies and lifted their morning spirits.

People out of his line of sight began to rhythmically drum and bang on things to make noise. 'Boom,' 'Crash,' and the noise grew louder across the field.

The horn sounded for the third time, longer and louder, drawing out its call until everyone in the entire celebration joined in. The deep sounds swirled and rushed around the field, skipping across the ground, bouncing off the trees, and swirling around one and all in its path.

And then it stopped, and so did the people. A slow drone of bagpipes started, and the skirling notes started their day. Everyone cheered.

Brother nodded to his friends. "Let's go."

They went to breakfast, and sure enough, Brother was swept away by more loved ones, well-wishers, and friends from long ago. He was happy to see everyone, but wished he could be anonymous again so he could join his campsite friends as they all drifted off to their destinations. Mei and Judyta rocketed off toward the dance stage, the musicians went to the session group's play area, and Steve and George faded into the crowd. But it was all good.

Brother caught up with Pop, Arik, and Sarah for a time. He quickly learned to ease his band of well-wishers towards something he wanted to see, but far enough back to avoid disturbing the event. In this way, he got to watch Mei and Judyta dance, Michael compete in the caber toss, and the last few minutes of Steve's lecture on the saber. Watching George's cutting demo was impressive. The way George normally walked was more of a lumber, but when he held the saber in his hand, he became fluid and much more graceful.

Brother wasn't surprised when Judyta did her sword dance. Nevertheless, watching her in action was remarkable, especially for someone her age. She had a gift.

Brother made a point of going over to watch Trinity, Audrey, and Marla play a few sets with other local musicians. They sounded every bit as good performing in a cow pasture as they did on stage with all the sound tech support. No wonder Mary Flynn took an interest in their careers. He still felt proud of that introduction; bloody wound story be damned.

In between sets, he talked to Audrey and Marla. Trinity was occupied talking music with a fan. Besides, whatever was building between him and Trinity, he still admired and cared for her two sisters and wanted them to be happy. He focused on making them the center of his world while he talked with them. He thanked them for sending letters and emails while he was in the service. They thanked him for the gifts he sent from around the world. They joked, took selfies, petted Boudicca, talked about Mei and what their family was up to. He learned the conversation was the kind he'd missed without realizing it. All too soon, it was time for them to play, and he needed to go. He made sure Trinity saw him leave, and since they didn't get to talk, when they locked eyes, he smiled and winked at her. She responded with the kind of smile that made his day.

Brother saw George and Steve, so he handed off Boudicca's leash to George so he could watch her during the ceremony. He felt odd letting someone else look after Missy B, but George would do a good job. It was almost time to meet with Mei, but he became involved with parents of his old friends. They were great people, and after all of the shenanigans Brother made them endure when he was a teen, he felt like a jerk for wishing them to hurry and move along, but time was running late.

Fortunately, Mei came to his rescue.

Chapter 92

Mei Mei

Looking for her Brother, Mei went by the food tables and picked out a sandwich. Munching away, she found him talking with a group of people near the athletic fields. In reality, the group of nice people were holding him hostage, oblivious to his subtle hints he needed to leave. Mei turned her attention to several big guys competing on the athletic field; throwing heavy weights and cheering one another. Most were almost as big as Brother, and she thought it odd but cool to see them wearing kilts. She was relieved they wore trunks under their kilts. She would've felt embarrassed for them to see bare behinds flashing while they competed.

She watched for a while, but the group of people around Brother wasn't going away. Summoning an unusual burst of courage, Mei skipped through the crowd and took Brother's hand and waved, a broad smile on her face. "Thank you for finding him!" To Brother, she said, "It's that time. We have to go."

"Oops," Brother said in mock surprise. "I'm sorry, everyone. I can't keep Miss Janice waiting." He allowed Mei to pull him away towards the house. The group waved goodbye.

Mei clutched Brother's hand and shared her lunch with him. They walked across the fields to Pop's driveway. They managed to avoid other well-meaning people wanting to stop and talk. As they approached the front door, Brother waved at someone through the living room window Mei couldn't see. He let them in, and they removed their shoes in the front hallway.

Miss Janice poked her head around a corner. "Is it time for you two to clean up?"

"Yes, it is," Brother said. "I think I'll need to put in extra work on Mei's hair."

Miss Janice waved her hand. "Nah. She'll be fine. All your things are hung up in the back bedroom, and you'll have the back bathroom all to yourselves."

"Thank you!" Brother said, then led Mei past the kitchen full of ladies and down a hall to a bedroom. Inside, his uniform was hanging up, along with Mei's best new dress and other clean clothes. He took her into the bathroom and pointed out towels, washcloths, soap, and stuff for her hair he must have bought at the salon.

"Take the washcloth and big comb and go shower," he said. "Take your time and scrub well. We need to get all the war paint off and wash your hair well. There's a small mirror in the shower, as well as the big one in here." He smiled and patted her hair. "I think you might have a bird's nest in there. When you're done, dry off and put on your shorts and tank top. We'll team up on the rest." He lay a quick kiss on her forehead, then left the bathroom, closing the door behind him.

Mei stripped off her clothes and stacked them in a pile. As she undressed, she realized Brother let her keep her throwing knife. It had become a part of her. She set the sheathed knife on the bathroom counter, then looked at her reflection in the big bathroom mirror. She was grubby from top to bottom, and her hair looked a mess, but she was also tan, taller, and her eyes were bright, clear, and brave. She felt good. She undid her hair and let it down, quickly brushed it out, then picked up a clean washcloth, a long-handled scrub brush, and went in and turned on the shower. She gasped as the first blast of ice-cold water hit her in the face. Fortunately, the water warmed up quickly, and she went to work. Her hair was tangled, but she worked it over with shampoo, crème rinse, and a wide bristle comb. She washed herself from top to bottom, spending extra time on her hair, then got out.

She wiped the steamed up mirror with a towel so she could see herself. Yep, she'd missed some war paint here and there. She worked the spots with her washcloth, then dried off with a fluffy towel and dressed in her tank top and shorts. Finally, she combed her wet hair, then wrapped up with a towel and went out.

Brother was sitting at the kitchen table with a sheet wrapped around him. He'd washed, or at least wet his hair, and Sarah was giving him a haircut. "Hey!" he said with a smile. "There was a person under all that happy dirt."

"Stop fidgeting!" Sarah said.

"Once Sarah finishes with me, we'll fix your hair," Brother said.

Mei hoped that meant he would do her hair. She liked Sarah but wasn't sure she knew how to do her hair, and today was important. Maybe some other time it would be okay, but not today.

Sarah snipped away with her scissors, then looked around Brother's head with a critical eye. She stopped and looked at a prominent scar behind one of his ears and into his scalp and gently ran a finger over it.

He twitched. "What are you doing?" he asked.

"You still have that old scar here," Sarah said.

"Well, yeah."

Mei noticed the mood in the room changed. Sarah abruptly got misty eyed, Brother got sheepish, and Miss Janice pointedly turned her head away so no one could see her face. Mei didn't like the change hanging in the air, so blurted out, "Brother has scars all over. Why is that one important?"

"I got caught up in a fight a long time ago, nothing to worry about," Brother said hastily, then unwrapped the sheet and stood. "It's no big deal." He ran his hand through his hair. "Thank you, my dear lady," he said with his charming and sincere voice.

Sarah just shook her head and sighed in mock frustration, but stood on tiptoes and kissed the scar.

Brother blushed, then turned. "Come on, Mei Mei."

They went back to the bathroom. Brother lifted Mei up onto the counter next to the sink and went to work on her hair with the comb, brush, hair dryer, and detangler. He was firm but surprisingly gentle, even when hitting a few tangles. They smarted for a minute, but it wasn't too bad. Mei's hair had grown longer since living with Brother and doing a formal hair style was a challenging task. She tried hard not to fidget while he patiently continued. Sarah came and stood in the doorway to watch, without comment. At one point, they chuckled when he combed a small twig out of Mei's hair.

After he'd untangled and brushed out Mei's hair, Brother used a hair dryer and then braided her locks, then he finished by coiling the braids into a tight bun. He lifted her off the counter and onto a stepstool.

Mei was surprised at the change when she looked in the mirror. She looked like a different girl. Her hair was beautiful, but her face, and especially her eyes, looked different since she'd lived with Brother. They looked more relaxed and calmer. Her eyes, once wide and afraid, now looked... Tougher? Wiser? She wasn't sure, but felt happy.

Brother leaned down and put his head next to hers, and they both looked in the mirror. "What do you think? Did I do okay?"

Mei grinned. "Oh yes, yes indeedy," she said, using one of his lines.

Brother chuckled and lifted her off the counter. "Go show the ladies in the kitchen while I shower. When I'm done, we'll get dressed in our formal gear."

Mei closed the door behind her and went back to the kitchen. She hadn't noticed Sarah had left the bathroom doorway, but found her in the kitchen with Miss Janice. The other ladies were gone.

"Well, look at you!" Sarah said, and Miss Janice turned and said, "wow!"

Mei felt immediately on display as Sarah turned Mei's head to admire from different angles. Sarah took pictures of Mei, Mei and Miss Janice, and Mei and Sarah. Mei felt odd being the center of attention.

Miss Janice looked at Sarah. "I'll be damned, but he did a great job. Then again, he was always good at whatever he put his mind to, but never tell him I said that."

Both ladies laughed.

"What does that mean?" Mei asked.

"Mei, your brother is very special to us, and he has a weird superpower," Sarah said.

"What's that?" Mei asked with raised eyebrows.

"When he sets his mind on doing something, he'll research and work at the task until he gets it right," Sarah said. "He makes no excuses, and he's so brave he's not afraid to make mistakes."

Miss Janice added, "It's his willingness to work and make mistakes that helps him succeed. You should have him teach you that."

"It also makes people jealous of his success," Sarah said.

"Why?" Mei asked.

"I don't know. Maybe they're not as willing to fail in front of everyone, or maybe they're not as willing to work as hard, but he's never mean about it, he just does it."

"Oh," Mei said. "So, it's a superpower I can learn?"

"Oh, yes you can," Miss Janice said. "In fact, it's important that you learn it." She handed Mei a glass of juice, then paused in thought for a minute. "Baby girl, you've had it rough, no mistake about that, but you have your brother now. The very best thing you can do for yourself is to apply all the lessons he's taught you. Some things won't be nice to hear, but they're important just the same."

Mei listened intently.

Miss Janice was clearly thinking hard for the right words.

"When he teaches you something, you need to keep two things in mind. One, he won't teach you anything until you're ready, and two, what he'll teach you are things most people don't learn until they're adults, if they ever learn them at all. Just keep that in mind."

"I will," Mei said.

"Okay, I have to get back to work," Miss Janice said, then returned to the kitchen.

"I don't hear the shower anymore," Sarah said. "Maybe Brother's done. Go check."

Mei went back down the hall and knocked on the bathroom door.

"Is that you, Mei?" Brother asked.

"Yes."

"Okay, just a second."

Mei heard sounds to indicate he was dressing. The door opened, and as steam rolled out, Mei saw Brother wearing a pair of trunks and the flannel shirt with the cutoff sleeves. His face was lathered with shaving cream. He turned back to the mirror, picked up his straight razor, and shaved. At an opportune moment, he asked, "did my work pass inspection with the ladies?"

Mei grinned. "Yes, they said you did good, but they expected it because they said you win at everything you set your mind to." She paused for a moment. "You win because you work hard, learn, and are brave enough, and don't care if you make mistakes."

Brother looked at Mei in the mirror's reflection. "Oh, is that right?"

"Yes, and they said it's one of your superpowers, and you would teach me."

"Is that right?"

"Yes."

He continued shaving. "I don't always win. Did you stop and think maybe I was already doing that?"

Mei thought for a minute. "I didn't think of that at first, but when they were talking about it, it sounded familiar."

Brother winked at Mei, then finished shaving, and washed his face. "Before we get you all dressed up, why don't you use the bathroom?"

Mei used the bathroom, then joined Brother in the bedroom.

"Go ahead and dress yourself," he said. "When you're done, I'll help you put on the finishing touches."

Mei took the dress off the hanger. It was the prettiest dress she'd ever seen. Brother had it made just for her. There weren't any store tags inside and the cloth was unlike other dresses she'd owned. She put it on and it fit well. She put on her stockings and shoes, then glanced in the mirror. A beautiful young girl standing up straight and proud looked back. For a moment, she became overcome with emotions. A lump formed in her throat and her face flushed, but she was determined not to cry. She'd cried enough lately.

Mei coughed when she heard a knock on the door. "Come in."

Brother came in and stopped, looking Mei up and down. "You sure make that dress look good."

He always knew the right words. He thought she made the dress look good. He didn't say the dress made her look good.

Mei kept herself under control. "Thanks. You got it perfect. The color is perfect, and it fits just right!"

"Well, alright then, but there's just one more thing," he said, then walked up behind her, reached into his shirt pocket, and pulled out a black box. "Hold still." Opening the box, he took out a beautiful silver chain necklace with a pendant, then leaned down and hung it around Mei's neck. "There you go. The pendant is called a Dara Knot, and symbolizes an oak tree, which means strength, wisdom, leadership, and power. I thought it might be a good luck charm." He inhaled. "It was mom's."

Mei froze. "Mom's? Like my... uhm, our mom's?"

Brother smiled. "Nice catch. Yes, it was in her things I got from the estate lawyer." He looked at the silver necklace for a moment. "I didn't even know she wore jewelry like this. For that matter, I don't know her ethnic heritage. I suppose I'll need to find out someday." He kissed her cheek. "Is it okay?"

Mei lost control and grabbed him around the neck and squeezed. He hugged her back. She held on tight for a few moments.

When they parted, Brother stood up straight. "Well, it's my turn to get dressed. Go and show yourself to the ladies, and ask Sarah to take some pictures."

Mei walked back out into the dining room.

"Wow!" Miss Janice said.

"Oh Mei! You look fantastic!" Sarah added.

For the next few minutes, they rained down compliments on Mei. Again, it was a lot and Mei felt odd being the center of attention. She turned away and swiped on her mask, then took a breath and turned back.

Without Mei asking, Sarah took out her camera and snapped pictures from various angles. At one point, she stopped and looked Mei in the eye. "Mei, relax. It's okay to smile."

Mei tried to relax and go along with the program. She chatted with Sarah and Miss Janice when she heard the bedroom door open, then close, and Brother entered the room.

In his Marine dress blue uniform, he was an awe-inspiring sight. The dark blue coat was tailored for his big chest and shoulders and hugged his trim waist. The stock collar was custom fit his 'pit bull neck.' Several medals were pinned on the left side of his blouse and there was a gold badge pinned above them, and on the right were rows of multicolored ribbons. He wore a white belt with a gold buckle. The trousers weren't as dark as the blouse, and a red stripe running the length of his leg. His black shoes shined so brightly; Mei swore she saw light reflecting across the room. He wore white gloves and a white hat with a black brim under one arm. Because of the angle of his arm, she saw striped patches sewn on the sleeve.

Mei had immediately taken a mind picture of him standing in the doorway. He projected an awesome, no nonsense persona, that was more than putting on the uniform or getting the haircut. She wasn't used to seeing him in this light. His expression radiated a focused power and strength above and beyond his normal expression. She thought hard to explain the difference, but didn't have the words.

All the talking and fussing in the room had stopped, and everyone looked at Brother. He smiled and strode the rest of the way into the room with a deliberate, almost marching step.

"Well, you cleaned up nicely," Miss Janice said.

"Thank you, Miss Janice," he said with a smile, then turned to Sarah. "Will you do the honor of taking some pictures?"

"Try and stop me."

Over the next hour, more and more people of the Clan arrived. Sarah took dozens of pictures with dozens of poses of Brother and Mei, Michael and his girlfriend, Arik and Sarah, and all the kids also took pictures. The men wore their formal kilts, shirts, shoes, and jackets. Some also wore a Scottish hat called a 'Glengarry bonnet,' with a long tartan sash over their shoulders, and an array of swords and knives.

The ladies wore long formal tartan skirts, long sleeve white shirts with lace on the sleeve, and long tartan sashes in the same colors as their men's. The children wore a version of what their parents wore. Everyone was outside on the far side of the house, catching the last of the day's full sun for pictures, when Pop and Miss Janice came out of the house. They were magnificently attired. In all his formal finery, Pop looked like a true lord from the stories of kings and queens Mei had read. Miss Janice looked like a lady of royalty.

Brother stood straight and proud, and more than once, Mei noticed people staring at his medals. A couple of men shook his hand and talked to him. She couldn't hear their conversation, but it all seemed to suggest there was more to Brother than she knew. Important things. Regardless of what it meant, she felt proud to be there with him. Mei received many compliments on her hair and dress too.

Chapter 93

Mei Mei

They all gathered and took several group pictures. Soon, a bagpiper, Scott, joined them, and Pop called them together to line up as if in a parade. Pop and Miss Janice led the parade, walking arm and arm. Then Arik and Sarah. Brother and Mei walked behind them with Brother escorting Mei on his left arm, and others behind them. Scott was out leading the procession and pumped the bag on his pipes. They all proceeded at a slow pace out to the Ceilidh field.

It was all so exciting! With the dresses, the formal proceeding, the parade, and the loud, harsh but beautiful music of the bagpipes, Mei felt goosebumps rise on her skin! The procession headed across the property and onto the Ceilidh field, passing a cheering crowd. They moved at a steady pace to the stage area. People had gathered on the benches on a dance floor in front of the stage. Trinity, Audrey, and Marla were there, with Mr. White, Judyta, and George seated nearby.

When Judyta saw Mei dolled up, her eyes bugged and her jaw dropped. George's expression was one of surprise as he admired Brother's uniform. As the parade approached, the White family stood, drew their sabers,

and saluted.

As Pop passed the Whites, over the skirl of the bagpipes, he ordered, "Veterans! Eyes Left!" Pop, Arik, and Brother snapped their heads to the left. Pop snapped a return salute to the Whites, then sharply returned it to his side. Mei saw the proud soldier Pop once had been.

The parade walked the circumference of the seating area, then stopped between the stage and the seating area. Scott stopped playing and walked up the steps to the stage. Pop kissed Miss Janice on her cheek, then escorted her to a front-row seat, then returned to Mei and Brother, then turned and led them up small stairs onto the stage across from Scott. Mei and Brother were the only people in the parade to follow Pop up onto the stage. Everyone else sat in the audience, while a group of kilted men lit torches around the outside of the seating area.

When the crowd sat, they cheered Pop as he walked out to the center of the stage.

"Welcome, everyone," Pop said loudly. "Thank you all for coming to another Clan Ceilidh. It's been too long since we gathered here as kith and kin. Many of us are Scottish or Irish by heritage, but we're all Americans. We've tried to incorporate our Celtic traditions into this gathering. Maybe we don't do it to the letter of the ancient traditions, but hey, we're Americans. We do what we want, right?"

The crowd laughed and clapped.

"The important thing is, we gather here by choice to make a place where we all belong, and no matter where we go, we know we belong to people who are rooting for us, people we matter to, people who expect us to carry on with honor. The Ceilidh reminds us there's a place to come home."

The crowd applauded in approval.

"Now we can formally adopt people into the clan, and can also banish people for destructive behavior. I'm pleased to announce we haven't banished anyone this year."

Applause.

"Next, we welcome newborns, or we would if there'd been any born since last year, which is good, because I see some tired parents out there. I'm sad to say we don't have any wedding engagements to announce this year, but that's okay. All in good time. And I'm happy to say none of our dear ones have passed away this year."

Applause.

"Next, because education is important to us, we recognize those of us making themselves better by attending college or trade school. This year, we have Shannon Campbell and Jason Forrest heading off to college, so please stand."

The two young people stood to a round of applause.

"And a special mention to Nancy Thompson, who is returning to college to pursue her own degree now that her kids are grown and gone!

One of the older ladies working at the food tables stood up to cheers and applause.

"Good for you, Nancy!" Pop said. "We also honor trade schools, because they're important in our society, so I have the pleasure of recognizing Kaitlyn Foreman, who is going to mechanic school, and Keith Frazier, who is out of the Army and attending electrician school!"

Both stood and were applauded.

"We all might be Scots, Irish, Polish, Korean, Mexican, white, black, tan, or whatever combination our parents brought forth into this crazy world, but we're all Americans, and live in the best country in the world. We have a special place in our clan for our members that raise their hand, put their lives on the line, and serve us in the Armed forces. They deserve a place of honor as they go forth and serve for us. Please remember, even if they enlist to what sounds like an easy job or a comfy duty station, in a moment's notice they can be called to sacrifice their lives, and all they're ever had, and all they ever will be."

"We're all different faiths here, but all of us recognize conviction, and a verse from the bible comes to mind when I hear of anyone who puts their lives on the line for their nation." Pop took a breath, and in his steady voice, recited:

"And I heard the voice of the Lord saying, whom shall I send, and who will go for us?

And I said

Here am I, send me."

Pop paused to let the words sink in. "So, tonight, we honor Colin Macintyre and Conner MacDuff, who enlisted in the Army, and Jennifer MacGregor, who enlisted in the Air Force. Godspeed, and thank you."

Applause erupted from the audience as the three stood.

Mei was surprised. She had no idea girls enlisted, too.

The applause ceased, and Pop continued. "It is also our way of recognizing our returning veterans. As the old saying from Cicero goes,

'Poor is the nation that has no heroes....

Shameful is the one that, having them ... forgets them."

"So, we of this clan will never forget our people and what they've done for us." He cleared his throat. "Tonight is special for me because I'm proud to say, after a long and busy enlistment, my son has honorably retired and returned home from his service in the United States Marine Corps. I'm very proud of all of my sons and their service, and also glad they're all home." Pop was clearly bursting with pride as he turned and motioned Brother forward.

Brother gave Mei the hand signal to stay in place as he marched forward to stand next to Pop at attention. Then he clicked his heels and turned to face Pop. Standing face to face, Brother executed a slow and precise formal hand salute.

Pop looked caught off guard, but quickly recovered, came to attention, and returned the salute.

They both dropped their hands to their side, then faced front and saluted the applauding crowd.

"Okay, son, at ease," Pop said, assuming the role of announcer again, then put his hand on Brother's shoulder. "Now here's what we say to all our returning veterans. Be proud of what you've done. Now, go do better!"

Once again, the audience clapped and cheered as both Pop and Brother smiled.

Pop turned back to the crowd. "Since he's up here, I'll give my favorite and final kind of announcement. In ancient Scotland, the clan was the center of life. Without the community of a clan, life would be terribly, maybe impossibly, difficult. You could join a clan three ways. You could be born, married, or adopted into a clan. Adopting from outside of the clan was rare and only for special people, so it didn't happen very often. Since we're all kith and kin, you need to hear this story and maybe stop any rumors.

As if his deeds in the Marines weren't heroic enough, my son has honored us with a different kind of bravery. He's adopted a special young lady he's brought to us tonight. Due to a hard twist of fate, my son's young sister Mei became an orphan."

Gasps and murmurs circulated through the crowd.

"Well, my son, being who he is, couldn't let a child be abandoned."

"Because he's your son," a voice from the crowd interrupted, drawing loud cheers.

"And our brother!" Arik and Michael said in unison.

Michael laughed and added "We have the scars and the police reports to prove it!" to the laughter of the crowd.

Pop flushed, looked back at Brother and nodded. "Yes, he is."

"Anyway, I'd like to call Miss Mei Mei forth and present her to you tonight. You've probably already seen and talked with her this weekend, but she cleaned up and looks very different now."

Pop and Brother turned to Mei, and Brother waved her over.

Mei took a breath and let it out, then mentally put her mask on and walked forward. Brother had told her what was going to happen, but she still felt nervous. All eyes were on her. She stood beside Brother and they faced Pop. Murmuring overcame the crowd. Pop reached into his sporran and unrolled a long sash of tartan in the same colors and pattern as his kilt.

"Miss Mei," Pop said, "you're a special person to my son, and to me. We'll always be yours, and it's a big decision, but we want you to join us. I don't know if you know this, but a long time ago, your brother stood where you're standing right now, and we adopted him into this clan. But that was then, and this is now. Miss Mei, we, the kith and kin of this clan, would like you to join us, as your brother did. Do you accept?"

Mei said clearly, "I accept your clan's adoption and I adopt you right back."

Pop looked surprised, and Mei saw his eyes flick towards Brother, then back to her. Pop smirked, but continued. "Is there any objection?"

he announced.

No one spoke.

"Is there any objection?" he repeated.

No one spoke.

"Is there any objection?" he asked for a third time. "I ask three times and done!"

He unrolled the sash and pinned it over Mei's shoulder. "We

expect great things from you. No matter what you do or where you go, we expect you to be a decent person, kind, smart, thoughtful, industrious, and brave. You have a long line of everyday heroes behind you. Our people may not look like much, but we're the ones who stand up to evil, fight against injustice, work hard to make things better, laugh and love, make mistakes, pay the price, and return to do better. This is who we are, and this is who you are now.

"Welcome."

Scott fired up his bagpipes as the crowd roared and applauded.

Mei felt overwhelmed and rode a tidal wave of emotions, but to her surprise, didn't cry. She turned and waved to the crowd, then smiled when she saw Judyta cheering and waving her fists in the air.

Mei felt a tap on her shoulder and turned to see Pop gesture her to step back from the front of the stage. He held up a belt with a knife sheath, reached around her and up under her sash to buckle it. Oddly, the knife sheath lay along her waist with the grip of the knife pointed to her right within easy reach. Mei was pleasantly surprised to see the knife in the sheath matched her other throwing knife.

Pop leaned in close. "Fantastic job yesterday. All your practice at throwing and keeping your nerve paid off." He smiled and held up a finger. "Now, don't stop practicing."

"I love you, Pop," Mei said, and hugged him.

Pop hugged her back. "I love you too, Mei."

Pop pulled himself together. "Before we get the party started, I want to thank the Ceilidh Cooking Club, who have fed us with so much amazing food this weekend!"

The crowd gave him a round of applause.

"The CCC is going to have a big breakfast tomorrow morning to clean up leftovers, so let's pitch in and help them. And thank you to all the dancers, musicians, and highland athletics judges who went out of their way to make this event extra special. Thank you so much, folks! Now, here is what we'll do next....."

Chapter 94

Mei Mei

Pop continued talking to the crowd. As the sun set, everyone pulled the benches back to the edge of the dance floor. Others scooted tables around to the outside of the benches and put food down. They turned on the electric lanterns and lit more torches, and out in the middle of the Ceilidh field, others built a bonfire.

Brother came and escorted Mei off the stage. As they descended the steps, well-wishers swarmed to congratulate them with hugs and pats on the shoulder. Again, Mei saw a couple of people she knew were veterans looking twice at Brother's medals. He pretended not to notice, but graciously shook every hand and accepted every hug offered.

Judyta bowled thru the crowd like a pinball and screeched to a halt in front of Mei. She looked her up and down in admiration.

Mei noticed she wore her saber across her back.

"You look so amazingly beautiful, Mei!" Judyta said. "And you got adopted by the clan! Daddyo told George and me what a big deal that is! I'm so happy for you! I'd hug you but I'm pretty grimy."

Mei hugged her sister of choice, ducking the handle of Judyta's saber as she leaned in. "I'm still your sister, Judyta!"

"I know you are. I'm so happy for you!"

Brother came up. "Okay, music and dancing will start up in a little while. Why don't you two get some dinner and we'll meet up over there?"

As the girls turned to go, Brother stopped them. "Wait," he said, then leaned in to speak privately. "The dancing and music are going to be fun, and I encourage you to dance a lot, but just remember, neither of you two have to dance with anyone, and you don't need to make excuses. Just a 'no thank you' is enough. Got it?"

They nodded.

"It should be no bother. I'm just reminding you that me and Pop are on your side."

"Yes, we know," they said.

"Okay, go eat, dance, and have fun!"

Mei and Judyta waved at George, and when he nodded back, they pointed to the food tables. George nodded his understanding, then pointed to himself and made a slash gesture.

Judyta nodded, and the girls headed that way. Or at least tried to. They hadn't gone ten steps when they were stopped by smiling faces and hugs, congratulating Mei on her adoption. Another six steps, same greeting, and so on. The faces became a blur of compliments on her dress, her hair, her adoption, and her brother. Mei had no doubt everyone was sincere, but became overwhelmed.

Judyta didn't escape the kindness mob, either. She received compliments on her raider attire and war paint, and her saber dance performances. Both had their picture taken several times.

Mei looked around and spotted Brother, who had it much worse than she and Judyta. A mob surrounded him, talking, shaking his hand, hugging him, and pinning him in place.

Mei was just reaching her breaking point with all the attention when a strong, matronly, no-nonsense voice cut through the group of people gathered around them.

"Let those young ladies alone! They've had quite enough of all of our niggling for now!"

The crowd parted, and Miss Janice's friend, the ever-formidable Mrs. MacDuff, dressed in the height of formal fashion, complete with tartan skirt, longs sleeves with lace, and several thousand dollars in jewelry, walked through to Mei and Judyta. "Young ladies, have you dined tonight?"

Mei and Judyta shook their heads. "No, Mrs. MacDuff," they said in unison.

Mrs. MacDuff's regal manner commanded immediate respect. "Well, that just won't do. Come along." She held out her arms to the girls, and arm in arm they strolled through the crowd to the food tables. On the way, Mrs. MacDuff said, "Thank you for your patience and good manners, ladies. It's refreshing to see that great unbridled spirit in our young ladies of today."

Again, Mei and Judyta answered in unison. "Thank you, Mrs. MacDuff."

"You're welcome," Mrs. MacDuff said, as they reached the food table. "Here we are, ladies. Please enjoy yourselves."

"Thank you, Mrs. Macduff."

"You are most welcome ladies," Mrs. MacDuff said, then turned to leave.

Mei and Judyta looked at each other, and, in their own way, communicated without speaking. "Mrs. MacDuff," Judyta said.

"Yes?"

"Would you like to join us?" Mei asked.

"Why, thank you, young ladies. That's very kind of you, but I'm afraid I must decline at this time." The grand lady looked at Mei and smiled. "I intend to have your brother dance with me tonight, and I fear the competition for his company from other females will be fierce. But to be scandalously honest, he cuts a rather marvelous figure in his uniform, doesn't he? He was such a rascal when he was young, but what can I say? I've always had a weakness for handsome rogues."

She chuckled at the expression on the girl's faces then turned and headed to the stage.

The girls stood in awe. One lady serving food leaned over to them. "She isn't wrong. Your brother is a handsome fella."

"But he's all beat up and has scars all over," Mei protested.

Another lady spoke up. "Oh child, we know. We know!" she said, then looked at the other ladies serving food. "Right girls? Woof!"

Mei blushed while Judyta tried to hide a giggle behind her hands.

"Okay, okay, girls. Let's get you fed," the first lady said. "Would you like a second plate for your handsome brother?"

"Yes, please," Mei said, then turned to Judyta. "Should we get extra for George?"

Judyta shrugged. "No, it's okay. Part of the signal we passed was him saying he didn't want me to get him anything. It's not as if I'd spit a hocker into his food."

Mei raised her eyebrows. "No food for George?"

"I know, right? He must have something going on, but I'll get extra for my dad or whomever."

They walked through the line. Like the previous night, the cooking club made sure there was an incredible variety of food. Mei couldn't identify all the dishes, and combined with her worrying about spilling food on her dress, she played it safe with her choices. Still, she filled two plates.

Judyta, ever the daredevil, and unencumbered with concerns with a formal dress, plowed through the food like a wrecking machine.

Mei marveled at how much her sister stacked onto two plates. They grabbed utensils and a ton of paper napkins, then headed back to the table where George sat. They managed to land their plates on the table with no spills. Mei sat, then arranged napkins to prevent spilling on her dress. She looked around as she started eating. She saw Trinity and the sisters had set up their instruments on the stage and were tuning up to play. She caught glimpses of Brother circling through the crowd, then spotted Mr. White coming back to the table.

"Heya, Daddyo!" Judyta said from over her stacked plate.

"Well, hello, my most savage daughter," Mr. White said, and patted her.

"I pillaged the food table and brought back spoils of war!" Judyta announced. "Please share with us!"

"Why thank you, that's most gracious. No food for you, George?"

"I offered, but he mysteriously declined, Father," Judyta said. "I was going to address this very topic after dinner, but since you brought it up, I fear our George has been killed and replaced with a shapeshifter. I have no choice but to dispatch who or whatever this thing is for our safety." She held out her hand. "Please pass the silver blade, Father, and I'll deal with this." She looked at George. "Don't worry. Whatever you are, I will make this quick."

"If you touch steel, I'll gut you like a fish and drink your blood, you snot wad."

George growled at Judyta, then looked at his father. "I'm okay, Dad. The game is afoot."

"Ah," Mr. White said as he dug into his plate. "Message received. Carry on."

Judyta started to comment, but George held out a hand to shush her. She coiled to spring at her brother, but Mr. White stilled her with a word, then gestured across the table past them.

Pop had walked out on the stage. "Ladies and Gentlemen, members of our clan, we have a very special treat tonight." The crowd applauded. "Yes! You've seen them on TV, on the internet, and heard them on the radio, so they need no introduction. Please put your hands together and welcome our girls home to our Ceilidh!"

The girls on the stage shifted from a tune up to a slow, cheerful tune. People quieted down and found places to sit. Mei saw Brother excuse himself from a group of people and march over to their table. He slid in next to Mei and removed his cover. Without a word, Mei slid a plate to him. He started eating. He appeared as though he was 'peopled out.'

"How is it?" Mr. White asked, gesturing at the crowd.

"About like I figured," Brother said. "Good folks and happy for us. It's just a bit much."

"Do you want to get away? I'll keep an eye on the brood."

"No thanks, Steve. I'll be okay in a minute, besides I want to see the girls play. After all, when it's all said and done, I'm still their fanboy."

"Effort well spent, sir," Mr. White said. "You're in good company." He nodded to George.

Brother turned and looked at George, who blushed, but didn't deny it.

"Well played, sir," Brother said to George.

The performers warmed up and the tunes they played picked up. Trinity stood up from her chair and strummed her guitar, then spoke into the microphone. "Hello everyone! What Pop forgot to mention is that we got our start playing right here on this stage."

The crowd applauded louder.

"And we're eternally grateful for Pop giving us our big break. Pop is right. We've been away for a while. When you're performing professionally, it's easy to get blown away like a leaf in the wind, so it's great to come back to the beginning and play here again."

Audra nudged Trinity, who looked over at Marla. Marla nodded. Trinity smiled and leaned over to the microphone.

"We had an epic reminder of the first song we're going to play for you tonight. We're ashamed to admit we haven't played it in a long time. So, we'll start with the instrumental, 'Three Young Ladies Drinking Whiskey Before Breakfast.' It should help us warm up. So, here we go. Thank you." Trinity sat down, and the trio started to play.

When Trinity had announced the name of the song, the crowd applauded, while Brother and Mr. White roared with laughter.

Mei watched the girls play. Seeing them as famous performers was far different than she was used to as fellow campers, and they were extremely talented! Each performer handled their instruments with the fluid confidence of the experts that they were. They moved together like they were choreographed. But things changed when they began to sing. Their voices cast a spell that lifted Mei up and carried her away to another place where her body felt weightless and she was happy. The music reminded her of stories of magic and truth, and sad happiness, and more thoughts she didn't have the words to express, but her life was better. A quick look around the table revealed everyone else thought the same way. Judyta and Mr. White swayed to the music, and George was sitting thunderstruck, watching the performers.

Mei glanced at Brother. He had the same faraway look she did, as though the music was taking him away. His expression indicated he was in a good place. As the girls continued to sing, Mei saw the tensions of the day melt off Brother. And Mei didn't have the words to describe Trinity's voice! When the sisters joined in, the music became more like the sounds of struggle and triumph, and welcoming hope.

Rather than struggle to define what she felt, Mei just closed her eyes and let herself be carried away into the night. She felt like climbing to the highest part of Pop's barn, then finding a magic ladder of light to transport her into the starry night.

The sound of applause brought her back to earth. She opened her eyes and clapped along with the crowd. The girls had finished playing, and Pop stood on stage thanking them in person.

Mei leaned over to Brother and took a look from his point of view. Brother had an unobstructed view of Trinity, and unless Mei was mistaken, Trinity was looking directly back at Brother.

As the performers exited the stage, they were mobbed by fans. Pop picked up a microphone. "Ladies and Gentlemen, our honored performers have given us a special treat with their performance tonight. They appreciate your support and friendship, but please respect their space."

The crowd parted, and the girls came over to the table. Brother, Mr. White, and George stood up for them, and Mei and Judyta quickly followed.

Mr. White greeted them formally. "Ladies, I'm mostly Scottish and Irish by heritage, and I've lived in both places. I've spent more than my fair share of time in pubs and concerts, so please understand the depth of my compliment when I say unreservedly that your music is the finest of its kind I've ever heard." He bowed gallantly.

The musicians all thanked him with hugs. Mr. White was supremely pleased. Judyta and Mei pounced on Marla and Audra with hugs and dancing in place, then Audra and Marla took pictures, marveling at Mei's dress and hairdo.

Trinity and Brother faced off silently for a moment, then Brother's stern face softened. He stepped forward, scooped up Trinity in his arms and hugged her tight. Trinity squeezed him hard in return. The sisters, Mei, Judyta, Mr. White, and George all clapped and cheered.

Brother eased Trinity down, but instead of letting her go, he slipped his hand across the small of her back and lifted her chin with his other hand, and, in front of everyone, kissed her passionately.

Trinity threw her arms around his neck, and the applause became louder. Suddenly, but smoothly, Brother twisted Trinity across his body and dipped her backward without breaking the kiss.

Pop's voice boomed from the speakers on the stage. "That's the style, son!"

Brother raised Trinity and gently let her go. Suddenly, Trinity grabbed Brother and drew him back to her, and this time, she kissed him! They parted, but still held hands. Brother said something to Trinity, who smiled.

Mei wasn't sure what the kissing business meant, or whether she approved, but she wanted to be happy for her brother, so she guessed that she was ok with it.

Behind them, some of the amateur performers and musicians were setting up on the stage for an impromptu performance. When some started dancing, Brother put on his cover and led Trinity out onto the dance floor.

Out of the blue, George cleared his throat, held up a crooked arm, and said to Marla, "May I escort you to dinner, Miss Marla?"

Without looking at his daughter, Mr. White pointed a silencing finger at Judyta, who was winding up for an outburst.

Slightly taken aback, Marla said, "Why yes, George, I'd like that." She took his arm.

Audra sighed and pretended to pout. George immediately got a goofy smile on his face and crooked his other arm. Audra took it, then she and Marla both laughed. As the trio walked past the dance floor toward the food tables, Brother locked eyes with George, stopped dancing, and saluted the glowing boy.

After they left, Mr. White lowered his pointing finger. Judyta scowled and Mr. White said, "that was a very important moment for your brother. It took courage, so leave him be."

"Yes, father."

Pop and Mr. Norris walked up to the table. Pop looked at George walking away with Audra and Marla. "Well, good on the lad!"

Mr. Norris agreed, pulled a flask out of his jacket pocket, unscrewed the cap and raised the flask. "To the boy," he said and took a drink. He passed the flask to Pop, who followed suit. Pop passed the flask to Mr. White, who gratefully accepted and repeated the ceremony. Then he raised the flask and saluted Pop. "A fine Ceilidh sir! Very fine indeed."

Judyta nudged Mei. "Let's go dance." They joined hands and headed to the dance floor.

As always, Mei enjoyed dancing. The group played country dance numbers, jigs, and a few slow ones. A bunch of guys asked Mei to dance, but she enjoyed dancing with Brother, Pop, and Mr. White the best. She saw Mrs. MacDuff got her dance with Brother, and for an elder distinguished lady, she danced with gliding grace. When Mrs. MacDuff danced with her husband on the next song, they moved like a lord and lady dancing in a grand ballroom at court, instead of on a rough dance floor in a pasture.

Since Brother was the celebrity of the evening, he was mugged for a dance on nearly every song, but was gracious, and did his best with each partner. He danced with Mei right away, then got carried away by Miss Janice, Sarah, the food line ladies, Judyta, Audra, a couple of moms, some of the not quite adult girls Mei danced with the day before. One time, Mei saw him dancing with three little girls, all holding hands in a ring. He even danced with Marla, but George danced with her as much as he could.

Mr. White pulled Marla to the side. "If you get tired of Casanova, let me know and I'll hit him with a bucket of ice water. I appreciate your kindness and understanding."

Marla smiled. "He's just fine, and his manners would make you proud."

"Thanks."

When the band took a break, a young lady ascended the stage and stood in front of the microphone. "I'd like to dedicate a song to all our servicemen, students, and friends from far away who we haven't seen in a long time. It's a sing along, so please join me." She nodded at a lady with a banjo strapped over her shoulder. The banjo lady started plucking a happy tune, and some ladies from the food serving tables trotted up in front of the stage and started highland dancing to the music.

The singer started...

"'Was you ever in Quebec?'"

"'Bonny laddie, Highland laddie,'"

"'Dancing on a sanded deck,'"

"'My bonny Highland laddie.'"

The crowd sang and clapped along.

"'High-ho, and away she goes,'"

"'Bonny laddie, Highland laddie,'"

"'High-ho, and away she goes,'"

"'My bonny Highland laddie.'"

"'Was you ever in Callao'"

"'Where the girls are never slow?'"

"'(Whistles and cheers...)

High-ho, and away she goes,'"

"'Bonny laddie, Highland laddie,'"

"'High-ho, and away she goes,'"

"'My bonny Highland laddie.'"

Judyta copied the highland dancer's moves, while Mei hoisted her skirt and tried to follow along. She felt clumsy, but it was fun, and she didn't care.

"'Was you ever in Miramishi'"

"'Where you tied fast to a tree?'"

"'High-ho, and away she goes,'"

"'Bonny laddie, Highland laddie,'"

"'High-ho, and away she goes,'"

"'My bonny Highland laddie.'"

"'Was you ever in Dublin Bay,'"

"'Drinking porter all the day?'"

More cheers and shouts)

'High-ho, and away she goes,'"

"'Bonny laddie, Highland laddie,'"

"'High-ho, and away she goes,'"

"'My bonny Highland laddie.'"

"'Was you on the Brummalow,'"

"'Where Yankee boys are all the go?'"

"'High-ho, and away she goes,'"

"'Bonny laddie, Highland laddie,'"

"'High-ho, and away she goes,'"

'My bonny Highland laddie.'"

The singer shouted, "One more time," and the crowd poured it on.

"'High-ho, and away she goes,'"

"'Bonny laddie, Highland laddie,'"

"'High-ho, and away she goes,'"

"'My bonny Highland laddie.'"

So much fun! The dancers bowed to applause and cheers from the audience. The singer and banjo player both waved. Other people got up to sing while they had time in between sets, so people returned to their tables or gathered in groups.

When Mei and Judyta got back to the table, Mr. White and Brother were sitting with Audra and Trinity. "Oh good," Brother said. "It's time to head back to camp, get cleaned up and get to bed, after another long day."

Mei felt disappointed, but Brother was right. It had been a long day.

Brother said to Mei, "our most outstanding guests have prepped the camp while we were getting dressed up, so there shouldn't be much to do. Sarah was so kind as to bring our clothes and gear from Pop's house and drop it off at camp, so we owe her a big thanks for saving us the trip."

The group slipped away when the next song started. Brother held Mei back so just the two of them could walk together. "Did you have a good day?" he asked.

Mei threw her arm around Brother and arm hugged him as they walked. "It was one of the best days ever. I am still thinking about it, nothing but good thoughts."

"Good."

Mei sensed Brother seemed... a bit nervous? Anxious maybe?

"Mei, would you be okay sleeping around the fire with the gang if Trinity and I slept further away?"

What an odd question, Mei thought. "What do you mean?"

"I was going to have a sleepover, just Trinity and me, maybe out in the orchard." "Boudicca, Mr. White, Judyta, and everyone else will be with you at the camp. Would you be okay with that?" He asked with forced calmness.

"Oh, so you'll just be in the orchard?" Mei asked tentatively.

"Yes. In fact, I'll be no further from you than opposite ends of the house."

Mei thought about it. It would be odd not having Brother close, but he would still be nearby, and she wouldn't be alone. She sensed this was important to him, but she checked her feelings way down deep, and although apprehensive, she felt okay, except for one last hard question. "If I say you can sleep somewhere else, will you think I don't want you to be my brother anymore?"

Brother gaped and stopped walking. "What? No! I didn't want you to think I was running off on you."

"Oh no, not at all," Mei said, "and I don't want to suggest I don't need you, but I don't mind spending the night with Judyta and Boudicca. Besides, I know you'll come for me if I need you."

Brother pushed out a deep breath. "Oh yes, Mei Mei, always!" He gave her a crushing arm hug.

They walked back to the campsite in the dark, which Mei didn't mind on such a pleasant night. Besides, Brother was with her.

Everyone was busy at the camp. The musicians were stowing their instruments, Judyta was filling a pot with water, Mr. White was stoking the fire, George was laying out sleeping gear, and Boudicca was supervising.

Mei went over to pet the big pup and checked her water and food, then got her sleeping t-shirt and shorts and went to the privacy curtain to change. She found it comical to be in a private space yet still hear everyone. Listening to friends and family chatting as they went about their business felt odd. Mei made sure her mother's necklace was safely stored away, then stepped out to let Brother in, carrying a hanger and his garment bag. He handed her the hanger for her dress, then stepped in.

Mei heard him take off his uniform. She hung up her dress and got her sleeping bag and rolled it out next to Judyta's. Judyta and Mei snapped on Boudicca's leash and took her for a walk, stopping at the port-o-potty. Far off, people sang on the stage and gathered around the bonfire, still blazing in the night.

The girls returned just as the water in the pot was steaming. Brother, wearing his cut off Cammie trousers and sleeveless flannel shirt, poured water into two wash basins, then stood back and gestured to the musicians. "Ladies, I have water ready for cleanup." He turned to the White family. "Got another bowl for you guys here."

Mei brushed her teeth, let her hair down, and waited for more water to heat. The musicians took the basin and went behind the privacy curtain. Judyta couldn't care less about privacy and was scrubbing up a storm on her face and arms. George soaked a washcloth, then headed into the dark for privacy. Brother chatted with Mr. White, sipped whiskey, and petted Boudicca.

Mei found it all comforting. Soon more water was ready, and she washed up.

Brother tucked Mei into her sleeping bag, with Judyta next to her and Boudicca nestled between the two of them. The pup slept on her back with all four paws sticking up in the air. Everyone was settling in and relaxing from the busy day.

"Will you two sing for us?" Trinity asked Audra and Marla.

The sisters smiled and shook their heads.

"Awe, come on," Trinity insisted, then looked at Mr. White and Brother. "I'm known as the singer, but these two can really hit the notes. I'm trying to get them to sing more on our next album." She looked back at the two girls. "Please?"

"I'd like to hear some," George piped up as he sat on his sleeping bag.

"You know I'm down to listen," Brother said.

Judyta poked a thumbs-up from her sleeping bag.

Audra and Marla leaned in and whispered to each other, then nodded and sat up straight.

"Here's an old one we like," Audra said. "And we think it's right for here and now." Marla nodded in agreement

They hummed together for a second to get the notes on key...

"'On waves of love my heart is breaking'"

'And stranger still my self-control I can't rely on anymore'" "

'New tide, surprise, my world is changing'"

"'Within this frame an ocean swell behind the smile, I know it well'"

"'Beneath a lover's moon I'm waiting'"

"'I am the pilot of the storms, adrift in pleasure I may drown'" " 'I built this ship it is my making'"

"'And furthermore, my self-control, I can't rely on anymore'"

"'I know why'"

"'I know why'"

"'Crazy on a ship of fools'"

"'Crazy on a ship of fools'"

"'Turn this boat around, back to my loving ground'"

'Oh, no, oh, no'"

"'Who claims that no man is an island?'"

"'While I land up in jeopardy, more distant from you by degrees'"

"'I walk this shore in isolation'"

"'And at my feet eternity draws ever sweeter plans for me'"

"'I know why'"

"'I know why'"

"'Crazy on a ship of fools'" "'Ah, crazy on a ship of fools'"

"'Turn this boat around, back to my loving ground'"

"'Oh, no, oh, no, ship of fools'"

"'Turn this boat around, back to my loving ground'"

"'Oh, no'" "'Crazy on a ship of fools'"

"'Oh, crazy on a ship of fools'"

"'Turn this boat around, back to my loving ground'"

"'Oh, no, oh, no, ship of fools'"

As soon as they started singing, Mr. White's eyes snapped over to them, but then he looked off. Obviously, he was thinking of other times and places.

Judyta had reached over and stroked Boudicca's fur. George smiled dreamily at the singers. Trinity had stepped over and sat next to Brother and rested her head on his shoulder, and Brother had reached his big arm around her.

Mei took a mind picture of everything, stretched out in her bag listening to it all and drifted off to sleep on a cloud of joy she'd never known.

Chapter 95

Brother

Mei walked out to the living room to show her new look with her head high and her shoulders back.

Brother put on his uniform piece by piece. Say what you will, the Marine dress blues is a very smart uniform, and the medals, ribbons, and badges he'd earned didn't hurt the image. He was glad it still fit, although snug around the shoulders.

When he was in the Marines, his physique needed to be functional, but now he could buff up. His persona changed when he suited up. The old snap, polish, and professionalism were the order of the day. He took a last look and strutted into the living room.

Brother may have kept his "all professional business" face on, but he felt proud to be decked out in his "Semper Finery," and with his family. He loved his kilt and blades, but there would be time for that later. All too soon, it would be time to put the uniform in storage, so he'd enjoy it while it lasted.

"Sic transit gloria mundi."

Brother and Mei had their pictures taken dozens of times. Fortunately, the rest of the family came and joined them. Everyone was decked out in their Celtic best; kilts, bonnets, sashes, flashes, and an arsenal of swords and knives. Of course, Pop and Miss Janice stole the show. They were wearing the epitome of Scottish formal wear without a stitch out of place. Picture after picture. Sigh.

Later, Scott the bagpiper showed up, and after a few more pictures, Pop had everyone stand in a parade formation and they marched to the Ceilidh field and main stage. Brother gave Mei a quick rundown of what was going to happen.

Scott started playing and began marching. Pop proceeded, and so on, until everyone was in motion. Brother's anxiety spiked, and he struggled to keep it invisible. He practiced breathing exercises as the parade moved towards the Ceilidh, and was centered before they arrived. He snickered to himself, and sarcastic thoughts came without welcome. Some big war hero I am, stressed out by attending a jumped-up family reunion. He acknowledged the self-abusive direction his thoughts were headed, and immediately shut them down. Instead of spinning in his mind, he felt pleasantly surprised Doctor Tom's suggestions worked so well. He praised himself. "Hey! You caught that nasty thought before it got septic! Hell yeah!"

He settled down and resolved to appreciate everyone's effort to make the evening a success. He glanced at Mei walking beside him. She looked radiant in her dress and hairdo. He was proud of her.

Brother snapped out of his reverie when Pop sounded off with drill commands. Brother's Marine brain wasn't sure how the command was supposed to go, but what the hell? He snapped a parade ground perfect salute, returning the honor to his friends. Trinity, Marla, and Audra stood next to the Whites, clapping wildly. Marla was holding Boudicca's leash while George saluted. Brother saw Trinity look him up and down, then smile.

Take it easy, killer.

When the procession reached the stage, Brother and Mei went up the side of the ramp and staged themselves for the ceremony, waiting stoically for everything to start.

The event started without a hitch. Pop was a brilliant master of ceremonies. He was experienced enough without being pretentious, and everyone enjoyed the pageantry.

Brother's heart swelled while he watched Pop. Brother had always wanted to be like him. Without a doubt, he had loved his first father, but Pop had always been hard-working, wise, brave, a tough taskmaster, doing everything for the love of his family.

Pop's powerful words and sincere sentiments were welcome. Recognizing life's challenges and achievements, no one in the audience doubted Pop was talking directly to them. Brother wondered how many lives Pop had changed with this annual speech. Were there people who weren't sure if they should take a chance on furthering their education who remembered what Pop said, then chose to go for it? Was there someone out there on the ragged edge of giving up who thought of the spirit of Pop's speech and decided to press forward? Brother was one of those people.

Brother had stood where Mei was standing, waiting to be adopted into this tribe in the only way that matters, legal paperwork be damned. It had been one of the best moments of his life, and he hoped this expression of belonging and acceptance would benefit Mei as much as it did him. He smiled inwardly. Well, she could do a lot worse than go through life with a couple of hundred hard-working, hard-fighting, pseudo-Celtic maniacs on her side.

He stole a glance at Mei. She had so much promise, he just had to keep the fiends and legal parasites away as long as possible, not to mention doing everything possible as a brother to give her a fighting chance at life. So much to do. He quickly refocused on the present.

Even though it wasn't a surprise, Brother felt slightly embarrassed when Pop recognized him retiring and coming home. Fortunately, his moment in the spotlight was brief, and Pop continued with Mei's adoption ritual. The ritual had meant so much, Brother had memorized the entire process when he was a kid, and it stuck with him.

Mei performed her part to perfection. God, she was good! Pop concluded the ceremony with fanfare from the crowd. It was time for the music and dancing, and the vibe from the crowd suggested the night would be special.

Brother and Mei came off the stage and swam through the crowd as best as possible. People among the crowd offered handshakes and hugs, and offers to drink from flasks and bottles. Fortunately, Brother saw George in the crowd, who gestured that Boudicca was safe at camp. Brother felt relieved, then saw Mei and Judyta carrying plates of food to a table. It wasn't far, but he still needed to wade through the welcoming crowd.

It looked as though the musicians were preparing to play soon. Brother flagged down a team of the young ladies helping put on the music show and asked if they could make sure they had dinner for the musicians.

"Oh, jeeze! Yes! I should have thought of that."

"It's understandable," Brother said. "Don't worry, you guys are doing a great job."

"Hey, thanks," they said, then trotted off toward the food tables.

Brother saw an opening and slipped through the crowd to get to the table where Mei and the Whites were sitting.

Pop was announcing the girls on stage when Brother slid into a chair next to Mei. She was gracious to share her plate with Brother. He was hungry, but wanted to watch the girls play. Music had always been important to him.

Just before the music started, one of the assistant girls stopped by the table and hunched down next to Brother.

"I just wanted to let you know, Trinity, and the girls said I didn't need to worry about feeding them because they plan to dine with you after the show."

Brother nodded. "Thank you for letting me know. You're very kind."

"You bet, big guy!"

The concert didn't disappoint. The girls opened the show by playing "Three Young Ladies Drinking Whiskey Before Breakfast," much to the audience's approval. Afterwards, Trinity thanked everyone, especially Pop, because they got their start playing in front of an audience at Ceilidh. Brother didn't know that. It must have happened when he was overseas.

Audrey and Marla recognized the session groups for letting them play with them, which was a classy touch. Once the talking was over, the girls put on a show rivaling anything they'd done on PBS. Trinity's ethereal voice, combined with Audrey's and Marla's talent with their instruments and backup vocals, shone on the audience like stars. All three of them performing was far more entertaining than the sum of their parts.

Brother relaxed and welcomed the music to seep into his inner self, carrying him across seas, skies, and time. Fatigue, anxiety, and pain melted away, creating a state of bliss. He snapped awake to realize he'd been dreaming with his eyes open. Quickly looking around, he noticed Steve looking at him. His friend nodded and raised his glass in a toast. He put his own mask on to hide his impatience as he waited for the musicians to come off the stage, negotiate the crowed and join them at the table. Brother hugged each lady in turn, but deliberately hugged Trinity last.

Brother drew Trinity into his embrace. "Lady, as you are mine, I am yours."

Trinity blushed, then nodded.

"Let's dance," he said, and escorted her onto the dance floor.

Trinity was a lovely dancer, and Brother hadn't had this much fun in years. He was surprised when Miss Joyce tapped Trinity on the shoulder to cut in! "I've always been a sucker for a bad man in a uniform."

Brother laughed. Soon, Pop tapped Brother on the shoulder and cut in. "I have to be careful. She's a sucker for a bad guy in a uniform," Pop said.

Brother cracked up, then Mei raced over to dance with him, surprisingly followed by Judyta. The night continued, and although Trinity was foremost on his mind, Brother accepted every lady's offer to dance. It was great to see George dancing with Marla, and Steve caught a few dances with the lady he met the day before, thanks to Boudicca.

As the evening wound down and the bonfire crackled in the distance, Brother made sure he saved the last dance with Trinity. They embraced and rocked together. At the end of the song, he kissed her again, and they looked into each other's eyes. Without thinking, He said, "Sleep with me in the orchard tonight." She gasped, then pursed her lips, saying, "Yes, big man, let's."

A wave rolled over Brother, but he put on the brakes. "I'm sorry. I have to make sure Mei's okay."

Trinity nodded. "Absolutely."

The band played a sing-a-long, and the crowd drowned out the rest of their conversation. Brother kissed Trinity quickly, then slipped away to find Steve. He found him talking to Pop and Prof Norris, who Brother had seen come in earlier. Brother was in a full boil from Trinity's company, but calmed himself down.

He welcomed Prof, and shook his hand, then shared a drink from a flask offered by Pop. The whiskey had a pleasant burn, and encouraged Brother to howl at the moon. Instead of pleading 'happy emergency,' he took Steve aside and confided his situation and plan for the evening. "Steve, I know I'm a shit for abandoning Mei."

"Nonsense, my boy, you're a man, you have needs, and a most splendid opportunity. Now, you won't be more than what? A hundred yards away?"

"Maybe less."

"Good. So you'll be close if the need arises. Furthermore, she'll be surrounded by her most protective family, and you'll be back before breakfast." He patted Brother on the shoulder. "You've watched over my children so I could go out. Now it's my turn. I have, as you Marines say, got you covered, little brother. Now go make us proud."

"Okay, I just have to break it to Mei."

Steve chuckled. "You're on your own with that one."

Brother returned to the table and talked with Audra and Trinity while waiting for Mei to come back from dancing with Judyta. The two crime partners soon returned, flushed and all smiles.

"Oh good, here you are," Brother said. "It's time to head back to camp, clean up, and get to bed. It's been another long day."

Mei looked disappointed but nodded.

George and Marla walked up. Marla was on George's arm as he escorted her along, as proud as he could be.

"We're heading back to camp," Audra said to the pair. "Time to wind down."

"George, I might have to take care of something, so would you see to Boudicca if I'm late?" Brother asked.

"You bet," George said.

Brother made sure that he and Mei separated from the group and walked by themselves. He found himself anxious about this next talk with Mei, but he knew his duty and that was to Mei Mei. He would not fail her. However, he found his own wants and needs calling, hopefully he could manage his duty to Mei and his duty to himself.

Brother thought carefully about what and how he was going to ask Mei Mei if she minded him going a ways off to "Spend the night" with Trinity. When Brother asked Mei if she minded, he got a big surprise when Mei replied. Her big worry was that he would think that she didn't want him around if she said that she didn't mind if he and Trinity went off together.

Brother nearly laughed in relief, but he managed to control himself. He didn't want Mei to think that he was laughing at her, when he was really laughing at himself for assuming that Mei would only answer one of two ways. He reassured her and watched her demeanor for sincerity. She was good and his relief was immense. He side hugged the little girl and the continued walking the rest of the way back to camp with their arms around each other...at least as much as Mei could.

At the camp, everyone was going about their business. Brother and Mei changed out of their clothes, then he showered Boudicca with petting and good words. He looked up and caught Trinity's eye. She looked a question at him. He nodded, worried she was having second thoughts.

Instead, Trinity looked back at him, gave him an impish smile, and mouthed, "Good."

That one word set off a symphony of music in Brother's mind. He swore he could hear the "Ode to Joy" playing across the night sky. It must have shown on his face, because Trinity giggled at him, but he grinned and resumed his tasks.

The first was to repack one of this duffle bags with essentials. Next, he rolled his blankets and futon mattress. With all the happy bustling around the campsite, it wasn't hard for him to pick up the bedding roll, grab his duffel bag and quietly fade into the darkness. After all, he was a highly trained Marine night hunter.

Ignoring his aches, he slipped into the orchard, and using the campfire and the starlight filtering through the trees to keep his bearings, he moved several rows back, then a few rows over. He found what he was looking for, a slight depression in the ground creating a bowl between the rows of trees. It would provide him and Trinity their desired privacy.

Moving quickly, he put the mattress and blankets down and lay down on them and checked. Yes, he was out of the line of sight, even more than expected. Perfect. He quickly unpacked and lay out windproof candles, beverages, and food, then took out battery powered warmers, turned them on and put them in the blankets. Still moving quickly, he scraped a patch of earth bare and placed a candle in it, lit it, then moved back several feet. When he looked at the campsite, he couldn't see the candlelight. Good. He dropped glow sticks along the ground to mark his path, then raced back to the camp to make sure he still couldn't see the candle.

He nonchalantly slid back into camp and wandered over to the kettle to get warm water for a wash up. Returning to the darkness, he took a quick sponge bath, then dumped out the dirty water and returned to the firelight.

Everyone had settled in. He tucked Mei into her sleeping bag, then sat down between her and Trinity. Boudicca had claimed her spot between Mei and Judyta. The setting was nice beyond measure. Trinity urged Audrey and Marla to sing for everyone. It took some urging from the group, but they girl settled in and together, sang an old Robert Plant song.

Damn! They could really sing! To be sure, they had their own style, but even Brother with his blast deafened ears could tell their talent was almost as magical as Trinity's. It also clicked for him that Trinity was sending a message to the girls that they were great musicians on their own, they weren't just accessories to make Trinity look good. Brother's thoughts were interrupted when Trinity leaned against Brother and rested her head on his shoulder, and he admitted he felt mighty fine with her in that position.

Mei and Judyta soon conked out, and Boudicca snored between them. Brother looked around. It was time. He stood, reached down and took Trinity's hand, and helped her up. "Good night, everyone," he said. Grabbing her sleeping bag and duffle, he led her to the orchard.

A chorus of 'good nights' and a giggle sounded after them. When they entered the orchard, Trinity said, "Wait a minute. Let me find my flashlight."

"No need. I can see everything ok."

"Okay, I'm trusting you."

Brother led Trinity straight to the campsite he'd made in the orchard with no problems, retrieving the glow sticks along the way. No need to make it easy for people to find them. When Trinity saw what Brother had prepared for them, she looked surprised.

"This is like something out of a fantasy book," she said. "When did you do this?"

"After we got back from the dance."

"Really?"

He chuckled. "Yes, for real. Watch." He laid out her duffle next to his to make a bigger wind break, unzipped her sleeping bag and laid it over the blankets for a bigger bed, and showed her how everything they might need was easily accessible in the near pockets of the duffle bags.

He then lit a few more candles and sat down next to the bed. Trinity kicked her shoes off and got on the bed.

"I don't want to kill the mood, but when was your last blood test and man-type checkup?" she asked.

"Two months ago. And yourself?"

"Two weeks ago, full spectrum of girl tests, and let me cut to the next question." She pointed to bumps on her upper arm. "Norplant."

"Okay, because I have..."

She cut in. "Why don't you come here and give a girl a kiss?"

"Oh yes, yes indeedy."

Making love with Trinity was like a joyous symphony for two on a beautiful spring day in a flower garden. Her silky skin, lovely muscle tone, the delicious curves of her body, fueled by her maddening pheromone scent mingling with the night air, and her enthusiastic exertion, created an euphoric celebration of everything good in life. Brother did his best to follow her responses down the path to what he had euphemistically referred to as a 'condition of swoon.'

He locked the images in his own mind palace. Trinity cloaked in shadow. Trinity in candlelight. Trinity silhouetted in moonlight as it filtered down through the apple trees. They curled together between sensual sessions, talking and exploring each other. At first, Trinity was timid, withdrawing her hand when she touched a scar.

"Oh, baby, I'm sorry. Does that hurt?"

"No. In fact, your touch feels much better than what initially left the scar. Please continue."

She swatted him playfully. "Don't be a shit. I don't want to hurt you."

He chuckled. "It's okay, beautiful girl, you can't." He picked up her hand and kissed it. "In fact, on a number of occasions, you and your music have taken away much of my pain and made the rest bearable."

Trinity's eyes watered, and she lay her cheek on his chest.

He pulled the blanket up over her to keep the chill away and rested his arm across her body, listening to her breathing and the sounds of the night.

"Sing for me, lovely girl."

He could feel her smile.

"Well, there's one song I have saved for a special man, a special time."

She started singing.

"'Take me now baby here as I am'"

"'Pull me close, try and understand'"
"'Desire is hunger is the fire I breathe'"
"'Love is a banquet on which we feed'"
"'Come on now try and understand'"
"'The way I feel when I'm in your hands'"
"'Take my hand come undercover'"
"'They can't hurt you now'"
"'Can't hurt you now, can't hurt you now'"
"'Because the night belongs to lovers'"
"'Because the night belongs to lust'"
"'Because the night belongs to lovers'"
"'Because the night belongs to us'"
"'Have I doubt when I'm alone'"
"'Love is a ring, the telephone'"
"'Love is an angel disguised as lust'"
'Here in our bed until the morning comes'"
"'Come on now try and understand'"
"'The way I feel under your command'"
"'Take my hand as the sun descends'"
"'They can't touch you now'"
"'Can't touch you now, can't touch you now'"
"'Because the night belongs to lovers'"
"'With love we sleep'"
"'With doubt the vicious circle'"
"'Turn and burns'"
"'Without you I cannot live'"
'Forgive, the yearning burning'"
"'I believe it's time, too real to feel'"
"'So touch me now, touch me now, touch me now'"
"'Because the night belongs to lovers'"
"'Because tonight there are two lovers'"
"'If we believe in the night we trust'"

"'Because tonight there are two lovers'"

Damn!

His voice was hoarse. Trinity had put her whole heart into the song. "Thank you, you lovely girl. I don't have the words to describe how beautiful that was. Your voice, you touch something way down inside me. Past all the black stuff I keep locked away. It makes me wish I was better, and I need to try harder, because there is still beauty and good things in the world, and they're worth fighting for. Even when I don't feel like I'm worthy of them. So, if you're singing the siren's song or playing coquette, please let me know, because I'm not playing."

He felt tears splash on his chest, and when Trinity looked up at the night sky, the light of the candles showed the anguish on her face in the light of the candles.

"I'm going to tell you something, and don't you dare make fun of me."

"What, why would..."

Trinity's hand over his mouth muffled his protest, as she sat up and wrapped a blanket around her shoulders. "Just listen and don't say anything." She took a breath. To herself, she said, "God save me from this big, bad, lovely man.

"I dont do this.." – she gestured around them with a hand "I dont go off with just any random guy."

"I have been in love with you since I was eight years old. You were like sixteen. You saved my brother Chris from those bullies who were beating him up all the time. He told me that you were like a real-life hero. I'd seen you running around here at the Ceilidh and over at my brother's school sometimes. You were big and kind of scary, except you were always joking, cheerful, and kind.

You probably don't remember this, but a few months after you helped Chris, We were here at the Ceilidh. I was a little kid and I had gotten lost in the crowd during the big night dance, and I was frightened because I couldn't find my mom and dad, and the music drowned out my calls to them. You came along and saw me alone and upset. You were all cheerful, stupid, horny teenage lug, and you were so sweet. You lifted me up and put me on your shoulder and carried me around until I found my mom and dad. Then you carried me through the crowd to them, then just smiled your big bastard's smile and went off."

She was right; he didn't remember that.

"And it didn't end there. I was little kid sad when your Pop announced you were leaving for the Marines. You didn't even know I was alive. Then I was thirteen when 9/11 happened, and I heard you were going to war. My class at school had a project where we wrote to a serviceman, so I asked my mom to ask Miss Janice for your address so I could send my letter to you. And you wrote me back and sent a picture of yourself because I had asked for one. I was the envy of all the girls in my class. I had my own Marine writing just to me. Then one day it sunk in you were in a war and could die." She took a breath. "You stopped writing me, and I got on with my life. But I was still so worried for you for so long, then Mom would show me the articles in the paper when you won your medals. Then we heard you were wounded, but were okay. You came home then were gone, back to war again. I couldn't keep up with where you were or what you were doing. Then you didn't come home for a long time. By then, I'd started singing with the girls and things were going well for me. We cut that studio demo, and, on a whim, I decided to send you a copy. I think your pop said you were in Afghanistan at that time. I didn't hear back from you, and then months later, I got the phone call out of the blue from Mary Flynn. Mary Flynn! For real. She told me she met you,

you were her biggest fan, and she had to listen to our demo. I can't believe you did that for me. Then Audrey, Marla, and I tried to call and thank you, but we couldn't get through. You'd become this combination of mystery man and frustrating guardian angel.

Then, after Mary spent time with us and got to know us, Mary told us the real story about how you met her. It was in the hospital when you'd been wounded and how all you could think of was helping us. When she showed us your blood on the drive you gave her, the four of us cried on the spot.

We called and emailed and bothered your folks, but still couldn't reach you. Then we went on tour and cut that disc and things started to take off for us professionally, travelling, and doing concerts and all. Then I heard you got wounded again, but worse this time. We toured near the hospital and wanted to come and see you, but your Pop and Miss Janice said you wouldn't let anyone see you, not even them."

She yelled. "You selfish son of a bitch! Damn you for that!"

Brother opened his mouth to defend himself, but Trinity ignored him. After calming herself, regained some of her composure and she pushed on. "Finally, we heard you were going to live, and then we heard you were a father. Oh my god, was I mad! I knew you were a tomcat, but I was so mad at you because I thought you had knocked up some bar fly bimbo. I thought, fine, my little girl crush is over and I could move on with my life with a clear conscious."

She took a breath. "Then I found out you hadn't knocked up some bar fly, but you had rescued a little orphan girl." She held her hands up in frustration. "Who does that? You can't be for real. So, when I heard you were going to be here this year, I informed the girls we were going to come, and they were all for it. However, I made Pop promise not to tell you we'd be here. I wanted to see you with my own eyes and hopefully find enough flaws to get you out of my system. Or at least maybe a quick bang with a bad man, and then I could run away and never look back. But oh, hell no, there would be no freedom for Trinity. What did I find? A giant scarred guy with a little girl and a puppy! A puppy, of all damned things! How am I supposed to get that out of my system? And then you sang and welcomed us to camp with you. Your arm over me while I slept, and even though I played the tease, you didn't make a lecherous move. And then, then, you brushed your little sister's hair right there in front of everyone. I swear I could feel my ovaries pop. You bastard! When you were brushing my hair, I got so fired up smelling your evil man smell and feeling your touch, I had to stop myself from losing my dignity and start purring like a cat.

"Then there was the whiskey before breakfast thing. That was very cool, by the way. Then tonight I made the mistake of asking Mr. MacDuff what your medals meant. Not only did he tell me, he showed me how to find your citations on my phone online with the complete story for each one."

"Since I'm already throwing my dignity at you, when I came here this weekend, I was worried I might want to sleep with you. Then I saw you and I became worried I wouldn't get to sleep with you." Her head bowed. "So there it is, big man, all .... All of it. I got nothing left."

Brother wasn't a dummy. He knew naked vulnerability when he saw it. He sat up, put his fingers under Trinity's chin, and lifted it up. "Thank you for sharing all that, lovely girl....I had no idea..."

"Oh shut up" Trinity cut him off.

So he kissed her. Softly at first, then with increasing heat. They solaced each other until the early hours of the next morning.

No regrets.

Chapter 96

Mei Mei

Mei awoke slowly. As usual, before she opened her eyes, she listened to her surroundings. Like the day before, she heard birds chirping, felt a morning breeze, and people moving around the camp.

She opened her eyes and looked up at the morning sky. It looked to be another beautiful day. Feeling snug and comfy in her sleeping bag, she felt Boudicca's weight pressing against her. Not wanting to disturb the big puppy, she lay in her sleeping bag and enjoyed the morning serenity.

The previous night she'd awakened with an anxious moment, worried about Brother in the orchard, but she'd used mind tricks to calm herself, and felt proud she could get back to sleep. She was proud that she was starting to be able to manage some of her troubles all by herself.

She heard someone putting wood in the fire pit and someone pouring water into a pot. She wiggled around enough to escape Boudicca's bulk and sat up. Sure enough, Mr. White was carrying wood over to the fire pit, and Audrey was using small pieces of kindling to coax last night's campfire into flames.

Mr. White noticed Mei, winked cheerfully, mouthing, 'good morning.'

Mei waved to him.

Audrey waved a silent good morning, and Mei waved back.

Mei wanted to help, so slid out of her sleeping bag and stepped over to one of the storage boxes. Carefully, she lifted the big teapot out and held it up. She waved to get Mr. White's attention, then pointed to the teapot and lifted her eyebrows.

Mr. White clasped his hands together in an exaggerated 'thank you' gesture.

Audrey flashed a double thumbs up, then patted her heart in gratitude.

Careful not to disturb those still sleeping, Mei took the teapot over to the water jug and filled it, then carried it over to Mr. White and handed it to him. She then stepped over to the other storage box and got out tea bags and mugs. The mugs clinked together louder than expected, but when she turned and gestured to Audrey and Mr. White, they put their hands together to gesture applause.

Mei smiled, then hopped over and got back into her sleeping bag. Or at least she tried. Boudicca had apparently decided the warm space Mei left was up for grabs, and a perfect spot for a sleeping puppy. Mei tugged and fussed as quietly as possible, and finally, Boudicca grudgingly relinquished her spot and squished next to Judyta. Mei burrowed back into the sleeping bag.

Although Mei warmed up from the morning chill, going back to sleep wasn't going to happen. After a while, she sat up and took in her surroundings. Nearby, Judyta and Marla still appeared to be sleeping. George, wearing a t-shirt, sweats, and a towel draped over his shoulder, walked into the camp. His wet hair and clean skin indicated he'd found a private place to clean up. Brother and Trinity and their sleeping gear were absent, so Mei figured they'd spent the night together in the orchard. She didn't feel thrilled about him not being there, but felt mostly okay with him spending time with Trinity. She wanted him to be happy, and he seemed happy during those times. Trinity was pretty and talented, and Mei appreciated the fact she didn't act mean or snotty.

Mei sat in her sleeping bag, daydreaming happily. She watched Mr. White pull the teakettle off the fire and fill the mugs with boiling water. He saw Mei looking at him and pointed to a mug and raised his eyebrows.

She nodded.

He got a box of herbal tea and held it up. She flashed a thumbs up, and he dropped the tea bag into a mug and poured in boiling water. He set the kettle down and handed mugs to Audrey and George.

Rather than drink from the mug, George took it and walked around the fire pit to Marla's sleeping bag. He reached down and quietly set the mug close enough to Marla so she would see it when she woke up, but wouldn't knock it over by accident.

He stood up and turned beet red when he saw everyone watching him. Audrey smiled, and Mr. White raised his mug in salute. He walked back around the campfire and made another mug of tea. Mr. White walked by and handed Mei a mug of hot tea smelling of berries.

Boudicca's head jerked up. She locked her eyes toward the orchard, then let out a 'chuf,' which Mei knew preceded a loud bark.

Brother emerged from the orchard, carrying a load of blankets in one hand, holding Trinity's hand in the other.

Seeing Brother, Boudicca thumped her tail vigorously, which was unfortunate for Judyta, whose sleeping bag rested in the impact area of the big pup's bullwhip tail. Fortunately, Judyta just rolled around in her bag for a second and went back to sleep.

Brother and Trinity lay down their stuff and Brother walked over to Mei. He hunched down and put his forehead to hers and hugged her. "Morning," he whispered.

"Good morning," Mei said.

Brother reached over and petted Boudicca, then looked down and pointed at Mei's tea.

Mei smiled and handed it to him.

"Thanks. Did you sleep okay?"

"Mostly," Mei said, then noticing Brother's look of concern, patted his arm. "But good enough."

"Cool. The big breakfast brunch won't start for a few hours. How about I make coffee to go with the tea? Maybe there are still scones to hold us over."

His suggestion was met with a round of nods.

Brother got up and made coffee, and everyone lazed about and enjoyed the morning.

Marla stirred in her sleeping bag, then woke up. She looked up and forced a smile at Trinity and Audrey, then noticed the cup of tea waiting for her. "Oh, how nice," she said in a hoarse morning voice, then reached over, picked it up, blew on it and took a sip. She looked at Audrey. "Thank you."

Audrey grinned. "Not me."

Marla squinted at her sister. "Huh?"

Audrey smiled and pointed across the fire pit to a blushing George sitting cross-legged on his sleeping bag. He smiled shyly and waved.

Overhearing what was going on, Brother stopped and looked over the situation, then looked straight at George. "Well done, sir, well done."

This time Marla blushed and smiled at the likewise blushing boy. "Thank you, George. That was very thoughtful of you."

"My pleasure, Miss Marla."

Brother and Mr. White both put coffee pots on the fire. "Good call," Brother said. "We're a thirsty bunch."

"This way we don't leave anyone out," Mr. White said, then looked at his daughter burrowed in her sleeping bag, braced up against the big puppy. "It's about time for her to be up," he said, then reached down to rock his daughter, but Boudicca picked her head up and locked eyes with him, creating a tense moment between man and dog.

"Perhaps you could inform your pet yak that it is in fact okay for me to wake my daughter," Mr. White said.

"Oh, good God. Sorry, Steve," Brother said.

"Not at all. She's a good pup doing what she's supposed to do, protecting her kids."

Brother snapped his fingers, and when Boudicca looked over, gave her a command. Boudicca got up and trotted over to him. "Yes," he said, and scratched her head.

Mr. White reached down and gently shook Judyta. "Hey, daughter. It's a new day."

"Ugh, hmmppfh." came from the depths of the sleeping bag.

"That's it, time for rising and shining." Mr. White said, and continued rocking.

"Ugh." from the bump in the sleeping bag.

"Okay..." Mr. White started to say, but before he could say anything else the sleeping bag exploded in movement, startling everyone around the campfire. Mr. White jumped back as Judyta jackknifed into a rigid sitting position, her eyes closed, bedhead hair standing on end, arms outstretched. Her resemblance to a zombie was creepy. "Dog!" she grunted.

"Jesus, kid!" Brother exclaimed. The musician girls gasped, and Mei froze.

"Dog! Now!" Zombie Judyta grunted, and in an exceptionally creepy expression, she opened one eye halfway.

"I think she's requesting the attention of your most excellent pup," Mr. White said in a forced reasonable tone.

"Okay," Brother said with a shrug, then pointed at zombie Judyta. "Boudicca, go get the girl."

Boudicca wagged her tail, then trotted over and began licking Judyta's face. Judyta wrapped her arms around the dog with surprising kindness and leaned against her for a hug. Boudicca wiggled for a few moments, flopped across the girl's lap, then rolled onto her back and waved her paws in the universal request for 'rub my tummy.' Judyta obliged.

Brother exhaled. "Alrighty then, I think it's time for coffee."

"After that, I'll take a shot of whiskey in my coffee, if you don't mind," Mr. White said.

"Good idea," Brother mumbled.

As he got up to get coffee, Mei got up and went over to her adopted sister and her dog. She kneeled down and helped Judyta rub Boudicca's tummy. After a moment, Judyta looked over at Mei, and as her eyes focused, she said, "Good morning, Mei Mei."

"Good morning, Judyta."

"Boudicca is a most excellent dog," Judyta said.

"I agree," Mei said, and they sat quietly petting the dog while Judyta came to her senses.

Everyone at the campsite cleaned up, packed, and stored camping gear. Mei and Judyta dressed in a variation of their raider clothes and tied their hair back, but today Mei wore the sash of tartan Pop put on her last night. She felt proud of it and wanted to show off to everyone she belonged to the clan now. She put on her new throwing knife and Judyta strapped her saber over her back.

Brother and George took Boudicca for a walk, and Mei and Judyta sat with Trinity while Audrey and Marla taught an impromptu music lesson. The lute Marla loaned to Mei felt awkward, but she enjoyed trying it out, awkwardly strumming chords. Mr. White snapped pictures as everyone went about their business.

After a while, the morning horn sounded. Long and loud, its notes rolled across the Ceilidh field. After returning from walking Boudicca, Brother motioned everyone to get to their feet. The horn sounded again, and this time Brother raised his hand and counted down with his fingers. When he reached number one, he led everyone in a war cry, just like the day before.

The horn sounded a third time, and the campsite roared again. This time, Mei heard other campsites joining in. When the war cries and cheers died down, the bagpiper started playing. The entire performance still sent shivers down Mei's spine and got her excited, for the day just like it had the day before, but today the music played with a tinge of sadness. Maybe because it was the last day?

As everyone gathered what they needed for the day, Mei found the face paint and called Judyta over. The girls took turns crudely painting each other's faces until they were properly ferocious. Mei noticed Trinity and Audrey watching, and waved. "C'mon," she said cheerfully. "We'll fix you up."

"Well, okay," Trinity said, "but just a stripe or two. We have to teach today and don't want to frighten our students off."

Audrey and Marla giggled, but all three came over and leaned in patiently so Mei could daub a stripe or shading on each of them as Judyta supervised.

Brother and George walked up, both wearing their kilts, and George was wearing his saber. To Mei's surprise, George wore one of Brother's vests (which was big on him), and one of brother's black bandannas tied over his head like a pirate. He looked pretty cool.

Brother took the camo paint from Mei and painted shading with a few slashes onto George's face. He stepped back and looked at his work. "What do you think, Miss Marla? Am I mistaken, or does our young man have a bit of dash to him?"

George blushed through the face paint.

Marla smiled. "He's got an excellent combination of rogue and gent; his people should be proud of him."

Brother answered with a manufactured Scottish brogue. "Och, Aye Lassie. The laddie started this trip as a wee bairn, but we canna deny he's a strong Lochaber now."

To everyone's surprise and delight, Marla responded with a fake brogue of her own. "Oh aye soorr, he's a grand lad, so he is."

Brother laughed and high-fived a smiling Marla. "Let's get a couple of group pictures before we all go our different ways, okay?" he asked.

Everyone agreed and spent the next few minutes snapping pictures. Mr. White even flagged a passerby so everyone, including Boudicca, could pose in a picture together. Afterwards, they all headed over to the breakfast. Mei and Judyta skipped ahead together, and George escorted Marla and Audrey on his arms, and they all walked along with Mr. White. Brother held Boudicca's leash in one hand, Trinity's hand in the other.

The food line was a another happy crash of breakfast and lunch foods from all over the world. Mei and Judyta loaded a plate of different foods to share. Mei got half a waffle with syrup, scrambled eggs with cheese, and a big Irish sausage link, then headed to a big table where Brother had tied up Boudicca. Judyta sat next to her with a plate full of berry scones, buttered garlic naan bread, a small steak, and a pile of peach and pineapple slices. The girls pushed their plates close together so they could reach either one easily. They dug in while chatting about their plans for the day.

When George and the musicians sat down with their breakfasts, George looked at Mei's and Judyta's plates. "What a schizophrenic breakfast."

"Save your breath for cooling your pies," Judyta snapped.

"Did you just drop a line from the movie Snatch?" Audrey asked impressed.

"Well done, miss!" Marla said.

"Yes, well done. Now don't ruin a nice day by getting into a scrum," Mr. White said, sitting down with his plate of food.

Soon after, Brother and Trinity joined them.

Marla looked at Brother's plate. "Is that what I think it is?"

Brother grinned. "Yeah, it is, haggis and eggs, the breakfast of champions."

"Oh my, for breakfast, right in front of everyone," Marla said. "You're not even remotely joking, are you?"

"Joking about breakfast? Whatever would I do that for?" Brother asked as he shoveled a scoop of the Gaelic offal and took a bite.

Marla grimaced. "What if you want to kiss Trinity later? Are you going to kiss her with haggis breath?"

"I thought of that," Brother said, then reached into his sporran and fished out a flask. He unscrewed the cap and held the flask up in a toast. "Slainte." He took a pull, swished it around and swallowed, then leaned over and surprised Trinity with a kiss on her mouth. "Mmmm," he said with a goofy grin. "Pancakey."

He had a giant goofy grin.

Trinity slapped his arm good-naturedly. "Don't be a bore."

"I might be sorry for being a bore, but not for stealing a kiss," Brother said, then resumed eating.

"Keep your hands and your everything else off that girl, you big beast!"

Everyone turned around to see Auntie standing next to Pop..

"Auntie!" Mei said, then got up and ran over to her.

Auntie threw an arm around Mei in a side hug. "Has your brother let you go completely feral out here?"

"No, Auntie. Last night I wore a dress and put my hair up."

"Well, okay then, but I'll need to keep an eye on him."

Pop looked at Trinity. "You'll have to forgive my son. Beautiful women bring out the fool in him." Pop paused and thought for a second. "And some not so beautiful women."

Everyone broke out in laughter. Trinity turned and cast a salty look at Brother, who suddenly looked interested in the sky. He turned to Mr. White. "Looks like we're going to have good weather this week."

"Don't drag me into this, my boy. I've already done my duty by you," Mr. White said, then scooted himself and his plate of food away from Brother as if a lightning bolt might zap out of the sky and hit Brother.

"Really?" Brother asked in mock disappointment. Dramatically, he took a deep breath and turned back to Trinity. "So, it's like this."

Trinity raised her hand. "Ah, ah, ah!"

"Ya know, you can't open the book of my life and start right in the middle," Brother protested.

"Oh, he dropped a Firefly quote," Audrey whooped.

"He's a smoothie, he's a smoothie," Marla added.

"See? Now they are being sensible and understanding when to let things go on by," Brother said, deliberately creating more chaos.

Mr. White scooted further away from Brother. "Oh, shit."

"Hold on!" Trinity yelled. "Hold on!"

"I'm afraid the council has spoken," Brother said.

George and Judyta laughed along with Audrey and Marla.

Trinity shot to her feet and glared at Brother, then without taking her eyes off of Brother pointed a warning finger at the snorting and giggling foursome.

Meanwhile, a small crowd had gathered around to watch the show.

"Hold on, beautiful lady," Brother said, holding his hands up in surrender. "Would a proper, no haggis breath type kiss make peace?"

"Oh, good night of living," Auntie mock groaned in disgust. "Don't let him off that easy."

Brother shot an exasperated look at Auntie, who smiled back at him cruelly.

Trinity narrowed her eyes. "Maybe," she said, relenting slightly, "but it better be a good one. Like a really good one."

Brother stood, wiped his mouth with a napkin, and repeated his mouth wash routine with the flask. Then he rolled his head back on his neck like a boxer stretching. When he was finished, he stepped over to Trinity. As he leaned in, Trinity raised her hand to stop him.

"A really good one," she said.

Brother paused for a second, then in an explosive but gentle move, swept Trinity off her feet and planted a passionate kiss on her.

"Whooooo!!!" Everyone cheered and clapped, except Auntie, who was merciless. "That's nothing! If he can't do better, throw the big bum out! He kisses his dog better!"

Mei laughed at the spectacle.

Finally, Brother set Trinity down and cocked an eyebrow, awaiting sentence.

Trinity was obviously in favor of Brother's efforts. Flushed, she crossed her arms and pretended to think, then broke into a big smile. "Okay, that was pretty good.... You're a bad, bad man."

The crowd cheered. Brother stood erect with a big grin on his beat-up face, but this time, Trinity reached up and pulled him down into another kiss.

The crowd roared its approval.

Auntie chimed in again. "Boo! Don't let him off that easy! He's a lug!" She burst into laughter, along with everyone else.

Soon, everyone calmed down and went back to eating breakfast. Auntie and Pop joined everyone at the table, and all enjoyed chatting about plans for the day. Mei was talking with Judyta when Brother leaned over. "Pop has offered to take you and Judyta riding today, if you'd like."

"Really?"

"Yes."

Mei turned to Judyta. "Do you want to come riding with me?"

"Let me ask Dad!" Judyta said, then turned to Mr. White. "Dad, can I..."

Mr. White cut her off. "Yes, you can. Just stay calm and follow instructions."

"I will!" Judyta turned back to Mei. "We ride!" and Mei clapped.

"Okay, you put on shorts to ride in," Brother said. "So go on, we'll wait here."

The she-raiders ran back to the campsite at breakneck speed.

After breakfast, they cleared the table. The girls came racing back, and everyone went their different ways. Mei and Judyta went with Pop to the corral side of the barn. Trinity and the girls walked part of the way with them, talking with Pop as they walked along. The musicians went to the session group. Arik, Sarah, and Michael were saddling up the horses to get them ready.

"Oh!" Sarah said. "The she–raiders are going to ride with us. Yay!"

"Hi, Sarah!!" Mei said. "This is my sister of choice, Judyta! And Sarah is my other Brother's wife, so she's a sister-in-law. Man, this is getting complicated."

"Hello, Judyta!" Sarah said.

"Nice to meet you, Sarah."

Mei introduced Judyta to everyone. Michael and Pop told Judyta they saw her saber dance the day before and admired her skill.

Arik and Sarah were impressed. "Looks like we missed some good stuff." Arik said. "Next time, huh?"

"You bet," Judyta said.

"I'm going to learn the saber too!" Mei said.

"Good," Arik said. "Anything you learn is like putting money in the bank."

As they prepared the horses, Pop and Judyta talked about Polish military history, and both were impressed with each other's knowledge about the subject. Pop gave a safety lecture on riding and had Mei list the 'do's' and 'don'ts.'

When the horses were ready, they saddled up. Since Mei had riding experience and Judyta was taller, Mei held the reins while Judyta sat behind. Their horse was gentle old Sally. The senior horse was easy for the beginners to ride. Pop gave the signal, and they rode out across the pasture, out the gate onto a well-used trail, leaving the happy racket of the Ceilidh behind.

Sun shining, they rode their horses along the trail, enjoying the day. Mei loved riding. She felt so tall she thought she could see for miles. She liked the strength of the horse and how it rolled and swayed as it walked. Even the gamey smell of the horse didn't bother her.

Michael rode in front of them, and his horse would occasionally fart, causing no end of amusement for Mei and Judyta.

"Sounds like George after curry night," Judyta said, after one particularly amazing thunder blast from Michael's horse.

They could see Michael laughing at Judyta's comment, too. The trail eventually came to the top of a small hill with a magnificent view of the farm and the surrounding area. Mei took a mind picture of the spectacular view.

Sarah had brought her camera and was taking pictures of the view and the ride. She'd just taken pictures of Michael and Arik when she looked at Mei and Judyta. "Would you two mind if I took pictures of you? We can wait until your dad and brother are around to ask."

"I don't mind," they said in unison.

Judyta bopped Mei in the shoulder. "Jinx."

"Okay," Sarah said. "But we're going to text brother from here and get permission from him and Mr. White. Never let a stranger take your picture without your brother or Dad's permission. Got it? If they try, just say, please don't take my picture without permission from my brother or father."

"Yes, Sarah," Mei and Judyta said.

"If anyone does take your picture without your permission, you must let Brother or your dad know. You won't get in trouble, but it's important for your safety."

The girls agreed.

As they lined up for pictures, the permission texts came back. "Okay," Sarah said, "we're good."

Sarah took pictures of the girls sitting on the horse from different angles. They she took pictures of each girl sitting on the horse by themselves. In one picture, Mei was holding her throwing knife in her teeth and holding the reins as if she was riding hard, but Michael and Pop were just outside the picture keeping the horse still.

Sarah took pictures of Judyta alone on the horse as well. In some of the pictures, Judyta was holding her saber in her hand, resting it across her front. In others, she held a pose as if she was charging with her saber out, and others as if she was fighting an unseen enemy. Mei thought her sister looked fierce and cool.

Pop put the two girls on the horse together, and Sarah asked everyone to gather around for a group picture. Mei enjoyed being part of the group. She might be the youngest and smallest, but she felt one of them now.

Pop couldn't be gone from the Ceilidh for very long, so they headed back down the trail much sooner than anyone wanted.

As they rode back to the barn, Mei thought it felt odd leaning forward when the horse went downhill, very different from riding in a car. When they reached the barn, Arik helped the girls off old Sally, then removed the saddle and gear.

"Pop," Arik said, "you need to see to your guests. Go ahead, we got this."

"Well..." Pop said.

"Go on, Pop," Michael added. "We'll take care of horses."

"Okay, I'll change back into my kilt and head over." He clapped Michael on the shoulder, then looked over at Sarah. "Keep these guys out of trouble for me, will you?"

"I can't make any promises, Pop," Sarah sighed. "But I'll try."

Mei and Judyta wanted to help with the horses but were just too small. Instead of leaving, they stayed to watch and help when they could by fetching things they could carry. Arik, Michael, and Sarah took care of all the horses. They took the saddles, blankets, and bridals off, then checked the horse's hooves for any rocks stuck between the horseshoes. They finished by brushing down the horses.

Mei had an inspiration and led Judyta by the hand out of the barn. "I'm going to ask some family kind of questions of the guys. You don't have to stay."

"I don't mind staying with you, but if you want privacy, I'll go," Judyta said.

Mei was torn, but summoned her courage. "I don't want to hurt you, but I think I need to do this by myself."

Judyta hugged her. "I understand Mei. I won't be far away," she said, then tapped the grip of the saber still slung over her back. "If there's trouble, I'll come get you."

Mei nodded, her heart swelling and lurching at the same time. She came close to crying, but held back.

Judyta headed out and Mei went back inside where Michael, Arik, and Sarah were still brushing the horses. She stood quietly and watched.

Arik looked over and saw her. "Did your pal go?"

Mei nodded. "Yes."

"Everything okay?"

"Yes," Mei said, and took a deep breath.

Arik stopped brushing. "What's wrong, kiddo? You look like someone stepped on your shadow."

Mei's emotions were flooding and splashing around inside, but she needed to find out. "Nothing bad, but I need your help."

"O-k-a-y. What's going on?"

"Well, I don't know how to say it, so here goes." She stopped when the words stuck in her throat.

Arik frowned with concern. "Jesus, Mei. You're freaking me out. Is this a girl thing? Do you need Sarah?"

"What's going on?" Sarah asked when she heard her name.

"Come here. Mei's in some kind of distress."

"Mei's in trouble?" Michael shouted.

"It's Mei!" Sarah said.

Michael stopped and trotted over to Arik and Sarah, standing in front of Mei. "What the ...?"

They all tried talking at once, but only made the situation worse.

Mei held up her hands. "Wait! Wait! This isn't going right." She took a deep breath. "I'm nervous, because I wanted to ask you to tell me about my brother. I don't know him like all of you do."

A long and stunned silence hung in the air before Arik breathed a sigh of relief. "Jeeeesus."

Sarah and Michael had similar expressions of relief.

Seeing Mei struggle with her emotions, Arik smiled with understanding. "It's okay, Mei. You had us scared there for a minute. I think we can help you with your question, but we gotta talk and work at the same time."

"Oh yes, that's cool," Mei said, trying to sound casual.

"Okay then, come on," Arik said, and they went back to the horses, working on one at a time, so they could still focus on Mei's interest in her brother.

"So, you want to know about your brother?" Arik asked.

"Yes, please," Mei said.

"Well, there's a lot to tell, so we won't get to all of it right now, but I think each of us here," he gestured over his shoulder at Sarah and Michael, "can share something."

"Good!" Mei said.

Arik talking while brushing the horse.

"Well, your brother came to us later in life than most adopted kids. He was eleven or twelve when he moved in. His foster mother was your auntie's mom, but she got cancer and passed. I never met her, but according to Pop, she was quite a woman; smart, old school classy, and a real fighter for her family. She had met mom and Pop at the VFW, and they all became friends. She was older when she adopted him, not like grandma old, but not a young lady either. Anyway, her cancer caught Mom and Dad off guard, but before she went, she made them promise to take in your Brother because your auntie was going to college on a scholarship. And your brother's mom didn't want Auntie to give that up to stay home and finish raising him." He paused and smiled. "She's a stand-up lady, just like her mom, but that wouldn't have been right, so her mom made the arrangement with Mom and Dad." He looked over at Mei. "You following all of this so far?"

Mei nodded.

"I don't know how long Brother had been with his foster mom, but, DNA or not, he was her son. She sent him to private school, which is probably why he did so well when he got to public school. She also had him in all the classic sports; wrestling, boxing, baseball, and football, so he was strong there. He was smart, funny, a good worker, and stubborn!"

Mei heard Michael and Sarah laugh.

"But you know what? He fit in with us right away. Lots of adopted kids don't, but with him, it felt like he was a close cousin right away, rather than some kid our folks were taking care of."

Michael nodded. "It didn't take your brother very long to become one of us, and he kinda went from distant cousin to a real brother really quick like. He pitched in with chores, did well in school, and got in trouble with us, so we never really felt like he didn't belong."

Arik continued. "Generally speaking, he didn't give Mom or Dad any trouble, and was generous with his things. He loved to joke and goof off, you know, kid stuff. And he was a total munching machine."

Michael laughed. "Yeah, by the time he was fourteen, he could eat a whole pizza by himself. If he was making breakfast for everyone, he'd start with a dozen or more eggs, a whole ham, and like a loaf of bread. Pop said he needed to go moose hunting to keep up with his appetite. He could home in on a baked pie like he had radar."

Mei laughed.

"It's true!" Arik agreed. "One time mom bought pies on sale, and just before your brother came home from school, she had Michael climb up on the counter and stash all three pies in the top cupboard above the fridge. Then everyone pretended nothing was up."

"Really?" Mei asked.

"No joke!" Michael said. "So, your brother comes home, puts his stuff down and walks into the kitchen like normal. As he passes the refrigerator, he suddenly stops and gets this, like, puzzled look on his face. Without moving, he looks around, puts his hand on the door of the fridge, but doesn't open it. Then he pulls his hand back and slowly reaches up to the freezer door. But again, doesn't open it. Then he slowly turns his head and looks up at the cupboard door and says, 'What's in the cupboard?' It was crazy!

Now he was a bit different than us. Not bad different, just like he was his own man. He saw and did things differently, and when he hit his growth spurt, although he was already big, it was evident he'd get really big."

Arik chuckled. "I was older, but he was almost my height and thicker."

"How else was he different?" Mei asked.

Arik tapped his chin. "Let me see if I can get the words right."

"He said be honest with Mei," Michael said.

Arik nodded and then grinned to himself. "Yeah, your brother could be a real shit sometimes."

"No!" Mei protested.

"Hold on. I said he could be a shit. I didn't say he was one all the time. In fact, he was never a shit to anyone in the family."

"That's true," Michael agreed. "We had lots of arguments and played jokes on each other, and he was a good sport, but if anyone outside of the family tried to do something to one of us..." Michael blew his breath out, "Damn..."

"That's a good point," Arik said. "He could take a joke or argue with one of the family, no problem, and could argue or joke around with someone outside of the family, but only if it was with him. If someone did or said something about one of us, or Mom or Pop, then your brother would go after them."

"Like how?" Mei asked.

"Mercilessly," Arik said. "There were a couple of incidents."

"What do you mean?"

Arik shrugged. "Fights and other stuff. Not important right now."

Michael cut in. "Mei, he seemed to think he owed us for adopting him and wanted to protect us. A nice thought, but unnecessary. Mom and Dad spent extra time with him to help him understand it was okay not to fight everyone about little things; what was important and what to ignore."

"That led to Mom and Dad making it clear what our boundaries were, their expectations, and practical courses of action on how to handle things effectively," Arik said. "For example, since Mom was an accountant, she was good at showing us ways to find exceptions to rules and loopholes to deal with bureaucrats. And of course, we were already excellent fighters. Besides chores, we all loved working out, watching MMA, and practicing martial arts."

"Your brother is very protective," Sarah said, "but he's also kind and thoughtful. He opened doors for people, and liked animals."

Arik stopped brushing the horse. "Yeah, I forgot about that. How is this for weird? Your brother would hunt and fish with us and even help with butchering, but he was never mean to the animals around the farm, and he spoiled our dogs."

"And don't forget his cat, Rufus," Michael said.

"That cat was a furry gangster!"

"What about Rufus?" Mei asked.

"He was just a scruffy cat your brother adopted, kind of like our mascot," Arik said. "He lived to an old age and passed away after he was spoiled rotten his whole life."

Sarah joined the conversation. "I remember things about your brother these guys haven't even mentioned."

Arik and Michael looked up.

"He'd go out of his way to do funny and outrageous things," Sarah said, then thought for a moment and gestured. "Not always bad stuff, but if a random epic thing happened, he probably had something to do with it."

Mei looked puzzled as Arik and Michael started laughing.

"Okay, here's one. In 10th grade, our teacher in American history class wasn't very good. Your Brother didn't like him because this teacher always gave his political opinions to everything. But one time he offered extra credit if the students did an extra history project. So, your brother somehow scammed a regional civil war re-enactor group, the people who dress in Civil War attire, to come to school and set up a living history camp. But he didn't get permission from the school or tell anyone, so, the first thing the school administrators know, the athletic fields were occupied by a platoon from the 20th Maine, a detachment of cavalry, and an actual cannon!"

Arik laughed. "I wasn't there for all of it, but the way I heard it, the principal looks out and there are pickets on guard, tents going up, a campfire burning, and horses crapping on the soccer field."

"Needless to say, there was a fuss over that one," Sarah said. "But the best part was when your brother got busted. The principal, a few teachers, and I think a couple of school board members on one side, with a bunch of guys in full Civil War uniform on the other side, along with an enormous crowd of students watching it all. Your brother is standing in the middle, just as cool as can be."

By now, Michael was cracking up at the memory. "Tell Mei what he said."

"I was there for this part," Sarah added. "Cool as ice, your brother looks at the commanding officer of the union re-enactors and says, 'Colonel, that school administration rabble are all southern democrat secessionists. I think your best course of action is to turn the cannon around and shoot a couple volleys of cannister into them, then finish them off with a bayonet charge.'"

Mei's eyes widened and mouth gaped. "He told the soldiers to shoot cannons at the teachers?"

"Yes!" Sarah was laughing so hard she could barely get the words out. Arik and Michael were laughing along with her.

"Did he get in trouble?" Mei asked.

"Oh, God yes!" Arik said. "The adults eventually got everything calmed down and the re-enactors put on a great historical display and show for the whole school, but whoo hooo, did Brother catch hell for that one."

"He might not have been in so much trouble, but he was audacious to the end," Michael added. "He looked at the history teacher and asked, So I get an 'A' and extra credit for this, right?"

The teacher was stunned and said no, so of course Brother went after him. "I have to plot and scheme to demonstrate actual history that you deliberately ignore and you're going to cheat me?" He turns and points to the cavalry re-enactors, and in his 15-year-old's command voice says, "You two troopers! Lend me your sabers! My honor has been wronged by this riffraff, and I demand satisfaction right now! Quickly now, this won't take but a moment!"

"He challenged the teacher to a sword fight?" Mei asked.

"Yes!" Sarah gasped between laughs. "I thought Mr. Engles was going to wet himself. He tried to get control of the situation and said something like, young man, I'm not going to give you satisfaction."

Brother immediately cut him off and went in for the kill. "Yeah, I think I heard your wife warned everyone about that problem of yours."

"How dare you!" the outraged teacher yelled, and Brother cut him off again. "Fine, maybe it was your husband that was unsatisfied, whomever, or whatever, the rumor is, your spouse, much like your students, isn't happy with your performance."

Mei was shocked. No one was supposed to talk to teachers like that, but here Sarah and the uncles were laughing about it.

"So, by now, despite everything, the students and re-enactors are roaring. Even the principal was struggling to keep a straight face. The teacher loses his cool and lunges at Brother, who dances back a few steps, and goads him. Oh, so now you find your spleen! Come on then, have at thee, villain!"

"Mr. Engles was really upset and looked like he was going to charge again, but Brother was ready to fight. Fortunately, the Principal intervened and calmed down the teacher, while Brother was marched off to detention. He got a two week's suspension, a month of detention, wrote a boatload of apology letters, a long grounding and extra work at home, and I think the admiration of the principal, who fixed everything with the re-enactors and invited them to come back the following year."

"Wow!" Mei said.

"Oh, that's not it by a long shot," Sarah said. "Your Brother had this need to inflict his will on his own life, and didn't let anyone get in his way. Like he didn't know how to play guitar, but didn't care and started a band anyway. If there was a girl he liked, he'd call into a radio station and talk the DJ into playing a song for her." Sarah laughed, while Arik and Michael groaned and shook their heads.

"What?" Mei asked. "What did he do?"

Michael and Arik looked at each other. "You tell her. No, you tell her. No ...you ..."

"Guys!" Mei insisted.

The brothers faced each other. "Okay, on three?" Arik asked, raising a balled-up fist.

Michael raised his fist. "Yes, on three."

They pumped their fists. "One! Two! Three!" and snapped their hands out.

Arik's hand came down flat, while Michael's hand showed two fingers pointing out.

"Scissors beats paper," Michael said.

"You always go rock," Arik protested.

"Which is why I changed it up today. Now stop stalling and face the music!"

Arik muttered curse words. "Okay, but you finish the horse."

"Yeah, yeah..."

Arik turned back to Mei. "I have to be careful with how I tell you this, but here goes. When your brother was about thirteen or fourteen, he discovered girls."

Mei started to speak, but Arik politely cut her off. "This will make sense when you're older. Hold on for now." He took a breath. "At that age, everyone is interested in each other, but your brother had it bad. Really bad."

Michael and Sarah laughed.

"That knucklehead fell madly in love with girls all the time." Arik shook his head with a mixture of fondness and sadness.

"And they fell in love with him too," Sarah added.

"Gross!" Mei said.

"Part of his daring do was he was brave enough to talk with girls he liked and didn't care if they pretended that they didn't like him back. Teenage boys can be dummies but girls can be mean."

Arik added, "Anyway, his appreciation for girls caused us no end of trouble. It was his weak spot. By the time he was fifteen, he was dating, going to dances, calling girls, riding his skateboard cross country to some girls house, and girls were calling the house at all hours. They had fights, breakups, and all kinds of drama. But he was never mean to any of the girls he liked. He liked them all; homely girls, pretty girls, popular girls, or shy girls. The fact is, he seemed to prefer nerdy smart girls the most."

"Yes," Arik said, "he was the Don Juan of the pocket calculator. Now let me get back on track. You'll understand all of this better later, but trust me, this infatuation with chasing girls was the one thing leading to more trouble for your brother at school. He got top grades and did well in sports. His big problem was girls."

"It was pretty much the only thing he did that bothered my folks," Michael said.

"Okay, enough with all the ancient Brother history," Arik said. "It's time to finish up here and get back to the Ceilidh. But before we go, we think the best thing he ever did was get you. We're very proud of him for that, and glad you're with us now."

Mei, overcome with emotion and gratitude, jumped off the hay bale and pounced on her brothers. They hugged and laughed, then Arik said, "We can't promise you this," he gestured with one hand, "but if anyone can win a court fight it's your brother."

Mei sobered up and nodded.

"He's always been lucky that way," Arik said.

"No way man," Michael said. "He makes his own luck. I've seen him do it time and time again. Our Brother can think things through like nobody else. When something is important, he always thinks four or five steps ahead. Now think of all the time he was in the hospital, especially from the time he found out about Mei. How much you want to bet he was thinking this through while trying to heal? Okay, maybe not this court fight exactly, but something close enough that when those trash popped up, he wasn't surprised because he was already ahead of them."

"That does sound like him," Arik said.

"Just like him," Sarah agreed.

Mei nodded with them, partly because she wanted to belong, but mostly wanted it to be true. She didn't want to leave Brother, Auntie, Pop, and her new life.

Sarah put an arm around Mei's shoulders and both leaned in.

"Okay, enough of all this," Arik said. "Let's get back to the party before everyone leaves."

They all agreed. They'd finished brushing the last horse while they talked, so they picked up the brushes and gear, put everything away, and headed back to the Ceilidh.

Using a term she'd heard from Brother, she said, "I need to ask a hard question."

Everyone stopped and looked at her.

"Sure, Mei," Arik said in a solemn tone.

Taking a breath and summoning up her courage, Mei asked, "Brother's got a lot of scars and old hurts. Is he going to be okay?"

Arik and Michael both nodded tentatively. "Yeah, he is, sweetie," Arik said. "He's going to have more ups and downs because the recovery process never goes in a straight line, but he's on the right track, and he's motivated to get where he wants to go."

Sarah put her arm around Mei's shoulder. "Don't worry about his scars. They only tell a story. Sometimes they tell a silly story, sometimes a serious story. But sometimes, they tell a story of greatness. Your Brother has all those scars."

Mei was quiet for a minute, then nodded to herself. "Thank you, everyone. I really appreciate everything you shared with me." She hugged everyone then headed back to the Ceilidh, feeling they were more family now than when they started off on the ride earlier in the day. She pushed her worries about the court case to the back of her mind, then looked forward to enjoying every remaining minute of the Ceilidh.

Chapter 97

Brother

Brother's travel alarm woke him much earlier than he'd prefer, but he couldn't complain about his company or circumstances. In fact, his current situation was one of the loveliest and poetic in his entire chaotic life. Trinity was most agreeably curled up with him underneath a pile of comfy blankets, semi-hidden, in an apple orchard on his father's farm on a late summer morning. It sounded like a poem or story that usually happened to someone else, but today it was Brother's story. Bliss.

As he snaked a hand from beneath the blankets and shut the alarm off, Trinity shifted. "It's so early," she said.

"Yeah, I might have accidentally set the alarm to wake us earlier than we needed. Accidentally of course."

"You, oh you, bad, bad man."

Brother gently lifted her face and kissed her a most glorious good morning.

All too soon, it was time to pack up and head to the campsite with the others, much sooner than Brother preferred. As he dressed and broke camp, stacked the duffle bags and rolled up the bedding, he felt the kinks, cramps, strains and ached. Lack of sleep didn't help, but he was not sorry.

Trinity took longer to get ready, and she'd been watching him. "You move much quicker than you seem to."

"Years of practice, my dear lady."

"Oh, yeah? I bet you've had years of practice doing lots of things."

Brother noticed a slight challenge to her tone, so he stopped and stood up to his full height and looked down into her eyes. He didn't intend to challenge her, only to find the meaning of her words. To his surprise, he saw uncertainty and vulnerability.

She looked away, then forced out a breath. "Well, you're the expert in the morning after stuff, so what's the plan? Go off and brag?"

"So, you think you performed well enough to brag to the girls?"

She tossed her head. "I, well, I meant you bragging."

Oh, man. This poor, lovely creature. He hadn't been with a woman in a long time that wasn't jaded. It was the nature of the life he'd led. He hadn't handled his feelings well in general, but since his time in the hospital, he'd learned to live a new life, so why not try being sincere? He walked over and took the duffle bag from her hand and set it down, then embraced and kissed her. "My dear, lovely girl. Thank you for sharing yourself with me." He sighed. "And I was really touched by your story you shared. I had no idea."

Trinity started to speak, but he gently shushed her. "It took real bravery to be vulnerable and give me a piece of your heart. You can't know how much that means to me. I hope you're not sorry about last night, and I'm hoping for more of..." He struggled for the right words. "... this, us. I know you have a bright future, and I have Mei and need lots of healing, but I'm not going away anymore if you want to try. You don't need to give me an answer right this second, but I wanted to tell you how I felt."

Trinity nodded, then pulled him down into a kiss. "I wanted another one of those."

"Good," he said, then they picked up their gear and walked side by side through the orchard back to the campsite.

Chapter 98

Brother

Boudicca's throaty, warm bark greeted Brother and Trinity as they emerged from the orchard. "Chuff! Chuff!" Once the pup recognized them, she stopped barking and started thumping her tail.

Brother put down his load and went over to pet the dog and check on Mei. Aside from the bedhead, she looked well.

Trinity put her things down and sat next to Audrey. They leaned against each other in sisterly support. Audrey looked up and caught Brother's eye and nodded. Apparently, she approved.

Not sure what else to do, he simply nodded. He busied himself by adding more wood to the fire and putting the coffeepot on to complement the tea Steve made. Judyta was still dead to the world, but Marla woke up and spied a cup of tea waiting for her. Apparently, George was flexing his gallant muscles and trying against all odds to win her heart. Good for him! He'd go far in life with that.

When Steve went to wake Judyta, he found Boudicca had appointed herself Judyta's guardian. He appreciated Missy B protecting his daughter, but Brother called Boudicca over so Steve could wake up Judyta.

Watching Judyta wake up was like watching a horror movie where you know a monster is going to jump out and scare you, but when it happens, you're still freaked out. Just like the day before, Judyta exploded awake startling everyone again. Brother had not seen many things quite as weird. Judyta was a cool kid to be sure, but without a doubt, weird.

Brother and Steve both splashed a bit of whiskey in their coffee.

"Oh, my, that was good," Brother said.

Steve glanced up at Brother and winked. "You'll want to take a sponge bath as soon as you can."

Brother did his best to keep a straight face. "Alrighty then. Thank you, sir."

Steve saluted with his coffee cup.

Everyone got busy with snacking, washing, dressing, and packing. Brother and Trinity shared occasional looks and smiles while drinking coffee together. Nice.

Heeding Steve's advice, Brother eventually got a pan of warm water and slipped away for a field style wash down. After dressing, he and George took Boudicca for her morning walk.

Brother lit a cigar. "You doing okay, George?"

"Oh yeah, I had more fun than I expected."

"Good."

"Hey, I appreciate all the extra stuff you did for me. I was wondering what you were doing, telling me what to do and all, but Dad pointed out what was going on, and it all made sense."

"I'm glad to help. You're showing a lot of potential, and I'm glad to be your friend. But to be clear, your dad's word is law. I won't go against his rules."

George nodded. "I really like Marla."

"You should like her. She's brilliant, kind, extremely talented, and let's be honest, very attractive. And she's patient."

"I don't have a chance with her, do I?"

"Not even a tiny one little brother," Brother said as tactfully as he could. "She's twenty and you're what? Twelve?"

"I'll be thirteen."

"Yeah, so besides illegal, there's too much of an age difference. But do you want your big brother's advice?"

"Yes."

"Keep on showing your good manners and spend time talking to her. It'll be good to get to know her. That way, you'll know how to act around girls your own age."

"Okay."

"Get her email address, buy her music, stay in touch, but do so appropriately. But when you find out she's dating or getting married, keep your shit together, wish her well and hold your little kid feelings in check. I know it's a lot, but if you have questions, ask your dad or me before you go do anything crazy."

"Okay."

"You'll learn your own style and become a lady killer with a ton of babes before you know it, so there's no need to rush off and do something to disgrace yourself."

"You really think that?"

"What?"

"The lady killer thing."

"It'll take some time, but yes, I do."

"Cool."

"Don't worry. You'll be fine."

They walked Boudicca back to the camp. Mei was sitting with Audrey and Marla who were coaching her how to play a lute. Good stuff. Brother got George extra clothes and gear to wear for the day to go with the borrowed kilt. George left to dress.

They'd all finished dressing and were ready to eat breakfast when the horn sounded. Call to the blood! Long and loud, its notes rolled across the Ceilidh field. Brother motioned everyone to their feet. The horn sounded again, and this time Brother held up his hand and counted down with his fingers. When he reached one, he led everyone at the campsite in a war cry in response, just like the day before.

The horn sounded a third time, and the campsite roared again. Everyone across the fields joined in, and today several bagpipers joined in raising everyone's spirits. God, he missed this.

Mei and Judyta were making themselves look extra fierce with war paint. Mei waved over the three musicians and gave each of them accent stripes. Brother thought it was great of them to indulge Mei and Judyta. They'd probably become fans for life.

Brother went looking and found George fussing to get his clothing right. The vest was too big. Brother gave him a hand tying the bandana and strapped on his saber. He looked good. Brother winked. "Hang on and follow my lead, little brother."

Before George could have second thoughts, Brother dragged him out in full view of everyone and painted his face while everyone watched.

As he figured, Marla sat among the spectators, so Brother engaged her to comment on his work, George's new look, and George's conduct in general. Much to his joy, the beautiful young musician indulged him and complimented George with the grace that would have George eating out of her hand for the rest of their lives.

Brother caught Steve's surreptitious nod of approval and slyly returned it. After gathering everyone together, the group headed off to breakfast.

The breakfast line was a happy riot, and because the Celtic Culinary Club was getting rid of everything they'd brought, the food choices were varied. Brother didn't eat much dinner the night before, and all the dancing and time with Trinity made him hungry. He made sure Mei made good choices, but he needn't have worried. She and Judyta teamed up with their selections and were sharing their plates.

He loaded his plate and joined everyone at a table. There was the usual cheerful banter at the table, and it wasn't long before everyone started teasing him for choosing haggis and eggs.

Trinity looked dubiously at Brother's breakfast, and Audrey and Marla teased him about kissing her with haggis breath. Brother took the opportunity to show his forward thinking and stole a kiss in the process.

Auntie surprised him by showing up at breakfast, where she proceeded to bust his chops, big sister style, in front of everyone. Mei jumped up and ran to Auntie for a side hug. Auntie didn't go for crowds much, so it was good seeing her, and twice at the same event was a big deal.

Not to be outdone, Pop threw Brother under the bus with Trinity with implications about his Casanova past. Awkward.

Steve happily joined in by adding to his distress.

Trinity didn't look thrilled, and Brother's attempts to put the slide and glide on her were going nowhere fast. She wasn't having it, and a crowd was gathering. Before long, people would start contributing memories of transgressions best left unsaid and forgotten.

Instead of turning the conversation on Trinity and her romantic dalliances of yesteryear, Brother threw everyone off balance and offered an unconditional surrender as his best course of action. His abrupt change of course worked better than he'd planned, and he ended up giving Trinity a most lovely deep kiss in front of everyone. My god, she's intoxicating. Even better, she felt encouraged by his shameless public display of affection, and insisted on an encore. Brother needed to be careful not to get carried away. Yeah right.

Everyone eventually calmed down and prepared to go their separate ways. Pop mentioned he was getting 'peopled out,' and was going to take a quick ride. He invited Mei and Judyta to go with him.

Mei lit up like a Christmas tree. She looked to Brother for permission. He nodded.

"You can go, but you're under Pop's authority and rules. Don't embarrass us."

"I won't."

"Okay, you need to run back to camp and put on shorts, then come back and find Pop. Go on."

Mei zoomed off at full speed, with Judyta at her side.

I wish I still had that kind of energy, Brother thought.

They finished breakfast while waiting on the she-raiders.

"What are you up to today?" Pop asked Brother.

"Boudicca and I are going back and pick up the camp."

"You mean you're going to go back to bed?" Trinity said.

"Indeed. Would you care to join me?" Brother offered, much to the amusement of the crowd.

Trinity blushed. "Uh, I guess. I walked right into that one, didn't I?"

"It wasn't a trap. It was a sincere offer," Brother said.

"Uh, I have to go play in a few sessions."

"Alas, duty calls. I understand. But I'll come find you when I wake up. I still love hearing you play."

"Deal."

"I'd be honored to escort you and the other beautiful ladies on my way to the corral," Pop said.

The girls agreed.

Steve and George were going to watch the heavy athletic events. Brother noted the athletic fields were next to the stage where the girls would be playing. He winked at Steve and nodded slightly in the direction where George sat talking to Marla. Steve surreptitiously nodded back, then gestured in another direction.

Brother glanced where Steve gestured and saw the lady he danced with the night before. Brother nodded back. He was happy for his friend.

They all talked for a while and were cleaning up the breakfast dishes when Mei and Judyta returned. Mei hugged Brother briefly and headed off with Pop, Judyta, and the girls. Pop was still the man.

Brother took inventory of himself. The unacknowledged pain spikes surged in his body, and fatigue manifested itself as a huge dark weight on the back of his neck. Nap time was calling. "Come on, Boo." Man and dog headed for the camp.

Brother changed into trunks and rolled out his futon and blankets. The morning was pleasant, with the soothing sounds of the Ceilidh in the background. Brother broke down and took a painkiller, then crawled into bed and fell asleep before he could tell Boudicca to quit hogging all the blankets.

He'd been sleeping hard for a while when Boudicca woke him by thumping her tail. He figured Steve or George was getting something when he felt a tug on his blankets. From years of training and habit, Brother coiled up and rolled over, ready to strike, when he saw a surprised Trinity. He clamped down on his instincts and reached out and gently touched her shoulder.

"Oh!" she squeaked.

"I was worried I was dreaming of a beautiful lady coming to join me, and if I was dreaming, I sure didn't want to wake up. And if I'm awake, I don't want to go to sleep."

Trinity tried to look outraged. "I'm sure you have lots of experience with ladies climbing into your bed."

"Not as many as I would have liked, I am sorry to say."

"Oh, really?"

"Oh, come on. It's too nice a day to fight about things that don't matter," he said, and pulled her onto the futon with him and threw blankets over both. He nudged Boudicca over and cuddled up to the beautiful musician. "I'm glad you're here."

Trinity held her breath for a moment. "I don't even know what I am doing."

Wisely, Brother said nothing.

"I'm not like this. I swore I'd never throw away my dignity and throw myself at a man like this, but here I am." She pressed her lips together. "Damnit."

Brother put his arm around her and she cuddled in closer, lying together in silence for a minute.

"So, don't you have anything to say?" she demanded.

"I am glad you chose to come here and be with me," Brother said. "It means a lot."

She sighed. "I have so many thoughts and questions bouncing around in my head. I need to know what you're thinking."

"I just told you what I'm thinking."

"Ugh," she grunted in frustration. "I swore I wasn't going to come over here, but here I am."

"Good," Brother said. "That means I don't have to chase you down, so I can ask to see you again."

Trinity exhaled. "Really?"

"Yes."

"I had hoped," she said, then chuckled. "Your dad is an old villain."

"Yes, he is, but what's he got to do with this?"

"When he walked me to the session, he pulled me aside and told me he'd seen you with a lot of women, and they were all gone. And he could tell you like me. And if I wanted something with you, I had to be smart enough for both of us and claim you."

"He needs to keep his teeth together, but he's right."

"So, what do we do?"

"Well, since you've been checking up on me, has anyone given you a reason to doubt my word?"

"No."

"So, why don't we make the best of this awesome weekend together? Unfortunately, we'll have to part at the end of the day, but when we go, we agree while we're apart to do some soul searching and see if we want to continue?"

"I don't want to go."

"Me neither," Brother said. "I'm intoxicated with you."

"You are?"

"Oh, God yes. I'm crushing hard on you, so I know better than to trust myself. I'm a sentimental idiot and can't afford to be anymore because of Mei."

"Okay."

"So, what do you think?"

"I think that's best. This is all so new."

"Yeah?"

"Yes, mister man. I haven't had all kinds of dalliances or anything, a few boyfriends, but after we started touring with Mary Flynn, there wasn't time, and most guys don't want to wait around. And Mary warned us about not getting involved with anyone on tour, especially random guys. And she was right."

"In a way, sounds kinda like being in the service. You deploy a lot, then when you're back, you're in training schools or in the field."

"But you still had lots of women," she said.

"A few, sure."

"Ugh. I'm stupid jealous of them."

"You don't need to be, but I understand. That sounds like something you need to sort out when we're apart."

Trinity abruptly turned to him. "I don't want to talk about it anymore."

"Me neither," he said.

She was quiet for a minute, then said, "Sing me a song."

"Really?"

"Yes. I loved when you sang the other night."

"But you're the singer."

"Don't you think that chefs like it when someone cooks for them?"

"Point taken. Let me think for a minute."

"Something sweet," she said.

"Okay, okay." He thought for a moment.

"Okay, I don't know if I remember all the words, but I remember an old one that will do."

"Good," she said.

He squirmed around to breathe correctly. Then, with his best gently singing voice:

"'I have lost all my pride'"

"'I have been to paradise'"

"'And out the other side'"

"'With no one to guide me'"

"'Torn apart by a fiery wheel inside me'"

"'I won't hurt you'"

"'I won't hurt you'"

"'I won't hurt you'"

"'I won't hurt you'"

"'An untouched diamond'"

"'That's golden and brilliant'"

"'Without illumination'"

'Your mouth, a constellation'"

"'The stars are in your eyes'"

"'I'll take a spaceship and try and go and find you'"

"'I won't hurt you'"

"'I won't hurt you'"

"'I won't hurt you'"

"'I won't hurt you'"

"'My pale blue star'"

"'My rainbow, how good it is'" "

'To know you're like me'"

"'Strike me with your lightning'"

"'Bring me down and bury me with ashes'"

"'I won't hurt you'"

"'I won't hurt you'"

"'I won't hurt you'"

"I won't hurt you'"

"'I won't hurt you'"

"'I won't hurt you'"

"'I won't hurt you'"

"'I won't hurt you'"

"Oh, God, do they teach you the art of seduction in the Marines?"

Brother chuckled. "No. When you look like me, you have to learn how to be super charming."

She playfully smacked him. "Stop it."

They napped, they loved on each other, then spent the rest of the morning chatting. Finally they got up and dressed and took Boudicca and rejoined the Ceilidh.

They had a grand time talking with friends and watching the events. Trinity got to sit in with a few sessions and play with her musician pals, while Brother listened with a joy he wasn't ready to admit. After a bit, Steve and George joined him. Later, he saw Pop passing by, who told him his brothers and Sarah were down at the barn telling Mei all his secret stories from when he was a kid.

"Oh, man!"

Pop chuckled and kept walking, but waved at Trinity as he passed. She gave Pop one of the most brilliant smiles Brother had ever seen.

That old villain!

When Trinity and Audrey and Marla finished their session, they came over and joined Brother and the guys. Together, they migrated over to the food tables for a final meal. They thanked the grand cooks of the Celtic Culinary Club. When Steve tried to make a contribution, Nancy, the head cook and CCC VP, declined.

"The big fella already contributed; we're good."

Steve turned and shot Brother a look.

Brother grinned. "Hospitality."

"Oh, you bastard!" Steve said in good-natured exasperation. "Manners and highland history point? This will not go unanswered, my friend!"

Brother laughed.

They had a grand day, but all too soon, it was time to pack up the campsite and prepare to go home.

Chapter 99

Mei Mei

When the foursome returned to the Ceilidh, it was obvious things were winding down. Music and dance sessions were still going on, but people were packing and heading home. Mei thanked and hugged her new brothers and sister. Then she wandered around the grounds until she saw Judyta shuffle dancing with the group of young ladies. She was still wearing her saber across her back.

Mei stopped for a minute to watch Judyta dance. She thought Judyta looked incredibly cool. Judyta saw Mei and waved. Mei waved back with the signal everything was okay. Judyta nodded and continued dancing.

Mei jumped in and they danced a few more sets together. Dancing still made Mei feel as if she was washed in magic. When they stopped for a break, they shared a bottle of water.

"How did it go?" Judyta asked. "Did they tell you any crazy stuff about your brother?"

"Yes!" Mei said and gave Judyta a quick recap.

"What?" Judyta exclaimed a few times and looked shocked more than once. Mei plowed forward with what she'd been told. They sat out the next few sets because Judyta wasn't satisfied with the short version of the story, and asked Mei to retell it with every detail she could remember.

When Mei finally finished, Judyta said, "That's an amazing story! But it sounds like it's something Brother would do. I think I told you my dad and Professor Norris were talking a while back and said Brother was one of their best students. He's not just smart, but puts in lots of extra work and asks questions until he gets it right."

"Really? They both said that?"

"Yeah, totally."

Mei exhaled a sigh of relief. "Okay. I want to believe everything good about Brother, but sometimes I get scared that, I don't know, he's really not that good, or this new life of mine isn't as good as it seems. It's hard to explain."

"Oh, hey," Judyta said, patting Mei's arm and looking her in the eye. "It's true. And it's good. And you're here with us now."

"Oh, I know, Judyta," Mei said, patting her hand. "I appreciate your concern, but I'm okay. For real."

Judyta narrowed her eyes. "You sure?"

"Oh, yeah! I'm so much stronger now than I was before and will only get stronger! And smarter! And be a better dancer!" With that, Mei ran back out onto the dance floor and started dancing hard. Judyta shouted with joy and followed.

The girls danced themselves into a happy exhaustion, but too soon everyone had to go their separate ways. Mei and Judyta wandered past the food tables and saw everyone packing up. Still, the girls loaded up and munched from the big plates of snacks sitting out. They waved and thanked the cooks before wandering back towards camp.

When they reached camp, everyone was busy packing and chatting.

"There they are!" Audrey said, when she saw the girls. They were greeted with a chorus of welcomes.

Brother scooped Mei into a hug. "Hey."

"Are we leaving?"

Brother sighed audibly. "Unfortunately, all good things must come to an end. That's why we live and love and celebrate whenever we can with the best people we know, so when it's time to leave, we part with good grace and sincere farewells."

"Well said, sir," Mr. White agreed while folding clothes into a duffle bag.

"Okay," Mei said and kissed Brother's cheek.

"Thank you, Mei Mei," he said as set her down. "Get your things together and we'll put them in the truck. When that's done, lend a hand with the other stuff."

"Will do."

With everyone working together, it didn't take long to get the camp picked up. Mr. White and Audrey got their cars and drove up to the site, and with everyone pitching in, the vehicles were loaded in no time. No more campsite.

Mei felt sad but relieved to be with Brother, and knew there would be more times like these.

The Whites were the first to leave after a round of hugs and thank yous. When it came time for George to say goodbye to Marla, he tried to say something gallant, but unfortunately it led to a stammering episode. Marla gave him a big hug and a kiss on the cheek, causing him to blush.

"I'll see you around, big guy," she said. "I expect you to go out and become the proper knight I know you can be. Conquer worlds, right wrongs, break hearts, learn much, and teach more."

George nodded and finally found the words. "When I do stuff like that, your music will be my soundtrack."

This time Marla blushed. "Well now, that makes me very happy." She pulled off a scarf she was wearing and wrapped it around his neck. "A young knight should have a lady's colors when he goes out questing, so I hope you'll wear mine until you can find better."

A push from a feather would have knocked George over. "Never better."

Mr. White spared George from having to say anything else, pointing his thumb at Brother. "You've been learning moves from this big gorilla."

Brother held up his hands and feigned innocence.

Mr. White turned to Marla and the two other musicians. "Beautiful ladies," he proclaimed in his most gallant tone, "I mentioned before I've lived in Scotland and Ireland, and have never heard better music played anywhere. It's been an absolute honor and pleasure to spend this time with you, listen to your music, and make your acquaintance. We're your fans and we'll be cheering for you. If I can ever be of assistance, please reach out to me."

Judyta pounced on Mei, following another round of hugs. "I love you, Mei Mei."

"I love you too, sister of mine," Mei said.

"See you soon," Judyta said as she climbed into the car.

Brother and George bumped fists. "Well done, little brother," Brother said.

"Thanks, Brother," George said.

The White family loaded up and drove away.

"What a great family," Audrey said. Marla and Trinity nodded.

"Yes, they really are, aren't they?" Brother said, then turned. "Miss Marla, thank you so much for being kind to George. He's good people."

"Oh, thanks," Marla said. "He really is a special young man, and I'm sure he'll make everyone proud before he's done." She paused thoughtfully "Especially with his dad and you coaching him."

"Thanks. I think so too. But the goodness and patience you showed him will change his life path. For the better, I think."

"Well, it's not every day a girl has a say in the proper rearing of a junior rogue, now, is it?"

They all chuckled. Brother talked with the musicians for a minute while Mei checked on Boudicca. Brother said he was going to go say goodbye to Trinity in private. Mei joined Audrey and Marla in sassing Brother mercilessly.

Mei laughed. She could tell they weren't teasing to be mean.

Trinity stepped over and took Brother by the hand, and they walked off into the orchard with the girls and Mei cheering them on.

Mei and the musicians played with Boudicca and talked amongst themselves.

"Does your brother have any girlfriends?" Audrey asked Mei.

"No. He's all alone. It's been just the two of us since I came to live with him."

"Thank you for sharing," Marla said.

"Thank you for this weekend," Mei said. "No one will believe I'm friends with famous musicians."

"Aw, thanks Mei," Audrey said. "We're your friends and appreciate you sharing your Ceilidh with us. We had the best time ever!"

"Really?"

"Oh, yeah!" Marla said. "Most of the time events like this involve work, so we don't get to relax and have fun like we did this weekend."

"Cool!"

"And we liked meeting you and seeing Brother again," Audrey said. "We knew he had bad times and were worried about him, and even though we're pretty sure he doesn't share our faith, we prayed for him. Seeing him here with you ...well, it's like our old pal is back, and even though he's a little bit different, he's pretty much better than ever."

"What do you mean, different?" Mei asked.

"Oh, nothing bad. He's just more grown now. Your brother always had a heart of gold and was just a doll to all the girls at school, but he could be really wild." Audrey said.

"Oh, his brothers said that too."

"I bet."

"So, where are you all going when you leave here?"

"Well, we'll stay at our parent's house for a few days," Marla said. "It's not too far from here. But we have school starting the week after next, and there's talk of another tour with Mary Flynn. So, we'll see."

"But no matter how far we go, little Mei," Audrey said, "we're still your friends, and we want you to go do good things too."

"Yes, we do!" Marla agreed. "Like we told George, live and learn, win wars, right wrongs, conquer, laugh, play, sing, and succeed at whatever you want to!"

Mei blushed. "Do you really think I can?"

The sisters both laughed and grabbed Mei in a team bear hug. "Of course, you can," Audrey said. "We wouldn't lie to you."

"But I can do it if I put in the work. Right?" Mei asked.

"Yes! You're your brother's sister, all right."

As they waited for Brother and Trinity, Mei and the sisters continued talking and playing with Boudicca. The sisters gave Mei their email addresses and asked her to send pictures of Mei and Boudicca. Mei asked about music and traveling. As they talked, Mei realized the sisters talked to her like a regular person rather than like a little kid, like her favorite adults did. In fact, everyone she'd interacted with during the whole Ceilidh had talked to her and treated her the same as the sisters. She didn't understand every topic discussed, and wasn't privy to every conversation, but she felt as though she was a capable person and mattered.

Before coming to live with Brother, it had never been this way, but she now realized this was the life she wanted.

They were still chatting when Brother and Trinity walked hand in hand out of the orchard, holding Boudicca by the leash. Trinity walked over to Mei while Brother said his goodbyes to Audrey and Marla.

Trinity squatted down so she was eye to eye with Mei. "I'm leaving, Mei," Trinity said. "I want you to know it was great meeting you and camping with you."

"Thank you, Trinity," Mei said. "I had a great time, too. Your singing is beautiful."

"That's so sweet of you to say," Trinity said with a smile. Trinity's voice became careful. "Most of all, I want to thank you for sharing your brother with me. " She took a breath and let it out. "He's very special. Take care of him."

"I will, Trinity. And even though you didn't ask, you're special too, and Brother likes you right back."

Trinity's voice caught in her throat, and she hugged Mei tightly. "Thank you," she said and stood up. She stroked Mei's cheek with a finger, then turned and walked to the car. Audrey and Marla were mugging Brother for hugs and kisses on the cheek, and the three of them were laughing and talking.

"Well, I guess we're ready to go," Trinity said, then gave Brother a quick peck on the cheek and got into the car. Audrey and Marla looked at each other, then at Brother, who had a blank stare. They said a last round of goodbyes, and Brother helped the sisters into the car. Audrey got behind the wheel, Marla piled in the back.

"You all drive safe and text me when you get home, so I know you're ...safe, okay?" Brother said. He struggled a bit to find the right words.

"Will do," Audrey said and Marla waved. Audrey started the car and Brother stepped back. The engine motor kicked to life and rolled forward as Audrey shifted into drive.

"Stop!" Brother's voice boomed. The car stopped so abruptly, it rocked on its frame and jolted everyone inside. Brother stepped around the car to the door, where Trinity looked at him in surprise.

He opened the car door and, ignoring the questions of the sisters, leaned across Trinity and unfastened her seat belt. As he stood up, he took Trinity's hand and lifted her out, then wrapped his big arms around her and kissed her deeply. Trinity wrapped her arms around Brother's neck and kissed him back as Marla and Audrey cheered from inside of the car.

When the two broke the hug, Mei noticed the tears running down Trinity's face. Brother said something Mei couldn't hear. Trinity nodded, and Brother helped her back into the car, then reached across and buckled her seat belt. He stood up and closed the car door, knocked twice on the roof, and Audrey pulled away slowly. Mei waved at everyone inside and they waved back.

After the car left their sight at the gate, Brother turned to Mei. "Are you ready to go home? It's been quite a party, but I think I'm ready for my own bed."

Mei nodded. "I have lots to think about."

"I bet you do. Well, take your time and think it over, and ask questions if you need help." He took Mei's hand, and they walked around the truck and trailer. He showed Mei how to see if everything was okay and ready for the drive home. After they put Boudicca in the truck, they got in, buckled up, started the truck and rolled across the pasture out onto the road.

"You know, you should try to sketch mind pictures from this weekend."

"I might," Mei said.

"Well, it's something to think about."

"Oh, damn!" Brother said. "I forgot to tell you to say goodbye to Pop when we left. Please don't let me forget to write him a thank you note."

They rode in silence for a bit.

"I really liked Ceilidh. Is it always like that?" Mei asked.

"It's always a good time, but this one was unusual with the girls returning and performing, me coming back, and the clan adopting you. But there's always lots of music and dancing, good food and good people. So, it won't always be exactly like that, but might be better in other ways."

"Is Trinity your girlfriend now?" Mei asked.

Brother froze, and after a moment, breathed deep and exhaled. "I'm struggling with that very topic, but the short answer is no."

"Why not? Don't you like her?"

"Yes, I like her very much."

"I think she likes you," Mei said.

"That's true."

Mei sensed this was a touchy subject. "I like her."

"I think it's safe to say she likes you as well," Brother said.

"Is there a bigger story here I don't know about?" Mei asked.

"Seeing Trinity and the girls was a big surprise for me. It was an even bigger surprise to see how much they'd all grown and changed since I saw them last, which is stupid when I think about it. The biggest surprise was finding out we were attracted to each other."

"Why? She's nice and fun and pretty."

Brother grinned. "Oh, yes, she is. Yes, indeed."

"And a bunch of ladies at the Ceilidh think you're handsome and brave."

Brother choked on the iced tea he had been in the process of trying to drink "What?"

"Yep, there sure was..."

"Please! Don't tell me." He mopped up the iced tea with a paper towel. "I'm afraid of making things awkward with whomever it may have been."

"Okay."

"This is a private conversation between you and me. " Which was Brother and Mei's phrase meaning not to talk about a topic to others. Before I got wounded the last time, I never thought I'd get married again."

"What? You were married?" Mei asked.

"Just briefly. It was a mistake and didn't last. I also had a few girlfriends and lots of lady friends, but the life I chose to lead wasn't one a wife would tolerate for very long. Besides, I liked it. I liked being selfish, doing hardcore Marine stuff, and doing things my own way. Now, everything's changed for me. I'm not sorry about it, but it's all new to me and takes time to internalize it all. You, my health, the court fight, and the life we're trying to build are my priorities. I'm not sure where a girlfriend would fit in."

Mei's stomach twinged at the mention of the upcoming court fight.

Brother continued. "Trinity has a lot going as well. She's going back to college to get her master's degree, and Mary Flynn wants her and the girls to record a new album and maybe go on tour again. That would mean new opportunities for her and her music, so it would be selfish and wrong of me to ask her to drop all that to stay here and be with me. But my heart isn't so sure." He thought for a moment. "Anyhow, she might come by for a visit before she goes away." He snapped back to focus. "We'll see what happens, but in the meantime, we have work to do."

The evening air held a chill, so Brother turned on the heater. Mei felt the warm air on her feet, then moved up, raising goosebumps on her legs. Between the warmth, Boudicca's comfortable weight, and the soothing rumble of the truck's engine, Mei drifted off to sleep while Brother continued driving.

Her mind raced to process it all. It had been an unbelievable few days. The people, the music, the food, everything. It felt like a story, and it had all happened to her! She wasn't sure what was next in her life, but knew, with Brother around, even if things got tough, it would be amazing.

She couldn't wait.

Chapter 100

Brother

After eating their final lunch, the campsite group slowly wandered back across the field to their home by the apple orchard; It was such a simple place but had come to mean quite a bit in a very short time.

Before packing, they all stopped for one last look to acknowledge their sentiments. For a minute, it was quiet, then Steve broke the silence.

"I find myself sad this weekend has come to an end." he said, then turned to Brother. "My good friend." he said formally. "Thank you for helping my children and I to have an amazing and memorable weekend with friends, ...the food, the music, and laughter, all things that I will cherish." He extended his hand.

Brother stood up extra straight as if at attention. "The honor was mine, good sir," he said, and shook Steve's hand.

Audrey spoke up.

"We aren't shaking anything, come here," then she and Marla hugged Brother, Steve, and George.

When Trinity hugged Steve and George and not Brother, he asked, "No hug?"

"You already had a hug today," Trinity teased.

"I also saw the sunrise today, but want to see more."

Everyone whooped, while Trinity laughed, shook her head and rolled her eyes.

Brother smiled and then, aches and pains be damned, he stepped over to beautiful musician and gently swept her in the air. Then he kissed her before setting her down.

Good times.

They were just packing when Mei and Judyta ran up. Brother said it was time to go. He felt proud of Mei. She looked disappointed but didn't react negatively.

The entire camp took their time packing their gear. The weekend had been special, and no one was in a hurry to see it end sooner than needed.

George brought the kilt, vest, and gear Brother had loaned him. Brother took the vest back but told George to keep the kilt and bandannas. "I can't have my little brother running around in pants all the time. Keep a hold of that kilt and wear it in good health. I want to see you wear it when you get your engineering degree or something important like that. If you do get rid of it, give it only to me or your son. Got it?"

George nodded and choked up.

"Oh, one more thing. You wear my man skirt, you always, and I mean always stand up straight like a man ought to. As a matter of fact, whether you're apologizing for something stupid or marching to a firing squad, always stand up straight, look them in the eye, and make them understand that George is a real man."

"Will do. Thanks, brother."

"You bet."

The Whites were the first to leave. Steve and Audrey got their cars, but Steve and the kids loaded up first, preceded by a round of hugs and goodbyes. Brother didn't hear what Marla said to George, but afterwards, the young man stood straighter than he had before. Marla also kissed his cheek, then wrapped her scarf around him as a parting gift. George looked as if you could bounce bullets off him.

Brother walked over and bumped fists with George and said his goodbyes.

Steve, ever the gallant one, gave a courtly bow and wished the musicians a most sincere farewell. Judyta and Mei hugged and danced in place. Brother hugged Judyta and shook hands with

Steve. "We'll see you and the hell spawn sooner rather than later," Brother said in farewell.

"Damn right, little brother," Steve said.

Steve was the first non-family and nonmilitary person who called him Brother. And Brother felt proud.

"What a great family," Audrey said to Marla, and Trinity nodded.

"Yes, they really are, aren't they?" Brother said, then turned. He thanked Marla for all of her patience with George.

"I think you helped make a hero this weekend."

They all chuckled, then Brother turned to the musicians. "May I offer some advice?"

The ladies nodded. "Sure."

"Stay in touch with Steve. Send him an email in the next few days, share your pictures, maybe send an autographed CD. He meant it when he extended his offer of friendship and help. And he's not only a brilliant professor who could help you with your academic careers, he's one of the most brilliant people I've ever met. Having a friend with that quality is a good move."

"Oh, really?" Audrey asked. "We weren't sure he really meant it..."

"I think he sees past your music, just as you see past his academic status."

They all nodded.

"Mei, ladies," Brother said, "I'd like to take a short walk with Miss Trinity before you all go, if you don't mind."

"Ooo la la!" Audrey and Marla chimed in unison.

"Oh, come on. " Brother protested. You were nice to the boy!"

Audrey smiled. "Well, he was a lad."

"And you're a scandalous rogue of the worst sort," Marla said, laughing.

"No mercy! No mercy! No Mercy!" the girls chanted.

Trinity stepped over and took Brother's hand, then they walked off into the orchard with the girls and Mei cheering.

Brother was dreading this goodbye. Normally he didn't mind goodbyes, because with most of his previous assignations, it was understood that it was for a dirty weekend or other limited time situation Now, he was in unfamiliar territory. He was smitten with Trinity and wanted more. So, he'd go with that.

Trinity teased him to break the tension. "Are you going to take me back to the spot and roll me in the grass again?"

"How did you guess?"

She blushed, so he pressed on. "We barely made it through half a chapter of the Kama Sutra, and there's so much more badness I want to do with you."

Trinity's eyes flashed open. "Well, now." She mumbled.

"It's only fair, you know. You can't be all gorgeous, talented, brilliant, and brave, and expect me not to want you."

Trinity gasped as her eyes searched his. "You mean it, don't you?"

"With every beat of my heart," he said, then paused to find the right words. "I'm afraid of trying to articulate more for fear of sounding trite or stupid, so I hope you believe me. I've traveled far, seen, and done way too much to play games."

Trinity saved him from his awkwardness. "Well, I want to roll with you in the grass again, and I'm glad you're going home with my smell on you, in case other bitches get any ideas."

Brother chuckled. "The only bitch in my life is Boudicca, and I don't think of her that way."

"Well, good, now shut up and kiss a girl a good one."

He did her bidding. Trinity enthusiastically kissed him back. He loved how she showed affection with total abandon. For such a petite thing, she really was a force of nature. They finally broke away.

"If we don't stop, I'm going to reach the point of no return," Trinity breathed.

"O-k-a-y," Brother said. "right. We have people waiting on us. Putting on the brakes."

"Yes, and I've already scandalized the rest of my band."

"What?"

"Marla said she heard us last night."

"No! Well.... Steve suggested I should bathe this morning."

"I got that hint, too."

"Really?"

"Audrey asked me to stay downwind from her and Marla because they were worried if they walked downwind from me before I bathed, they'd get pregnant with your babies. Then, to add salt to the wound, they said they weren't sure they'd mind so much if the babies were yours."

"Uhmmmm."

"Oh, shut up, mister man. I don't think they were serious. Those were jabs at me. Just be happy that they like you like a pal. And they're happy for me. They say you might be a rogue and a bad man, but you have a good heart." She paused. "And I agree."

"I'm proud to know them."

"They really did worry about you when you were overseas and prayed for you, too. And they cried when they heard how badly you were wounded. So did I."

"I'm sorry really doesn't say it, does it?"

"No, it doesn't."

"I still am. I never wanted to hurt anyone I care about. That's why I stayed away for so long. I was selfishly having a ball doing all the alpha man stuff and didn't want good people here at home to see me in case they saw me for the monster I really was.

"But you are not anymore." She said it as a statement.

"I still can be, but I'm older and have more experience in keeping him in his cage. Especially now that I have people to live for. I guess I always did."

"Yes, you did."

"Thank you," he said, then took a deep breath. "Can you let the girls know how much I love them and appreciated their letters and emails? They're very special to me."

"They know how you feel, but you need to tell them yourself."

"You're right, and I will. In the meantime, come here and make me glad to be a man, then we need to go."

"Oh, you bad, bad man."

They held hands and walked out of the woods to where the girls waited. Trinity walked over to where Mei stood, holding Boudicca's leash, and squatted down. They talked quietly, obviously wanting privacy, so Brother turned to Audrey and Marla. He held out his hands so the sisters could each put their hands into his.

"My most talented and beautiful ladies...... My dear, dear friends. This is overdue, but I wanted to tell you both in person how much all your letters, emails, kind words, music, and prayers meant to me while I was away. Your kindness helped me through some very black days. I'm sorry I was such a shit and didn't call you back." He smiled at both of them. "A bad man could do a lot worse than having the both you on his side rooting for him when things get rough."

"We were, I mean are, so proud of you," Audrey said

"You're our real-life hero," Marla added.

"I don't know if I'm worthy of those accolades," Brother said.

"Yes, you are," Audrey said. "Not just because of what you did in the war, but you could have let yourself become an evil guy and you didn't. An evil guy couldn't have saved Mei Mei. Now stop it, not everyone gets a hero, so you do not get to take ours."

He cleared his throat. "Is this where I shut up and take yes for an answer?"

"Please do," Marla said with a smile. "Sometimes less is more, ya know."

Brother laughed, and nodded. then he gently but firmly hugged and kissed each young lady. "If you need help, any help, you can always call me."

"We will."

They faced each other while shifting their feet awkwardly.

"Well, I guess we're ready to go," Trinity said and pecked Brother on the cheek, then got into the car. WTF???

Brother watched the girls get in, then started to say all the platonic goodbyes. Then he realized he couldn't let it end like this. Sounding off in his Marine Staff Non-commissioned officer's command voice, he roared loud enough to make Audrey hit the brakes and stop the car abruptly. With direct and deliberate movements, he walked over to the car, reached in and lifted Trinity out of the car.

He pulled Trinity into his arms and with heart pounding like a cannon firing, he kissed her deeply. Trinity melted into him and returned the kiss passionately.

"Because of circumstances I can't come to you, but come see me soon." Brother whispered

Trinity nodded.

He helped her back into the car and they drove off across the field to the gate and were gone.

Brother watched them go and with his head still spinning, finished getting Mei and Boudicca loaded up. They slowly left the Ceilidh and headed out onto the highway. He chatted with Mei as they drove. Brother struggled to try to be present enough in the moment to answer Mei's questions about the events of the past weekend, then she asked him point blank if Trinity was his girlfriend now.

His mind immediately locked and swirled at the same time, so he forced himself to pause and carefully answered his little sister as honestly as he could.

He really didn't know, and he told her so. Mei Mei asked more questions, and they had an open discussion. Before he realized, he'd confided some private thoughts, and even admitted to a failed marriage.

Mei was surprised and asked more questions.

Brother summed it all up with the truth; that only time would tell.

Brother could see Mei fading off to sleep, so lowered his tone and talked in his 'late night FM radio DJ voice,' until he was sure she'd fallen completely asleep. He felt jealous. He'd love to have someone else drive so he could conk out. He felt worn out from so many unexpected and forgotten feelings in a short amount of time. But that's what happened when you put yourself out there. Despite feeling uncomfortable with his new feelings, he wasn't sorry. He knew that was the price to be paid for growing.

He drove down the road into the setting sun and shifted his thoughts to the days ahead. Refocusing and doing his 'think' thing would help keep him awake and help to calm his mind so maybe, just maybe he could sleep later.

The first and most important topic was Mei. My God! It all came together for her this weekend! The competition, the dancing, and the friendship with Judyta, all of it gave his baby sister the opportunities to show herself who she was. Brother didn't want to admit the Ceilidh had been a test, but it was. The surprise for him was when he'd realized on the first day, the entire event was more of a test of himself as a budding parent, more than for Mei as a child. Both siblings had been tested this weekend, but ultimately it was

Brother who was responsible for both passing. He snuck a quick look at the grubby, sleeping girl in the seat next to him and felt a surge of pride. She had real hope of being successful. Granted, there was still so much more to do, but for the first time, he knew deep down, that they were on the right path.

He reflected back a lifetime ago, to sitting in the hospital bed marinating in his depression, when the Chaplain had come into his room to tell him that Mei not only existed, but needed rescuing. Knowing his audience, the Chaplain didn't sugarcoat the truth. Instead, he hit Brother between the eyes with the fact if Brother didn't step up and save the little girl, nobody would. In his quiet, calm, but stronger than steel Caribbean Island voice, the Chaplain had posed the question:

"When two orphans meet in such terrible circumstances, can they form the bonds needed to become a family of choice? And do you have what it takes to grow those bonds so you can save that little girl and yourself?"

Brother had spoken the words aloud from his heart before he had time to overthink.

"Yes, Padre."

And he now knew it was true. He had what it took and felt relief. He thought of his personal motto's that meant "challenge accepted";

Semper Fidelis.

Fide Et Fortitudine.

Here am I, send me.

Brother snapped out of his reverie and refocused. He'd turned on his phone when they'd left the Ceilidh, and messages immediately downloaded to his phone. He plugged in an ear bud and checked his messages. Sure enough, the private investigator had left him updates on the course of action he set in motion against the fiends before leaving for the weekend. Predictably, his actions had stirred up a firestorm. The PI ended the update to caution him the fiends might finally be onto him, so he needed to take all legal and physical safety measures to protect himself and Mei.

"Listen, man, these people aren't like everyone else. They don't need courtroom proof whether you're the one causing the pain in their lives. They need only to suspect you, so they can justify that coming after you is the righteous thing to do. Hopefully, they won't figure out what we've been up to until it's too late, but be safe anyway."

Noted. Brother was glad he'd been layering his defenses since that time back at the VA when he found out someone was hunting Mei and him. It sounded as though things went according to plan, which meant while he was at the Ceilidh, the fiends got a rough lesson they weren't hunting him, rather, he was hunting them. Just because he wasn't initiating violence doesn't mean he'd sit by and let anyone hurt his sister.

Brother checked himself. During the short time he was processing the information about the fiends, his feelings went from warm and sentimental to calculating and arctic cold. He was glad he could still flip that emotional switch. Clearly, the chances were good he'd need that old skill to serve him again, sooner rather than later.

Finally, Brother thought about what he classified as the "Trinity" scenario. Everything had moved so fast. That situation was pure chaos. He let his mind slip into a stream of consciousness.... It had all gone from, "wow, you grew up," to "Are we really attracted to each other?" to "Yes we are," to "How will this attraction play out?" to, "I love your nonphysical beauty as well your physical beauty," to "What the hell is going on-because-I-am-crushing-on-you-hard-I-dont-want-you-to-go."

What a mess! What a glorious mess!

He smiled to himself. Of course, he'd had whirlwind dalliances before, but most of them were short-lived and, he was ashamed to say, a bit cynical. This didn't feel the same. He sorted through his thoughts and feelings and came up with pointed questions needing answers before he could decide his course of action. Was Trinity safe for him to lower his guard and let into his life? What would that look like? Could he revive his gallantry and romantic sincerity? He was pleased to find he dared to hope so. Holding hands and walking with Trinity in the summer sun had sure been fine, and when she demonstrated that she had bravery and beauty, his attraction rocketed out of sight. However, Brother's practical nature knew there were other forces that would influence whatever would happen between him and Trinity. He had to keep his control freak influences in check.

The next few days would reveal what would happen, and he could do nothing but wait.

In the meantime, he didn't know what everyone else was going to do, but he knew what he would do. He'd take it easy, decompress, and plan for what he and Mei would do next. He knew the two of them were on only the first steps of a very long road, but he was determined they would be traveling on the Glory Road and not a Highway to Hell.

Most of all, he hoped to spend time with Trinity before the fiends did something desperately stupid or the police came to get him.

Fingers crossed.

Acknowledgments

Note.... a not-so-humble brag... I owe so many "Thank Yous" to many people for this effort I am sure that to my shame I will miss someone. So I would like to say thank you to all of the teachers, bow hunters, instructors, Marines, family of choice, rabble rousers, Celts, highlanders, college pals, professors, shooting pals, blood kin, Masters of Mayhem, and all of the other people who have been there for me.

My "Uncle" Richard Schwender who taught me so much about hard truth, logic, reasoning, and especially what family of choice is.

Marc MacYoung was the first person who saw something in me and encouraged me to start writing. My first published work appeared in Marc's brilliant anthology; "Beyond the Picket Fence." My story is written anonymously but after your read "The Orphan, The Marine, and the Mastiff" it wont be hard to find.

I don't have good words enough to honor all of my beta readers. In my ignorance as a beginning writer, I inflicted rough draft after rough draft on them and I am embarrassed for that, but still extremely grateful. Many people have read passages but my stalwarts are the ones who have read the entire book(sometimes more than once as each version was written....sigh..sorry.)

Mandy Skowera – The one and only Pizza Girl! I am not sure why you took a chance on reading the story from a giant maniac, but I appreciate it. Your words of encouragement "Shut up and keep writing!" gave me the notion that I might have something here.

Jessica Humphrey – I say to you with all the love...... "Hi Man! Heard any good ones lately?"

Rory Miller – Your critiques were timely, spot on, and inspired me to dig in and do the needed work.

Kami Miller-Thank you for all of your coaching.

Denise Heiser- I dont know how to say "Thank you" enough...for everything. Love Always.

Sarah Estus- Gemini Girl!!!

Arik Estus – Thank you Brother...seriously.

Michael Estus- Just listening to my audio processing sure helped.

Sara Ryan - You Rock Bro!

Joyce Burns - Thank you so much..... and no, you can't have Boudicca.

Chris Licking – Let's go find an Andelusian Bull!

Bunny and Kerry Davis – Kilts and Celts Forever!

Raven Littleriver - Got a Java?

Scott "Prof" Norris – Mentat, cigar lover, and best kind of good friend.

Gail Metz – Semper Fidelis!

Doris Klein-Sehr Gut!

Liz F, Nancy K, Dave and Maggie B, Steve B, Terry T, Jae R, Jennifer M, Amy K, Clint O, Jeff S, Ben L, Jennifer K, Louretha G, Melanie W, Kat E, Stacie S, Laura S, John C, Tom and Diane W, and so many more..........

A very special acknowledgement to my bonus daughter Penny Cooper who's exceptional art graces the cover of this book. Her talent is magical!

About Author

About Josh

Josh Amos was born and raised in Olympia WA in the 1970s and 80s. Spending a great deal of time learning to love reading, competing in archery tournaments, learning karate and being a general knucklehead. Despite a stunning lack of natural physical talent, Josh enlisted in the Marines. While in boot camp, Josh found out that he was going to be a father at the ripe old age of 18 (because being a pudgy white kid at MCRD San Diego wasn't enough of a challenge).

Nonetheless, Josh pushed on and earned the title of US Marine, whereupon he served for years as a logistics specialist where he attended many schools and learned lots of hard lessons that would pay off in his future.

Honorably discharged after four years, Josh returned to Olympia as a disabled veteran (no regrets) where he spent the next parts of his life working various jobs, making mistakes, and trying hard to be a good dad. As a committed lifelong learner, Josh continued with his love of reading and trying new things. Eventually, Josh progressed from noncustodial parent to single dad. Somewhere along the way, Josh earned the esteemed status as bonus dad to his amazing daughter.

After his kids left home, Josh fulfilled a life goal when he went to college as a near 40-year-old "old guy." Going from zero to MBA in under 5 years while working full time wasn't easy, but he did it with a 3.75 overall GPA.

It was in his last Semester of grad school when Josh got a call from his long time friend and author Marc MacYoung, who asked Josh to contribute to his anthology book "Beyond the Pickett Fence." Josh's contribution was recognized by several authors, who encouraged Josh to continue writing.

Josh still lives in Washington State with his long hair apricot Mastiff Boudicca, and he enjoys good books, fine cigars, and his family of choice.

Don't miss out!

Visit the website below and you can sign up to receive emails whenever Josh Amos publishes a new book. There's no charge and no obligation.

https://books2read.com/r/B-A-TQEZ-WYYKC

BOOKS 2 READ

Connecting independent readers to independent writers.

Also by Josh Amos

The Orphan the Marine and the Mastiff

Milton Keynes UK
Ingram Content Group UK Ltd.
UKHW011940010124
435297UK00001B/61